THE 28th DAY OF ELUL

Richard M. Elman

THE
28th DAY
OF ELUL

CHARLES SCRIBNER'S SONS ▪ New York

Author's Note

As early as 1960 a set of documents and some correspondence came to my attention; I read them, put them aside, and attended to my business. The following April I started work on a long short story in which it soon was apparent that certain documentary characters had emerged. The more I subsequently tried to put them out of my head the more their lives crowded in on me. Luckily, I was not pressed for time and was able to put my hands on additional relevant materials in the public library. By the following spring, I had completed a first draft of a much longer work which I then condensed, revised, and rewrote on the Magdalene Islands in the summer of 1963 and, subsequently, on two other occasions. At various times I was sustained by the good counsel of my friends Ronald Sanders, Joel Blocker, Al Fried, and Dan Jacobson and, in a special measure, by the encouragement and good will toward the work of Morris Renek and Gunther Stuhlmann. To all of them I am, of course, deeply grateful.

Richard M. Elman, New York, 1966

Book One

Did not your father eat and drink?
  He did what was right and just,
  And it went well with him.
Because he dispensed justice to the weak and poor,
  It went well with him.
Is this not true knowledge of me? says the Lord.

Jeremiah 22

Dans ce denuement sordide, une des plus suprenantes conséquences est la destruction de toute hiérarchie de l'âge. Toutes les conventions qui maintiennent une certaine civilité à l'égard du vieillard sont anéanties. Le vieillard est soumis aux contraintes communes. Il est de droit qu'on adolescent le frappe et l'injurie, le chasse de sa place pour la prendre et se servir. Le vieillard est un objet de dérision et de mépris pour sa faiblesse. C'est que la puissance seule compte.

L'Universe Concentrationnaire—DAVID ROUSSET

A Letter

"Sir:

"You write (have written?) to tell me that my late uncle, the former Bela Yagodah (changed to James) is my benefactor through his estate in Merton, Ohio, of which you, in New York (sic) are the principal executor.

"You are also most kind to advise me that under the terms of my late uncle's benefaction, as expressed in his last will and testament, witnessed by you and dated September 12, 1939 [the 28th day of Elul, 5700], I, Shandor Yagodah, the son of my late uncle's brother Newman and his wife Ilona, that I am to receive my portion as one third of one third of the total estate, since Uncle Bela had two sisters as well as a brother, and since his only brother had three children: myself, my widowed sister Sarah in Melbourne, Australia, and my sister Perl, who I no longer see and who I presume you have traced and found to be alive. As I have no doubts she still is.

"You then assert (sic, p. 3 of the document) that you can deposit on demand in a special account at the Bank Leumi in Tel Aviv the sum of 120,000 Israel pounds (approximately $40,000)

3

for which I must in my own manner present positive identification of myself as Shandor, the only male heir of Newman and Ilona Yagodah, and for which I must further attest (according to a separate codicil in the Will dated October 12, 1939) [the 29th day of Tishri, 5700] that I am a professing Jew and that I intend to raise all my descendants (such as they are and may someday be) in the ways of the Jewish law. All this you have stated to me in your letter of June the twenty-ninth [the twenty-seventh day in the month of Sivan, 5722], received only last week. I repeat what I understand to be your meaning so that we can be of one mind about the question at hand: namely, that my dear late uncle has died in America without immediate heirs, leaving me the sum of forty thousand dollars at this time plus additional monies and properties once his said estate is liquidated by no later than the first of next year . . . Roman calendar . . ."

Yagodah's sputtering pen caused a large opaque ink blot with frayed edges to form along the normal route of the script. Beyond this barrier, which was not unlike a pair of butterfly wings, the prose hesitated before resuming, slanting off then in a different direction, the letters now smaller, beadlike, having greater spaces beween them: "My head is coming to a point!" There was another blank space. Nothingness—where Alex had leaped away from his desk. . . .

Very simply, he thought his trousers were on fire. To Alex, the smell was unmistakable—burning wool. And there was heat too. Why couldn't he manage to be more careful?

He searched for an ash tray, hidden by his many papers; then he threw the stub of cigarette against the sill and jerked his body against the back of the chair.

Leaning away from the offensive odor, Alex slapped at the spot on his lap, again and again, like a judge wielding a feeble

4

gavel against some threat of disorder. When he went off the mark and his open palm stung soft genitals, he doubled over with pain.

Then he paused, breathed deeply a moment, examined himself, especially the singed spot at the seam. His immediate gesture was to light another cigarette, whereupon he observed, as the match flared, no hole, only a small discoloration in the place where the nap had been burned away. Mutely, Alex scratched the spot with a bitten remnant of fingernail before sitting down once more to write.

As soon as he started again on the letter, his lips were in motion. Dense with sweat, his balding head also seemed to nod in accord with what he was saying to himself. Alex trembled and swayed back and forth above the sheets of paper with pen in hand and the smoke streaming around the contours of his face like incense fumes about the face of a Buddha.

When the smoke made his eyes run he doused the second cigarette. Then he scribbled another moment, leaned away, surveyed what he had done with a practiced eye, and bending forward ever so slightly, scribbled a little more, catching a drop of sweat as it ran down his cheek with the sleeve of a dingy white shirt which reached to his elbow, and, a second time, with a thin hairless swipe of his forearm. "How disgusting," Alex had written. "How deplorable." Then he had given up again.

Yagodah was a meager, stooping fellow with narrow cringing shoulders; it was only the high dome of his head and the stooping of his frame from the waist up that was at all Buddha-like. His most characteristic grimace seemed attuned to expressions like "deplorable." It was a kind of worried facing at you which sometimes deepened into the frown of perplexity and which always managed to force the steel frames of his heavy spectacles in place against the fleshy red volutes of his ears. The lenses of these same spectacles were cloudy and scratched; they magnified the size of his eyes, making them seem huge, bleary, the eyes of a be-

5

wildered person at times while, at other times, they gave you the impression that they belonged to a man who had simply been drinking too much. Alex needed to wear glasses for close work but he could view the world well enough without them. If he never cast the heavy frames to one side but went about always encased in them it was because he preferred the adversity of looking out from under glass, or to the sides of it, at the raw expanse of scenery which he now inhabited. Alex treated his eyes as if they were confined by a set of blinders, even when he sat back at last to admire his bold, straightforward penmanship.

It was a very humid evening late in July. The lamp sputtered current. Insects rioted softly against the window screens. Beyond the dust and grit of the sill, people were still in their yards or sauntering home from chores. The lengthening dusk held a promise of coolness, of quiet, long deferred. The tiny settlement waited. One could almost hear its communal sigh of disappointment with the continuing dusty heat. Now it was nearly nine. Through the small window overhead Alex was confronted when he looked up by a glow of arc lights at the perimeters. Beyond this point the density of the darkness was confirmed by its outer limits: hills, ruined vehicles, barbed wire, an eroded burial mound, then another, spectral against the arc lights, and, beyond, the final black barrenness through which he thought he could barely make out the flaring match-fire point of an encampment. It was rather like looking into a dark pit; you saw more than was actually there, and that meant the night was now complete. Alex started to write once more, a fly bothering the tip of his nose.

The surface over which he was working was, in reality, the top of his wife's sewing machine, their most treasured possession. Breathing thickly, too aware of his balding head and burning eyes, Alex was alarmed by every scratch of the pen, and seemed unable to trust the movements of his own hand. What he whispered to himself was unintelligible and imprecise, a series of groans usually accompanied by that fetish gesture of his free arm

6

up toward his forehead, intended to assuage the point of pressure between his eyes, beneath that densening crown of perspiration. Alex would write, groan, then write again, peering up between bouts to ascertain the state of the night's oblivion while, in the only other room of the small, whitewashed shack, the child he called his daughter practiced rhymes for her English class; and the woman he called his wife plodded noisily from sink to stove, preparing a late supper.

For the third evening in a row, Alex had attempted to start the letter immediately upon returning home from the hospital, but, when he had tried to concentrate on the salutation, it felt as if his head was not sitting properly on his neck. His mouth tasted like chemicals. It was a thing unto itself, isolated from all the other organs of his blind senses, as if all communication between the different parts of his head and body had been disturbed.

When his daughter had found him out, insisting that he coach her with her English lessons, Alex thought he could smell burning flesh. "Speak to me. Speak like an American to me," she teased. Feeling used up, sullen, the taste going strong and bad under his gums, an ache encapsulated in his head, as well, which began far back in his sun-baked leathery neck (the only part of his body still tanned) and even flashed between his eyes when he opened his jaws to mumble a correction (as if he had a clasp of searing iron about his head), Alex had coached her in the clumsy repetition of English verbs, staring blankly into the dark hollows of the child's face as she cajoled him and beseeched him to say more; and he continued to try to work a certain arthritic stiffness out of his fingers.

Dampness bothered Alex of late, but his daughter's singsong recitations were even more irritating. The very presence of another person exacerbated his feelings of self-loathing. Alex wished the child didn't look so much like an Arab girl. He wished he could make her stop using so much Arabic and American slang, but he knew that for all the children in the settlement this was

7

but another form of play-acting in what was, after all, a rather dreary place of sameness.

Pulling the child to him and stroking her head to signify that the lesson was over, Alex nevertheless shuddered when she, becoming womanish, softly curled herself against his shoulder. "Go. Your mother wants you now," he said, aware that he was being cruel and that the girl knew it.

Moments later his teeth began to ache. His whole jaw felt as it was spreading, enlarging. His limbs grew cold. He thought of fetching a chair into the tiny vegetable garden behind the house to smoke, to warm himself, and, as the sun burned low, to reconsider the strange set of documents he had been sent while waiting for the supper which he didn't want but knew he would not be allowed to refuse.

"Call me to the table," Alex had muttered on passing his wife.

"Where are you going?"

But, when she saw the look on his face, she added: "If only you would be more direct. The way you are about this letter you would think . . ."

"Never mind!"

"You never mind, my friend," Esther replied. "Looking at you these days even I lose my appetite. Why you feel you must be everybody's conscience except your own . . . it's something I don't understand. Tell them what they want to hear. Forget what you think you know. Your father thought he knew a great deal. Look where it got him. What do they care? There are plenty of your kind of stories in *Yadvashem*. Was it any different in my case? I ask you . . . So why must you always be so unpleasant about ancient history. Even if you can't use the money I can . . . and the girl can . . ."

Never previously had Esther expressed herself with such vehemence about his "papers." Her sudden discourse stopped Alex in mid-passage. He cleared his throat, and brought a hand up to his head, mumbling: "Oh never mind. . . ."

8

"You never mind," she countered ferociously, once again.

"Well?" Stubbornly, nodding his head, Alex added: "What *should* I do?"

But, looking toward the doorway, he quickly whispered, before she could answer: "These Americans . . . first they spit in your eye. Then they say pardon me . . ."

Afterward, when Alex waited for her to comment, she remained thoughtful, as if truly considering his remarks.

"*So? What should I say?*" he pleaded finally.

"Don't be so intelligent," Esther said. "Do whatever you please. Write a nice letter. Tell him what he wants to hear and be done with it. . . ."

Leaving the house then, Alex had settled himself under a fig tree in his garden, having neglected to bring his papers, chain smoking but with an unopened detective novel on his lap. Lately he was becoming quite addicted to this kind of reading, only he usually found that he was never able to get to the end of the story without cheating; always he had the compulsion to skip ahead to learn who the culprit could be. Tonight Alex found himself so provoked that he needed to know *who* from the moment he had set his eyes upon the paper-covered volume entitled *Murder She Said;* and so he couldn't bring himself to trespass even its opening pages.

Why did he waste his time on such trash?

Why stare at such a tawdry imitation of a pretty woman's face?

Fingering the slick book jacket, Alex confessed to himself that he thought his new habit was degenerate. He put it to himself that he actually felt now as if a stinking black fog or cloud separated him from what he called "wholesome life," even penetrating into his brain (and thus making him utterly incapable of piercing through it to the light beyond). Within this obscure region of mindless anxiety, he focused hard upon his book once again, as if he believed it would help him to reach beyond his present funk to

9

that place where the outlines of memory could be traced as sharply as the cutting edge of a knife.

Alex was unsuccessful. An even greater darkness was advancing now, shade upon shade, so that he could almost taste the black brine of distant seas, the mist and fog of mountainous places, together with an all-pervading stench of corpses. In the deep chasm of his being he felt a sudden twinging near his heart; and he actually thought he might be taking leave of his body. Then he told himself that he could feel his ears standing above his head like those of a cat, and he tried to force himself to weep.

At the far end of the settlement, a band of youngsters were singing a popular ballad:

> Strangers in love . . .
> In war strangers . . .
> When the night blooms . . .
> And the lemon sheds its scent
> Who shall come together. . . .

Although this was intended to be a melancholy song, the youthful voices betrayed only elation, inhibiting any sense of unhappiness. The singing, moreover, was simply too carefree, presumptuous, even though off-key; and this sank Alex into a further dejection. He kicked at a stone, shivering. The golden heat of the day was waning. He felt a sudden cold breeze against his shoulders. A neighbor's goat, trotting part of the way over to stare at him, was startled by his harsh throaty sounds. It backed away, sprang up, lifted its heels, kicking at the dust to all sides as it moved.

Coughing, with short, sharp bursts of air, Alex passed his tongue across his lips to keep them moist. Then he became aware that he was smiling. The back of his head also felt enlarged. It seemed to him that he could hear his own laughter, as if from afar. In the neighbor's window a face appeared; a long thin finger shook. He continued to laugh, but now it seemed that he had re-incorporated the sound as a part of himself. He put a hand over

10

his mouth and gagged, but the face he touched didn't seem to be his. And when he waved at that now-blank window frame, his mind was clear, too clear, as if the dampness had all evaporated, and the air was suddenly thinner, cooler, more purified. Against the bones of his skull he felt an unfolding, a thumping of blood. Visions of a street, a house, a town square, at odd angles and perspectives began to jump in front of his eyes. He would say what was wanted of him. The face of a young woman with combs in her hair swam into view, and he wanted to shut his eyes, to enjoy this vision—so unlike the face on the book jacket—awhile longer, but the conjuration was sadly finite. His closed lids merely revealed a purply blankness, then the orange flames of funeral pyres, palling smoke, cinder storms. Truly, Alex seemed to be trembling over a pit. He got up, hurried across the pathway to the shack, still trying to call the face back to view, but leaving behind chair, book, and his precious cigarette in the blackened afterglow. Fifteen minutes later he had already filled ten closely lined sheets of his daughter's cheap school stationery, although he had hardly begun to articulate what had been asked of him.

1

RUBIN:

According to Jewish law the son of a Jewish mother is a Jew forever. There is your answer. If only I could answer for your civil law in which the estate is to be liquidated. . . .

Liquidated! In German *liquidiert!* Which can also be described as *ausgemerzt!* or *erledigt!* You may be sure I know of such words. Many now use the polite vocabulary. They speak of the *holocaust* as some regrettable lapse in manners, or, if they are fund-raisers, as if to refer to some heroic event in the Bible or Greek Epic. Although I much prefer the bluntest words for what happened, by now all words are traps. Let us simply say those who *were* are *not* any longer; and it wasn't their fault. No! Not in the slightest! You can't find fault with them. They are *not*. They were treated like niggers . . . What happened was ugly, petty, great only in the scale of the undertaking—and I assure you, dear sir, no puns are intended when I say such a thing.

My late uncle married but there were no children. Sad. His wife is dead? Are there cousins in America? Sweet little ones? How I should like to know of them. But they are probably not.

12

The only members of my family who returned from the camps were my half-Jewish cousin Hilda and my father's great-uncle, Dr. Erdos. After the war I was for a short while in Bavaria with the occupation. The Germans complained. The English did not trust us. We were sent home. Fortunately I was able to revisit my mother country beforehand—on leave, an allied soldier in ill-fitting civilian clothes. I still knew more of my mother tongue than I dared let on. Thank heavens! What could I learn that I did not know already? I saw strangers, made inquiries. The living told me stories about other people, never themselves. The curtains had been drawn and all the villains had rushed out through the wings to change their costumes. Russian troops now occupied the stage. Once more there was the rule of the bayonet. A whole people cowered. I was no different. Afraid to be conspicuous I asked timid questions of the tradesmen, who answered me in parables. This one sent west two weeks before the Liberation. Another in a contingent of *Vorarbeiter* sent north, slave labor, the firm of Wagner & Biro in Austria, a factory for the production of U-Boats where the older people were put in a special barracks called Interlag 22 which was deliberately placed alongside the railroad ties next to the factory at Statlo because the Germans hoped to save on Zyklon gas by having the allied bombers do their executions for them . . .

In one trainload five in my mother's family perished. Her stepbrother Mihaly died with the message on his lips that his wife had been his only love and that he would truly never forget her. This I was to learn in Jerusalem, thirteen years later when speaking with one of those investigators for the Jewish agency who had no vocal chords and made words by swallowing and belching out the air from his belly.

What of those who did survive? Half-cousin Hilda returned to an empty blue house, a sagging porch, stillness. It was the winter of 1946. The peasants had only roots and sunflower seeds to eat, but they were still wearing their lovely woven costumes—the apple-cheeked women with brief leather jackets in which the fleece was turned inward. Hilda traveled to Miskolc in a train burning charcoal. A Communist family from Szabolcs with eleven children had moved into her old flat. Hilda didn't even own a bed. She remembered that her mother and my mother had owned some land in common near Kishavas. When she went to the Ministry of Land Owners to inquire after it she was told the poor peasants were working the land. They told her the land was no longer hers because she had not been in the underground, because she was a bourgeois who went with the Nazis, because she did not wish to be a Communist.

I met Hilda again in Haifa in 1953. Really, she was luckier than she would admit. Although she had not been allowed to go to Rumania where there was other family property, the authorities did consent to her deportation to Czechoslovakia where it was arranged for her to come here to Israel. When we met she was working in a *Konditorei* as waitress. I hardly recognized her. Saved from one oblivion she seemed prepared to enter another. Not only had she grown fat and blowsy, but she looked so tired, a woman old before her time. When I inquired about the Vienna Meidling (where the U-Boat factory was) her eyes crossed suspiciously. She would say nothing. Only once could I get her to speak about her own experience. She was telling me of Uncle Erno's death. I asked if she could remember the exact date. Hilda said: "In the brothels we never knew when it was Sunday or Monday."

. . . So you may be sure, although I had no knowledge of the existence of my dear late Uncle Bela other than those occasional dinner-table allusions to him which my bereaved father, his brother, made to my bereaved mother when I was naughty and he wanted to compare me to somebody who had come to no good, and that although I am still not positive that your deceased client was indeed the same ungrateful monster who was then

14

spoken of, and that although I cannot yet comprehend how you were able to seek me out here—despite all these factors plus the inability of a poor man with a family to seriously consider a fool's errand in Tel Aviv—despite my weakness, my various illnesses, my envious neighbors, and my Government (which no doubt will attempt to acquire all the money as payment for the "mercies" they have shown me)—despite the fierce summer climate, which does me no good and, as I say, all these significant factors of illness, envy, greed, I am now ready and willing to come to your representative in Tel Aviv for the purpose of attesting to my name and identity before sworn witnesses and relieving you of that burdensome store of money and other worldly goods which my late uncle accumulated in safety in America at a time of great suffering for me and my entire family.

As WHO WOULDN'T BE? Ask what I wish to do with my uncle's bribes. *To have just for the sake of having?* I tell you, dear sir, I intend to wallow in these riches. It will give me as great a joy to help in the "liquidation" of what remains of Uncle Bela as he (in his own way) was instrumental in helping our enemies *register* and *account for* and then *liquidate* us.

Only tell me, sir, what was it perished in the camps—Man or the idea of Man? If I seem to be putting the above assertion tentatively, almost in the form of a question, is it because I do not wish to hear your judgment before I have offered my evidence? Come now. You must know what I am speaking about? I refer you to war stories and little jokes currently to be heard in the cafés of Jerusalem. Here is one: It is in Europe, shortly after the war. A man meets his former boss on the street. The boss is surprised. "Joseph," he exclaims, "I am pleased to see you alive."

"Natürlich, I am too," the other man replies, dryly.

There is also the tale of the two former Nazis who met in Buenos Aires. *"Heil Hitler!"* One greets the other. "Oh don't mention it," the second one protests. "Times have changed. You must

15

change with them. Now even the Party has a new slogan." "Why, what is that?" the first one asks. The second fellow answers: "Next year in Jerusalem."

Do you understand better? Isn't that the way we are living? What else might we have expected? Do you think we didn't know that people like Bela felt this place wasn't good enough for them? Probably he thought all the Jews of Europe would change their names and have their noses corrected. Believe me, there just wasn't time. We had too much pride. Can't you see? You Americans are snobs even when you are being democrats? The lot of you. . . .

But how to prove that I am still Jewish? What can I show you? What must I do? What can I now prove that our enemies did not prove for us? You joke, of course. It is plain to see that my uncle had a keen sense of humor. Prove you are still Jewish. Funny. Why not simply tell me if you think I am not? I do not find my uncle very amusing. It is plain what kind of man he was—a perverse old fellow with certain hidebound ideas about things, people, institutions. Is it true he was a miser who bought all the friends he ever had? Stingy. He never even had children. Was my aunt barren? Yes. I think so. No doubt she was cold to him. He took mistresses and every year when they forced Bela (as an act of expiation) to give a few dollars to build schools and plant trees in this *gehenna* which he never even dared to visit, or on those Days of Awe when even the air has a different savor, my lousy late uncle, this man who called himself Bela James, told himself a nice little story to put himself to sleep that his nephews and nieces in the old country, his brothers and sisters and grand-nephews and grand-nieces as yet unborn, that all the sentimental-ized generations of his father's and father's fathers, that all the Yagodahs were leading fine Jewish lives somewhere, anywhere, preferably in a place he would not have to visit, a place he had long ago fled in his anger and shame. Sir, do you call that funny? The nerve of such a man. Didn't he know of the camps? *Every*

16

third one of us here lost somebody to one of those places! Didn't you bother to tell him of such goings-on? Or was he already senile, in his dotage, this Mr. James, an old man in a home for old men? And, if so, must I continue to respect the wishes of a senile old man? I ask you this one final time: how could you allow him to continue to believe such things, to believe in fairy stories, you, a man trained in the honesty of the Law, and he, illiterate and aging, dependent on you, no doubt?

Or is the law different in America, as it was different again in Europe? Still you must have known better. It occurs to me that such a bequest cannot be probated; it is not even valid. In a proper court of law I could contest. But then, where would the money go? To your kind. More lawyers. More waste.

You have stated (sic, p. 4) and I am quoting exactly from the set of documents you were good enough to send along:

I give, devise and bequeath to such lawful issue the survivor of us surviving the share or shares which the parent
or parents would have taken had *he, she,* or *they* survived the survivor of us, to be divided among them
equally, share and share alike, with the proviso that if
one has left the Jewish faith, forsaken Jewish worship,
concealed Jewish identity, then his shares shall be divided among the others and the survivors of them surviving *per stirpes.*

My compliments, dear Rubin. I believe it is not possible to have put the matter more precisely. Yes. It was very decent of you and my uncle, Mr. James, to aim to be so exact. But did he know when you were composing this masterpiece of jurisprudence about the policy called *Judenrein?* Did you think that policy a failure? Because that was also based on jurisprudence.

Allow me to return to my initial proposition: Bela, the old miser, who never once tried to help his dear ones when they really needed him, who pushed and cheated and stole (and no doubt went to synagogue regularly on the Sabbath), now he is

17

sitting back behind the curling smoke of an expensive cigar, gloating over his circumcised member, and wants to know if my wife goes to the baths? God help him. I haven't got a wife. My wife that would have been is dead. Murdered. This is only some woman I live with out of charity, a cook if you like. And who is to say I am acting badly—will it be Bela James again? Would you have him judge me when already he is forcing me to falsify myself if I wish to benefit from his works? I hope he is in hell for rewarding me in this manner. Liar! I have nothing but contempt for his gestures. Can I help it that he felt guilty? Guilt is also a principle of life. You Americans pretend to know little about it, although it touches you, I'm sure. In that respect you are just like the Marxists you pretend to hate so much; you live as if there were no guilt when in fact you are just as guilty. In one grimace of flame and smoke didn't you destroy three hundred thousand Japanese? Eighty thousand Germans dead in a single raid over Hamburg. Another eighty thousand burned alive in the fire storms above Dresden. And high in the clouds, in the seemingly neutral heavens, Americans. . . .

Why even you, Mister Attorney, you must know what it means to feel guilty. Have you ever been forced to make love to your own hand?

Or perhaps you have a relative over here some place, an old widowed aunt, a cousin or grandmother whose health or whose whereabouts make you slightly uneasy, but who you are resolutely prepared not to search out, to do as little as possible about her until it is too late. Perhaps you anticipate her approaching death with misgivings. She may be an invalid, who cannot come to you for help, so you tell yourself: "What can I do? We all must die sooner or later. Be calm!"

And she need not be here in the "Promised Land" but in some long-ago neglected or deserted neighborhood of Brooklyn, New York; Chicago, Illinois; Venice, California; or Newark, New Jersey. In books there are such old women, living among the black

18

people. You tell yourself you will visit her soon, before it is too late, but something always seems to interfere—business in the courts, family problems, selfish things. You never seem to find the time and, since you are, at heart, relieved that this is so, when the morbid day arrives, you make a big show of things at the funeral. You try to throw yourself into the grave beside her like Hamlet. You cry: "Oh don't let her lie there in the cold ground." You come back for the unveiling. Every fall you buy so many candles for the *Yarzeit* that the house is like a furnace. Or you start to give contributions to some charity in her name.

Believe me. It doesn't have to be a relative; it could be an old girl friend, a discarded mistress, a former business partner, the *sendak* who held you when you were eight days old, somebody who has shared in your life or been kind to you in some way, or, perhaps your former servant. . . .

And it doesn't happen only in America. People everywhere are always left lying about in London, Tel Aviv, or Miami Beach to make us feel guilty. Since there are more of us than there are them, they only manage to touch us occasionally. We write them off with tears, money, food packages, anything and everything— just as my uncle now tries to buy me and my history.

Damned fools. What would you say if I told you I have discovered the secret of our Disaster in three words—repression, rationalization and greed? What else can there be? Does Bela truly believe he can cry out from his grave, inquiring whether I wear phylacteries, or fringes, or keep kosher? As if these old habits could still matter here.

In his *Last Will and Testament,* my dear naïve uncle, Mr. James, disinherits those who have "concealed Jewish identity." Who among us has not done this and worse? Concealing such an odious thing was a small enough price to pay for survival. It was even done when he lived in our old country. Is it sufficient for the survivors to plead extenuating circumstances when, after all, it was an identity that none of us treasured in the first place? You

19

were damned if you were and you were damned if you said you weren't. Only fools or abject sentimentalists chose to brazen through it all. Very simply, our identity was shaped by murder, oppression, the scorn of our neighbors, our own self-hate, many thousands of years of it. Hitler was merely an opportunist. He did not invent anti-Semitism. He seized upon what was psychologically correct for both Jew and gentile. The terror of identity. Some of the Polish Jews were so ignorant that they called each other Harry Snot, Isaac Crap, and Leah the Squint, not having any proper names. And there was a Jewish peasantry in our country, too. How could Bela have forgotten about the so-called "minority problems" of his own motherland? What kind of country is your America that a man can come to it and obliterate in his mind all the things that impelled him there to begin with? Didn't Bela realize that we were just like the despised *tziganes?* A black spot before men's eyes. Hateful to each other as well. Being so before we came here we cannot simply change now to suit his or your fancies because the British Government gave us lessons in field sanitation, or because certain other governments after 1936 ruled on our *Blutsenteil,* deciding who was a *Mischlinge* and who was not, or even because you people, again out of guilt, sent us thousands of little blue and white flags, gave us a piece of land, a pair of shorts, Hebrew lessons? What does he suppose his money helped to build—a *cheder?*

When will we Jews let up on ourselves?

This is not a religious school, mister! There are people living here. Rashi is dead. We have burned all his books. A whole culture is in cinders. We inhabit the promised land now and grow our own food which sometimes tastes like ashes in the mouth, and when we shit we make it stink like any other country, only it is a Jewish stink, of that you can be sure. So do not ask me to swear that such a stink is not also mine. How could it be otherwise? But if you insist upon asking me to swear am I also proud of it then I must tell you no; I am not proud. Do I seem like such a fool?

20

How can somebody like myself be proud of anything after what I have seen with my own eyes . . . No! And after what I have also done. No! I humble myself in the midst of such a stink. So do not ask me to say that I think it may be *eau de cologne* when I know it to be shit. Shit! It is shit. We are all being shit upon, here and in your own country, only we Jews in Israel are now so used to it that we have created a country where we could each shit upon the other. And if we get tired of this, there are always the Arabs to be shat upon as well. They even seem to enjoy it in their own ways. . . .

Let me ask you, therefore, again: how am I to affirm to your satisfaction that I am still a self-conscious observant member of the Jewish religion when I can no longer affirm to my own satisfaction that I am a member of what men have often optimistically called the human race?

What, after all, is the Jewish religion? A bunch of beards in *Mea Sharim?* Is that what I must now swear to? Beards without Jews? Offal! I have nothing in common with such parasites. If these Guardians of the City, these Jewish fascists, are what you call the Jews, I want no part of belonging to them. But if you continue to ask me what I am if I am not Jewish, then I must tell you that I am nothing if not Jewish . . . and yet I am Jewish and still nothing. Nothing! Even when—like all Jews—I begin to get bleary-eyed about my so-called Jewish identity.

21

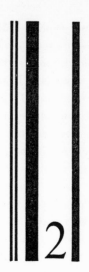

2

THE child you have inquired about has a black skin. In your country she would be called nigger! I call her my daughter. A lie for her sake. She was born in a mud hut in the Southern Hejaz where she ate food cooked over dried camel dung. Her real father and mother? Hopefully they are dead, spared any further misery. You must write and tell me whether she, as an adopted child, is also disinherited. The girl is sweet and kind, and, were it not that one of her hands is crippled from the poliomyelitis, Ofra would grow up and make some man a fine wife and mother of his children. As it is, I wonder. Every night she cries out in her sleep. She says she cannot remember her real parents. Again I wonder.

I told you my wife is a good cook but she would make a far better plow horse. Her time of fertility is past. The child was never hers. A foundling. It does not comfort me to know that Esther has killed men in our War of Independence.

Esther Protruding Lip, as they called her, was born in Bessarabia. Even in Europe her family had land and could farm it. They were not much better than peasants. Esther's first husband, a Jew

22

from the town of Cziffer in Slovakia, died of typhus in one of the camps. How she managed to find two such suckers is a mystery to me, for she was never what you would call feminine. Now she has a mustache, looks ten years older than me, complains terribly. I do not like the way she smells. Sometimes I have affairs with other women. In general, they are always too demanding. My heart is weak. The doctor tells me I must not overstrain myself. Esther takes care of me; she will not allow me to eat fatty meats or drink carbonated water. I have a stone. It is misery when I pass water. What else can I tell you that you don't already know?

I lied to you about my sister Perl. She now lives in Beersheba, has remarried, to a man from the potash works, an emigré from Kishinev, a very simple man whom she rules over like a queen. I don't see them if I can help it but I hear about them often from some of Esther's Kishinev relations. They tell me Perl still tries to have children and that they always miscarry. Her womb must be made of sandpaper. She was always that way. Harsh!

Given: my parents are dead; my future obliterated; my lovely Lilo—she who would have been my wife, the mother of my children—what did they do to her? Surely you know the answer to my questions. Just because what happened was unspeakable does not mean that one should forget. Almost every night late one can hear the shootings, rifle fire at the border, not thirty kilometers from this place. Presently the mortars and light machine guns join the show. They make a frightful noise. Then the UNO patrols are seen rushing through our settlement, their red lights cutting a deep swath in the miserable night. To cause the guns to stop, to find the dead and then return the corpses to the proper authorities on either side of the line, it must be a tiresome job for these Swedes. Why don't we do them a big favor and stop? When even now murder is always close at hand, it is not a question of one side or the other side being right or wrong. We just seem to like to kill each other. We are not deterred by the waste. And yet you and your late client dare to ask me when I

23

was last to the study house. Very funny. Would you also like to know if I still believe in God?

Because the answer is I do. I believe even as I know that what I believe is a blasphemy, that it doesn't matter whether I believe or not. For me all such fine distinctions are now useless. Finished. No amount of your money can buy back what we have lost in that respect. Still I believe and exult in my belief. How could it have been otherwise? If not God, then who else was responsible? Hitler? Horthy? Rudolf Kastner? Alois Brunner? The Papal Nuncio in Budapest or the Jewish Agency? My father? Maybe Bela?

Was the death of six millions the work of anything less than a God?

For that matter, we Jews, His people, did we spring up out of the amoeba or the cheese louse?

It is obvious that we were formed in His Image, even to our women with their vicious tempers, their nagging voices; and so I believe in Him, in everything; and I hold every bit of what happened against Him.

Only He betrayed us. He profaned us. He took our prayers in vain. He mocked us. He rewarded us with cruelty. He listened but did not hear. He was there and He was not there when we needed Him. He led us into injustice, into this place of asylum and exile where there can be no asylum and exile since we are all stricken with the same history, have the same horrible memories.

I ask you, Rubin, was that the work of a pigmy? It was the Jewish God. The God of Sinai. Our Father. . . . The Lord God of Hosts. If not He, who then? If He could make the Creation, was the Destruction too much for Him? Or do you think He felt not like His usual self on that day when the order was first fixed and left it up to a bunch of clowns at Wansee to do His dirty work for Him?

Eichmann and Krumey and the rest. What were they but cretins and clowns? Whoever may have thought he was responsible, whichever way the thing was eventually carried out, in the end only He was responsible. We placed ourselves in His hands and He did not disappoint us. I tell you there is a straight road from the Ark of the Covenant to the ovens at Ravensbruck, Treblinka, Auschwitz, Statlo, and the other places, and it is lined on both sides with the bleached bones of my fellow Jews. I believe in those Jews as the work of the Jewish God. Only They will never fail me. I believe in Them far more than I believe in the State. The bony sockets of Their eyes stare blankly past all of us toward the Disaster to which They bear witness as God's Chosen People. And we, the living, cursed with our lives, bear witness again and again to the facts of Their death. That is why we are here. As if you didn't know that. How could you not know? Did you think you can put an ocean between yourself and such guilt? You, in America, saw the pictures in the newsreels, the books, the sleazy magazines, and no doubt you winced and then turned away with water in your eyes, a tightening in your throat, giddy with revulsion, lightheaded. Sometimes memory is like a kind of vertigo; one has to struggle to avoid the trap. I know the feeling well. So why now am I giving you more lectures on the same subject? Because, I tell you, what we are trying to avoid stretches endlessly before us. Even in my dreams, which come in separate frames just like the newsreels, only they never seem to end. We have all broken faith with those Jews. My life in this country is a blasphemy. I hear the victims cursing me, crying out in my sleep, the true Believers in the world *as is*. What if tomorrow we should find another War Criminal and hang him from the highest post in the land? What vengeance will have been served? We cannot murder ourselves. Our only punishment must be to remain alive. Be still. Be still. I know that I am talking too much. For thirty thousand or forty thousand American dollars, as the case may be, I am prepared to forego rhetoric and tell you simply that I am

25

your brother, a Believer, also Jewish. I will swear to it if you like. Why not? The world *as is* is more dishonest than the world *as if*. That is as it should be.

   Should be what?

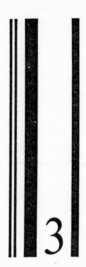

3

Should be what, I say? What kind of business is this?

Alex could not control his head from jerking up, as if on a string, yet it was only Esther again. She must have heard him mumbling. He sensed that she had come into the room and was now standing directly behind his chair. He covered his papers. "Busy," he croaked in English, forgetting that she hardly knew the language.

Then he took a soft pencil and wrote all across fresh paper the word *PEACE*. He held the paper over his head so that it faced Esther.

"What happened to your tongue?" the woman asked.

He made a grotesque gurgling noise.

"Anyway," she said, "it's your brain I worry about the most."

After another moment, she added: "Who cares? Do you think this lawyer in America cares what you think?"

Alex was more offended than he wanted to let on. He could not control the humiliating blush that burned on his face. Twisting his frail body about to face her heavy sullen presence, he grimaced without thinking at the streak of black down above her upper lip. *"Who cares?"* she was shouting.

Alex bit his tongue and looked away. He was short of breath. The stone was pressing against his kidney. From the way Esther continued to accuse him with her stares he could tell that supper was already on the table. He heard her say abruptly: "Will Yagodah Pasha eat or will he continue making a fool of himself?"

Alex replied, cringing: "A minute. A minute more."

But Esther wouldn't turn away.

"Please. A minute more," he pleaded then, turning away himself.

"Yes Pasha!"

Immediately Alex found he was able to resume the letter. Indeed, it was as if, in a blink of the eye, his hand had sought out the exact same spot on the page where he had left off. He felt the pain begin to ease, a relaxation, a pressure oozing downward from his head during which he was aware of his thoughts racing quite rapidly along certain well-prescribed routes. It was another long while, though, before he heard the woman cough and shuffle out of the room.

The long summer heat in Israel affects me badly. I am working as an X-ray technician, salary pretty low, and we are four, counting my wife's mother, now in the hospital.

Mister, consider what I tell you as a message to Man. I do not write because my fingers are itching. I shall not spare myself or other Jews. I wish to be fair. And I shall not be quiet about the so-called humane gentiles, even Germans.

Where I was born in Transylvania people called themselves alternately Hungarians or Rumanians. This was the ancient Erdély, a place richly endowed in minerals, grain, forest lands, and vineyards. Hostile armies had fought over us for centuries. Many different peoples swarmed among us: Poles, Slovaks, Ukrainians,

Gypsies, Magyars, Saxons, even Bulgars, Turks, some French and Germans; and we were but a separate minority, lost in their midst. The result of this constant confusion, this constant changing back and forth of nationalities, was that we never knew to whom we belonged, or even what shire or judicial district we were in, and we didn't care. Politics were impossible—a bloody game of petty ideologies in which we were always up for grabs along with the salt fields, the marshes filled with butane gas, and whatever else could be assigned a value. You cannot imagine how difficult it was to be a nationalist when you had to change your loyalties almost as often as you changed your shirt. And every time we washed our hands of one regime to suffer under still another, the trains were made to run in a different direction.

It is stated that when Rumania's first king, in 1866, was invited to take the crown, he drew a line connecting Hamburg with India on the map of the world. When he saw that this line was running right across Transylvania, he uttered what were considered prophetic words: "Transylvania is a country with a splendid future!" What nonsense! We were a backwater of the Old Kingdom where the peasants still hid their money in their socks, rather than trust the corrupt bankers of Bucharest, and where men like my father were active in a Jewish community that numbered nearly 150,000 throughout the provinces—"the foremost Jewish community in the Balkans," to quote one gazetteer of the period. But did that make us any less of a backwater? The fact is we were thankful for our backwater status. Some of our trains still ran on the old large gauge of Imperial Russian capitalism. The currency fluctuated like quicksilver. The police were greedy and lazy and the criminals inefficient. There were the masses and the leading classes. There were also the "minorities" and, among them, the Jews. Some find it significant that our chief exports to Western Europe at the time were always listed as walnuts, beans, and cheese. All nonessentials.

When I was born during the reign of King Ferdinand and his

29

beloved Queen Mary, in Bucharest, it was a period of relative prosperity. Rumania was slowly paying off her war debts, and Her Gracious Majesty, a pretty German lady with a vapid smile, fond of wearing tiers of beads, or a laurel wreath in her hair, was always sending greetings to her royal cousins in England. The king and his ministers, meanwhile, were addressing themselves to "the minority problem." What was the use? Rumania had more than 500,000 orphans from the Great War. The people were poor. Eighty-two per cent worked on the land. Bucharest was hundreds of miles away from the new province where we lived. In Clig even the liberals talked like anti-Semites. But while they talked they did little and we lived comfortably amid our *numeras clauses,* never knowing for very long to whom we belonged until August, 1940, when the Queen's son Caroli fled, pursued by the bullets of the Hungarians. Once more Hungary annexed our territory. We were reunited with our Magyar brethren. Hungarian troops occupied Clig, which became Koligsvar. The trains rolled westward.

Funny. Even today I possess documents of one sort or another which confirm that I have been a Czechoslovak-British-Israeli soldier, a British policeman in Palestine (under the CID), a Salvadoran citizen, a cattle farmer from the Dominican Republic, a ski instructor from the town of Celerina in Switzerland, a Portuguese croupier in Macao, and a member of the Turkish Red Cross. At this late date it is difficult for me to remember which is a forgery and which is real. Yiddish, or even Hebrew, is not my native tongue and I would be grateful for help with my English. Probably you wouldn't believe it but I have passed a London matriculation in 1946, while waiting to be demobbed from active service.

Now do you see what you are asking of me when I have to swear if I am still Jewish? Do I want your pity? Yes. Of course. But I also must make you see. . . .

People say Yagodah is a Sephardic name with a Russian spelling for the Hebrew Yehudah. From others I have heard of an ancient Aramaic formation meaning "the eye of God." In either case, my family was driven across Europe from Spain to Galicia and into the Ukraine, but at the time of Hetman Chmielnicki they fled southwest again to the seven cities, first to Kronstadt, then northwest to the town of Kligensfelt (Clig, as I shall call it), where they remained and prospered. My maternal great-grandfather made his fortune as a cooper. Appropriately enough, when names were given out, he took Fass. When my mother met my father the Hapsburg Empire was on the point of dissolution, although the impact of pan-Germanism was still very real. It is not surprising that my parents should have identified with the moderating influences of German culture and German Jewry. My father served with distinction in the Austrian army in the Great War, first with the Bosnians, then with the mountain cavalry as an NCO. After being slightly wounded at Lespdíi, he was discharged in 1917, came home, married my mother (whom he had met before the war) in the German Jewish synagogue at Clig. I have seen a copy of their wedding certificate, sealed with red and yellow wax stamps in French, a novelty. It was at that same synagogue that we were taught our Jewishness. Although we were not observant we learned quickly. You may judge for yourself if the lessons were of any substance . . .

In Transylvania there was no war until 1942. Hungary was left autonomous. No German administrators were appointed. We Jews went about conscious that something somewhere was dreadfully amiss but never absolutely convinced that it would or could affect us. The local authorities from the Ministry of the Interior continued to treat us with the same historic mixture of envy, contempt and civility. Even when they were changed from Rumanians to Hungarians their attitudes were no different, and the local population, mostly Szeckler but with numerous pockets of other minorities, remained hostile but respectful. In that sense our town was not like the villages of Slovakia or Poland. There were no dominant groups and each minority made use of the other for whatever political leverage they could have. Moreover, if we had been given a choice, we would have certainly preferred the Hungarians to our former reactionary governors. My father said: "In Hungary the people are more progressive-minded." In the Hungarian Parliament others argued: "This war is not our war. Our enemies are our friends and our friends our enemies." We felt confident that these distinguished gentlemen were not merely showing off their powers of oratory.

And our hopes were confirmed even when the various Nationalist factions took power under the Regency. There were Jews serving in the armed forces. The news boards and town criers continued to show us no malice. If there was more of a bureaucracy, it was not necessarily directed against us. The seasons changed: crops were bought and sold; the gold and salt mines worked steadily. My father, by profession an advocate, had many other interests. Working with my mother's fortune, which he had no doubt doubled and trebled by investing in the mines as well as by lending money at interest to the peasants, he hoarded a large part of his wealth in gold for my Berliner art education after the war.

Economically, Father also fancied himself a liberal. Not that he was a meddler or a do-gooder, but he was a firm believer in the social contract, a man who thought people should be encouraged to advance through their own efforts; and he recognized that the German had his grievances. In this regard Father was fond of reminding us how even Aristotle saw no basic alteration possible in the status of master and slave. He would say, "The different states of men are advantageous for all. Some beings command and others obey." Yet Father was also convinced that the politicians and the "responsible classes" would not allow Hitler to have his way for much longer, convinced that civic life must shortly take a turn for the better, convinced—in fact—that Nazism was just some temporary aberration of the German personality, comparable to those earlier eras which had produced legends about trolls or elves. Once he even compared the jack-booted SA to our own Kossuth movement, and another time to the crusaders against the Ottoman Turks.

To make matters more complicated, Father had little love for Bolshevism. "In an imperfect world," he used to say, "the socialism of Ivan is the socialism of the firing squad." Father considered himself a political realist. He was always saying that without a reformation of national character the class system was a necessary deterrent to the passions of the uneducated. But Father thought Germany was more likely to provide such a reformation than any of the other faltering powers! Thus, on the one hand, he had a high respect for the German mind and German progress, while, on the other hand, having ideals and a strong sense of Jewish tradition, he simply refused to take Germany's pretensions at organized Jew hatred seriously—although, as I have indicated, he did have a high regard for all things German, culturally as well as in the commercial world.

Now you may ask: How was this possible?

To begin with, understand that my father was educated in Vienna. Additionally he always seems to have had a rather Germanic sense of punctilio. Father's favorite reading was the *Official Gazette*. Indeed it may be said that he modeled his way of thinking after the various ordinances printed therein. He put on that he was a serious man, and had a rather high opinion of himself and his attainments, which we were all taught to respect, but he was basically only a petty bourgeois puritan who knew how to push.

All that my father took seriously, in fact, was business, the family, and my education. He also was a bit of a gastronome, but he lacked any real flair. And if he got along well enough with people Father had few really close friends, perhaps because he could seem so tight-fisted and cold. . . .

If pressed hard I would have to say that my father was a ruthless man, but that was, no doubt, because he had been very early frustrated in his efforts to make a successful practice of the law; and he swore, consequently, that he did not want me to enter trade. Father belonged to no political parties. He was not always finagling for power. Neither did he approve of any of the various youth movements which, beginning in Germany, were springing up all over that part of Europe. He had a college friend in Prague whose son was a shining light of sorts in the *Wandervogel*, and he was constantly setting the particulars of young Blum's irresponsibility before me as little moral exempla. The other great lesson to be learned concerned the daughter of his old friend Lebovitz in Krakow. Hannah Lebovitz had emigrated to Palestine and was killed in an Arab raid on her settlement. Father concluded that Jews died in Palestine just as they had died in our part of Europe during the pogroms.

After the Great War my father had been a young man of promise. Well-connected through marriage, he had served briefly on the provincial board of trade. There was a scandal; I never knew all that happened, but I do know that before his dismissal father was able to tour most of East Europe and had even written a brief monograph, entitled *My Impressions*, which was printed privately at his own expense.

Father's views on the economic future of neighboring Poland may serve to give you a better insight into what kind of basically humane man he was. "Poland," he wrote in *My Impressions*, "needs, more perhaps than any other country, a powerful government. The masses can be of value to their country if they are guided by a clever hand who knows how to get the best out of them and who can put each individual in his most productive place."

My Impressions also contained a fascinating series of tables on the median age, height, family size, and income of the Polish village of Sopronowiz in which my father estimated that the Sopronowizers were of the median age of 24.2 as opposed to 29.7

34

in the rest of Poland and 31.5 in the Warsaw area and also that Sopronowizers had median households of 3.56 persons as opposed to 3.27 for the rest of Poland and 4.1 in Warsaw and environs. Based on such guidelines, relying, too, on the fact that over 35 per cent of the population of Sopronowiz was under fourteen years of age (as opposed to 29 per cent in the Warsaw area) Father recommended that his fellow capitalists undertake a rigorous program of vocational training for the young Sopronowizers in their own best interests! "When the factories of the future look to Sopronowiz and villages like it," my father declared, "the children of Sopronowiz must be ready to greet them with the assurances of a diligence based upon their learned attainments. . . ."

Father concluded by quoting Homer's description of the civilization of the Cyclops: "They have neither assemblies for consultation nor *themistes*, but everyone exercises jurisdiction over his wives and his children, and they pay no regard to one another." After elaborating on Savigny's jurisprudential distinctions between *Volksrecht* (the positive law of the people) and *Volksgeist* (the spirit which begets that law) and stipulating how *Volksrecht* must spring from *Volksgeist* but *Volksgeist* is not to be confused with "mere custom," my father departed from this tangent to discourse again on the necessity for Poles (and all other East Europeans) to extend the *Patria Potestas* of domestic life to the full range of civic, domestic, and commercial affairs. "In the genesis of political ideas," my father wrote, "it must be assumed that kinship in blood is the sole possible ground of community in political functioning. . . ."

"Shall the shuttle weave and the lyre play by itself," my father paraphrased the great Nicomachean. "Shall the architect be without servants, the tiller steer without the sailor? Who shall man the looms of the future?" he demanded. "How can we best yoke these turbulent energies of unrest?"

My father proceeded to answer his own questions: "When I look around me I see unbelievable breakdown and sloth. A petty egotistical individualism supplants ancient rules of procedure; and they are being pampered whose only resource may be their physiques. All of Eastern Europe cries out for discipline. Why are the poor so afraid of hard work? I fear for these people—as I do for the pitiful multitudes everywhere."

Unfortunately, the only thing I inherited directly from my father was his extremely wooden prose style. He thought of himself as inevitably one of the "leading classes," but I wished to be a vagabond. If only I could say that I was also an idealist, but like him I tended to be selfish, which I justified by finding reformers and socialists alike ill-humored, dry. My father was constantly admonishing me to improve my mind so that I could someday *lead*; I think he would have settled for a respectable ne'er-do-well, or even a Bohemian poseur; for he never whole-heartedly disapproved of my painting, and, if I had nothing better to do, he often told me to read books. I will say so much for him; he approved of books; and he didn't seem to care what I read. We had a gramophone and he liked to tell me stories of the concerts he had been to in Vienna and Budapest and Prague as a young man. He always said we would be going again *soon*. Yet even though we often discussed the trips we would take when "the hostilities" would end, we never had any thought of leaving our town permanently. The few Zionists we knew were a laughing stock. Charity cases. We did not take their disciplined ways seriously. More often than not, we scorned them for their priggish sobriety. When they, in turn, called us "empty" or "selfish" or "cowardly" we learned to recognize the obvious jealousy that motivated their insults.

Life was too good. And we didn't believe in suffering. It was especially fine to live in our little patch of the countryside until the German occupation in spring, 1944. My friends and I, we read mostly books in the German language, Wassermann, Carossa, Swannauer, Bettinger, Dehm, Fahidy; even Marx was still

36

being printed in inexpensive Hungarian editions. What matter that if a hundred or so kilometers away they were deporting some Jews? What could we do to help them? Besides, these were not of our kind—these *Ostjuden*.

I must remind you that even under the strictest interpretations of the Nürnberg Codes my father was exempted because of his prior military service. Since the codes were not even in effect yet in Hungary, we believed we had nothing to fear. My mother used to say we were even better off than the half-Jews or the baptized ones. "Your father," she would say, "fought for Austria and was decorated. They will not turn against him now."

Mother, you see, had her own malignant variety of simple-minded faith in the permanency of Germanic values. What she liked she called German in contradistinction to those things of which she disapproved; these, she argued, were provincial.

Mother could be shrill about the loutish behavior of our neighbors who squatted in their tiny blue shacks along the slopes of the Sellagvar citadel, but there was no higher compliment she could pay one of the locals than to call him a German gentleman.

Her attitudes were conditioned by her upbringing and education. Mother's father, Istran Fass, had been a typically Balkanized dandy, a fancier of fine horses and loose women, who had deserted his wife to run off with a dancer from the café Nagy Gabor. Although Istran Fass had inherited enough money at the death of his father, the pious Andras Meyer, to continue supporting both his families, he did so grudgingly, without any outward show of affection toward his only daughter. When the first wife died, Istran—to spite his dead wife's relatives—bought a cemetery plot with three graves, one for each of the women and one for himself. Then he had my mother sent to a Protestant school near Debrecen which was founded by some latter-day opponents of Matthew Corvinus.

Mother had come from a comfortable, pious Jewish household where the women still wore their heads shaven under wigs. In

Debrecen she had to turn away from such a life and was then re-buffed by the new. I doubt if she ever got over the shock. From his home in Budapest, Istran Fass continued to provide her with an ample clothing allowance, money for treats, special tutors; nothing could improve her situation. There was no denying that she was different; unpopular. Forced to live as a perpetually en-vious outsider to a culture in which she could never share, she had to tolerate constant slurs, insults from her schoolmates. At the age of fifteen, she fled the despised place and came back to live with her mother's relatives, a wealthy aunt and uncle, but by then the damage was done. Mother was not of one world, hardly of the other. When her father summoned her to Budapest to live with his new family, she refused in a lengthy insulting note in which she called him "a lecher . . . a goat . . . a parvenu . . . and a criminal," whereupon it was said that he settled an ex-tremely large sum of money on her and never again communi-cated with her until the day he died.

Mother's experience in the world outside Clig had left her with very little respect for our kind of education, the written word. Her father had considered himself an educated man; he had often traveled to Lemberg, to Basel, to Berlin, and Paris. Mother could never forgive him for what he had done to her, so, by some strange mutation of hurt, she passed over all the obvious flaws in his moral character and blamed his sins on his worldliness. Mother always said she did not like worldly people. She despised them almost as much as she despised the Hasidim who would oc-casionally wander down to us from Sătmar, a hundred or so kilo-meters to the north. She called them "bastardizers" and "deceiv-ers." No wonder. Mother's aunt and uncle had been strict *mithnagdim*. In their home the only "worldly" books that were permitted were the yearbooks of the Jewish community, the census, certain of the collected homilies of a certain Rabbi Adler, and a bowdlerization of Leonhard Trank's *Polish Metaphysics*, a truly depressing work. Consequently when she found us reading

38

books by some of the great German Jewish intellectuals whose work was making such an impact on Jew and gentile alike, she would caution us tentatively that these authors were not to be regarded as wholesome fare. She found it of crucial significance that Karl Marx was the son of an apostate Jew, not because she still held strong views on the virtues of Judaism, but because she believed such people were always "troublemakers."

Mother's own reading obliquely recalled the numerous hurts she had suffered in the lost world of her childhood. She took a German-language fashion magazine from Vienna, read a German Bible, liked to have the classic Yiddish stories read to her (since she claimed she could no longer make out the Hebrew characters), but her favorite author was one Max Winkleman, a second-rate, assimilated Jewish author of potboilers about honorable fathers and mothers and their wayward sons and daughters which were chiefly set in places like Carlsbad, Monte Carlo, or the Swiss Alps, and which usually encompassed a couple of lugubrious death scenes and concluded with the union of two honorable family names through marriage. Mother was constantly recommending to my sisters that they look into Winkleman's work, which invariably amused my father and myself. Father did not like any fiction. He read histories of the Bourse in Paris, essays about heavy machinery, or learned explanations of how Saint Paul had meant to remain a Jew. Believing, as he did, in only two of the arts—music and portrait painting (and portrait painting above all else)—Father was both vain and philistine. He always had to be coaxed to perform for us, although he could sing passably well (arias from Mozart and Rossini), and was a fine mimic. But, whenever the subject of Winkleman would come up, Father always chose to show his lighter side by delivering a perfect imitation of a character in one of the novels. Chiefly I remember him saying: "Dear Frou-Frou, won't you pass the *fraises du bois?*" Or: "Baden is quiet now that the Guardsmen have gone off to Sedan? *Eh?*" Although my mother pretended to be cross with Father when he teased her so, we children usually found their banter delightful.

Yes. We were a very merry group. Though we read all the bleak headlines in the newspapers we felt that what was happening on the front page of *Pester Lloyd* was quite remote from our town where, that winter, there had been a record snowfall and the promise of fine fruit crops in the spring, and where my sister Sarah was about to give us her second child, and plans were being made for my sister Perl's wedding to the apothecary's son, Adam. Finally, I was so taken up with my own affair of the heart that it was evident even from the way I walked or hung my head on my shoulders so that everybody talked about me and applauded me for my audacity.

Was I really such a rakehell? No. I had chosen much like my father. But I was the youngest, a bit of an idiot about things like butterflies, histories of the Japanese Islands, and Chopin nocturnes. I was also Father's favorite. The only son.

Father's sense of anticipation about my future alliance with my cousin Lilo was noticeably superior to what he felt about the girls and their chosen ones; and my mother identified completely with this poor little orphan girl.

Father and mother were distant cousins. Though they teased me often it was always with a spirit of good-heartedness and wonderment that I had chosen so well. Their reasons for being proud of me were seemingly too numerous to count: being in love with one's own cousin (even though she happened to be a cousin once removed) was not, as you see, an unusual circumstance in a small town like ours where there was a real closeness among the better Jewish families, but it could be an especially piquant occurrence when the cousin was an orphan who, again, had been sent to the best Jewish boarding schools in Switzerland and who now lived with a maiden aunt and possessed a fortune in securities and gold certificates of her own valued in the millions. Ah! That was bound to set some tongues wagging, bound to make me think that I had been blessed with outrageously good fortune and was about to set off on a remarkably unique course.

What lies I told myself. In moments of pique it would occur to me that my father had as much regard for Lilo's fortune as he did for our proposed alliance, for he was always speaking openly to us of our future together by which I chose to think he meant the future prices of Lilo's stocks and bonds, her gold certificates, Rumanian treasury notes, all the leis, kronen, and Swiss francs which Father was constantly transubstantiating as dollars, pounds sterling, bolivars, marks, francs, gulden, and vice versa.

Father was the chief executor of Lilo's father's estate, and he jealously guarded every pengö. He took a boundless joy in demonstrating to our assembled families at the end of a year that he had done far better by Lilo than he had done by his own investments. Pretending to care little for money in those days, I used to make elaborate shows of my fiscal naïveté for the benefit of Lilo and her aunt Pepi, afraid that people might otherwise confuse me with one of those fortune-hunting creatures in a Winkleman novel and not realizing, of course, that my father had probably acted in the same way with my mother.

How little originality I had when it came to Lilo. Yet who would have dared to question the genuineness of our relationship? Adam and Perl might be setting up a family, my mother always said, but it was not the same with "her little ones," who were in love. And, Mother added, "When I married Newman he was also the poorer one. What does it matter when we are all now so comfortably well off?"

Such complete identification of my mother with Lilo was a continual source of astonishment to me. Mother could never allow our relationship to seem happy, merely casual; it had to be a delirium. She was always pointing to the way we walked together, what we said, our silences in her presence, as sure indications of a passion that went beyond mere friendship, companionship, or in-

41

fatuation. Mother infused our lives with a kind of fairy-story madness of preparations and decorous formalities, arguing, for example, that the observances of our betrothal, although a matter of course, needed the most painstaking planning if nothing was to be overlooked which might promote our future happiness together.

How we were pampered! How we were talked about! Mother was our fiercest advocate. If she so much as thought she heard people saying that there were other girls advantageously placed, besides Lilo, she would immediately proceed to recatalogue all of Lilo's advantages. And when people said, with some justice, that I was a sickly boy, sallow-faced, unworthy of Lilo, she would then spring to my defense, as if completely unaware of the laws of paradox.

Mother's favorite way of silencing such critics was by a long, hard glance of her large dark eyes, a whisper like a cat spitting, or perhaps by merely saying in a calm and dignified manner that her son was going to give Lilo a home at long last. Mother was careful, of course, never to pass such gossip on to me. I learned of it much later from Lilo who explained how she had crimsoned when she had heard the whisperings and how she had tried not to listen, to look away.

My darling Lilo! She had fair skin, the clearest brown eyes, dark blond hair which she wore long in plaits or, occasionally, braided above the crown of her head with tortoise-shell combs. Lilo was dainty, her skin waxen with soft pink highlights. Her most striking feature was her expression—sudden, intense, like that of a wax model's face coming alive; it could strike a pose, mixing puzzlement with petulance, the blood surging just below the surface of the fine silken skin. Lilo was lovely but maddening at times the way she would purse her lips when she glanced at you, as if she were suddenly about to be kissed. In general, though, her reserve was perfect: she had been taught to flirt at boarding school, yet she was not a fickle girl but prudent, gentle, and soft-spoken. Some said she did not look Jewish. Her eyes bulged delicately with amused surprise under the molded hinges of her soft white lids. Her body was small: her waistline slim and delicate. Her manners were also delicate, the product of that same boarding-school education. She was not a snob.

Lilo called me Alex, occasionally Shandor, which was also my father's way. I had no special pet names for her. She had learned a smattering of English and she could speak French with a charming accent. She was an accomplished pianist, a good water-colorist, and, though theater was scarcely to be found in our provincial patch of the countryside, she knew the names and leading roles of all the famed actors and actresses of Europe. She was also skillful in identifying wild flowers and in writing acrostic poems in German.

In none of these ways would she show herself off, however, or attempt to compete with my friends and myself. I learned of them only by observation, for Lilo was retiring, and she preferred to appear mild, almost withdrawn, sometimes even a bit silly. If she was ever sharp with anybody it was with my father, but that was to be expected because of the affairs they had in common. And because she looked quite young, nobody ever thought to mention that she was a full half-year older than me.

Like me, Lilo lived a large portion of her life through books. Her manner with strangers was such that she always seemed to be warning them to be kind to her. Some thought her overly shy; others took her as she presented herself—a happy but naïve girl. They did not, perhaps, notice her eyes, or the charming, quiet, but nonetheless brazen petulance of her smile.

I had not expected my little cousin to fall in love with me. In all the years that she was away from Clig I had merely wanted to possess her as mine. It turned out upon her return that the war made her choices more limited than I had realized. So many of our friends had fled and the remainder were not always sufficiently cultured. Presently Lilo seemed as devoted to me as I was to my parents, and as my parents were to the welfare of both of us.

A happy time, I tell you. We were all contented with ourselves. We were even optimistic in those days, like newly rich peasants. If we never spoke of your late client Mr. James, Rubin, it was because we hardly ever thought of him. When we did, our thoughts were never flattering. Poor Bela! You must recall that he left under a cloud of disgrace. A certain Slovak officer planned to shoot him on sight. My father liked to tell the story! There had been much drinking, a quarrel over a horse, a woman, a brawl, and Bela had bitten off the man's ear. Alternately, Father would be either boastful or shamefaced about his only brother whom he never failed to call "Poor Bela." Once my father confided to me that Bela was a syphilitic, and had been simple-minded at birth. Another time he said Bela deserted from the Austrian army. Father never failed to describe his older brother as unhappy, a drunken prankster, lonely and cut-off, miserable in America, well-to-do perhaps but definitely on the wrong side of the authorities, and in a strange land which my father intentionally mispronounced as "Ahoy" when he meant "Ohio."

Father said Ahoy was a country full of locusts and gangsters. He said there were no towns, only farms. He described it as a place where Jews were forced to eat pork and marry with Negroes, where Jews and Negroes wandered together as homelessly as gypsies. The cruelty and the beauty of the world did not evade us completely where we were. "Black bread," my father said, "always tastes better when you eat it in your own country."

Thus, pitying Bela's alienation, we rejected every one of his boasting letters as mere bombast, blatant forgeries. What was there for us to envy when we were so comfortable here on our own? And why—if Bela truly was so well off—why had he changed his name like a criminal? Why didn't he send evidence in a form that would have mattered to us: money or gifts or tickets for a holiday in America? Unlike our other relatives in the big

44

European cities, Bela had contributed nothing toward his parents' headstone; he never even visited us and he didn't send presents. Surely you can understand now that though we told ourselves we did not need for anything, we would have taken whatever he sent, if only to feel better about our poor near relation whom we thought to be cut off from his roots, alone, four thousand miles across a hostile sea. Also it would have been a way of indemnifying my father for the pains he had gone to on Bela's behalf when he had first gotten into trouble and had to flee. How can I make you understand? From the refugees who left Clig we received infrequent letters about the hardships of the Depression, of your bread lines, Murder Incorporated, and the Jew-hater Father Coughlin, and we expected more from that ingrate than mere materialistic boasting about the extent of his holdings. Was Bela James just another American gangster? We had no way of knowing. But when we got no further assurances from him, life went on without dear Bela, as if he were already dead. A *kaddish* was said over the distant corpse and we worried about the living. . . .

I believe I should stress this point, Rubin, because I know that a man such as you no doubt feels superior to a man of my background and that, in fact, is the basis for your pity. But you must disabuse yourself of such pity at all costs. Our Clig standards of living sufficed to make us envious of nobody. Clig was a backwater, yes, but so is Denver, Colorado, and yet your General Eisenhower goes there to recuperate from his heart attacks. And what, pray tell me, is Merton, Ohio? No! Only prigs should feel superior to our Kligensfelt community.

Sometimes you live in a backwater and it seems like the principal spot on earth. Does the Arab squatting over his dung in Amman or Sena think of himself as inhabiting some ignominious pest hole? I will not have you sneering at Clig. Rubin, I have in front of me my schoolboy's diary (one of the few pieces of memorabilia I was able to take with me). Turning to October 12, 1939, the day Uncle Bela first made his benefaction (while no

45

doubt sneering at that little dung heap from which he told you he sprang), I find the following entry which I shall be pleased to translate for you:

> *Exceptionally early snowfall. The snow heavy and soft, falling continuously now for seventy-two hours. The passes between here and Dej, between Zalau and Satu-Mare, are closed because of the snow. Even Clig lies buried. In the Public Gardens trees stand up to the heavens and are lost. All night the snow fell. To Gidelves and all along the Little Szemos it is dangerous to cross because of thin ice. Every so often the sun appears, then disappears. What warmth can melt this thick covering? The air rings with the silence of falling snow. Birds do not sound. I am without a proper pair of snow shoes. The snow spins through the air like clots of cotton or heavy pollen, yet I feel as if I could reach out through the window and touch the spires of St. Mihaly, save that the air bites my fingers. In three days' time we are to journey to Debrecen so that I can register for my examinations. To Debrecen it is a trip of more than half a day in clear weather. Father says Mr. Ignotu of the Ministry is not one of those who expects presents, but my mother says: "Give and worry about offending the man later." I must remember to buy zinc white and a wide sable brush in Debrecen. Hopefully, then I shall return in time to paint this wonderful first snowfall. Tomorrow perhaps I shall work in crayons if the cold is not unbearable. But now I must practice my Latin verbs and it is just as well. . . . It is snowing in Carpathians from Ruthenia in the Ukraine to Bukovina. . . . Can the roads be cleared in time? Father says there is a politician in Britain named WC . . . and my uncle sends us belated greetings for the Jewish New Year from America . . . 5700. . . .*

46

And so, dear Rubin, my point should now be obvious. Was it Blake who said one finds a universe in a grain of sand? Well, the particular grains of sand between the Moldavian Plain and the High Tatra was our universe; and Bela no longer inhabited that universe. If he was still worrying about us, we had long since grown apathetic to him. Go ahead and think of us as savages out of the *National Geographic*, but recall: At the Municipal Exposition in 1941 three of my drawings in Conte were purchased by the Rajk family, a leading family, including one self-portrait. Did Bela really tell you that we had little save our troubles to distract us? True enough, we did not have clothes-washing machines and two cars in every garage, as you Americans do, but we had values. As my mother used to say, quoting I Samuel [15:22]: "To obey is better than sacrifice, and to hearken, than the fat of rams."

But what would you, or your late client, know of such things?

4

In the town, my family lived in a handsome house with a large garden in the back of which my father had planted expensive French poplars as a screen. The garden was large enough to have at one side a rare Japanese cherry tree, and flowering bushes of all sorts. There was also a patch for sunflowers, a rose garden, a gooseberry patch, and a grove of elders under the shade of which was a tiny summerhouse tendriled with withered grapevines. During the winter months the vines and wooden posts would acquire a covering of rime and hoarfrost the way a magnet attracts iron filings. During the Feast of Tabernacles we would decorate this place privately, undisturbed by our gentile neighbors. Father used to say he was giving thanks for the success of the peasants' crops by the sale of which they had again managed to repay all his loans with interest on time.

Our house was in a new quarter—a long ride by tram from the Fóvár, the old Saxon castle in the center of the city where the palaces of the local nobility who wintered in Clig were to be found. Most of the houses in our quarter were painted a uniform blue, but ours was of brick—ocherous brownish red with deeper

48

brown trim. It was located not far away from the principal brick factory and a German champagne warehouse, but it was protected from these eyesores by a wide square fringed with elders and linden trees and with a grassy fountain area at the other side of which was a branch-line railroad station, an electric tramway connection, news venders, and market stalls. Concrete benches dotted the square; there was also a row of market stalls facing us, an outdoor tavern frequented by the leftists, and a tiny bandstand. Our house dominated the immediate area.

I do not know if the place is still standing but it was a fine old structure, four stories high with a copper Parisian roof (which had turned green years before), and many large sunny rooms. From a window in the mansard one could survey all the neighboring region: the hotels California and King of Prussia, the Magyar University, the Museum, the suburb at Gidelve.

My father had acquired the place as a bad debt from a bankrupt wine merchant, a crazy mercurial drunken sort of fellow said to be half gypsy who, because of his nasty manners and bleary eyes, we called simply Skirzeny der Schike. This same fellow was far from simple. He had once been quite well-to-do and had important friends among the petty nobility, as well as in the local bureaucracy, but now he lived in a log cabin in the woods with his wife and brats of which he had no less than seven, the oldest being a stepson, Miklos, about whom you shall hear more in a moment.

Skirzeny senior used to say: "The Jew is to the gypsy like strong brandy. A little is enough to make his life miserable." But he was not an anti-Semite. Nor was he such a bad sort of fellow. In fact, my father liked to say he was "harmless." When his business went bankrupt, the old man pretended to be a hunter, distilled illegal spirits, and smuggled contraband. He also continued to pay us visits, shotgun in hand, accompanied by his brats, or else by a band of besotted friends, as if to reoccupy his place. "The goy is a drunk," my mother would chant the old song, but

49

my sisters and I were always told to humor the fellow when he came to show off his former estate, stinking of alcohol and strong mastic bark, his boots caked with mud or manure; to let him wander about the place like the village fool; and even to present him at the end of a visit to my father in his study; where they would share a glass of wine together, or perhaps a cherry schnapps, and reminisce about the Great War, and even about the business through which the estate had changed hands.

This was a very strange way for my father to behave. It left me permanently feeling about our house as if our occupation of the old place was only a marginal thing, as if we were only temporary lodgers who might be dispossessed any day by the ragged Skirzeny and his band of brats. By Miklos in particular.

At the gymnasium Miklos Skirzeny had been my former classmate. If anything he was even less likable than his father. Some may have thought him merely a detestable, callow human being but I had personally tasted of his venom. A year or so younger than I, Miklos was as cruel as a hardened criminal. Though he often appeared slightly simple-minded, he was definitely not: Miklos had the cunning of a wild thing but he had very early learned to disguise what he thought behind a pale, expressionless, thin face, the mask of waste, or to make a joke of his viciousness, to play the clown for the other boys. He was quite strong, you see, having matured earlier than any of us; and it was said that he could masturbate with either hand. We middle-class children often called him "the white-skinned nigger," but, though we hated him, we also envied him and feared him. It was even rumored that Miklos kept a mistress—a cranky old whore named Bracuta who lived in a wooden cabin on the dark shore of the Szemos.

Miklos and I had played together as youngsters, a kind of hostile, armed truce, but when his father went bankrupt, war was declared outright, and I became his principal enemy. If he knew my parents were gone from the house, Miklos would come and

50

stand beneath our windows, taunting me to meet him on the darkened street, or he would follow me home from school in the dark days of the wintertime, shouting Romany curses at me, foul strings of Magyar and German.

Schiss-stücken," he would call me. *"Juden-schiss."*

One afternoon before the Christmas holidays, Miklos fell upon me in the snowy alleyway near the market place and beat me with his hands and feet and then with a stick. Having demonstrated his physical superiority, he next decided to torture me. He rubbed dog turd in my eyes and tried to make me eat it, but I gagged so often and so loudly that he became afraid somebody would overhear us, and left me there against the snow bank. I came home that evening bruised and sore. Afraid that Miklos had damaged my testicles with one of his kicks, I tried to run upstairs to examine myself, but my parents found me out. Then I had to lie to them that I had taken a bad fall from the walls of the Fóvár and they forbade me to climb there ever again. From that day on my father would tease me about how I had landed in a cow pie.

Miklos Skirzeny disappeared from Clig the next day, presumably because he was afraid that the police might be searching for him, but he simply hadn't reckoned with the fright he had given me—a fear so overpowering to my conscious efforts to resist him that I would have continued to lie, even under a police cross-examination, rather than reveal what had actually taken place between us.

And from that day on, though I was to see little of Miklos' person except in my dreams, he possessed me as the devil himself. My private nemesis always managed to keep me informed of his activities. *"Der weisser Teufel,"* as he was also called, did not return to school after the holidays, but I was able to learn from the other boys that he was working for his father. It was said that he spent most of the time at their cabin in the woods, killing squirrels, although some argued that he slept in Bracuta's shack and that the two stole jewels and reliquaries from the neighboring

51

monasteries. Still others believed him to be his father's chief smuggler. If this was so, Skirzeny der Schike remained mysteriously silent on the subject. When the old man used to come to visit my father, he would tell us only that his son read too many books. He said the boy had a good head on his shoulders only he was too wild, too brash. Miklos and his father were, in fact, extremely cordial enemies. The boy favored his mother, a dark squinting woman who occasionally served the peasants as a midwife. It was said that she could mix potency cordials, and knew how to embalm dead bodies. Skirzeny always seemed afraid of her but Miklos and she were as close as thieves. The only thing Miklos seemed to have acquired from his father was a love of shooting things. The two would often go out together after the chamois or the bruin. Presently it was rumored that Miklos was the best marksman in Clig and he had a band of young admirers who trailed along with him wherever he went.

When the German training cadres first arrived, Miklos Skirzeny started coming to town more often again. The less time he spent in the woods the more conscious he became of his manners and his attire. He joined the official Youth Movement, swore a blood oath, was on the streets every night organizing demonstrations, and volunteered to serve as a group leader in the home defense. But I am going too fast. The fact is Miklos did many things: he was nasty to the priests, brazen with the officials, showed no respect for his elders, and seemed to enjoy all the legends growing up around him—that he had made love to his own sister, that he practiced pederasty with the younger boys, that he and Bracuta had a spawn of black children—all this and worse. Miklos Skirzeny was a celebrity in a world turning upside down. He came in and out of his father's woods like Wilhelm Tell, and was feared by all to the point of blind idolatry—a kind of free spirit.

What more could he then have wanted?

But what had he wanted in the first place?

If he had simply been a bully, craving notoriety, would I have

52

been so afraid of him? And would my fear have been so paralyzing? What to others was mere devil-worship was in my case a blinding ultimatum of self-hate and self-torture. I could not pass Miklos on the street without a sudden cold shiver going down my back. When Lilo was with me, these feelings grew even more intense. Then my face would turn the color of ashes, my mouth would taste like a caldron of lye; I would spit bile; my eyes would burn and water and yet remain bloodshot; and I would tremble as if from a palsy.

Miklos had a way of staring at me from behind his long blond lashes, as if the cold blue of his eyes was really just a glass surface masking an intense red gleam of fire, or the red eyes of a snake. Why? Why had he picked me out to torture and humiliate? We never spoke but we had an understanding of mutual enmity. Was it because we were equals? Was it because he envied me, wanted to be me, wished we could change places?

I am not making these insinuations idly. Some of the more rabid anti-Semites in our town contended that there were blood ties between the Skirzenys and my mother. How do you suppose an impressionable child, such as I was, might have fancied that? I can remember when we were playmates how Miklos used to interrogate me about the old man, Istran Fass. What did he look like? Had I ever met him or seen his photographs? But I could recall no such person. There was, of course, a tiny little man with a Vandyke beard whom we were occasionally taken to visit in a house near Gidelve. He wore cutaway coats and striped trousers and sometimes greeted us in his smoking jacket, rubbing his pudgy hands together which always smelled strongly of lilac water. As I recall, he was rather nearsighted and his eyes were always running. Before kissing, he used to offer us breath mints from a flat silvery tin with a castle on the lid.

My sisters had been told that the old man was a friend of the family to whom my father, out of the goodness of his heart, had granted a small pension. I was hardly a toddler in those days.

53

They said nothing to me. Personally I doubt if such a sad little fellow could have been my mother's father. Once, years later, I even mentioned all this to the paterfamilias and he resorted to his favorite colloquialism, a bit of English slang: "Quite rich!"

Later, too, when Miklos and I were enemies, I even came to fancy that he bore a resemblance to that pallid old thing with his breath mints and rheumy eyes, but I was always able to shake myself free of such an aimless delusion, always able to discern the distinction between fact and fantasy. Still, whenever we passed on the streets, whenever our eyes met in a crowd, I shuddered at the sight of Miklos because I had this feeling that if such a thing could be possible, I was a guilty party to the affair; and I would be the one forced to yield and to atone. Since I could never manage to outstare Miklos, I would be the one to give in to him. We would be forced to exchange places. He could then cast off his brazen pose of notoriety, the shame of his blood, his class, and of his father, and I would be the despised "white nigger" while he was enjoying my friends, my family, the accolades of the community, yes, and Lilo. He would have Lilo, too.

Surely I came to fear this more than anything else, but the house chose itself as the symbol of all my fears. To this day I find the experience has affected me; I do not like the company of visitors, and I prefer not to live in a place which others have vacated. For example, I prefer even this jerry-built shack, made with my own hands, to any of the larger cabins in the settlement which others have vacated. So if you come to visit us, Rubin (as I hope you will), do not expect any sudden changes in my way of living. Now that I am used to bare necessity it is hard to envisage renewed affluence as a state of grace.

I exaggerate of course. Was I ever truly aware that I was so unnerved? What did old Istran Fass mean to me? The answer is nothing. In those days my sense of life was different; it had a different flow. Like it or not, I was trained to be a Winkleman

54

sentimentalist. Disturbed as I may have been by the constant visits to the house of Skirzeny and his stepson, I still managed to retain some very warm feelings about the old place. It was a great accomplishment, the supreme comfort, and it would be my inheritance.

Once upon a time it had been the palace of a powerful Hasidic wonder rabbi. When that cult disappeared from our part of Transylvania, the house was renovated by a family of German-speaking Szecklers, immigrants from the East, who had the new wing added on in which were kitchen, dining room, and study, and who, after installing water closets, bidets, and other such luxuries, had fitted above the study a wooden placard carved out of a birch log which, when translated from German, declared: "Long live the Magyar race and the Magyar tongue."

This same family had also installed the noisy, knocking central heating system about which my mother was always complaining. She insisted that we modernize; she said we lived not much better now than our gentile neighbors. When Mother had trouble finding maids to do the nasty work about the place her complaints grew even more shrill. Then she would call the place her "curse." Or she would berate my father with memories of the substantial establishments she had known in Debrecen. Of course, their attitudes were bound to be different in that respect, reflecting the differences in their responsibilities: Mother regarded the place as a series of chores to be organized and taken care of every week whereas my father was truly *signorial*. He thought of the house as his domain, a castle of comforts and good things of every sort, as well as a means of defining his status. If he was successful with me at all, it was in inculcating that same feeling.

Let me see if I can describe the place still. You entered through two great doors into a baronial hallway with dark waxed floors, wainscoting on the walls of birch and cedar, and a high arched ceiling stretched with rough-hewn beams. Overhead was a handsome chandelier of painted wooden spokes set with glass flowers, pillaged—no doubt—centuries ago from an Austrian church. To the left of you then a strip of oriental carpet floated on the glowing floors toward the parlor and living room, at the front of the house, two complete rooms of heavy stuffed furniture upholstered in chintz from Vienna, a final wedding gift to my parents from Istran Fass. If you turned right you faced the banister that wound up the stairway to the bedchambers. Further still to the right was another anteroom where the floors were left naked, rubbed a deep cherry brown as if with a fine cloth. This led past a hall closet and a water closet to the immense dining room, beyond which was the pantry and kitchen and alongside of which, abutting from the main block of the house into the garden, was my father's study.

There was also a variety of suites and apartments on the second and third floors: bedrooms, sitting rooms, baths, closets of every description, hallways where the floors had been stained the color of steak sauce, attics, basements, and sub-basements, a primitive garage in the back where oxen had once been kept, a privy for the kitchen help, and, behind it, a small hay barn and greenhouse.

As I say, to walk through the place was an adventure. The stove had a monstrously deformed human shape. It stood on tiny metal legs, wore a giant stock pot for a hat, had eyes of yellow fire. Next to it was the old hearth which burned charcoal, wood, and sage. From the ovens built into its face there was a constant roar like the ocean, sending forth the warm smells of special dishes, local delicacies or Jewish favorites, baked goods and puddings (for my mother regarded some forms of moderation as a kind of stinginess); and in the deep damp pantry next door, where the potatoes, onions, and confitures were stored in earthenware tubs, one could always smell the summer fields.

There were rats, too, in the pantry—large friendly brown fellows with eyes like beads of red fire; this could not be helped. If my mother blamed them on the Skirzenys, the fact is that she was never very successful in destroying them, although she never stopped trying. But in a million other ways she did her best to make one aware, as one walked about the place, that everything else was well cared for: the walls in the kitchen whitened with fresh flaked lime; the wooden furniture and floors, the wainscoting and the beams in the ceilings all properly waxed and oiled with essence of citron or beeswax; the upholstery puffed out, the strips of Bokhara carpeting and the small flowered bedroom rugs shaken clean; and the dozens of chair protectors, the linens, the cloths all fresh and starched white.

You cannot imagine how I identified all my future needs and comforts with such a place. Even the stuffed animal heads planted over the wainscoting of doorways by that Szeckler family were a source of delight. My sisters and I gave them names. The moose with the sparkling glass eyes who looked like an immense rat we called Radu. The bear's head was Prince Bibescu. And the brace of mallards, continually molting along both sides of the Magyar legend over the doorway leading to my father's study, these we called, for some forgotten childish reason, Mush-Mush.

And so our life together until late spring of 1944 could be truly described as a series of games, dragging heavy meals, long naps, and lazy holidays when the family would gather in the garden or in the living room, if the weather was inclement, to hear music on the gramophone, to argue about foolish things, and to tell preposterous fortunes with the cards. I stress this because it is important that you know how limited our view of the future really was: when I was growing up, I definitely thought that I would want such a place for my very own—if not this same place—once my parents were to pass on. What else could one have wanted? That my parents not pass on? Who lived forever? Besides, I was certainly not much of a radical in those days. The prospect of being stifled in my own lair never even occurred to me. One traveled, I thought, but one always returned *chez maison*. If, occasionally, some of my less advantaged friends teased me that I was an unadventurous person who stayed too close to his own garden, I used to quote a favorite story of my father's, that shortly after coming to the place he had been walking on the attic floor when he chanced to notice a panel set in the wall that had never caught his attention before. When my father leaned against it, the wall gave. Much to his astonishment, then, he found an entire suite of unoccupied rooms set into the roof like an eagle's nest. There were some old scrolls of the law, naked of their coverings, a genealogical history of the village of Nemiskert, and a tarnished silver pointer in an ancient cabinet. There was also a set of manacles for both the wrists and the ankles, rusty and incapable of being unlocked, and there were empty bottles and other trash. When the place was swept clean three gold French coins were found among the trash.

"And so," I used to conclude with a shy wink, never sure whether the story was true or merely apocryphal but always afraid afterward to go unaccompanied up to the attic, "who knows what I shall find by sticking close to my garden?"

And again, who can say what intuition gave me such clairvoyance?

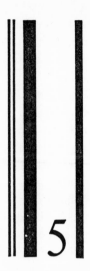

5

LIVING together, as I told you we all did, my father, mother, sister Sarah, her husband Maurice and their little boy Anatole, Perl and her fiancé, Adam (who spent most of his time in our company), we quarreled often but we also did not have to seek very far afield for companionship. Our quarrels were to be expected —being such entirely different personalities. But, in good times, we provided delightful contrasts when together.

Father, for example. He was not the sort of man one could easily disregard. I even used to find myself adopting some of his poses, although we were not alike physically—he being quite a large man, imposing, one might say, with a pale, handsome but heavy face, jowled at times when he was not slimming, but even then imposing, his lips delicate, fine blue eyes, fine white teeth, a nose with only the slightest curvature at the end, and fine habits, fine manners.

Father always walked with his shoulders squared, like a peasant carrying a great sack of flour, but his delicate hands would be folded behind his back so that his belly protruded only slightly. At table he managed to fold these same soft pink hands before him after each course without ever appearing effeminate or uncomfortable. Despite his great bulk, he could manage to seem like a delicate person, sensitive to others, almost noble at times.

Mother, on the other hand, was dark, plump, pretty. She brooded, exploded, or else she was silent. It was plain to see that her straight black hair would never turn gray. Her manners were not as fine as my father's; when she ate she picked her teeth with her fork or a fingernail, and her laughter tended to be shrill. Mother had a way of accusing you with silence. Just when you thought she had relented, a torrent of shrill insults and provocations would gush from her mouth.

Mother could also manage other kinds of emotional blackmail; by the effort of holding herself aloof and foreign, she got you sooner or later to agree to her most absurd whims. I have a favorite memory of myself sitting in the darkened kitchen opposite my mother while she pretended to chastise me with silence for a bad grade in school. Mother was convinced that children should be disciplined often with a disapproving silence. Despite her upbringing, she had a good deal of the peasant still in her.

Another memory I retain is of the day Sarah announced that she wished to marry Maurice. "Do you want to kill your father? My heart!" she kept repeating, solely because Maurice was the son of a carpenter.

As for my sisters, in temperament and looks, each resembled a different parent. Perl was my mother's daughter; Sarah my father's child; but they both managed to intensify in themselves what had been merely striking in their parents.

By all accounts, Sarah was the gentlest and most noble-spirited girl in our community. Her first husband, the student Herszeg, had died of influenza less than a year after their marriage, leaving her alone with a month-old infant, yet I cannot remember her even then being envious or complaining that life was too much for her, or that she was being treated unjustly.

Perl, on the other hand, seemed always to be accusing us of dishing her portion out to her from the wrong side of the plate. Manners were important to her, perhaps because she was so coarse. Her lips were always chapped. Her hair was greasy and unkempt-looking, although she fussed over it for hours. On her dark skin Perl had the shadows of eczema scars. She was short, and seemed, as a child, meager, and, later, stouter than was actually the case. And since she particularly enjoyed reminding me that I was the youngest, I was closer to Sarah and to her second husband, Herszeg's friend Moshe Shad (whom we called Maurice), and to certain of their friends.

Rubin, now as I look back over those days, I know there must have been horrors for some and pettiness for all, but I cannot recall any of that. When I remember our life in Clig it is as a place of stability in the midst of chaos where there was ample opportunity to enjoy life, and enough variety to keep us at arm's length from the ennui. What did we do? How did we pass the time? Across the older border was Debrecen, where my mother's stepsister (really her cousin) Gerda and her glass-eyed husband, the accountant, kept another large establishment. They also had a villa in Lillafüred in the mountains where we would swim during the heat of summer. Another maiden aunt Gussy, really my father's cousin, had established herself as a lady doctor in Budapest. In Miskolc our cousin Imre was highly placed in the Hungarian Bar Association. Between these points and other points such as Plevnitz, Halmi, Geralt, there was a constant exchange of mail: greetings, condolences, announcements, admonishments to lead good Jewish lives which—despite the unfortunate circumstances of war—we must have all felt we were then leading as Jews in the country of our choice. Once a year my mother and the girls went to Gussy in Budapest for a gynecological examination. At Yuletide presents were exchanged in the Christmas wrappings of the gentiles. Hitler and his camps? We did not like to believe in rumors.

61

Some may have even thought that precautions were justified in the case of "certain extremist political groups," many of which were already seeking to undermine our uneasy tenure, but I recall the term of approbation we most often used was hooligan. "You cannot fight hooligans with hooliganism," my father used to say. How many times have I tried to recollect what we professed knowing then and what we said to each other about such things?

Our press told us only what we wanted to know. Our press lied, knowing this would please our prejudices. Thus, though we read copious dispatches about the wars in Spain, in Finland, and later in Russia, like most East Europeans we had no special fondness for the Bolsheviks. Memories of the Tsar were too strong for us to be pro-Russian and we knew that Ivan was going to give our holdings to the *muzhiks*.

As for the Anglo-Saxons (a term used together with the appellation John Bull to describe the Englishman), wasn't their quarrel with Germany all a matter of trade? A minor squabble over markets and merchant routes, and a cruel treaty which had deprived Germany of most of her riches?

Spaniards and Italians—they were all foolish pietists. Perhaps the Fascists would bring them into the twentieth century. My father had once been to Italy and he complained that all the food was doused in tomato sauce. We all admired the French, but we didn't take "a nation of pederasts" seriously. Father said they had "sex on the brain." And the Czech Social Democrats, he said, "are just like your Bolsheviks." My father extolled Scandinavians and detested Swiss. He would argue: "Whereas the one is industrious and hygienic, the other is greedy and hygienic." Remembering his World War I service, Father also had little use for Islamic peoples. "The Turk," he would insist, "doesn't eat pork because it is too clean for him." Rumanians "practiced incest" and Greeks were "dishonest." Croatians were "blockheads," as were most Polacks. As for you Americans, the phrase we most often used to describe your condition was, as one might say, a dog was "mongrelized."

But sometimes my father would also add that you were "shoddy materialists."

"John Bull rules the waves," my father used to say, "but the black man pays for his steamship tickets!"

Or: "Hitler could be worse. He *could* be a politician. . . ."

Or he would joke about how Napoleon had to be exiled to St. Helena by an English duke, "but the King of England goes to Bermuda with an American divorcée. . . ."

Can't you see how simple it was for us to be callous at such a time? We were not like any of these people. We were Jews of good family, residing in a nation that had taken us in and had treated us as well as could be expected. This was our mother country: Clig, Miskolc, Hermannstadt, Kronstadt, Debrecen, Budapest; this was our world. Berlin was an exhausting journey by train with many change-overs on route. Once or twice a day trains went through Clig on the way to Vienna. There was also the train to the East which few in our town now found an occasion to use. We never knew all the horrors of the emigrations and deportations, and some of us lived like the last Acadians.

In the late thirties I remember Bela writing to us about the boycotts, later about the so-called "crystal night." Hideous as these events surely seemed to us then, we believed (and with some justice, I think) that the Jews of Germany had brought disaster on themselves—by intermarriage, the assimilation, by aping the gentiles. That was the extent of our Jewish identity: we were critical of others but remained opportunistic and quite optimistic when it came to our own situations. None of us would have thought of marrying a Hungarian (because the women were all said to be whores and the men all cruel) but, as we wished to continue to do business—and that necessitated being neighborly —we disregarded Bela's letters and went about our business.

A cousin in Belgrade had an illegitimate child by a Serbian woman. He went off to Palestine. Still other cousins in Galicia obtained exit visas for Cuba. My father joked: "What a great distance to travel for a good cigar." By and by, when the Hungarians repealed the Rumanian so-called "land reforms," we were the beneficiaries. Everybody commented upon the improvement in the general tone of life under the Hungarians. In the schools we were made to swear: "I believe in the revival of Hungary," and to sing of living and dying on Hungarian soil, but we also wrote many letters to our relatives, exchanged wedding and birthday greetings, planned trips back and forth once normal railway service was restored. All of us had our friends in the Arrow Cross movement. It seemed that an exception could always be made by these people if one were a friend. Friendship was considered a matter of personal honor. Ah, Rubin, in those days our letters always contained phrases like "personal honor" or "my good gentile friend." It was so until the day the mail stopped coming to us. Shortly thereafter, our outgoing letters were also not accepted at the post.

To be precise, that was some weeks or months after you in America declared war on Germany. A bitter day for all of us. We thought: what right did you have to make the conflict spread? And then, slowly, mail stopped coming; there were no more letters from Bela. At first we blamed the *Ostbahn*, the local railroad authorities. A meeting was held. The Jewish Council was empowered to inform our nominally Fascist local authorities that we were prepared to strike a bargain: no more letters would be sent through Switzerland to England and America if they would allow the rest of the mail to come and go as before.

These local authorities were still acting courteously toward us at that time. Indeed, how could they afford to do otherwise? Due to the inflation, currency speculation became a way of life and many had borrowed on their annual salaries, as well as on their superannuations, from men like my father who, despite the Aryanizations, still controlled nearly everything of liquid value in Clig. If left to their own resources of pettiness and corruption, I am confident that these local people would have continued to co-

64

operate with us. But that was not the way it was to be. Within a month's time they were all replaced or reassigned. A new set of officials came among us—transferees from the Banet, Austrians, White Russians, and owl-eyed Hungarian clerks with blond hair and fair skins, cashiered from the black markets of Budapest, or transferred by the Ministry of Defense to the Eastern Provinces for disciplinary reasons. Again district court jurisdictions were switched about. The news boards began to taunt us with new ordinances and proclamations. That same month we saw our first German soldiers, not occupying troops but training cadres for the militia. Things were now changing even more rapidly. A company of Ukrainians occupied the town, billeting themselves in the mansions of the nobility, in the Fóvár and the Sellagvar, and the agricultural and technical schools. More Arrow Cross police were to be seen. A curfew was installed. "Defensive Guards" were placed in front of the remaining Jewish businesses. We were told to register like foreigners with the Ministry of the Interior (your State Department), at the Jaroscrag. Being peace-loving citizens, if all they wanted was your name, then you gave it.

The process observed laws of its own; it built on its own momentum. First the gendarmerie expropriated one of our neighbors' homes. Then we were all asked to pay a ransom on our homes. A sum of fifty kilograms of gold was extorted, another sum, a third. By spring nobody walked the streets at night except the sentries and the town drunkards. We were ordered not to play our wireless after dark. We had to receive special permission for bank drafts or to send telegrams. We had last priority on the trains for which we had to pay a special permission fee of 30 pengö. Still my father found himself arguing: "Was it any different during the last war? . . . And when the Germans left," he argued, "all the peasants were inoculated against smallpox."

Father's belief in German public health measures probably blinded him to the novel excesses of this new bureaucracy. Soon the authorities knew where every Jew was and where he could be found, also where his father, uncle, and aunt lived in case he was not at home. The peasants very quickly learned which way the wind was blowing and there were presently many forfeitures on notes, barn burnings, mass rallies. Somebody poured poison in our live-carp pond. We could no longer get servant girls. Even the gentle Magda, our cook, whom I shall always remember lovingly, admitted to us one evening with tears in her eyes that it would endanger her husband's chances to be foreman in the brick factory if she were to stay.

Magda, at least, was sorry for what she had to do. Others were of a different mood. Once, when my father drove out on a morning to collect on a note long overdue, he was stoned by a gang of local ruffians who broke all the windows in his handsome Mercedes.

But, even then, it was not as if a decree was signed, posted on the street lamps and the hoardings, stating: "From tomorrow onward all the Jews of Clig are going to be sent to die." The fear and terror came upon us so gradually that we never knew exactly when it was that we were first cowed. Very early, my father's Mercedes was expropriated by a *Stadtkommandatur* on the excuse that there was not enough benzine to go around. Then we were told by local authorities not to go out of doors unless it was absolutely urgent. Then—if we valued our safety—we should not make the jobs of these public servants any more difficult by attempting to "antagonize" the local population. When men like my father still complained that they had no such ideas but were merely trying to collect on their notes due—bad debts—debts which authorities had always recognized in the past to be within their rights—they were told: "The past was corruption. These loyal citizens also have their rights. We are merely trying to reestablish a bearable relationship between Jews and gentiles."

They were also told: "You are a minority in the midst of a great people. Be thankful that nothing more drastic has been done to you than to right past wrongs."

Finally it was said: "When the State orders Justice nobody must stand in its way."

Do you know there were some among us who actually believed what was being said? They seemed to feel so guilty they were willing to accept any personal mortification for what they imagined were their misdeeds. What did such men have to tell us? Some wrote letters to the authorities in Budapest about the expropriations. They got together delegations and signed petitions. "We emphatically declare our loyalty," these men said. "Nor do we seek to redeem error with arrogance. Nor do we wish to perpetrate malice. Nor are we even seeking an audience in order to lodge complaints about the merit of the measures adopted, but merely ask that they be carried out in a humane spirit." Later they would shrug their shoulders and tell some of us: *These are a determined people. It is scarcely in our power to oppose these orders effectively. . . .*

Fortunately my father was too busy with his own affairs to be so involved, yet even he did not preach resistance but tried to be tolerant, to view the crisis we were living through from the other man's point of view. The crucial fact to be remembered is that we remained. We did not flee like some. We made no effort to dishonor our names, but lived as best we could with an ugly situation, persisting stubbornly in our belief that "it is never wrong to be a patriot."

From the Brand story we now know that some of our leaders learned about the gas chambers as early as 1942, but I assure you we were never told. My father had said: "The authorities are hard pressed. They cannot act otherwise."

"Hungary," my father declared, "has absorbed many new peoples. It is like an industrial concern with people of all kinds of nationalities and with different customs, whereas before it never had more than ten or twenty.

"We must give time to the new administration to find its bearings in the governing of such a new territory, and be patient and

67

indulgent toward positive mistakes that must happen if a country develops itself in such a short time."

All this my father said.

When the deportations began we were told that people were only going to work in Germany for the war effort, that they would be treated as workers. We believed or else we could not have lived on. In every prosperous household of the Jews, if there were no soldiers billeted, families gathered, growing even more close because of the adversity. When one of our neighbors was dispossessed, they too moved in with us for a short while. We shared our larders and made room. One fed the other, cared for the other, looked after the other, and thought it ungrateful of the other when, as in this case, the first opportunity was used to slip south across the borders.

That spring we did not celebrate the Passover for fear of antagonizing our gentile neighbors who were celebrating Easter at the same time. Although a sense of loss grew stronger within us with every passing day, we kept busy, hoping in that way not to let events get the better of us. When Hitler shouted at us over the wireless, blaming us for all of Europe's problems, past and present, except, perhaps, the Kishinev pogroms, my father complained that his German was atrocious, and my mother said there was too much interference to get his message clearly, but they both pointed out for our benefit that he would need to simplify matters for the benefit of the "average uneducated German."

The first deportations from our town were ordered for the sons of the working-class-quarter Jews from Dohnani Street and for some unmarried girls between the ages of eighteen and fifty-five to go to Poland or west around Sopron and Gyor for important war production, no others. It was explained to us then that, as we were not working class, we could not be expected to do physical labor. Thank God, we thought, our brains and special skills are still needed. The Jewish council was asked to lodge a vigorous protest with the commanding officer of the special police in charge of the resettlement but, as the day of the order came due, my father and his colleagues hastily gathered together to help draw up the lists.

Two policemen called for each girl. That is significant. Toward the end, when they were taking whole families, one policeman was enough for ten persons, but that was only after the Allied bombings began, when to leave Clig did not seem like such a terrible disaster. Now it was quite different. All were asked to wear Jewish stars but that was as far as they dared to go with their executive measures. The mothers were told to pack sandwiches and warm blankets for their daughters. People actually waved to the trains as if they were embarking on a holiday.

In that initial draft I was spared for the obvious reason—my father had pulled strings—and you must know that I was thankful he had. True, there could exist many worse things than death, but, I thought, why look for trouble? "Life for an hour is also life." And I had Lilo to think about.

The war in the East had destroyed nearly all of her paper fortune. An early bombing raid had also obliterated her ancestral home. Therefore, she and her Aunt Pepi were forced to move in with us. Living together, our life took on a new intensity. Because the puppet government was allowing Jews to earn only five hundred pengö a month (about $100), marriage and a separate establishment were out of the question, but we were as close as one could expect. Aunt Pepi was simply too old to play duenna. She preferred to look the other way, or she knitted. On rainy days Lilo and I studied English and French together, and listened to my father's gramophone recordings of the elder Slezak and Mme. Antonescu. When the warm weather came I set up my studio in the summerhouse. Morning and afternoon, then, I would spread my tubes of paint upon an oilcloth. Seated beside me in the high grass with a book in her hands and our lunch basket next to her, Lilo, in her summer dress, would sometimes pose for me in the manner of the French Impressionists. I did hundreds of drawings

69

of her Dresden-doll face peering out through the lattice work of the trellis, and of her brief, alert young body, about to spring up toward the indefinite horizon.

Even then, the war seemed a great distance away. Sometimes for hours we did not hear the sound of marching feet or the roar of the military trains as they rushed quaking through the village toward the Eastern Front. Through the bow window in her sitting room, my mother would smile down on us and think to herself: I am gaining another daughter.

About the summerhouse that spring peonies bloomed in a fantastic variety of pinks, blues, and purples. After a rain, they would mix odors with the roses intoxicatingly. These were not the ordinary bulbous shaggy blooms that one sees, for example, in the French countryside, but a special array that sometimes lasted a fortnight on their stems. Underneath them were planted pansies —and there were great mauve dahlias growing wild in every quarter of the place. When the sunflowers came much later they were the tallest ever, and they never seemed to wilt. It was my intention to perpetualize all these blooms on canvas. All day the air would have a fine golden luster in which the heavy scent of flowers and fertilizer, combining with the soft warmth welling up through the ground, bathed the eyes and sweated the forehead.

As I painted in my thick careless impastos, Lilo read or she made caricatures of me in a Florentine leather schoolgirl's diary. The lengthening spring days kindled against our skins so that they tingled with the coming of nightfall and were, themselves, perfumed by the peonies. We were as natural as a pair of barnyard animals. Since both her aunt and my parents had already given us their blessings, it was no wonder that one day we should have wandered together behind my father's barn where—not far away from a simmering compost pile, alive with butterflies and blue bottles—a small patch of mustard seeds had bloomed on the soft turf. The place was surrounded by privet shrubs of such overpowering scent that they gave one a headache. Even so,

70

Lilo's sexual curiosity was no less than mine, and when I insisted, she did not find it convenient to refuse. On that very same spot, with much fumbling and embarrassment, but scarcely any pain or bleeding, our nuptials were consummated before the actual ceremony; and I withdrew not a moment too soon.

Lilo wept, of course, but that was for the sake of the play. She was proving her love for me. And if she seemed grudging about it at first, her behavior was just as unreal when she later pretended abandonment. Lilo wept even when she was giving herself to me in an abandoned way (imagining herself, no doubt, as some kind of tragedienne), so how was I to know that by that single unguarded act, which we both presumed to be passion, that I was to bring about her eventual downfall? If I had known—I ask myself now—would I have behaved differently? Never! That very day I had placed camellias in her room which she swore she "adored." Although we both told ourselves later that we had lost control of ourselves, we knew better. The act had been calculated from the very first warm day of spring. By coming together so, we had shaken ourselves loose from the grip of our families. Our very idleness had conspired to lead us down such a path at such a time, and if we were not as pleased with each other afterward as, say, Paolo and Francesca, or Héloïse and Abélard, or any other truly mythical pair of lovers, we were also not ashamed, but each rather proud of what he or she had individually done.

At bottom we must have known that public life in Hungary was now hopeless so that when we joined together the shock of naked flesh against naked flesh it was by way of reaffirming our individual beings, our mutual hopes, and the privacies we still hoped to share.

Even inexperienced as we both were, we managed to learn quickly through repetition of the act when to try and where to hide, the next day and the next, and once, late at night, after meeting together in the attic above my parents' bedroom. Presently I began to take a clinical interest in Lilo's menstrual cycles;

71

the intervals immediately before and between her flowings were times of unbearable worry for me. Lilo did not like my asking so many personal questions about "her time of flowers." She used to call me "nosy little Dr. Ispansky," but she claimed she could understand my concern and she tried hard to oblige me in all ways.

But never were we quite successful in the clinical sense of the word. Though Lilo made every effort to give herself to me fully, I was always aware of a momentary retraction and retention on her part, and she, no doubt, was equally put off by a certain coldly methodical competence in my manner. Perhaps it had to with my necessity to withdraw before ejaculation. Or perhaps it was my training, such as it was, through imaginary experience, street-corner colloquies with my friends, and pornographic novels.

I might also explain that we generally preferred to perform the act out of doors, believing that in the few moments we could steal from sight we would be more free. Thus we rarely had an occasion to sleep together, or to gain expertise from our previous errors by repetition of the act. Lying in the deep shade behind my father's hay barn, we told ourselves we might be anywhere: Paris, the High Carpathians, or the Alps, but our ruse was not always successful. Usually I remained too aware of the light acrid smell of hay and compost combining with the stench of father's carp pond, as a consequence of which my attempts at unusual competence tended to unman me.

You mustn't misunderstand. I was still able to believe—as no doubt Lilo believed—that the effort in itself was bound to have rewards, and, for that reason alone, though certain allegedly "ultimate joys" evaded us, our lovemaking beside that dung pile continued unabated, each taking what pleasure he or she could from the silent gestures our effigies made against the hay, while the lines of tension that creased our tanned faces grew no less severe. After a while, I found, also, that I had little time for my painting activities. Most of the day I was in an erotic stupor, or worse, hypnotized by my own calculations; in fact, we were both usually exhausted. Presently Father began to tease me about the unguarded easel that always stood near the summerhouse. "Just what are you working on behind the barn?" he wanted to know. Yet we were confident that we had been prudent enough in stealing away so often, and that he did not really care to know the whole truth. Besides, we told ourselves that such secrecy was no longer urgent. Two months after our initial embrace, however, the thing happened that was to change the nature of our relationship.

That day in late May had begun overcast, after an unusually heavy dew. We had come late to the summerhouse, having spent most of the morning after second breakfast in the attic looking through family possessions. On the radio in the attic we heard about the Allied fire-bombing raids over Linz and Ploesti. We also heard the Vatican radio discussing the fate of Mussolini. By noon the sun began to split open the low cloud banks. The stairways and halls stank of the yellow soap used by my mother and her daughters for the cleaning. As we came downstairs, Lilo remembered that it was her turn to make up the beds. Concerned lest one of my sisters should scold her, she had the look of one who has come from total isolation into a roomful of noisy people. She was very lovely, nevertheless, in a flimsy silk thing with a bare back, twirling an antique parasol she had found among the trunks upstairs. Presently we heard voices coming from the main alcove.

Skirzeny, the gypsy, had arrived. Now, for purely opportunistic reasons, a minor official in the Hungarian party, he also pretended to have important dealings with the Deutsche Gesellschaft, the agency in charge of Aryanization, and he never went anywhere without a shabby leather brief case which had replaced his shotgun. Skirzeny was also dressed more fastidiously, in a new corduroy jacket with matching cap and plus fours. But his chief claim to status had to be the case—a pouchy thing of pigskin that looked more like a commercial traveler's gladstone than a repository for important documents.

Farnas Skirzeny was standing in the vestibule, coughing into his hand, when my father came to greet him. From our observation post on the second landing of the stairwell we were able to follow the movements of these two large balding figures as they hailed each other and then came together, embracing, then stepping backward, squeezing each other's hands and exchanging meaningless pleasantries.

All seemed to be in order. Skirzeny said he had stopped by on the way to a parade in the Public Gardens. He declared it would be unwise for us to try to attend.

"Naturally," my father snapped back. He led his guest into the study. The door closed on them. It was quiet again by the time we descended to the bottom of the steps.

Then I heard an angry voice: ". . . The way you talk to me, Newman."

Lilo reached for my hand.

"Be careful, Newman," Skirzeny shouted.

"Lower your voice," said my father.

"I will do as I please," Skirzeny replied, "and you will be careful how you speak to me."

When my father returned the threat, Skirzeny adopted a different tone, a wheedling that rose and fell and was never continually audible. He seemed to be making his usual plea to buy back the house on terms, but he now had added to it a cajolery that was both comical and embarrassing. Farnas Skirzeny said he wanted to be paid in gold for the eggs and butter he had been delivering to my mother but this was merely a pretext for still other cajoleries. He seemed to wish that "the little ones" should get to know each other better; he wondered if I would tutor his son Miklos for his civil service examinations, and he was also hinting that there would be further deportations. Since it was extremely difficult to hear more than isolated phrases, it was next to impossible to make out the context of all his remarks.

Once he repeated his threats: "Be careful, Newman. You treat Skirzeny shabbily when you need a friend and you will not al-

74

ways have a friend; times change and you must now change with them."

Again my father chose to bluff, but his laughter was rather obviously forced: "Change? How should I?"

Skirzeny was stamping about the study. First he demanded wine. Then we heard his fist thunder against the desk.

"Farnas, behave yourself," Father warned.

Too late. Hearing the uproar, my mother had rushed over to the locked door. "Just what is going on in there?" she demanded to know.

"Go away," said my father.

"I will not," she shouted back.

"Do as your husband says," Skirzeny added.

Mother would not be deterred. When the locked door did not yield to her pressures, she hit against it many times with her fists, demanding to be let in. Still trying to cope with the gypsy, father would not even answer her questions. Then, for a moment, there was quiet, as if the two men had put their heads together to whisper. Mother turned imploringly toward Lilo and myself: "Children, what have they been saying? What are they planning?"

Lilo gasped. I had lost my tongue as well. The thick oak doors to my father's study were so successful in muffling the voices of Skirzeny and my father that what we did hear sounded all the more terrifying; and, although I wanted with all my heart to set my mother's worried mind at rest, what honestly could I say?

Really it was rather like being in the dentist's anteroom while another patient is in the chair; you cannot always tell if the garbled sounds you hear are those of pain or haggling over a bill or, perhaps, mere conversation, and even when you are sure that somebody is suffering terribly (and you can hear nearly every particular of his moaning and lamentations), what you hear are just sounds, divorced from the suffering body, shut off, void of any sense of the immediate place where you are.

75

In a like manner, the only way I could answer my mother was to ignore her. To stand idly by listening to these two men going on and on about "kronen" and "lei" and, as it were, allowing the imagination to color in the blank spaces, this would have been too painful for all of us. We would know soon enough what was to come about. In the meantime, if I was unable to comfort the two women, I thought I should try to help them resist morbid and speculative thoughts. I would divert them as best I could.

"Mother," I said, "I hear little Anatole. Sarah may have forgotten to change his napkin. You had better go to him quickly."

She looked at me then as if giving me to understand that it was Sarah's business, not her own, but when I turned next, as if to ask Lilo to go in her place, Mother protested: "Oh no. I'll look in," for she didn't want Lilo to think she would be a bad grandmother.

Moments after she started up the stairs, we heard the argument resume: "Damn you, Newman! Where is your memory? Can you really afford to be so obstinate?"

I took Lilo's hand and rushed out through the kitchen and the dark pantry with her toward the summerhouse.

"Ah, won't you ever give me some help?" Perl called after us, from her post near the wash tubs.

I clapped my hand over Lilo's mouth so that she could not reply. Then I pushed her inside the summerhouse and threw my arms about her to quiet her.

But Lilo was too conscious of the sound of Skirzeny's voice which could still be heard, as if magnified by a *haut-parleur*, through the open window in my father's study and across the echoing green landscape. After another moment, I pushed her with me out through the other side of the summerhouse and down past my father's barn and under the cattle skulls on the ornate back gate.

We ran then like happy thieves across our neighbor's property. Once Lilo had to stop by the well to take off her sandals. Then we skirted the small private park adjoining the monastery of

76

Kolasz, and reappeared in front of the brewery with its beer garden, where the old men with their pipes were already gathering for luncheon. Afraid to be seen, we climbed to the brow of a small hill and fell down again.

Beyond this place was a patch of unposted forest land through which ran a tributary of the little Szemos. Catching our breaths we stared over the crest of the hill down into the city. In the noon sun we could clearly make out our square, my father's garden, the railroad terminal, the double chimneys of our house and the gate with its twisted iron serpents—all distinct as cut-outs in a jigsaw puzzle. There was Hunyady Janos making his rounds with the post, as he had done every day for the last twenty-seven years; and there was old Wenkheim from the bank with the money bags for the workers at the brick factory. Clig dozed under the sun, as if after a heavy meal. The streets were deserted; the shutters next to the windows in the little blue houses clapped in the breeze but we could not hear any sounds.

Presently there was a rumbling; a cloud of dust filtered down toward the square. From the citadel road a squadron of militiamen on motorcycles were cruising—it seemed—toward our street. "What do you suppose they want?" Lilo asked. I got up, took her hand again, would not even allow her to brush herself off before leading her into the forest.

What did I hope to avoid? I assure you I had no reason even then to put two and two together about anything. I merely wanted to dodge the uncertainty, all that questioning when we could not possibly know the true answers. Suddenly my nostrils were stuffed once more with the strong smell of my mother's yellow soap. I saw our little garden as a prison. The only way out was through the forest.

My father had often warned us not to stray beyond the square or the authorities would not be responsible for us, but, once we had entered the woods, we could not stop ourselves. Our shadows strayed among the tall beeches. Here we could talk as loudly as

77

we wanted to without being overheard. Crashing through the heavy growth, I called over my shoulder to Lilo: "We can go as far as Lillafüred if you like." When the ground came trembling up to meet our feet, she answered me with a giggle: "To Sztoika. I wish to try the natron springs."

"I understand," she continued in a deliberately affected way, "they are said to be wonderful for a number of feminine complaints."

Our laughter did not stop us from wandering on at a good pace.

Presently we were completely enclosed by the dark shade of the beeches. It grew very hot. Mouths sprang open in the leafy tree tops. Tongues of searing sunshine licked our foreheads. We commenced running again.

Breathless, after only a short time, we came first to a marshland, then to a river side where there was a narrow strip of unfettered sand beach. Tall trees were draping immense fernlike branches over the place. A piny scent rose from the ground like a heavy mist. The water, no more than three hundred feet across, rushed over rapids in places the color of red clay or rust, but there were also deep blue channels in between and along the shoreline. On the far shore the forest thickened again.

I took Lilo's hand so that I could lead her when we waded across but as soon as we came to the sand beach, she cried out in a happy voice: " 'Please. I cannot, Shandor. Must we?" Then she fell to the ground and lay crumpled up on one side, laughing, it seemed.

For a moment I stood listening to the many birds and the distant rushing of a gorge. Then I took off my shoes, and fell down beside Lilo to kiss her on the forehead.

We were both sweating profusely. The air was like a cauldron of boiling dust. Even here there was no breeze. I was so thirsty that I thought I would faint.

Going to the stream, I cupped my hands in it until they were numb and tasted the sweet cold water. "It's warmer than you think," I said, splashing Lilo where she lay all crumpled up, but she did not reply. Then I went to her again and placed my cold wet hands on her forehead. She shivered but reached out to embrace me tentatively.

"It would be nice to swim here," I said.

A flame lit on her cheeks. "Ah, but what shall I wear?"

"Why must you wear anything?"

"But Shandor, we will catch pneumonia . . ."

"And perhaps a frog or two," I added, laughing.

I didn't dare to look up right away, but when I did I saw that Lilo was carefully taking off her clothes and folding them in a neat pile. Quickly I shed my things and followed her. Naked we raced to the shoreline and stood together on the verge, our buttocks flexing nervously. I went to cup my hand over her small warm breast. Again Lilo shivered and shied away but when I touched her another time she took my hand and pulled me with her into the rushing waters.

First we played splash games. Then we held our breaths under water and tried to say I love you to each other. Coming to the surface, we frightened each other with stories of water snakes and poisonous leeches before diving under again.

Never had I felt so aware of my manhood. In the cool rushing of the brook we could dip down low and drown the ugly ringing in our ears of Skirzeny's wrangling voice, or we could touch lips under water—kiss, pass our hands over each other's parts. The moment we entered the stream, I felt restored, quite emphatically male, alive. I even lost my own fear of the deep dark places under the trees and dove everywhere with Lilo alongside of me, Presently our skins were like gooseflesh. Pebbled with the cold, we dove down one final time. Then I guided us ashore. Blindly we shook our bodies dry in a patch of the sun before falling together in another embrace.

Slowly, then, our bodies warmed to each other. I had wilted

79

but now, again, I grew hard against Lilo as she moved underneath me. Entering her was like sticking one's foot in a patch of slime. She was warm; for the first time I felt her body ease, then arching suddenly, she began to move against me with an intense quivering motion.

I was spending myself even as I continued to plunge blindly on and Lilo abruptly pulled me to her then, forcing me to kiss her closed lids, then opening my mouth with her lips, so that we were thrashing about like a pair of snakes, fast together at every part, hands pressed to each other's buttocks, our tongues merely imitating the thrashing gestures of our other parts as I grew hard, came again, and even then began to pump once more.

In another moment I was on the verge of a complete dissolution. My trembling flanks could no longer struggle against the abyss, for I had grown numb to the body beneath me which was still heaving against me, although also overcome with darkness and delight. When I fell away from Lilo she cried out: "Alex. . . ."

"Alex," I heard her a second time.

My jaws had fallen slack. I opened my eyes to the torture of the sun, my body feeling like a small, naked thing as I rolled over onto my back. Then I could see only my bony kneecaps and a patch of hair along my chest.

"*Alex,*" exclaimed Lilo a third time, even more urgently.

I tried to use my hands as a visor so that I could look into the sun. Was it Lilo's leg I saw dangling from the tree overhead?

But Lilo was beside me. When I turned to her she was clapping one hand to her bright triangle while pointing up with the other hand toward that same tree where something seemed to be thrashing about at us.

Had we been observed?

I stared up at the sky, as if transfixed by the thrust of the figure seated in the crotch of that high branch. A man with a narrow face and straight blond hair was peering down at us, but I could not making out his features; and I was afraid to address myself to him until he had spoken first.

For longer than a minute we observed this protocol of silence. Then I heard: "Bravo. Excellent, Alexander." The figure began to applaud.

"Who are you? What do you want?"

"Who am I? What a silly question?"

"But who are you?"

"Oh you are silly, Alexander."

At first, equally dazed by the taunting apparition in the tree, Lilo could do little beyond trying to hide herself, but now the sound of our voices roused her once more. She started belatedly for her clothing, only to stumble against a nearby rock, trembling, quite humiliated by her nakedness.

Then I turned again toward the figure in the tree. "Now do you see what you have done?" I shouted. "What do you want here. Who are you?"

With a sound like the flapping of giant wings, this thing came falling down out of the foliage, pulling leaves and branches along with him, then landing upright before rolling back against his heels. He shook some long greasy blond strands of hair out from over his eyes. "Do you know me now?" asked Miklos Skirzeny.

6

At age ten Miklos and I had been friendly with Ignace Vinterland, the son of the publisher. It so happens that young Vinterland, who was even too refined for my taste, preferred the company of Miklos Skirzeny to that of a fellow *chedarist;* and I was often exceedingly jealous of the pair. The way they would hide out together. The way they would go off on excursions and outings without ever inviting me. I assure you my childish jealousy was not unprovoked.

One spring day after final examinations I followed the pair to the tram terminus at Gidelve. They were headed for the Protestant cemetery to steal brass crosses that we would sometimes sell to a small foundry near the market place for pocket money. Once they spotted me, of course, they were very cruel. Young Vinterland said he would have Miklos beat me if I did not desist from shadowing them, but when my anger and jealousy caused me to strike the little sycophant, the wrath of his protector did not materialize. "Don't be so stupid," Miklos told his protégé, as he led him onto the waiting tram.

That was before his father was to suffer the last of those business reversals which led to our taking title to the mansion. Even then the Skirzenys were living under a black cloud. Strange, therefore, that I should have cared, or even remembered such an incident at the very moment when my own humiliation seemed imminent. "Don't be stupid, Miklos," I found my naked self cautioning him out loud while—to my inward self—I was adding: If Miklos had come to town with his stepfather, if he had waited on our front stoop or in the alleyway, if—seeing us leave the house —he had followed us quite innocently, as I had once followed him, staying out of sight all the while . . . and if. . . .

If if if if if! Where were my speculations leading me? Why was I now so anxious to make excuses for this animal? Miklos was not like me. He was the son of Skirzeny der Schicke. What more was there to say? Even during the few seconds it was taking me to reconstruct his deceit he had not once ceased smiling. Why, it seemed as if he was actually forcing himself to make those lips curve upward long after his amusement at our nakedness and helplessness had been dissipated. Miklos was just a dirty, grinning gypsy bastard! The fact was Skirzeny wasn't even his real father. People said he was some tinker from Bessarabia. . . .

For once my hatred of Miklos overmastered my fear of the fellow and I wanted to throw myself on him, erasing that expression from his face which was really no natural thing but something forced, a void, the absence of all feeling. Or so it seemed to me then. . . .

But what chance did I have to do any such thing? Miklos Skirzeny was as strong as he dared to be. He stood with hands on hips before my naked fiancée and myself and, when we cowered, he seemed to grow more immense. He was wearing his party uniform, too, with some kind of fiery insignia of rank above the crossed arrows on his shoulder patch; and, naked as I was, I reached to my shoulder, where the Jewish star had been, for security, protection, identity. Then Miklos rekindled his smile. Again he seemed to dominate us and the landscape so that when

83

he diminished we became truly puny, minuscule, but he always sprang up again before us once more, straightened and growing taller, like the wind-bent beech trees.

"Haven't you any decency?" I challenged him.

"Who is to talk?"

That face softened, a bland mockery of itself. "Come now, Alex," Miklos said, as if to mimic the way Lilo used my pet name, "you will not deny an old schoolmate his pleasure. Remember we were once pals. Have you forgotten? Ah, but how can you have forgotten that afternoon in the alleyway. Now Alex, I won't say you didn't perform ably. Why, you surpassed all my expectations. But—" Miklos interrupted himself to turn toward Lilo. Then he added: "Our friend here is very skillful with what we call the push-push. . . .

"Why, he is unflagging," Miklos went on. "Push-push," he mimicked, shimmying with his hips obscenely. "But," he continued the previous thought, "two are always needed to make a competition. So you must give me an opportunity to show off my abilities with your lovely little cousin."

Lilo spoke before I could, a kind of keening voice: "You'll regret this. You'll regret this."

"Miklos," I interrupted her, "do you think all you have to do is fall upon a woman? You are a coarse stupid fool."

He didn't even seem to hear me. Putting his hands on his hips, he leaned slightly over and again addressed himself to Lilo:

"Come here . . . little Miss Gero. Slut! Come here, I say."

When Lilo actually started up from where she had been sitting, in a position of modesty, Miklos seemed astonished. But then she made another dash for her clothes, and it took him a moment to realize what was happening and to start racing after her.

Lilo screamed. Then we were all screaming at different times like children at the beach. "Goddamn you, Miklos!" I shouted.

He was chasing Lilo toward the woods. Too late! Would I be too late? Rushing as fast as I could on all fours I tried to fall in front of Miklos, hoping in that way to trip him up so that Lilo could escape, but I was unable to move myself fast enough. All the while I had the sensation that my arms and legs were like many soft pairs of mandibles and that there were tight bands of steel wound about my head. I felt winded and dizzy. When I stretched myself out ineffectually toward Miklos, he fell on me, and we clung together like a pair of fierce insects until he was able to struggle to the top.

"Oh you filth! You dirty filth! Please, somebody, please!" I heard Lilo screaming into the woods as Miklos was pinioning my shoulders to the ground with his heavy knees.

"Get away while you can," I shouted back to her.

"Where will she go without her clothes?" he laughed.

Now Miklos was almost choking me. His lips were so close to mine I could smell the garlic on his breath. Miklos kept slobbering and spitting, falling against me with his heavy sweaty body again and again so that I thought I could feel the point of what was clearly his erection.

Again I shouted, "Hurry, Lilo!"

Her shadow started to move but not quickly enough. One of Miklos's thrashing elbows caught the point of my jaw and I was dazed, almost knocked senseless. When I recovered it was to see that dirty bastard falling across my little Lilo, who, with her step-ins down at her knees, was resisting him fiercely, as fiercely as could be expected.

I rushed over toward them. Miklos was whispering something avidly at Lilo who was writhing under him—a parody of the sex act.

I ran around to all sides of them, trying to see if he had overpowered her.

Presently Miklos howled: "What do you suppose I'm doing to you?" Then his eyes closed. The brute grunted and began to shudder. With her free hand Lilo slapped feebly at his face.

His eyes opened wide again. Astonished by the ticks of laugh-

ter that were convulsing him against his wishes, Miklos allowed
Lilo to throw him off to one side of her just at the moment when
he seemed about to enter: "Slut!"

Indeed, he could not help himself from shouting some obscen-
ity, if only to control the demonic laughter which, just then,
seemed to tyrannize over his lean body, making his flanks leap in
spasms, and his arms and legs to jerk like those of a puppet, even
as he was ejaculating onto the pine needles. But no sooner had he
uttered the word a second time than he was able to throw back
his head, was stiff in a seated position, and, strangely enough,
mute.

In another moment he was whispering again in German to us:
"I take what there is to take. Nothing else."

Neither of us knew how to reply. Seated in that humiliating
half-circle, against the slope of that sandy beach, what self-
disgust we both must have felt. Yet we seemed afraid to make the
next move, afraid even to glance toward the other. Miklos, with
his breeches unbuttoned and only one heavy military boot kicked
off, seemed like the clown once again. The cast of his eyes was
obscured by his hair so that one had to try to define his expression
solely by the curve of those thin blue lips. He wore a bruise on his
chin, a smudge of denser blue, but his face was otherwise un-
scratched. Crouching forward toward us now, with the shadow of
his long narrow head between his knees, the prepuce poked
through his pants like a weeping eye (or some other delicate
organ of sense). By the artificial tranquillity of his pose he
seemed to be measuring his mood against ours, as if he thought
he could discern through such a comparison each new phase and
nuance of our disgust.

Finally Miklos seemed to sense that he was unbuttoned. He
fastened together the gap. Pretending boredom, he yawned. "You
are at liberty to dress now."

I was the first to move. Although afraid to turn my back on

Miklos, who sat observing me stolidly—like a piece of garden statuary—I began to back away from our little circle toward my pile of clothes. Then I tried to force myself to look directly at Lilo but it was as if my neck was all awry; a good half of my vision had been blacked out. Fortunately, when I was reaching for my trousers, my cigarette case fell out of a pocket and I could see Lilo reflected in the metal surface, grossly distorted, like a gnome, as she pulled her step-ins over the swelling of her hips.

The sky turned overcast. Lilo's image was again obscured. Against my shoulders the chilling breeze grained my skin like leather. As I stepped into my shoes I glanced up obliquely and saw Lilo, upright once more, with her arms folded in front of her breasts; her face pale and agitated by the violent tremblings of her body.

"She won't put on her clothes," Miklos explained. "Perhaps she is afraid that I will look at her."

Again he threw back his head and began to laugh—laughed so uproariously that again it seemed as if he had lost all control of himself, but this mood was also to be ephemeral. Just as he seemed about to collapse, unable to sustain those hollow pealing sounds any longer, his lips blanched, compressed on themselves and, abruptly, the laughter was interrupted. "Alex," he said, "do you know what it means to take? I'm sure your father does."

"My father?" I shouted back.

"Well then, perhaps not," Miklos reflected. "But," he went on, "you know what I have in mind? To take! To have anything one fancies . . ."

When I started, protectively, for Lilo, Miklos hissed at me like a snake. "Don't worry. If I had wanted her I would have taken her too. Let us not confuse sport with serious business," he added. "But," said Miklos, "you may go and comfort her if you like. Go. Tell her how I am scum. A brute. The son of a petty opportunist gypsy whom your father has bested in business dealings more times than any of us can remember. A bastard, too. Yes, illegitimate, Alex. And now I have done this shameful thing to you and her. Well? Why not tell your father about it? Or my father? Or the police? Go. Speak to the police. Well, why don't you, Alex?"

"Allow me to tell you why!" he shouted. "Is it because you are Jews? At least I am not a Jew. Not that! But isn't it also because this girl . . . she is not as virtuous as you would have others think. I saw you together, you know. Like barnyard animals. Disgusting. Neither of you are saints. Moreover," Miklos added, fancying his turn of phrase, "if you do make a complaint to the order police you know there will be trouble. Race-mixing is a capital offense. I am a very good liar. I will say I was seduced by the Jewess here. Then what will happen to you two . . . and to your families? Think about it, Alex. There will be bad trouble."

Miklos rose off the ground again and began to limp toward his still-upright boot. Stepping into the thing, he reached into the pocket of his tunic for a cigarette. He was standing with his heel upon my lighter so he stepped away, picked the thing up, sparked a flame, drew smoke, and stowed the shiny metal object in his pocket. Then he rushed over to where Lilo was sitting. "Don't you want to make me happy? Is he such a charmer? Am I such a horror? Don't tell me you weren't interested. Slut! I dare you to say you weren't."

"Miklos, you know that isn't so," Lilo replied.

"Jew slut," he said. "If only men could believe you women." He seemed on the verge of kicking Lilo with one of his great boots. "Jew slut," he whispered again, as if for my benefit. Then he winked, spat on the ground, turned away and walked off into the woods.

Not until the crash of his footfalls in the brush had become indistinguishable from the rushing of the gorge, or the sound the wind was making through the trees, did Lilo think it safe to rise, and, when she did, she cowered like an old woman. Turning from me when I moved toward her, she stole down to the river to wash. I remained behind, deliberately. With lowered head and eyes averted, I tried to finish dressing. When Lilo came back I was standing fully clothed with her dress and underthings slung over the cradle of my arm, ready to pass her each article as she asked for them. I also tried to apologize. "I might have known better," I said. "If it hadn't been Miklos somebody else would have seen us here. Lilo. I am sorry. Next time we shall be more careful. I shall make sure of that."

The words rushed from my mouth and were swept up by the breeze. Lilo didn't even seem to know I was speaking to her. Tears glued her eyes shut. She would not take any of the clothes. At points along her arms, under one breast, and on her right thigh, were small yellow knots, submerged injuries, bruises. My immediate thought was that I had given her these. "Lilo—" I started. When I went to cover her with my body, she seemed to gag, and then turned shrill.

"Leave me be. I don't want you and you don't want me. I hate you."

She pushed me away. Then I felt the sting of her hand against my face! "Pig shit. Coward! Haven't you had enough of my hole?"

Really I didn't know what to say. Could I simply tell her to come to her senses? How would she interpret such remarks? If her hatred was to be directed at me, could I dutifully kiss her brow, as I so wanted to do, and move backward from her, turning away at last out of some now incongruous sense of decorum as she took the proffered clothes from my hands and began to dress?

I honestly thought not. To my way of thinking I had to try to mitigate the hurt. I could not simply hold my tongue. Foremost was the compulsion to apologize, to smooth over the injury, even if my efforts were to expose me to more severe outbursts of contempt.

"Lilo," I spoke quickly, hoping not to be interrupted, "if only we had not come to this place. If only there was something I could have done. But he. . . ."

"Yes. You were the perfect brave little soldier. . . ."

"That isn't true—"

"What isn't true, Alex? *What isn't true, little baby? What?*"

Our dialogue had come the full circle; once more, I was the guilty party. And there was no way I could answer her, for her questioning was so gratuitous, merely another form of insult.

It took me a moment to gather my thoughts. Then I said: "At least you will take the proper precautions?"

Lilo did not answer. The only sound that could be heard was the croaking of a frog on the banks of the stream.

"Lilo," I dared to speak again, "you know what I mean, of course?"

"Yes, stupid. I know," she replied, "but you needn't worry, stupid. Why, he hardly even spoiled the wave of my hair."

And before I could remonstrate with her once more, she was adding: "Get out of sight! Quickly now! Out of sight," she insisted.

I misunderstood her, did not look up in time.

A timber barge was slowly moving downstream along the open channel. The men on deck, three or perhaps four in all, were glancing our way. One was even waving at us. As we fled behind a screen of low bushes, the foresters hailed us in passing with a chorus of ribald jokes and laughter:

"Say there, is that a mustache between your legs?"

"Young man, what happened to your—"

"Don't be stupid," another laughed. "He's a young lady!"

Then all was silent again, save for the croaking of the frogs, the increased lapping of the water against the shore. We were standing in a patch of wild thorny framboises.

I picked a few of the berries, washed them in the stream, and brought them over to Lilo in the cup of my hands.

90

"Insensitive bore! Pig shit . . ."

Biting her lips to deter still another outburst, Lilo struggled with a final catch at the back of her dress. She made a noise like retching.

When I happened to look down at my hand it was the color of fresh blood.

7

WHEN my friend Bashansky died not far from here in the Galilee six months ago after a raid, I immediately went to pay my respects to the widow. Naturally the poor woman was distraught. He had left her with growing children. It had been a stray bullet. Probably the raiders hadn't even been aiming at poor Yehuda. And I had been by his side.

"*Why him? Why not you?*" the poor woman had screamed at me. "Why Yehuda? What did you do to deserve to live?" My dear Rubin, what could I say? You can imagine I felt helpless.

Likewise, when a woman has been very nearly raped by another man while the man she is supposed to marry stands by, helpless, as obscene as any third party at such a moment, would it be astonishing for her to direct her animus against her fiancé, and not toward the actual culprit? I will say this much for Lilo: she tried hard not to be entirely consistent. Although it is quite true that we had no intimate commerce together for another week, our relationship in all outward appearances remained quite as it should have been, and that made our actual estrangement even more excruciating.

On that terrible afternoon we walked home like strangers. Our hands did not touch. Not once did we stray toward one another. We were separated by no more than a hand's breadth of space, but that was sufficient to estrange us completely so that when Lilo lagged behind a moment I did not dare to hold the forward motion of my rigidly marching body until she would be beside me again. I continued walking, frowning, as it were, straight on toward the horizon where the roofs and church steeples of Clig had all turned purple before the final butchery of the sun.

It was like a dusk at the end of the world. We could tell that tomorrow would also be another searing day. The sky was spattered with fresh blood and the shadows of the clouds and the antiaircraft balloons, passing over the soft hills of the adjacent countryside, made it seem as if an ever darker gore had dried along the parched earth. Heat lightning flashed. From time to time there was a dry crack of thunder that presaged no rain. The freshets of blood and golden pus, rent from the bursting clouds in that final eruption of day, seemed to bloom as darker flowers along the course of the river which mirrored the whole sky—like a giant suppurating wound.

Facing into the sun as we walked our lips were purple, our brows glowed orange, then mauve, in the shadows, as if they had been stained with vegetable dyes. If we took no obvious delight in these strange refractions of the bleeding firmament, we also did not let our true feelings toward each other emerge. To return home safely, escaping detection, was enough of a chore, and we both applied our minds to it with an automatic acceptance of the relief it was to provide for us. When we came to the well near the monastery Lilo again stopped to slip into her sandals. Once we were safely back inside the confines of Father's garden, she insisted that I take her hand: "Alex, must you look like suffering Jesus?"

Lilo was pretending her usual petulance. She even affected a concern that we would be late for supper. Then she made me inspect her skirt, front and back, for stains. "Come now," she finally said, "it isn't as if I liked what happened," and ran ahead of me into the house, making sure as she went from room to room to greet everybody with extraordinary care (and to tell each of them in the same monotonous voice the lie we had made up together about falling asleep behind the barn) before she hurried upstairs to her room in order to change her clothes.

Nobody could then have suspected from her outward demeanor what I alone knew to be the truth—that she was in the throes of a terrible revulsion. On many occasions I had seen Lilo sad; I had also seen her delicate sensibilities angered and hurt. When my father was forced to tell her about the decline in her fortunes she was naturally despondent but, as she seemed to want to be consoled, it was accomplished easily enough. In a day or two she had recovered and could say to me: "Why should I care? I will never starve." But then I remembered her at each of her parents' funerals. She had been like stone. She actually seemed to be mocking those who tried to comfort her. "Oh yes," she said to one aunt who had journeyed all the way from Miskolc, "I'm sure you feel that way if you say you do."

"Oh yes, Cousin Erna, my mother felt no pain . . . none whatsoever. . . . That's true isn't it, Uncle?" She had turned to my father: "It was just like going off to sleep . . ."

Now, once again, Lilo was like stone. She could say nothing to me except to make hollow jokes, but her jokes and the silences in between were also acts of accusation. Once again she had been stricken, beaten down, so violated that to give utterance to her feelings might have outshrilled all the criers in hell; and so she pretended to be a petulant little girl clinging stubbornly to the former surfaces of her life, hoping in that way to preserve some semblance of herself as she had been before the encounter.

That evening at supper Lilo made sure to join the rest of our family. The talk was all pettiness. Perl went on and on about a certain family who were being baptized. Lilo's aunt said that in

Dobruja under the last tsar some Jews had refused to circumcize their children. My mother talked of oleomargarine, nothing but oleomargarine. But, you see we were all carefully avoiding any mention of Skirzeny's visit until such time as my father felt it appropriate to raise the subject; and Lilo was playing her part in the little charade as well as any of us. Toward my father she was kittenish, charming. She made it a point to discuss the coming auction sale of the bombed-out site on which had been her parents' home, but was that anything unusual? Lilo enjoyed baiting my father into one of his harangues about the abysmal state of her affairs. Then she could say to him: "Ah, Uncle Newman, if that is the case, then I'm afraid I must ask the courts to find me a less profligate guardian," and, having agreed beforehand that such a remark could only be meant in good humor, we would all join in the hilarity, as if upon signal.

But that evening Lilo's comments had a shrill cutting edge as she listened to my father expounding on all her financial setbacks. Once she was heard to say: "How can I trust this man?" Seeing then that she might have given out some hint of her true feelings, Lilo added: "Oh, but of course I can. *You all do.*" Whereupon she lapsed into a deathly silence.

My father had reverted to relating the war news, droning a rigidly self-censored version of the facts at us, filling our ears with casualty numbers and strange places and names; and we listened with a rapt attention about the Russian incursions in Moldavia, if only to escape our own turmoils.

And suddenly it was time for dessert. The honey cake was being passed about. Lilo passed what was handed to her, cut a small wedge and dropped it carefully on one corner of her plate, but she never once touched a fork to it and she didn't volunteer to help out with the cleaning up.

If this had been anybody else, poor Mother would have turned scold, but Lilo had already been roused on two or three occasions to help with the clearing of the first courses and the serving of coffee, and that effort had appeased my mother, unused as she was now to so much housekeeping.

So, when our coffee cups were taken away and I persisted in staring at Lilo so that nobody could ask permission to leave the table, thinking there had been something left unsaid, she didn't even bother to glance away, and it was my mother who declared: "These love birds never have enough of each other."

"So we are birds, are we?" Lilo said, pretending to be amused. Then with a quick shrill giggle she ran to help Sarah bathe the baby. Only my father remained at the table. To shield my embarrassment I had to make conversation: "Why did Skirzeny come today?"

"That," my father announced slowly, considering the impact of every word as it was articulated, "is my affair. It is not yet your affair."

"Well spoken, Uncle Newman!"

It was, of course, Lilo again. She had come down the back stairs. When I rushed over to her, she edged further away: "Not now, Alex. I'm so tired." Then, making sure for the sake of appearances to give me a cousinly good-night kiss on the cheek, she left again to go up to bed.

8

THE next day and the next Lilo exhibited the same sort of behavior to me but at different times in differing ways. The slow hot days of June were proceeding on their course. Almost every night now there were air raids. Or false alarms. The harpy voices of the sirens punctuated our sluggish daily activities. When they were stilled, again the vacuum of abstractions by which we lived was completed. Enveloped by clouds of dust and heat, Clig slumbered as best it could, everywhere except perhaps in my own heart. If I could manage to stand Father relating to us the taunts and insults of his defaulting creditors, or the brutalizing sun, or the closeness of my sleeping quarters which made oblivion something one thrashed after unsuccessfully for hours on end, I still could not tolerate Lilo's continual siege of melancholy, that doldrum of guilt and accusation into which we had stumbled together as if against some thorny hedgerow.

"Lilo," I used to say, "we ought to talk about this thing . . ."

"Lilo, it isn't right . . . all this coldness toward one another . . ."

"Lilo," I would insist, "are you quite sure that this is what you want?"

I tell you if my skin had been flayed from off my body with the sharpest knives, I would have felt no worse. I became the victim, Lilo my incubus. Since we were all thinner in those days because of the subsistence rations, I was not unusually concerned by her pallor; this merely accentuated the dark patches of shadows, like bruises, under her eyes; and they were my accusers. The steadiness with which Lilo could hold me in her gaze, like an insect suspended above a candle flame, always made me flinch. It was impossible to take refuge from her anywhere within the big house. Traces of Lilo were in every room, on every chair and table. Quite deliberately she seemed to be always leaving things about to remind me of her presence. When she walked her tread was purposely heavy, ominous, and she was trailed by the strong scent of her bath water and salts. The estate became a Bastille. Lilo was my cruel warder. Even when I thought I was alone with myself, she would reappear. That chink of light in the prison door would be her eyes. She would make herself known to me by staring, by fixing her gaze on the back of my neck or on my cold, clammy, fidgeting fingers, by whispering too loudly to my sisters about the corridors, or by that shrill choked laugh of terror in response to one of my father's ill-chosen jokes at the dinner table. As the days passed we found fewer opportunities to speak together in private, but we were always aware of each other; Lilo seemed to make it her business to be at my side when others were absent so that if I suddenly turned around she was there, almost a shadow of myself.

It became so that I began to resent this treatment very quickly. First I pitied Lilo, then I grew angry with her. The prisoner and his jailer shared every emotion of love and fear, hatred and disgust. Sometimes I would try to convince myself that what I was presently experiencing was illusory, the effect of my jangled

98

nerves, or that we were witnessing a play, a dumb show, in which the real Lilo and myself were only observers, not these two nasty participants. Or I would accept the illusion as a reality and still try to convince myself that Miklos had failed in his purposes and that Lilo in her treatment of me was simply being too squeamish. Then I would argue with myself: "What have I done? Isn't this a bit much—all her carrying on? Miklos is the guilty person, not I! Why doesn't she accuse Miklos?"

Then I wanted to scream accusations at Lilo—that she was a child, a spoiled baby, a squeamish spoiled infant.

"Lilo," I said once, "It's not as if you didn't want to. So it is just as much your fault as my own . . ."

She threw back my guilt at me. It was like a pinched nerve, like an astonishingly swift hand clapped over my mouth. Then the slow ache of memory would touch me again and again, a compress dabbed against an open wound. I recalled our life together before the encounter with Miklos, and I would feel my body cringing with misery.

Even when I was able to sleep, I was no better off. Sleep protected me like the oily surface in a pond under which a certain swarming dense inner life suffers final deadly paroxysms. Being deprived of Lilo was torment enough, but I would also dream that she had been murdered, that I was in fact her murderer, and in my dreams I would be forced to embrace her naked corpse. To make myself awaken was like pricking my body up through the surface of that pond again to swallow the heady air of day. But were my daydreams apt to be any better? I was constantly fantasying that I was standing exposed on a turbulent seashore while the waves kept sweeping over me, or even lying in some flimsy boat, being tipped by the waves, or even lying in my own sweated bed, choked by the bedclothes. And always there would be the same pressure against my chest—a constant indigestion, as if my ribs had been weighted down with cold bricks. What did I

99

really feel and what were simply guilty imaginings? Most of the time I went about as if my head had been enclosed in a vise. I had that same mandible feeling in my extremities. My lips were numb. They seemed to bleed too easily, as did my nose. I always seemed to need to scream to be heard, was never able to speak in normal tones—even when we were the only persons in the room.

Only once, however, did Lilo declare herself openly to me. That happened early one evening when a messenger came for her with a note. I had gone to the front door to give the boy some money. Assuming that one of Lilo's girl friends was merely imparting a confidence, I did not think of opening the note but brought it out to Lilo in the garden where she was sitting under the last fires of the sunset with some embroidery. She snatched the thing from my hands. "Did you open it?" she demanded, even though it was clear that I had not. Then she turned her back to me and tore at the envelope. From the way her shoulders were trembling, I sensed who her correspondent was.

"Give that to me," I shouted. "What does that fellow want from us now?"

"Liar! So you did open it."

"No. Never."

"Very well. Then you may have it to read now." As she ran up toward the wooden stairs leading to our kitchen, Lilo let the paper flutter out of her hands. When I bent down to the grass, I found myself staring bleary-eyed at a perfect square, perhaps two inches, across which Miklos Skirzeny had printed only one word in great block letters:

SLUT

That evening I tried to lure Lilo to come to my room, so that I could reassure her by telling her all the horrible things that Miklos had done to me in the past, but she was careful to elude me by going upstairs with Aunt Pepi before I could get to her. I spent the evening alone in the front parlor with my head between my hands. When Father purposely stopped by to inquire why I seemed so pensive, I remembered the way he had treated my questions about Skirzeny, so I merely stared at him as if dumb-stricken until he left the room.

What would I have gained by confessing all that had happened? Wouldn't he be obliged, if he knew, to speak with Skirzeny? And how could one predict what that wicked old man would do? More than likely he would be forced to construe the thing in favor of his stepson.

I said: "It isn't any of your business, really," and my father grumbled but he left me alone.

Morning came and Lilo searched me out after breakfast in my father's study. I usually liked to hide there when I knew he would be gone from the house. Sometimes I would go through his papers. Most of the time I would merely sit and try to imagine myself as master of the place.

That day I did neither. It was rainy. The leaded panes of glass in the window alongside my father's desk were pearled with dirty drops of rainwater and the light that filtered through covered my face with a smallpox of shadows. The general gloom of the old wooden chamber was like a stink, mildly suffocating but comfortable in a strange way, for it seemed almost palpable; it filled the gaps between you and the world of objects; it softened the void.

I was reading I don't remember what when Lilo approached. I suspect I may have looked rather startled upon seeing her, but, though she seemed to take note of my expression, she would not come forward from the doorway. I actually had to order her to enter and close the door after her and, once she had done this, she still continued to speak to me in whispers.

"Alex," she said, from the other side of the lounge on which we were both now sitting. "I think I've been making quite a fool of myself. I want to apologize. I know you couldn't help what happened. I only hope you don't bear me any grudges. We are both so helpless, Alex. You do forgive me, don't you . . ."

101

I started to protest that there was nothing to forgive, but she cut me off with a motion of her hand: "I know you think I've been avoiding you. The truth is," Lilo added quickly, "it could not be helped."

"What do you mean? *Helped?*"

Lilo's face reddened: "Women's problems."

The way she purposely stressed the phrase "women's problems" —it was the way some people behave when they are lying. They try to appear so casual that they call even more attention to what they are saying. For Lilo was lying. No more than two weeks before she had completed one "time of flowers." Although I felt my face reddening (and I found myself looking over my shoulder toward the doorway to make sure that we were not being overheard) I could not allow her statement to go unchallenged.

"When did all this begin?" I asked.

She seemed to sense my suspicions and moved farther down along the lounge, away from me. I repeated my question: "When?"

"Can't I have any privacy?" But when Lilo saw that I was not put off by her challenges, she said: "It happened the day after we went swimming . . ."

"You mean," I cut in, "the day after Miklos—"

"*What?*"

Lilo was angry with herself now, so she pretended to scold me. "I have forgotten all about that," she said. "Why must you keep reminding me? I advise you to forget about it. Do you hear me?" Then she added, whispering again: "So you see you had no need to worry . . . none whatsoever," she continued, shaking her head. "Alex, isn't that true?"

"Yes. It's true," I replied. "But I already knew that."

"Oh you infant—"

She didn't finish her sentence. There was nothing Lilo could say that would not further compound her petty lies. We stared at each other like a pair of condemned men on the scaffold. How could we avoid confronting each other now? Our silence was

102

mutual, considered, a profound interval during which we each pretended to be deep inside our own thoughts. I actually was trying to frame the words whereby I could say to Lilo that we must break with this infantile and deceitful behavior and try to face our situation squarely, as it actually was, but so profound was my reflection that I almost allowed her to slip unnoticed out of the room.

Lilo was at the doorway again by the time I saw her. There was nothing then I could do but to scold her: "Lilo, we are prisoners here, don't you see? We can't run from each other. We can't lie to each other. We have been too intimate.

"You know as well as I do," I continued, "what kind of a person Miklos Skirzeny is. In normal times they would have put him in jail. But Lilo," I went on, "these are not normal times and yet we must try to live through them. I have always loved you," I said, "and I still do—despite what has happened. I must assume it could not be helped. Thus, as soon as possible, we will get married . . . that is, if you still want me . . . if you are still willing to try to come to an understanding with me, in short, that what happened in the woods was just an unfortunate incident which will never happen again. We will see to that. I will swear it, Lilo. Do you understand? Well? Tell me what you are thinking . . ."

I had spoken longer than I had planned. Breaking off, I peered across the gloomy space at Lilo. Her face was enveloped by the shadows from the window; the stuff of her garments seemed to fuse with the heavy patternings in my father's carpet, so that only her eyes blazed back at me, larger than life, as if, in the darkness, a beam of strong light had suddenly been swept across her face.

"You do understand?" I asked.

"Yes," she whispered, "I do understand."

Peering once more into that corner, I saw that Lilo had fled.

The next three days were a novel form of torment for both of us. Love? We hardly spoke to one another. Neither of us could bear to sit through the long evening meals. We stole food when we could and wandered about the house on separate courses like rival spirits.

My sisters, sensing our alienation, now called me "lovesick." How we endured the teasing of our families I shall never be able to explain. To be greeted by everyone one meets as "lovebird" and "sad eyes" was almost too much to bear. It became so that I would purposely excuse myself from a room when it seemed that Lilo needed to make an appearance there, and she seemed to do likewise, as if by a common agreement. When we passed in the halls we nodded silently, but we never joined courses, never went off together in the same direction. Neither did we speak to one another if it could be helped. To distract myself I tried to paint alone in the garden but all that I could manage were mono-chromatic squares and circles bisected by jagged lines of hot harsh color.

Sometimes during those afternoons when I painted under the sun like some demented creature I would see Lilo peering out of one of the back windows, but when I looked again the vision had vanished; my eyes would be confronted once more with the monotonous black window frames lit here and there so that they were opaque by the strong orange glinting of the sun. Then I would tell myself that I had been imagining things again, but whenever I would turn away I had the sudden knowledge that her face had reappeared and that I dared not look again or she would only vanish once more.

We were now leading entirely distinct lives; even our silent warring with each other had reached a point in time whereby it was now largely perfunctory, a way of biding time until some new, hitherto unexplored patterning of emotional responses would form in ourselves to replace that previously quiet spell of animus. My father blamed me, but Mother claimed to think it was Lilo's fault. It was terrible. They actually seemed to think that I had acted like a scoundrel. "Your chances aren't so great at finding another one," Father said. When I told them there would never be anybody else, Mother said, "Why? Is she such a paragon?"

It is lucky Lilo didn't overhear. But she was probably by now just as immune as I was to such "good advice." It was likely, too, that we would have continued to exist numbly, in such a world of non-feeling, had it not been for exterior events over which, as you must know, we had no control. One evening a rumor circulated among the Jewish families of Clig that the Horthy government was planning to capitulate. If that happened, it was argued, the Nazis would occupy Hungary. Horthy would then be deposed; our army would be merged with the Wehrmacht. You can imagine how we felt about such a possibility.

My father was immediately summoned to a meeting of the Council, leaving me, under Maurice, in charge of the house. He went up to bed early. The house soon slumbered. I was alone.

When the hours dragged by and there was no further news, I decided to lock the front door, knowing that my father would have his spare key. I even went so far as to throw the bolt, until it occurred to me that my father's key would not work if this double lock was applied, so I decided to change into my bedclothes and stay awake by the fire in Father's study until such time as he did get home.

Going up the stairs to my room I again had the sensation that I was mounting a scaffold and when I felt the cold touch of death grasp at my hand I very probably blanched.

"Oh my poor darling. You are nervous!"

Lilo was standing, shielded by the draperies, in a dark corner of the landing. Her outstretched hand seemed disembodied, as if it had been merged into oblivion, but so caressing was her voice, the words she spoke, the tone of concern with which she uttered them, that my first thought was to reach out to her across the void, to embrace her and bring her close to me.

"Not here. Come to my room," she whispered then.

"Can we?" I found myself asking.

105

"Come to my room," Lilo insisted. She disregarded my timidity, making me feel so petty for having uttered the words that all I could say then was, "Lilo, should we?"

If only I might have been more impulsive, but I had my father to worry about. I cursed myself silently afterward for what I was forced to do, but the fact was I could not allow myself to be away from the ground floor when I knew he would be returning shortly.

Lilo sensed my confusion. "You have nothing to fear," she explained. "Don't you understand what I am trying to tell you?"

"Yes," I lied. "Only let us talk tomorrow. Tomorrow we can be alone in the garden."

"And now? What should I do now?" she asked.

I started to explain that I needed to be up to let my father in. "Wait here with me," I said.

"I'm afraid. I don't care to know what your father will tell us. He will only lie to us again."

"Don't say that!" I cried.

"Why shouldn't I?"

Lilo leaped toward me out of the darkness as if she was being pursued: *"Why can't I? Why mustn't I?"* she demanded. *"Aren't we ever to be truthful with one another again?"*

She was just as alert to my next protesting responses. Her hand brushed across my face, her fingers rested on my lips. She wouldn't let me speak. "Don't. Don't say anything more," she chastised me.

Then I heard her moving away. Lilo was disappearing above me into the gloom of the corridor so that, in another moment, I barely heard the shuffling of her muled feet against the polished floors.

When I followed she was already out of sight. A yellow glimmer filtered down from the dusty transom above Perl's doorway; the great corridor was thronged in obscurity. I stood alone, outside the rooms of my sleeping family, stricken by deceit and equivocation. To escape my own sweated body I would have probably given up life itself. I couldn't stay put. Feeling as if I had allowed myself to be used in the perpetration of some despicable fraud, I tried to hide from myself in my room, but when the door closed softly behind me, like the cocking of a revolver, I knew that I would have to go to Lilo as soon as my father was safely inside our house again.

I changed into my sleeping garments, lit a stale cigarette (for I was not then a frequent smoker and usually cadged from my father), stared at my watch. Fifteen minutes oozed by. Then half an hour, an hour, the stillness making me think I had been deafened. I went to the window. Nobody in Clig seemed to be observing the blackout. On the rocky hills the houses squatted like glowing caterpillars against a giant cabbage leaf. Although I had not once stopped sweating, I now felt chilled, as if from a fever. I bundled myself in a dressing gown; my head was like an immense carbuncle of pain. Drawing, swelling, pulsing, it seemed as if it would extrude all of my being into one point of agony and then suddenly split apart, like a water blister. Every time I tried to recall what we had said to each other I was forced to put my hands up to that angry object, as if steadying some quaking idol on a shelf. Finally I could neither repress nor bear the feeling any longer. I lay across my bed to read while waiting for Father. My eyes closed. I was soon unconscious. . . .

But not, even then, impervious to reverie or suggestion. That evening I dreamed our wedding ceremony was taking place. My bride and I stood under the canopy. The rabbi intoned the sanitary code of Clig in German and Aramaic. My parents and friends solemnly looked on. Even Lilo's dead family were present as was Skirzeny and his first wife. At last, the rabbi pronounced us as of one flesh. I was made to stamp feebly against a wine glass until it shattered like thin ice over a pond. Then the rabbi told me I should lift my bride's veil.

The head I saw was framed by the long blond tresses of Lilo

Gero but it was the face of Miklos Skirzeny, and I could hear my voice crying out: "You slut. You filthy slut!"

I woke to the sound of *haut-parleurs* in the square opposite our house. All the Jewish families were being summoned to assemble on the Street of the Oxen, adjacent to the brick factory.

Trying to rouse myself my body felt like a fuzziness, a blur of sensations, having no bulk or weight. Presently there was a knocking at my bedroom door.

My father!

"Alex. You are wanted. We are all wanted. You must get up immediately. Please son. . . . *Alex, do you hear me?*"

"Yes. I hear you."

"Well then, it's lucky for you, my boy, that I was out all evening, for you left the door bolted. I had to wake your mother to let me in this morning."

Again his voice sounded as if it was coming from one of the *haut-parleurs:* "Now will you be getting up or must I send Maurice after you?"

I rushed out of bed.

My clothes lay everywhere.

I couldn't find my shoes.

Light was streaming through the curtains, spattering itself against the flowered wallpaper like splotches of mildew.

When I sat down to dress I noticed my bedclothes were stained yellow with semen. Stumbling into pants, a shirt, sandals, I hurried down the stairs without having even attempted to cover over the shameful condition of my linens.

"Ah, there he is," my father said. "Will he ever be on time for anything?"

Father had already assembled our entire family alongside our front entrance. My mother and sisters were in their holiday best with Lilo and Aunt Pepi, even more splendid, squinting over their shoulders. When she saw me emerge from the doorway, Lilo tried to smile. My father said: "Probably he will be late for his own wedding . . ."

108

He stood next to this little grouping with his hands behind his back. By his other side glared Maurice, uncomfortable in his only ill-fitting business suit, his collar open like the Zionist he had once been. Moshe Shad seemed especially shoddy in comparison to Father, of course, who had assembled his very best outfit for the occasion.

Despite the heat he had managed to dress in his frock coat and striped pants. His sweltering magnificence was further formalized by a gray silk four-in-hand tie.

Yes, Father reminded me then of the man said to be Istran Fass, but, even more so, he was like one of those "proud but impoverished" Hungarian noblemen we came to know so well in Clig after the Rumanian land reforms. He had located his decoration from the Austrian crown prince. It hung on a ribbon around his neck like a talisman. When my father crossed his hands over his buttocks, swelling out his belly under his thin silk vest, I noticed also the fine gold chateleine on which his great watch was pendent along with a certain queer charm from his student days—a heart-shaped locket with a ruby set into it that was encircled by a dim rosette of old script.

To round out his self-esteem, Father carried behind his back the hat he wore on the High Holy Days—a great black beaver tub with a brim. When I joined our little circle, he clamped the thing down onto his head, but every few seconds the heat forced him to turn the brim in one or another direction so that he could swab a portion of his brow with one of those large, fresh, white linen handkerchiefs which he seemed able to pull out of his vest pockets and sleeves in series of two and three like the fabled white rabbits of some very great magician.

In such a company I was perhaps the shabbiest person present, except for Maurice, who, jobless, penniless, living off my father's charity, had conducted himself ever since the start of the labor drafts as if we were living in suspended animation, and who had never been particularly fastidious to begin with. Consequently, when Lilo first smiled at me, I thought it was because of my appearance, but when she continued to favor me with such amused glances, I felt considerably cheered. The *haut-parleurs* renewed their entreaties. I thought we were being observed by all. Recognizing the mechanical voice as belonging to one of his fellow Council members, my father jumped, as if startled: "Franke must be calling for us," he said. "We are probably the last ones . . . thanks to Alex."

With that he took a lunging step forward, stopped on the cobblestones, wiped his brow, and began again to make his promenade, dodging occasional piles of horse droppings, but even then never allowing his eyes or his head to be cast down. Indeed! It was as if he were threading his way through a course that he had helped to lay out.

Do you know we followed him?

Without thinking we departed single file.

Like Morris dancers!

Or as if, indeed, it was the Holy Days time, and we were merely about to make our annual appearance in the stalls of the now boarded-over synagogue.

What folly!

Years later in the cinema at Beersheba I was reminded of that scene. What I saw was not some Hollywood-created image. These were films captured from the Japanese—a blown-up eight-millimeter recording of a family wedding of some Japanese Christians, photographed only moments before a certain split second in August 1945.

Father, mother, bride, groom, the relatives and friends, all dressed in Western clothes, as if to deliberately parody our own style of dress. Or so it seemed to me then.

The amateur cameraman had not been very expert. He kept cutting off heads and feet and the family seemed to be walking as if on eggs. But, in those last moments of Christian innocence, effusively, as they marched off to the toy church ceremony, that procession of middle-class Japanese could have been ourselves.

110

Their grainy faces, their dress, their postures gave no indication that they knew they were moving past those rapidly fluttering lenses toward the glare of a brilliant sun to be atomized like dust.

Yet, in our case, one must take note of a certain shading of diff-ence: some of us should have known by then; others—like my father—more than half suspected. We had never before been summoned to come together as a group. Where did we think we were going? To the public gardens? To a band concert? The truth is we didn't ask ourselves such questions. This, you must remem-ber, was June 1944, and there were already so many rumors that they soon became confused with one another. It was difficult to sort them all out in a coherent way, next to impossible to know the source, and the work of an Einstein to separate the likely from the unlikely.

Rumors of every description we heard—that the Germans had already taken over in Budapest; that Hungary would sign a sepa-rate peace treaty, like Italy; that the Pope in Rome would inter-cede; that some of us would be ransomed to Turkey and others to Madagascar through Rudolf Kastner and his father-in-law. Al-ready it was clear that Germany was losing the war, but what could we make of that? Who would be our next set of masters? Would they be any kinder to us? We had heard that King Mihai of Rumania was about to join forces with the Russians. Could we endure another Rumanian occupation?

I tell you, Rubin, when one is exposed to rumor after rumor and some prove true while others prove false, but never as one would have hoped or even expected, the intelligence becomes mired by skepticism and distrust, and one's reflexes turn to rub-ber. In a short while it is no longer possible to respond to each fresh new speculation. One merely shrugs one's shoulders and mutters: "Ah, more rumors. Always rumors."

So if we did not seem to hesitate, much less resist, at that point, perhaps it was because we still did not know what we were resist-ing or whom. I can assure you it was never for fear of ourselves

111

but for fear of the retribution to those who we thought surely would be saved. When we thought of that retribution, it wore no face or uniform; it was, I tell you, completely anonymous, as vague as storm clouds.

Today you may feel differently, but I am telling you only the way we felt. I have nothing now to hide. Nor do I expect to soften any judgments you will make. Believe what you wish; just do not question our beliefs. They were not twisted out of theories. They were not the work of a bunch of historians. They grew out of the very life we were leading. Unarmed and ill-prepared, beset by murderers too, we saw and heard many different things. Then we tried to reconcile all the contradictions. When your history has been deceit, that is not a simple chore. We had been tricked so many times in the past by false prophets that we came to scorn the very act of prophecy. Remember, Rubin? Some of our ancestors had followed Sabbatai Tsvi? And what came after him? There had been the Slavophile movement and the movement for Transylvanian autonomy. Yes. Fancy that. Our little backwater wanted to be a great nation. Was it any wonder then that we grew immune to all rival speculations? To threats and prophecies alike? For us they were just loud noises, thunderheads in a sky thronged with clouds.

The cruelest fact of all may be that we who claimed to revere life, not as some petty abstraction but for the sake of being alive, of choosing life—that we were the ones who were tricked into the behavior of sheep. Or swine!

Be patient with me. I shall even try to show you how that came about. But you must not begin by doubting me. Be skeptical but reserve your judgment. Understand: the condemned man usually thinks there is another appeal. Even Eichmann went to the scaffold pleading legality. Even the slave learns to doubt the determination of his master. Consider: circumstances often change overnight. Miracles may not have seemed possible, but our history had taught us to respect the unpredictable. And at that very

112

moment, the Russians were at the borders of Moldavia. The famed Iron Guard would probably crack. A breakthrough into Rumania would mean a separate peace? Could Hungary then afford to expose its frontiers to the Russian hordes? And if the worst came about, we would flee toward the Bolsheviks. We had been told about Birobidzhan. Although we knew better than to believe in fairy stories, some thought they would have to take us in, if only to make propaganda, and we said to ourselves: "One can live under any law." Remember: even Berlin had its privileged Jews—its *Mischlinge* of the first and of the second degree, the men from the war veterans *Verband*, yes, and the war invalids and those in the *Judenrat*. We did not then know the word *Kapo* but we knew about Thieriesanstadt. If we knew of any camp it was Thieriesanstadt. What then could we have expected? To be admitted into the *Stamm H. J.*? The Aryanizations and the deportations were unavoidable, unalterable; we had heard that too many times already to believe differently. But weren't there still some Jews in our parliament? And how were the Hungarians going to be able to decide who was a *Mischling* and who was not when even Hitler had said that the blood stain lasted six or seven generations?

Do you see how narrow was the scope of the optimist in those days?

Do not misunderstand! I don't wish to suggest that we were actively hopeful. I think the correct word in English would be "quietistic." We did not have sufficient knowledge to be stoics. Nor were we so single-minded. Trooping beside my family toward the Street of the Oxen, what I wanted was to speak to Lilo; and she again seemed reluctant. My sister Perl asked: "What is your hurry? We'll be there soon enough." I merely snarled at Perl. When Lilo lagged behind to adjust the strap on one of her sandals, I seized her hand, squeezed it as if entrusting her to conduct me somewhere I had never been. I simply would not let go of Lilo.

113

Not that she protested, or in any way seemed alarmed. Her parted lips, her slightly myopic staring at me, this was not meant as accusation; Lilo was acknowledging my presence. The sun also made her squint. With the faintest of smiles, she returned the pressure of my squeezes. Her voice, when she finally spoke, was quite matter-of-fact: "Strange, Alex, that we should need an occasion like this to take a walk together."

I did not answer.

Presently I heard her speaking again. ". . . And if we are both deceived at least we were deceived together. We are together. We are together still."

". . . Forgive me, Alex."

"Why? What for?"

"Then you do forgive me?"

"How could I not?" I waited until the rank in front of us had turned the corner. "Lilo," I whispered then, "you are my bride!"

She says nothing, and we are forced to walk on. Presently other couples, our friends and their families, come into view. We have not seen some of these people in many months. They all look a trifle faded. A street full of ghosts. We exchange the usual greetings: heads bow; faces take cognizance of each other. Our eyes are never downcast, although as we come around the square to the place where the assembly has been called we are packed so closely in ranks that we hobble each other's shins.

Then all our ranks merge, shift, like the sea, some seeming to break into a run at the sight of the square, the preparations under way, the brilliant sun, while others are reforming in new little groups of sixes and sevens to stand without so much as a grumble in these hastily composed units, shoulders blotting from view their own boarded-over shops on the perimeters of that same square.

And all the while we are forming, a brass band blares "the song of the good comrade" through a multiplicity of statics from the *haut-parleurs* which have been erected on long narrow stanchions, like beehives on stilts, but at every corner.

114

And even when no gramophone music is being transmitted, when a record is being changed or sought after, or when the needle catches in a groove, these same contraptions continue to give off a steady buzzing or humming, not unlike the sound bees make when they are swarming about a hive.

At last, Lilo speaks to me: "I wish it would rain. Then all these arrangements would be spoiled. What do you think, Alex?"

"Long live Hungary!"

"*Alex, what?*"

No answer. I merely point with my hands toward the core of that same square.

A detail of Galicians (or perhaps Ruthenians) is in the act of constructing a large wooden platform. The thing is immense. It has been erected out of prefabricated sections directly over the basin of the fountain Empress Marie Theresa (so called to commemorate our former status as a "grand principality") but it is flanked still by those twin patriotic statues in bronze of Pastor Roth and Nicholas Horthy.

A preposterous moment. Our history—as much as theirs—is being blocked from sight. Even as we are formed, that gang of scarecrow laborers is hammering the last sections of a superstructure into place which seems to resemble a hat box on top. No! It's so much larger. A bandstand perhaps. Or the top decks of some great ship.

Squeezed between artless monuments to our Transylvanian autonomy, the immense anonymous scaffolding rises higher, wider, devouring every blade of grass in the square, until it seems to erupt out of a blankness of concrete and stone like one of those feldspars of salt one saw before the war in the countryside near Parajd.

Some think at first that it is a gallows. We are to watch a public execution. But then, where are the hanging posts? See! There are no trap doors.

Even as we speculate, the wooden sepulchre has surged another yard or more toward the clear blue of the sky on its giant stilts. Now it towers above our heads. Our shoulders ache. Large sections of flooring are being unloaded from a waiting lorry. Near the foundations of the structure an accumulated detritus has been carted into a mound so that an ordinary painter's ladder can be laid aslant this toward the top deck. Still, the hammering does not abate. Sluggardly, uncoordinated, it persists like muffled drums, but with such syncopations that our ears and tender shoulders twitch before, during, after every blow.

To everybody's astonishment the structure is allowed to rise to a height twice the size of a man. By the time work is permitted to slacken off, the grandeur of our statuary has been effaced; the sun, moving across the nearby roofs to glare down upon all of us directly, flares like match fire behind the faintest of clouds.

But, since there is no shade and little breeze, that emaciated gang of slave-carpenters does not seem very anxious to move on, away from the slight shelter provided by such an edifice. Some are casting furtive but accusatory glances our way from under great flaxen shocks of hair while others in that party of perhaps thirty men and boys pretend they are doing final touch-up work.

The intensifying sun makes such a charade difficult to prolong. Presently, every single movement of the men is accomplished in painful slow motion. It seems as if the saws and hammers they carry have grown giant-sized, weighing many times more than their actual bulks. The detail continues to lift these tools and to bring them down with a dullish thud against the face of that clumsy octagon, although it is now as if they are expending their last reserves of strength. One man planes at a block of wood until it is little more than a scrap. Another is holding a spirit level up against the slanting ladder, trying to appear quizzical. Nobody seems anxious to move on, least of all the guards.

Despite their close proximity to the workers, we can hear the guards complaining to each other about the heat. Then the men begin to grumble quite openly, a babel of tongues. They are obviously all thirsty, for some keep licking the sweat off their shoulders. One man, dressed in rags, tries to do a bit of personal housekeeping. Among a pile of saws he has found soap. Now he is trying to lather himself with his own sweat. I hear Lilo: ". . . Like hyenas, Alex."

"Long live Hungary," I answer, a second time.

Another pair of boys have hidden themselves among the under-stiltings of the platform, hoping to find a cool spot. At first they are not detected. Their eyes close. They roll over on their bellies to share a scrap of bread.

Then somebody shouts: *"Get away from there!"* Two guards run toward them. The boys are dragged out by the feet and beaten across their shoulders with rifle butts.

A minor incident. Nobody wants to show alarm. The majority of the Order Police, being themselves Hungarians or Ukrainians, stand by without offering to help. Some are grinning beneath their steel helmets, or perhaps they are merely licking the sweat off their own lips (for the heat is probably an even greater torture to them). Yet they have to stand by in proper uniforms until the structure has been properly inspected. Gazing up at the tower along with the rest of us, the faces of these older soldiers redden; tunics grow dark with sweat. They are like us; they do not seem disturbed by the efforts of their hostages to make more work for themselves.

The best way I can describe our reactions is to say that we are like spectators at a performance, bored perhaps, but not hostile. Let the circus go on. We would judge the worth of every act and applaud or remain silent, according to our moods.

Yes. Our manners were impeccable. We were the best of audiences. Having been shunted over to the shady side of the square for our main assembly point, we were not even uncomfortable at first but were what you might call the onlookers. At least we strained so as to appear as if we were. The speculative, grumbling rumormongers in our midst were forced to constrain themselves. Loudmouths were gagged. Our mood was contem-

117

plative as we followed the action. After a while, our passivity (or if you prefer, curiosity) was like a fatal contagion which caught us all standing with eyes bulging and lips compressed, as if posing for some specifically solemn group photograph. No one spoke. Eyes seemed glazed, or else they were like slits. Of course, we pretended not to notice the looks we were getting from the Galicians.

Before the Jewish nation was sent up in smoke it was changed into mud and dung. Don't believe it when they say people know how to die. People are created to live. We went to our death immersed in life up to the ears. When the heat, although indirect, became no less oppressive, we fanned ourselves with anything we could find, our hands if need be, but the breeze we scooped from the elder trees also brought horse flies which tickled our noses, buzzed about our ears, lighted on us and then tickled us or bit us again. I remember faces specked with bluebottles as with some plague, and I remember feeling the strange scramble of tiny hair legs across my lips, my brow, the bridge of my nose, my eyelids. When would that camera shutter finally snap? When would we hear the anonymous photographer declare: "Now please all say at once: *BITTE!*" We posed; some were gaping like peasant-tourists the first time in a city, the only sounds we heard being the occasional thud of a hammer.

Presently the "song of the good comrade" is amplified to a distortion. A squad car pulls up. An officer steps out. Salutes are exchanged. The familiar phrase is echoed: *Alles in Ordnung!* Our Galicians are herded together by their guards, each carrying what appears to be a different make of automatic weapon. They all march away in the direction of the brick factory.

"*Attention!*"

Troops of the regulars have now appeared at the four corners, more salutes are exchanged with the new officer in command who goes about on a brief inspection tour, a baton under one arm. Then he and a subordinate go the way of the work party, to be

118

replaced in turn by a rather portly colonel in the dark uniform of the Reichkommissariat.

"GREETINGS!"

I hear Lilo whispering to me: ". . . A proper little pig!"

"Maybe so," I reply.

"I want none of that. Do you hear?" my father speaks.

"Long live Hungary," I say, still another time.

The gentleman who stands before us now smiles as if by habit, but he also seems insistent that every formality be observed. He is, to judge from his looks, a man in his late fifties, with a kindly open face, wrinkled about the eyes and lips by incessant sunshine. We have never seen him before. Apparently our business is also new to him, for he seems rather uncomfortable behind the tinted glass pince-nez which he affects—so much so that there is a quality of absent-minded self-amusement in the way he attempts to total up our numbers with his index fingers, his lips moving all the while like those of a country schoolroom pedagogue while he meekly stabs his finger at us and loses count of his sums.

The poor devil. We do not envy him for what he has to do. We only have to stand and be counted but he has to do the counting and, perhaps, the choosing. Poor fool! He may very well have once been a schoolteacher, a provincial clerk, attorney for the now-defunct courts of the peasantry, an idealist, a land reformer, or a specialist in high-colonic irrigations. The man had that kind of face and he did not have a particularly military gait. His reservist's uniform was unspeakably sloppy, the leather pipings unpolished, his leggings in a deplorable state. He didn't even carry a revolver. The insignia he wore on the collar of his tunic was that of some obscure echelon, nowhere near the front ranks.

Even from my distance, I could read the man's lips as he mused: "What shit this is!"

On closer examination I was also able to observe (when the officer paced before us on the platform) that his eyes were puffy and bruised, the irises bloodshot from lack of sleep or too much drink; and that he carried his left arm rather stiffly, almost too high, crooked at the elbow too, as if with a slight paralysis. . . . So this is what they had sent to choose among us. It was easy to see why my father said: "They can't know what they are doing."

But he only said that to pass the time. It was like that officer cursing: "What shit this is!" Nothing much is meant by it.

Too bad I was never able to learn that officer's name. From his manner it was clear he did not have his heart in this kind of work. He wanted us to understand that he was not entirely sympathetic with the tasks assigned to him. Most often he did this by his manifest display of tics—that finger jabbing at the air, the slight deferential shrug of his shoulders, the foolish smile, as if always on the verge of making a joke calculated to lighten our mood, or by the way he had of looking down at the floor whenever one of us would attempt to stare hard into his eyes. Nothing much meant by it! A country lawyer. No doubt of it. Or perhaps one of the new military chaplains. I thought: this man is definitely out to waste as much time as possible. See how he keeps stepping down among us to straighten out our ranks. Watch him. Now he looks at his watch, lights a cigarette, walks among us. Once he even stops in front of my father.

"You are a Jew?"

Father nods.

"Both your parents . . . were they Jews?"

Again my father is forced to nod his head.

"But . . . did you have any ancestors who were not Jews?"

My father hesitates. Probably the temptation was great to invent a kinship with Horthy himself, but a thousand faces are staring at him. Finally father spits out another negative.

"How I wish this could be helped," the colonel says, backing away then.

Truly, I wish I could remember such an officer's name, for he seemed to be such a humane fellow, and it wouldn't hurt anybody politically nowadays to know of him. He was obviously

120

straining to forestall what was to take place as long as he possibly could, as if in hopes that by his inaction the morning would wane into afternoon and the afternoon into evening and we could all be sent home until another day.

How different from the companion who is shortly to join him—a rather severe-looking civilian, dressed in a costume identical to that of my father: striped pants, a swallowtail coat, decorations, a vest, a winged collar.

Between the colonel and this civilian superior there develops an obvious, although suppressed, inarticulate atmosphere of tension, an expectancy. Each keeps staring over his shoulder at some imaginary other fellow, as if to check certain of his actions against certain other unstated responses. The civilian is immaculate in all respects. He has the pallor of an asthmatic. He gulps twice at every breath, swallows hard. His eyes glitter as with a fever. One has the sense that just as he is continually picking pieces of lint off his funereal costume so he would also be, in official matters, a kind of lint-picker. It is also apparent that he is not from our part of Europe but has been swept our way from off the boulevards of some great city. There is definitely something quite citified about the ashen pallor of his face, set in an incredulous squint underneath that pall of shadows cast down by his large black hat. At all times, the gentleman leans heavily to one side on the crook of a magnificent, gold-handled walking cane.

The fellow reeked of officialdom, I tell you—so much so that I took him at first sight to be one of the new set from the ultra Endre faction in Budapest, but when I heard only a few phrases of the faultless, citified German he was using to address his underlings, I realized that our new friend had come a much greater distance, perhaps even from Berlin.

Anyway these two "gentlemen" make another tour of our ranks. Afterward they climb unaccompanied up to the platform so as to face the totality of our tiny community. Then more soldiers reappear, stationing themselves in our midst at more or less strategic

121

points, their object being to forestall demonstrations. How unnecessary. The music resumes momentarily, an anonymous Bavarian march. Meanwhile, other Greens—as we called them—are going about with their weapons at the fixed bayonet position across their chests. They are very polite as they chase away the nosy onlookers who are standing about on the other side of the square. I gaze up. Other soldiers are in the balconies of the shops. Their weapons are pointed down at us. Four have even climbed like monkeys to the tops of the stanchions holding up the *hautparleurs* while two others have mounted a light machine gun on the top of a medical van. Resistance? You dare to ask me. They are an army and we are a bunch of school children. . . .

. . . Although, I must add, everything proceeds with a general air of courtesy. Our murderers have fine manners. Once, by mistake, a young private accidentally butts one of our neighbors, the Spaniard Mendoza, with his rifle. Mendoza doesn't even flinch but the poor fellow almost automatically cries out: "*Entschuldig!*" Never shall I forget that startled exclamation of regret. It was clear that the young man was still unable to erase from his memory an upbringing based on traditional German politeness. "*Entschuldig!*" he cries again. When you step on somebody's toe you should always apologize, his mother had told him; and so he did. The strange thing is we are not startled or even cynical when we hear such an apology. These, after all, are Germans.

And so, had it not been for the oppressive heat of the pale vaporous sun in the sky like cellophane, our continuing attempts to maintain a semblance of order might have been more successful, but, though the sun had passed its high point, the day was getting hotter as if we had all together taken a sudden leap backward again into the infamous sirocco of 1939. A grumbling surged through our ranks. People started to drift about, gossiping in small groups. Some may have even contemplated walking home again. Such fantasies! Only my father acted as if he had no illusions. He wrote memos to himself in a pocket diary, mopped

122

his brow, handed about little slips of paper to his friends, tried to light his pipe, and reread—of all things—a letter from Bela, delivered to him weeks ago by the Red Cross. My poor sainted father! When his brother had offered to purchase exit visas for the entire family, he had scoffed: "And where shall we go? What would a man like me do in Santo Domingo?"

Now Father seemed to grunt every time he unfolded the wrinkled copy of his brother's last letter. His breathing was heavy; his face hardly more than a grimace. Presently I heard him winding his watch.

"What is the meaning of this delay?" Maurice asked sharply.

Father didn't answer. Air-raid sirens sounded, then were still. A false alarm. When Lilo reached out for my hand, hers was once again a live thing, although sweated and damp, like a claw. Pressing her head against the hollow in my shoulder, Lilo asked: "Must we stand here like this . . ."

"Please," my father said.

When I turned to him he was again staring at the ornate face of his watch. Father had removed the crystal. One fleshy pink finger was gliding over the gilt entablature of Roman numerals. It was now nearly one in the afternoon. We had been standing for over two hours. Father's finger was moving like a blind man's.

My mother spoke: "Isn't it bad enough to be treated like common prisoners? Must we also suffer a sunstroke?"

"Ilona, please!"

Next Sarah's child lets out a loud whimper, a bleating sustained as a series of gasping cries. "Give her to me," Lilo says.

My sister is too frightened. She can't relinquish her hold on little Anatole. Her endearments grow fierce. To Moshe Shad I hear her whisper: "Dare I feed him here?"

Lilo begs: "Oh, please give him to me."

Sarah wants to smile but looks unwell. The child is pressed against her bosom like a lump of clay. She stares. Maurice is sweating and cursing to himself. I feel as if I am about to cry.

123

Little Anatole's arms begin to flail. He makes a frightening noise. My mother tickles his ribs, coos. Lilo's aunt begins to hum a lullaby. Sarah's lips are barely touching the child's forehead. One can hear her saying: "Baby you mustn't. No baby." At last Anatole is quiet. Sarah starts to hand him over to Lilo. The child whimpers. Moshe Shad looks angry. "Now do you see what you've done . . ."

"Oh no . . ." protests Sarah.

"No . . ." Lilo echoes her.

Another voice is abruptly heard: "So they are taking notice of us at last."

When we turn hastily to face the platform we see that the speaker happens to be correct. The *haut-parleurs* have finally been disconnected so that even the buzzing noise has disappeared. The square seems stunned by the sudden impact of such a total silence. A detachment of medical lorries can be seen debouching from out of one of the side streets. The soft fluttering noise of their motors is the only sound heard.

Another command car guns its motor upon arrival. An officer of the RSHA runs toward the platform. He wears a red cross on one arm of his black tunic. Climbing up the ladder, he salutes his superiors. Jovial-sounding greetings are exchanged. The man turns, his right hand raised as if for silence. But it is only time to call the roll.

Do you know, Rubin, not a single Jew was absent? Would you believe it? Save for a few deportees . . . But when their names were called the authorities already seemed to know about them. One could see lips moving as they noted down the words: "Labor Force."

The rest of us were all on hand, duly accounted for, although some had arrived rather late, like dawdling children at a class day. These we cursed along with the authorities.

Never before had I seen so many Jews. So many different types. Rich and poor. We didn't even speak alike.

124

On that summer day the remnants of over a thousand families were gathered about that single remote little square. There were also quite a few unmarried men, some baptized Jews, a few working-class strays, refugee families from Spain, Rumania, Poland, Trasnitaria, the Kalmuck, and, in a block, an unruly gang of young and old seminarians brought in trucks from their settlement in the countryside near Dej. These people still wore kaftans. Their long pale faces, flanked by the reddish, brownish, and black twists of their forelocks, dripped sweat like wrung-out rags. None of us would stand next to one of these people, for we claimed to know they did not bathe, but we could not completely disavow their presence. They were among us. We could not disown them completely. Whether we liked it or not, we had all been lumped together. For the first time since the burning of the Temple we seemed as one community.

A minor miracle? No! A plague! A blight! It had never been our habit to disappoint our governors. Especially the poor among us. They were no different from peasants anywhere. What, we wondered, made them call themselves Jews?

Out of the ragbag of our community was poured every dirty little piece and soiled bit of Jewry within fifty kilometers. Even the underworld was represented, the men from the thieves' market, horse traders, the peddlers from the countryside, the carters who worked along the Szemos, the women who sold their favors on market day to Jew and gentile alike. There was a delegation of "ethnic Germans," another from the Veterans' Bund, another from the Kossuth Society. There were black-marketeers, former Kuhnists, followers of the Jabotinsky movement, followers of the baptized Wirschauer, even some Zemenhofites, certain members of the Bible Brotherhood and, of course, the *droit-commun*, the lowest of the low along with sturdy bourgeois *prominenti* like my father.

Rubin, I sometimes wish that men could see us as we were then. Maybe, if they could, all this nonsense about the Jew would finally disappear. The children of God! People of the Book! Chosen People! What Jews? Which Jews? Did my father have anything in common with the brawny little man with carbuncles on his face who stood next to us in work clothes, chewing on a lump of goose crackling? This man wore iron-toed boots. His hair was clipped short. He had ringworm on the back of the neck. He had horse teeth.

And what, indeed, could a fine well-bred lady like Aunt Pepi regard as mutual to the company of those three ancient harridans with wigs who kept pinching her skirting, oohing and ahing at its fine quality?

We Jews were perfect individualists. Objectively speaking (to quote the Marxists) the root cause of our troubles seemed to lie in our contradictions, but how rich, how very various, we seemed. Because our attendance was now so perfect, not one of us ventured to stand out by himself to mar the high solemnity of the event. We also listened with the attentiveness of those same school children, as if aware that each of us should take a personal interest in the proceedings but feeling that the problem presently under discussion was still rather remote to all our individual preoccupations and discomforts.

"Belinsky, Fido . . . Ben Hadam, Benjamin . . . Dubrov . . ." Now the tedious registration efforts of the bureaucracy in 1940 and 1941 were being more than recompensed by these scrolls of punishment: "Katz . . . Katzen . . . Landau, Gyor . . . Landau, Izrael . . . Lindauer, Gyozo . . . Lipser, Ferenc . . Marmelstein . . . Wanderman . . ." That was the way it was done. Last name first. First name last. The medical major did not even seem to notice how our attentions were wandering. No one was to be slighted. The roll had to be read. He had no intention of making mistakes. Be patient. We have waited this long. We will just have to wait a little while longer.

If that process was efficient, perhaps it was because great pains were taken that no oversights were allowed. That man's whole manner was one of pure function. Neutral, he seemed to be telling us still that he wished to avoid unpleasant excesses of voice or gesture, but was merely carrying out another "executive measure." What a convincing liar he must have been to himself. The medical major spoke each name with a Viennese (or perhaps Bavarian) lisp, a hesitation, as if he had to try out each syllable silently before daring to repeat them aloud. When he called out the family names in that perfect alphabetical order, the eldest male was told to answer for the lot. Satisfied that nobody was attempting to be troublesome, the major indicated his pleasure with us by a tiny grin that made his lips grow faint, like scar tissue.

Did it occur to me then or much later that the joke was to be on us? It must have been much later. At the time, the entire procedure so satisfied our sense of the way things should be carried out that when the major finished there was a definite relaxation in our ranks. Relief! I even heard one man sighing: *"Alles?"* Then the major made a little bow toward the colonel and his civilian companion as if to indicate—before stepping to the rear of the platform—that it was all a question of administrative talent, of knowing when and how to be firm with an adversary, and when to be lax. Perhaps he felt he needed to stress such a point because he had been so tardy, but it was clear from his manner that he was giving his superiors a valuable object lesson.

The major simply hadn't reckoned with the feelings of the colonel, who now seemed dismayed that there would be no further delays. After the calling of the roll, he took an intolerably long while to set his watch by the church tower, as if composing himself, before he dared to speak to us once again.

"Please. I must have silence."

But nobody seemed to be listening.

"Citizens, I am asking for your attention."

We are all quite startled. Are we truly to be called "citizens"?

Noting the way all eyes turn toward him and all faces are tilted upward, the colonel hesitates to smile. Both hands are raised in

127

the air like the master of ceremonies at a Christmas pantomime. A voice is heard from the crowd: *"These stuffy old fools . . ."*

The colonel pretends not to hear. He clears his throat. His companions are growing restless. Again he raises his hands. "I am reminded now," he begins, his voice quavering a bit, "now my friends" (another unusual mistake to make in our case?), "now . . . as I have been saying . . . my friends . . . for me it is . . . it is a great pleasure . . . and for all those under German protection a great honor . . . a great privilege, a great honor, I say . . . for me to welcome here today a man who . . . the emissary of the Fatherland who . . . as we have just learned . . . comes to you today to supervise the carrying out of orders of the highest authorities . . . the very highest of authorities, do you understand?

"May I present to you . . . therefore . . . His Excellency, Doctor Ernst Zingesser . . . formerly of the Foreign Office . . ."

The crowd makes a noise. Hard to tell what is meant. It's not applause, hardly even an acknowledgment. Just a tiny corporate squeal in which I have involuntarily echoed everybody else.

Our sound seems to make Zingesser's face brighten. Not the colonel! He is all streaks of shadows. He actually seems disappointed with us, as if we have been rude to him. He pouts, straightens the crease in his leggings.

I smell fresh excrement. It is clear that my little nephew has soiled his napkins. I put my hand to my nose.

Zingesser and the colonel are changing places on the platform. Lilo sways next to me. Someone is barking for us to be silent. But who is making any noise? Where we stand it stinks like strong, sour cheese, and we all look sullen . . . as people generally are when they don't know how to interpret what has just been said to them.

The truth of the matter is that none of us have ever heard of such a fellow.

Zingesser! It was the kind of name they gave to Jews during the Old Empire.

My father said, "An educated man . . ."

And somebody else was heard to comment that there were many such names in Swabia.

All ignorant speculations.

I have since found out that our Zingesser was born near Königsberg, East Prussia, the son of a watchmaker. He was never more than a petty functionary in the German machine who, with his Freiburg education, had placed highly in the civil service examinations for the legal department of the post office and from such exalted ignominy had worked his way up through minor party posts until the invasion of Poland when, because of his knowledge of Slavic languages, he was transferred to Von Ribbentrop's Foreign Office, promoted to *Botschafsrat*.

Herr Professor Doktor *Botschafsrat* Zingesser, VAA! Such a fellow would no doubt still be functioning in Germany were it not for the Russian terror bombings of October 1944, in one of which Zingesser perished to be replaced, no doubt, by another careerist named, perhaps, Heusinger, or Zimmer.

Such men persist in all bourgeois societies. They are cold, ruthless, methodical, not cruel themselves but always to be found near the scene of cruelty. We even have them in Israel, in high places in our government, with patches over their eyes. The perfect neutrality of their manners, their icy correctness, make them seem hard-headed, practical, and ideologically correct, as if their only ideology is to show a lack of sentimentality.

Very baldly, that was the way Zingesser tried to show himself off, as a man cautious, correct, businesslike. But whether he was precisely what he thought he was—that's another matter. Stepping forward to speak to us, his first words were to admonish us not to smoke. As he snapped open a brief case to remove a set of file cards, he asked our guards to take the names of any rowdy persons. We were then asked to pick up any fag ends or papers near where we stood. The guards were to move among us with receptacles. We were to deposit watches, rings, gold coins for the war effort. "This is a voluntary solicitation," Zingesser pointed out. "Give generously and Germany will be able to defend herself vigorously. It is in your own interests to volunteer a sizable contribution."

Zingesser's lenses glinted opaque against the sun when he made this observation. Speaking in the voice of one used to relaying messages, he pretended—while waiting for the collection to be finished—that he had no time to waste on trifles, yet by shrugging his shoulders and making faces at his highly polished shoes, he also seemed to be insisting in some minor desperate way that he really didn't care if we gave or not, he being just a cipher for the whims of others with whom, by the way, he did not necessarily disagree.

Bravura Stanislavsky! The text is not hard to remember:

Jews of Clig. Listen carefully. I do not intend to repeat myself. Your fate is in your own hands . . . your own hands . . . I say.

Exactly three days ago in the city of Plevnitz bandit elements within the Jewish population destroyed a benzine depot . . . fuel for the war effort. Five young cadets murdered. Millions of liters of much-needed benzine destroyed . . . *ausgemertz.* Hungarians, it should now be clear what we mean when we say that there are enemies in our midst. You are justly outraged by such renegade banditry. Barbarism! The higher destiny shouts for revenge but the Fuehrer is Justice . . . Justice, I say. Listen carefully:

Rumors that the fugitives have fled south to Clig may or they may not be substantiated. If such are among you, rest assured that they will be detained, prosecuted, shown no mercy. Strongest executive measures will be taken. *The fire will be quenched.* . . . But many of you Jews also have relatives in Plevnitz and there will certainly be the risk of further infestation. Word travels fast.

130

Winged words. You have burned all your bridges behind you. Now there can be no escape. The flame of insurrection cannot be allowed to burn so brightly. The fire will be quenched, I say. To protect you from similar temptations in Clig as they suffered in Plevnitz, to indemnify the Regency (as well as to safeguard vital installations of the Reich), our governments have ordered a special atonement.

Clig will be cleansed. The infestations will not be allowed to spread. All Aryanization projects for Plevnitz and adjacent areas will be completed immediately. Possible troublemaking elements will be resettled to points outside the danger zone. A work indemnity is ordered for all able-bodied males. May I stress on behalf of my government that there will be no exceptions made. Drastic measures taken have earned their just rewards. Silence! Do not let me hear your whimpering. You cannot say you were not warned. Adolf Hitler has repeatedly held Jewry responsible for the excesses of this conflict. Silence! Did you expect to be rewarded for bringing bloodshed to all of Europe?

Silence!

Immediately after this formation men between the ages of sixteen and fifty-five without physical defect will report to the railroad station for medical examinations. Unmarried women are to take separate examinations at the temporary infirmary in the brick factory. Mothers, Jewish elders, little ones, those who say they are too weak to work, await further instructions at your homes and tenements.

This is a Fuehrer order from which even you Yid war veterans are not exempted.

Jews of Clig, when some have called you a subhumanity, what crocodile tears were shed. Now let the world take note of your courage. Europe's final death struggle is nearing. Within forty-eight hours all of you will have seen the last of this place. You are to be resettled, given special treatment. The Reich will be indemnified. By serving Germany and her allies at this historic moment, you cannot avoid serving the interests of International Jewry and of your motherland Hungary. Failure shall only result in further misery; opposition may lead to a savage justice. We demand total obedience. Even now, harsh but just countermeasures are being taken throughout the Reich against the bandits and the rebellious among you. Work is available for all those strong enough to work. Until the day of final victory, those unfit can expect special treatment at camps so designated. You must expect great hardships. All will receive a scarcity subsistence but nonessentials must be left behind. The fire will be quenched. Hungary will be indemnified. Yid terror must not go unavenged. My government has empowered me to say that our decision is irrevocable. What Destiny has ordained your destinies must be. *Questions . . . can there be questions?*

There are no questions. Our colonel friend has deserted us. Zingesser is saluting the rooftops. Nobody dares to reciprocate. What happens next is rather extraordinary: before anybody can protest that treason is impossible if one is without citizenship and, moreover, there are no saboteurs among us, as anybody can plainly see, we are dismissed.

A judgment was pronounced. That was all. The officials— feeling so confident that any judgment about Yids must be correct—walk off their platform, and drive away in their waiting limousines.

Imagine our bewilderment. With stuttering hearts and prating voices, deafened by the resumption of the band music, essentially

132

leaderless, too, or cut adrift, we become logical, protest our innocence to each other, curse every Jew in Plevnitz for making such trouble, then turn toward our new leadership to make our protest aloud, only to discover that they too have fled.

Meanwhile, soldiers with bayonets, loud voices, the manual *haut-parleurs*, are prodding at us to move, as we had been ordered, to the brick factory, or to the railroad station. If nobody immediately fell into step, it was not because we wanted to be heroes. We were directionless. The only way we knew to turn was toward one another. Indeed! We fell against each other, kissed, embraced each other, as if for the last time. From that single square in Clig could be heard a great lamentation as impersonal as it was also obscene, for it was directed for the most part against the "troublemakers" in Plevnitz; nobody took the pains to rail against the SS.

Does that surprise you? When will we Jews let up on ourselves? If a hold-up man enters your store and, at pistol point, forces you to give him all your money and you do, would it be fair to say that you approve of the criminal? Are you now his accomplice?

Be sensible. The accusation of disloyalty demands that one prove loyalty. It does not mean that one goes about instigating insurrections. To what end? To prove that one was, after all, disloyal? You must understand; the presence of hope is what gives terror its logic; desolation is always a numb feeling. Those of us who cried out did so because we were not prepared to give in. Although we felt abandoned, momentarily lacked leadership— yes, and were suffering—that doesn't mean you can sit in your comfortable law offices with your code of ethics for free men in a free society and condemn us for being victims. That day in Clig, as we ran from one familiar face to the next, seizing bodies as they fell against us, propping them upright again in our arms, joining the lament, tears mixing with spittle, remorse, perspiration, every way we turned led but to another *cul de sac*, another

133

agonized familiar face, postures of anguish and uncertainty, a maze. . . .

Eventually the troops were able to quiet us by joining arms to form a cordon in which they marched against both sides of our mass, hemming us in until we were a dense compact mob of bodies and flailing arms and twisting necks.

Some among us now were trying to pass out handbills on which the Fuehrer order had been printed; these were most eagerly sought after by the older people who needed to have what they had heard confirmed in print—as if even now they wanted to be "the People of the Book." From the center of that milling vortex, Lilo and I must have trampled on hundreds of those yellow sheets of paper when we were suddenly separated from our family by a shoving of the crowd, and thrust arbitrarily here and there, first this way and then that way.

Rubin, have you ever felt a thousand hands on your body all at once? A thousand feet hobbling your shins? The noise? The stink? The sweatiness? The confusion? And the pain of imminence?

Lilo, I could tell, was angry, her face like granite. "*Look. Look. Look,*" she whispered. "*Our own people . . .*"

I could not bring myself to denounce anybody. Nor did I need a mirror to know that I had also turned ashen and was seized by chills, as if every face I saw was that of Miklos. When I held Lilo close to me by the shoulders, her dress was soaked through. Then I was forced to say: "Don't. The others will hear . . ."

"*These?*"

A new voice could be heard on the *haut-parleurs:* "Dismissed. Clear the square. Report to your appointed places . . . clear the square . . . immediately . . . Dismissed."

We had come the full circle. One of our people was speaking to us now, a council member. The effect was stunning: the pushing of the crowd about us subsided. At the very same moment our family rushed toward us in a mass, their eyes glass beads, moving like little stick figures. I hardly recognized my sister Perl until she began to speak:

134

"Are you sad, Lilo? But you heard the gentleman. Do you think you are the only pretty girl in Clig who is unmarried? Clearly we will both make some officer very happy. . . ."

"Perl! . . ."

Adam's face had turned the color of fresh lard. He stammered but could say no more.

"How can you speak that way?" asked Aunt Pepi.

Lilo shrugged, "Let her be."

"How nice of you, cousin," Perl said then, "and why don't all of us stand here feeling sorry for ourselves?"

"Perl, I forbid you—"

"Yes, Father. You forbid. That's very good." In the silence that ensued Perl struggled to master her anger, to adopt a new tone. Now that she had registered her disaffection she thought to deal with us more gently. There were no more saucy faces, no more pronouncements. In a voice so soft that at first I wasn't sure who was speaking, Perl said, ". . . a respectable young lady like our cousin would never think of fornicating with a German, but I tell you, Sarah, if it would guarantee my safety I would do that and worse. Wouldn't you, sister?"

"She invents these things. Don't listen to her," my father said, but Sarah's blush was hot and troubled-looking. She seemed to want Maurice to speak for her, until my father interrupted again: "Enough of this. It is ugly enough. I positively forbid any of you to go on like this." He was talking directly to me: "Shandor, I expected you to know better. Come with me . . . And you too," he added, as an afterthought, staring hard at Maurice.

Father even attempted a moment of levity. He would have said anything to cajole us away from the square.

"I presume you have all observed," he said, "that we are to get free medical attention. Your mother will tell you that I was just about to make an appointment with Dr. Gross for my heart."

But when nobody allowed themselves to seem amused he again turned sober: "What do you expect me to do? What do my children want? Do you think because your mother and I are no

135

longer young that we are prepared to sacrifice ourselves? Children, listen to me. You cannot afford to act foolishly. If we are to be saved affairs must be settled. We must make decisions. There are questions to be asked. We must use our brains. We simply cannot afford to act like hooligans."

Father spoke to us with water streaks on his face. I looked at him with a new set of eyes. Had he ever cried before? Had he ever pleaded with any of us? Usually he gave orders; sometimes he instructed; but never had he been conciliatory.

I actually felt sorry for my father. Recognizing that this was an unhealthy attitude, I nevertheless continued to savor the taste of my compassion, as if the feeling made us equals. It wasn't that I liked being cruel. Nor did I care to aggravate the situation. But, as it gave me a certain importance and elation to be one of the objects of my father's beggary, I prolonged the act longer than was perhaps necessary.

Finally I said to Lilo with a shrug: "I'm afraid we haven't much choice."

"Whose fault is that?" she demanded.

Then Father scrutinized his future daughter-in-law, his eyes clouded with pain. He was about to single her out for another rebuke when, as gently as I could, I seized Lilo and pushed her toward Sarah who, though she held Anatole already in the cradle of one arm, managed nevertheless to reach out for her, and hold her close to her. Frightened, the child again started to whimper.

"Come," Father said.

To Maurice, he added: "Take your family home. There will be a place for you on the queue."

A lone soldier sauntered by: "Schnell!"

Each of us responded to the injunction as if we had suddenly been struck. The air was turning smoky. Wind blew through the tunneled streets. A vast melancholia was clotting in the sky. We flinched, again stupefied. Beyond our immediate grouping, where the cobbled alleys crawled back on themselves underneath the

136

jutting porches of the old blue houses, other families were parting, or moving on, and at the brick factory they were changing shifts.

A bitter business nevertheless. No words or greetings were exchanged by any of us. In gayest holiday clothes the dense, funereal procession mixed with soldiers, vintners, florists' carts and butcher wagons. They were parted by a wedding party, for which they seemed to form an aisle of somber well-wishers, so that bride and groom could proceed the other way.

Giddying moments. All our costumes seem too flamboyant, like overexposed color slides; it is very hard to tell where faces and necks begin and scarfs, sleeves, collars are ending. A troop train shudders against the silence. Since we are facing east it seems as if we can actually hear the massed artillery fire, hundreds of miles away, yet here, closer at hand, the silence is immediate, really quite infinite.

"*Schnell!*" The young man in uniform barks a second time.

Heads bow. First Lilo and Perl depart, silent as ghosts. My mother, Maurice, and his family turn the other way as Aunt Pepi and Adam hurry to join up with them. Father and I are finally quite alone. The air smells of cordite. Up the hill to the infirmary the girls are crawling like insects. I say: "Father, you must forgive Lilo . . ."

"*Schnell!*"

The point of a bayonet stipples my father's vest. He can only move backward as he says: "Don't be afraid, young man. My son and I, we are not here to cause you trouble."

Book Two

Build ye houses, and dwell in them, and plant gardens and eat the fruit of them; take ye wives and beget sons and daughters; and take wives for your sons and give your daughters to husbands, and multiply ye there, and be not diminished. And seek the peace of the city whither I have caused you to be carried away captive, and pray unto the lord for it; for in the peace thereof ye shall have peace.

Jeremiah 29

1

The borders of our sleep are sometimes every bit as capricious as those of ancient Transylvania. Late in the afternoon of the next day, when Esther woke Alex, it seemed to him as if he had been jarred out of a blankness. His body felt stiff, as if encased. When he shuddered a yawn, Alex heard the squealing of an animal. Then all the hard edges of desk, books, and window framing seemed to soften. The air sparkled with a fine irridescent dust. He put one hand up to his eyes.

Alex couldn't get used to the intense light. He groped about to find his glasses and saw, at last, that his papers were flying about the room. "A fine mess," Esther was nagging at him like a toothache. The child, she told him, had gone off to school in the very same outfit she had worn yesterday. How could he be such a selfish father? Didn't he know that little girls needed care? What kind of man was he?

Still under the spell of awakening, it suddenly occurred to Alex that even his sleep had not protected him from Esther's voice. Only her sounds had penetrated that shadowy blankness, the dark void which had covered over his eyes so that he thought, for a moment, he was surely blind. Dazed by sleep, Alex had been stunned awake again by this voice—like the mad screaming silence of a nightmare—and now, alert at last, the noise was equally unrelenting, a series of hammer strokes against his temples. As he dared not look at the perpetrator of these blows, he finally pushed himself up from his cramping posture behind the desk, and started to collect his papers.

"They called me to the settlement office," Esther was saying. "A telephone message from the dispensary. They would like to know why you are not at work. I had to lie. You were quite ill. A touch of the sun, I told them. That plus your weak heart. Do you think they believed me? Your friend the manager is coming to see you. They will wish to examine you. Alex, do you wish to be sacked? What will happen to us then? Don't you care? Think what will happen to us. Since you are bound to write your memoirs before we get the money, what do you propose that we eat while you are making *belles-lettres?* And do you think the child and I are going to sleep another night in the kitchen, unable even to undress? You smell like a sheep. Fool! Destroy all this and write a simple one-page letter: 'Dear Sir, I believe I fulfill every stipulation in my late uncle's will, period.' All that lawyer wants to know is yes or no. Your mother *was* Jewish. What's the problem? Say what he wants you to say. Here. I brought you this air letter. It cost me forty grush."

Esther tried to hand him the tiny green slip of paper with its broken white borders but Alex backed away and let it fall to the floor. Tired as he still was, he was also aware of a tension returning. His guts were cold. His mouth tasted like curdled milk. A live thing coiled against his chest, ready to unfold, and he had the feeling of blood forcing itself into places behind his ears where he had never felt it flowing before. Without answering Esther he padded about softly, as if wearing thick carpet slippers, to collect his papers. Once Esther bent to pick up something for him, but

142

he tore the thing out of her hands. "Don't worry," she sneered, "I don't want to know any of your dirty little secrets."

Stricken with a twinge of sorrow, he slumped against the folding bed and held his head between his hands. Yes, his body did stink, but he was also hungry and he felt all dusty. Esther was standing above him, hands on hips. He cowered beneath her tremendous shadow: "What do you want from me? Why are you so aggressive toward me?"

"Because you are such a liar," she said.

With a little nod Alex acknowledged the remark. Then he started to sort his papers, putting them in order; he couldn't stand looking at so many pages of crabbed script. At last he spoke again: "Have I ever lied to you, Esther?"

"No," she said, "you don't even think that highly of me."

Alex wanted to convince her she was wrong. What was the use? All that escaped from his mouth was a little gasp, a protest of sorts. He heard himself and it seemed to him as if even his protests were deceitful. Seizing a towel from off their bedstead, he said, "Esther, you expect too much," as he left the cabin.

Yagodah took his papers with him when he went to the bathhouse. Yes. He was afraid Esther might destroy them, but he also liked to feel their thickness against his hand as he walked through the glare of the deserted settlement. It gave him a certain importance.

The trouble was he forgot to bring a clean change of clothing so that, when showered and shaven, he had to step out into the heat of the day in those same drenched, slightly stiffened garments. "Water is life. Don't Waste It . . . Be sure to wash your hands after leaving the toilet," somebody had scribbled with yellow chalk over the wooden lintels in the entranceway. Alex checked himself momentarily to make sure he had complied. But, as he left, once again his nostrils were assailed with the gagging stench of his own body. Cheeks nicked and stinging, he staggered along under the sun, papers in hand, kicking up the dust.

143

At the canteen he stopped again to buy strong cigarettes. Eric, the Lithuanian behind the counter, guessed immediately that his customer should have been at work. It was an event to find a man at liberty in the settlement at that time of day. To be using the bathhouse was, additionally, a wholly irresponsible act; for, if a man were unwell, he should be confined to his bed. Eric wore his glasses rather far down on his nose, the frames stuck together with strips of adhesive tape. He had a knowing way of looking out over them: "Your birthday? How old? Come now, Yagodah. Don't be shy—"

"I am forty-two," Alex solemnly declared, hoping that he could not be accused directly of lying to the other man. He wanted to go quickly but there was the matter of his change. "I know an intelligent man when I see one," Eric was saying until Alex stopped him: "Please . . ."

The Lithuanian nodded. He counted out some metal coins one by one and when they fell against each other in Alex's palm it was surprising to both men that they had so little weight, made no metallic sound. "These *grush* . . . Not like real money, eh?" Eric asked.

Alex nodded with a grunting sound, as if making it clear that he had no time to chat, that he would have to leave, but he was disconcerted upon hearing his feet creaking against the unevenly joined flooring in the little shack. Over the storekeeper's head a roll of flypaper dangled from the ceiling. It was beaded with black specks of still-struggling mortality. Watching the thing swing back and forth, Alex grinned and stepped away. "They don't seem to give you much of a struggle," he said.

"Even less with the DDT," the storekeeper explained, noting all of Alex's movements. "But I'm afraid of the DDT. It's just like poison, you know. This is a different matter—"

"You mean it isn't poison?"

"It's a very different matter," Eric shrugged.

Again Alex turned to go.

"You are writing something?" Eric stopped him again.

Turning, he said: "It's just a little something to amuse myself . . ."

"Don't tell me that," the little man replied, "its probably your memoirs. Everybody here thinks they have a story worth telling. The only trouble is, my friend, they are remarkably all alike."

"A nation of storekeepers and busybodies. Hardly a nation at all. A Levantinized offal," Alex was cursing to himself silently as he walked back along the dusty principal street in the settlement. The sun stretched out his shadow like an accusation. He passed the communal water tower, the observation post, some ramshackle cabins that were built for refugees and no longer occupied, the offices of the *Moshav.*

So far so good. The air about him was still fetid, but the manager was nowhere in sight. At the first cross street he turned right and practically stumbled against his daughter returning home from school.

"Poppa," she cried, greeting him with a kiss, but Alex could tell that even Ofra was offended by his smell. As they walked home together, chatting quietly about her morning in school, he went to put his arm around the girl, and she squirmed away, complaining about the heat. Moments later, when she met a school pal and they embraced happily, Alex snapped: "Come along now." He was actually jealous of the other little person. "Come along now," he said, his feelings quickening as he bit down hard at his lower lip.

The door to their bungalow was ajar. Alex led the girl into their kitchen where Esther had set out grapes and yoghurt, along with some scraps of Arab bread. A hastily scribbled note pinned to the wall explained that she had taken the jitney to a nearby town to shop.

So it is possible I can still be hurt . . . and by a little girl at that, Alex thought as he served Ofra and himself calmly, making sure to give her the largest portion of everything. They both ate slowly, enjoying the taste of each morsel. Afterward Ofra asked: "Where do I sleep tonight?"

"In your own bed . . . of course," Alex nodded. He smiled at her sudden unbecoming show of earnest concern. That he thought himself unloved was not important; he couldn't deny himself the liking he felt for this other person. Ofra was a plucky little thing. She was his heir. A fortune would someday be hers and she was still oblivious to it. . . .

Or so Alex tried to tell himself. He thought now that he truly loved this little girl, thought he wanted to encircle her, to make her purr at him once again, as she had done before. But when he came closer, she frowned another time, imitating her stepmother's squint. Presently Alex found himself asking: "Don't you have to be in school again?"

"Why of course. I was just about to go, Yagodah."

She left the place giggling.

He carried their dishes over to the sink and dipped them in a basin of soapy water, drying his hands along his white trousers as he parted the curtains with his shoulder and entered the other room.

It was quite cool now inside the little shack. Above his desk, a few pieces of wash were fluttering on the curtain rod in a crisp flutter, an effusion of desert and sea. When he went over to the desk to sit down his eyes were a torture, and he had to force himself to stay on his feet, to blink the pain away from his being.

In a little while he was well enough again to select a new point for his pen, but, since his inkwell had run dry, he had to rise, locate the Watermans bottle in the closet, fit the spigot to it, and then carefully pour himself some more. "Be sure to wash your hands after pouring ink," Alex mumbled to himself facetiously, appalled by the many black smudges on his fingers. Afterward he nervously shuffled the roughly sorted quire of papers between his thin waxen hands. Overhead, two jet planes raced their shadows

146

along the earth. Some children ran out from his neighbor's house and pointed up toward the heavens. The Mysteres seemed to careen against a total silence; moments later, the whole house shook as they accelerated beyond the speed of sound again. Alex waited for more silence before returning to his scribbles.

And again he smelled his mustiness. Indeed, now, he could almost taste it in his mouth. He lit one of his strong cigarettes, watched the heavy smoke swirl above his head. His tongue and his lips were acrid, caked.

When Esther returned, thirty minutes later, he didn't bother to look up. The woman stared at his hunched shoulders a moment, registered her disgust, came a bit closer, peered over one shoulder at the fresh blank sheet of paper, muttered: "Ech!"

"The management is grateful for your comments," Alex said sarcastically.

Esther replied, "Nasty thing! Can't you give some warning before you break wind?"

With her net shopping bag in her hand she parted the curtains at the adjoining threshold and went into their kitchen: "You saw the little one?"

"Yes thank you."

"You both ate?"

"Yes thank you."

"And now she has gone back to school?"

"A minute ago."

"A minute? Ofra will be marked late. Are you sure it wasn't longer than that?"

"Perhaps," Alex quickly replied.

"*Perhaps, perhaps,*" Esther mimicked him. "What kind of a fool do you think I am? Idiot! What kind of a sucker am I?"

"You tell me—" Alex started to say.

But Esther interrupted. "I want you to understand," she began, "you are trying my patience, Yagodah. I won't live this way. I don't have to. Unless you finish this nonsense by evening I am taking the girl. We are leaving you. Did you hear what I said?

"Alex, did you hear me?"

"Yes, loudmouth, I heard you . . . *I heard you,*" he insisted. Then he added, a whisper to himself, which he hoped she would overhear, "Big lip!

"Now will you shut up!" Alex finally shouted.

The woman entered the room, removed her sandals, let them drop to the ground, and fell against their bed: "Nasty thing!" Alex thought he heard her sigh but, presently, he realized she was dozing. He glanced down at his pen. Throughout he had hardly stopped writing. ‖ ▌ ▌

"Rubin my friend (and counselor?):

Can an onanist be a good Jew?

Don't sneer. I ask not to be contrary (perverse?). I know how Onan was punished by God. I have lied to you. Better to be punished than to lie to you. I like little boys. Yes, my heart is weak but I have undoubtedly enjoyed myself with very little boys. Call me a sodomite, if you prefer. The people of Sodom were also punished. They even say here that they have unearthed the spot. I don't believe it, don't believe in excavations. Here it is the national sport but I say it is never possible to know with any certainty about such things. For all we know every ancient city was Sodom, and Jerusalem was the most ignoble Sodom of all. What do we hope to find in ruins? If the grave could speak would you need Yagodah? Ah, if the truth were told, if you must know, if the grave could speak, I once kissed a certain thing with these lips of mine when I was very young . . . and that thing (which I leave to your imagination to conjure fully) hung from the groin of none other than Miklos Skirzeny.

Out of Jerusalem shall come forth the Law. Out of the lesser

149

Sodoms only filth. Say we were children. Little ones. Wild creatures in a sandpile. We made love like savages, thinking it was a form of play. Very happy we were too. When I kissed M on the penis (and without coercion) he didn't seem at all astonished, but was rather haughty with me only later. We were standing near my father's well. Like Narcissus, M shouted into the carp pond. Another voice spoke to us out of the depths. M said it was a spirit of evil.

Why remember? Who cares? Is it because I have always believed—even until this very day—that M's father and my father knew what we had done? Heavenly Father, was I always such a guilty spineless creature? A sniveler? But if I was such a dirty young man and am now such a dirty old man why must I tell you about it? Poor innocent. Do I tell you so that you will conclude two and two is four? But what, after all, is four?

Perhaps it is because I don't choose to have you know about four that I ejaculate nonsense like the seed of Onan. The Cabalists believe in the significance of numbers. What, I wonder, does the number four signify?

If truth were told, Rubin, I am still quite fond of little boys. My fours cannot mean repentance because now, even at this very moment, in the words of one of your American student-tourists, I am a "cocksucker." And if some smooth young gentleman from Tunisia or Morocco were to come along, at this very moment, I could not swear to you that I would not want to bugger him. Call it my shabby adjustment to the Levant. In any event, when they read me out of the British army, they had reasons. . . .

Of course they did. Her Majesty's soldiers shall not be "cocksuckers." Beefeaters, perhaps, but not "cocksuckers." Ask my Esther. I bugger little boys. Ergo, I am a dirty old man. A moral coward. Yes, that was the charge—moral cowardice. Esther could tell you all about it. Ask! Look at the way she lies there in the bed staring at me like a corpse. Esther has never gotten used to the drinking water in this settlement. She is frequently constipated, and it makes her very irritable, but she knows my heart is weak and she is always feeling sorry for me, always saying: "You nasty thing, you will die if you don't take better care of yourself." Can you believe it? I think she truly feels sorry for this little moral coward, even though she pretends to be made of stone . . . or salt. She and the little girl, Ofra. They will insist on feeling sorry for me. That is one thing about all our women; you will find them puritanical, hard! Which doesn't mean they lack compassion.

Who needs compassion? I seem to be going in circles again. The magic number is four and I cannot claim exhaustion because I have slept passably. Do I offend you, Mr. Attorney? What exactly am I trying to avoid? How insufferable to have to make of every petty moment of one's life a little Cabalistic mystery, or, at best, a ghost story. As if you could care. Who pays you to care? But, if I have told you so much already, can I suddenly turn coy? No! What I have to say is really a matter of public record. There are documents in the War Ministry . . . what was I saying? "Father's vest stippled with the point of a bayonet?"

"Vivid. Extraordinarily vivid! An excellent piece of *belles-lettristic* prose writing. Completely irrelevant, of course, because the poor soldier who held the rifle attached to the bayonet which stippled poor Father's vest was like a scared harmless little boy, and so were we. When Father backed away, that poor soldier no longer wished to stipple Father. He withdrew his point, and we then began to walk, as directed, to the railroad terminus.

A Walk never to be forgotten. Newman Yagodah and son, two of a kind, although they did not fully accept their common natures, trailed other fathers and sons, equally common, but made sure to keep their distance, always staying at least four paces behind the mob. They were snobs, you see. They may have seemed cocky and superior but they were really just self-absorbed. Indeed. Such was their peculiar trait in common to think that they alone were confronting difficulty; and that they alone were threatened. They simply never got any further outside of themselves than four paces would allow. . . .

I have borrowed the above description from a Max Winkleman

novel entitled *A Soft Life and a Doting Father*. My translation is
perhaps faulty in spots; *grieving* could be more accurate than *doting;* or perhaps it is *condescending*. What difference? Insofar as it
goes a certain accuracy is captured. Rubin, all of us in Europe
were more influenced by this Winkleman than we ever cared to
admit. And insofar as he went, we sentimentalists went along
with him. The trouble was this Winkleman and his kind rarely
went any farther south than Merano. Where we needed strong
medicine he offered us the grape cure.

The first Commandments in the Jewish religion are "Thou shalt
have no other Gods but me," and "Honor thy father and mother."
If it is true that we did not greet others as we walked that day to
the terminus, would we have seemed less dutiful and self-
absorbed—more receptive to certain environmental stimulus, as
they say—if we had glanced away from each other to stare at
those others who were similarly preoccupied as we were. Our
community was built on deceit and maintained by the discreet
application of self-deception. In our world it didn't pay to be always so perceptive. We had agreed long ago to lie to each other
with a smile, and we called what we did "good manners," or
being polite. Yes, we gave and we took our little grape cures in
secret, but carefully, so as not to irritate, as one might take a mild
high colonic. Is there anything else you need to know about our
dishonesty? Surely life in America is not so very different. When a
man is puking his guts along the street, you will still ask: "Are
there no receptacles?"

The truth is even when a man is lying in the gutter bleeding,
you will ask: "Did you hurt yourself?" Quite natural, I suppose.
Quite as it should be. . . .

Thus, rounding the corner away from the square, Father and I
may have said to ourselves, "A fine thing," but we did not choose
to observe those other fathers and sons stopping suddenly in
alleyways or the vestibules of tenements. In Winkleman certain
fathers were always disinheriting their sons as the leeches were

being applied and then, through some personal tragedy, being re-united and, as it were, reconciled at the moment of recuperation. In our case, strong purgatives were demanded but we felt well enough. When my father grabbed my arm above the wrist and made me repeat after him, four times in a row, "Swiss Bank Corporation, Basel, Account Number 4200424," it was just as the doctor had ordered, as if life was giving us another shabby imitation of the great Max Winkleman; and when he suddenly thrust a small wad of paper into my hands, the privilege and election I felt—was it really so unique? No! It was but the denouement of *Between the Acts*. It was the first chapter of *Mother Love,* or perhaps the coda to volume two, *In the Tuilleries*. Moreover, it was happening all around us and we didn't even bother to see.

Winkleman is dead! Long live the Winklemans! Why should it matter now that I also felt absurd, a mere fiction? My father and I stood like separate panels in an elaborate cartoon, expostulating nonsense, numbers, all the gibberish and imbecile cant of his transactions with that Swiss bank, but I found this mumbo-jumbo reassuring; and to an observer it might have only seemed as if he was coaching me in certain of my religious observances. "Honor thy father and mother." Among our type of Jews that was an article of radical faith.

The point was, Father simply wanted me to know that he had hoarded four thousand francs in a numbered account in Basel. I was to have the only record of his greed. What a stroke of luck! What honor! "Your head must be like a vault for safekeeping," Father said, pompous as ever, while he tapped his shining skull with a finger. Next he forced on me a real treasure, a piece of paper folded into a wad so wrinkled and soiled that at first I took his gesture as a way of covering up for his previous verbal confidences.

Not so! Father was depressingly solemn. Ritualistic as he had been, he quickly grew impatient with my playing Esau to his Isaac. Staring at my bloodless, clenched fist, he would look about in all four directions, to make sure we were not observed. Then he spoke to me again:

"Your future is assured!"

"It is?"

"Don't play the fool, my son. Open the paper . . ."

Spread out flat against the palm of my hand, the little crinkled sheet could have been contained inside a child's phylactery. Imagine my surprise upon discovering more meaningless figures in my father's scrawl, something torn from one of his ledger books. Fours divided by fours and multiplied by four numbers.

"The other side," I heard Father say. "Turn to the other side!"

When the thing was reversed I saw a hastily drawn map of the garden behind our house. Here and there were little curlicues in green crayon, intended to indicate shrubbery, while the house, in orange, was represented by a pyramid-shaped drawing of its sloped roof out of which the dotted lines of a path wound about a certain obstacle, the summerhouse, until it disappeared near the carp pond, at the very same spot where Lilo and I had investigated our passions so thoroughly, and—*there*—a series of X's were squarely marked off.

"You need not comment on the work of art," Father explained, calm once more.

But I hardly paid attention to what he said next, for I was about to confess everything that had transpired between Lilo and myself. A troop of ragged Ukrainians passed. Father put his hand up to my mouth: "Alex, if you look and listen you will not need to bother me with questions."

"And I would feel better," he interrupted me a second time, "if you would recite for me again."

This time my recall was slow but precise: "Swiss Bank Corporation . . . Basel . . . Account Number 4200424."

"Excellent."

And since he seemed genuinely pleased with me, he rested a hand softly on my shoulder the way he used to do at home when

154

he would help me with my lessons. "Now," he continued, "I want you to understand what my obligations have been and how I have made preparations for this day. Can you follow me?"

I nodded.

"Excellent," he exclaimed a fourth time, waiting for a horse cart to drag its way past. Then:

"A man like me needs to tell his secrets to others he can trust. I am old. I shall certainly die. Your future depends on this map. . . .

"Precisely at the spot where X's are marked I have buried gold last evening, good English currency, too, in a strong box, a few costly things belonging to your grandmother; some of Lilo's bonds . . . and some documents. These are yours and hers. As her guardian, it is my right to do as I have done. Have her respect that right. The others will also be provided for.

"But someday you will come back, you will need the means to make yourself a life here, and you will find what is yours. It is of no use to anybody else at present. Memorize the places. Do you see how I have carefully scattered everything under the shade of these bushes? Will you forget? Do you think you can remember? Look at the paper, Alex. Don't you see what I have done?

"Alex, we haven't much time. Will you please look?"

Some things are better left unsaid. For gnawing in the earth like a pack rat my father wished to be congratulated, but I said only, "I will remember," although my memory was already growing vague.

Then he grabbed the map, quickly struck a match, and lit the thing. The flame soon licked the points of his fingers so that his eyes clouded with pain. Poseur that he was, Father held the paper steady until all but a tiny corner was consumed in ashes. Sucking one of his blistered fingers, paterfamilias swallowed a piece of ash and had me recite another time.

"Swiss Bank Corp . . ."

"Excellent. Never mind. You really have it, don't you? But we should hurry or we'll be the last ones and they will punish us. Come . . . I really must pass water . . ."

Give a hungry dog a piece of flesh and he will bite off your hand! My heart was faint but my footsteps quickened. Odd that I should remember my father needing to pass water, even though I can't remember any longer where he buried his little excremental treasure heap. Or even the Swiss numbers of my birthright with any certainty. Odd, too, that in hearing the clap of thunder all we could do was to turn the old familiar Judaistic somersaults. As if we were trying to cure the backache. But, although I was flattered (who wouldn't be?) because my father had suddenly confided in me (and because he had bestowed a fortune on me) I was not satisfied that he was being absolutely candid. I thought he would say more if only I dared to ask questions. How to avoid ingratitude? What could I properly ask? When I said, "I wish I could be as cunning as you," Father ignored me. And that wasn't really what I had meant to say.

You see—what I wanted to know was why—if he had gone to such elaborate pains—why wasn't it likely that he had learned in advance what was to be happening? And why hadn't we fled? Why didn't he do anything?

Not a very polite question. Walking alongside my father, trying my best to keep up with him, I avoided asking him such things directly, and I prodded myself, as it were, with a deliberate masochism. Did I have a choice? I was, after all, Father's only son. To do otherwise was to accuse my only father. Of what? Did I always have to live under the shadow of his good intentions? Good or bad, as they say.

Presently my anger was transferred to others—the local Germans, those in Budapest, our co-religionists in the council. Wasn't my father an officer of the council? It was not a crime. By whose standards do we convict such men of criminal behavior? To believe so is to subscribe to all the blood libels from the crime of

156

Judas through the Protocols of the Elders of Zion which, of course, our Nazi persecutors did. But, if you ask me, do I believe such men are deserving of contempt simply because they took responsibility for the welfare of others, then I must tell you I find such thinking contemptible, intolerable. It is like saying that Mary gave birth to anti-Semitism when she became the mother of God. Although we Jews have a perfect right to such contempt, I find I must reject it. It confuses victims with victimizers. Never will I accept such logic. There are far too many anti-Semites in the world without adding Yagodah to their ranks. Which is why I shuddered at the wayward direction of my thinking even then, and tried to redirect myself to think only of my precious one, my Lilo.

Was this Winkleman again or the plays I had seen and the stories I had been told? Life imitating Winkleman or vice versa? My point is that I thought for the first time how this might be our last evening together for a very long while, and I tried to foresee what we would do and say and pledge to each other, and how I would now try to reassure her.

Again, of what? That her guardian had buried his fortune for us next to the family cesspool? Quite rich! I felt my ears burning, a pounding of blood against my eyes. When I turned to my father it was with a stony face: "Isn't it possible that you have been mistaken all along?"

"Alex. . . ."

"Answer me!"

Father chattered on rapidly, a prepared speech: "It is still not too late. We have all been deceived. Tragic . . . I have considered every possibility. Safety demands discretion. After the examination we will be allowed to go home to collect our belongings. Skirzeny will be there. He has promised help—"

"*Skirzeny?*"

"Alex, he is a very important man now—"

"And you are impressed with him . . . you old fool?"

"Alex . . ." We had come at last to the terminal entrance. Father muttered gravely, "You are worried, overstimulated, tired. I understand and I forgive you."

He drew himself erect, his smile a bit weary as he took me by the shoulders and placed a wet kiss against my forehead in the steaming shadows of the entranceway.

"I forgive you," he said a second time, kissing me again with his yeasty breath, as if that would make everything right again. "I forgive you, sonny. . . ."

"I forgive you," a fourth and then a fifth time.

"Why? *What have I done?*" I asked.

The sound of our breathing seemed to echo among the colonades like the snores of naked Noah.

3

THE great terminal at Clig was extremely overblown, even for a town of its size. It resembled a slightly smaller version of the Gare D'Orsay, which I did not see until after the last war, although I am told it was actually modeled after another place in Berlin. Cranes sometimes nested in the roof. Starlings soiled the long cathedral windows. This vast complex of barrel arches in fretted iron grillwork, glassed over, and with immense, lonely areas of marble flooring, marmalade walls, smaller domed waiting rooms, and colorful green and yellow metal kiosks, was grandiose, slightly anachronistic, as if it never quite could live up to the even grander pretensions of its builders.

Because of Clig's proximity to the old borders, this was to have been a kind of shunting-off place for cargo and passengers from the rich industrial areas of Slovakia and Austria. Here, the natural resources of Transylvania, of Silesia, the grain and oil of Moravia and Walachia and the Ukraine were to be intermixed and fed up into Mittel Europa through an immense glass-roofed terminus, where scores of shining iron tracks crossed over each other and then made pin turns back again; a decade of unrest had put an end to such plans. Only one single track was eventually laid down. Although Clig still managed to prosper in its isolation it was never to be thought of again as the crux of Mittel Europa, as the point of exchange, the great terminus which people like my father had envisaged it being only ten or twenty years previously. On the contrary! By the summer of 1943 the terminus was hardly in use. The grain exchange kept open only half a day. There was no more free trading. Three days a week the *Gelt Wechsels* were closed down, and all currency was now black-marketed. The rolling stock lay rusting at the ports of Braila and Galatz. The Russians had occupied Constanza on the Black Sea. Except for the movement and temporary billeting of some tatterdemalion troops and labor battalions, large areas of the terminus were now vacant, making it an ideal place to be put to other uses, such as the one for which we were now gathering.

I mention all this for two reasons: first, because it is an obvious piece of irony of the most shallow variety that my father should have been examined for deportation in the place he had helped to conjure up, to finance and create. Secondly, even if we can dismiss such irony for what it is, another important consideration almost immediately comes to our attention—namely, that it has always been supposed the Reich had to undergo severe privations to bring about the considerable deportations which began for us in a small way in 1943 and became the major concern of German authorities in Hungary by 1944 when the Russian breakthrough in Bessarabia and Moravia was complete and the Iron Guard had turned against its former allies. This was simply not the case! Even before 1944, ample facilities were always on hand. What was needed was a willing heart to implement such material circumstances. This was supplied by our Hungarian neighbors at the very last possible moment, as if they had been holding back for too long the hatred which they felt surging within themselves.

By 1944 even the cranes had fled the roofs of the great terminus at Clig to escape the sufferings of their hunger, but men

160

just can't fly away like cranes. We Jews were earthbound. We went up in smoke. Every time I see one of little Mr. Chagall's paintings of a floating Hasid I think of that. We were earthbound and we went up in flames, alive. True enough, Hungarian and Jewish interests had participated in the construction of our vast terminus in concert; and very early, it seems, these same Hungarians felt certain qualms about what was happening to their Jewish neighbors. They began to miss us as they missed their cranes. Pressures soon increased. Hungarians were dying at the front. German propaganda grew strident. The bombings started and these same Hungarians fell upon us like wolves. Only our common facilities managed to remain neutral; they had been built to be put to any use and they were: they were used against us in the year of liberation—1944.

And if this seems like more empty Winklemanizing on my part, let me please also state, for the record, that such cruelty was not unique to Hungary. Not to our part of the world! God forbid! As you have probably gathered, Rubin, the writer of these letters is a man of cultivation and sensitivity, a gentleman who is properly affrighted by events in the recent past of his present homeland as he was certainly touched by those events which drove him hither. If, therefore, I speak only of those atrocities which made a madhouse out of Europe (and not about what has happened since), perhaps it is because I am forced to believe that it was such events which conditioned all of Israel to the murder of innocent fellahin, the slaughter at Port Said of Egyptian families, the continual border sniping, yes, and the growing militarism, racism, and chauvinism of this place. Events here. Events in Asia. Murders everywhere. I tell myself we were not always so bloodthirsty; events made us so. Yet I reserve the right to be skeptical of my own apologetics. Did He who allowed such events to happen under His very nose then proceed to give us a place where we could carry out His dreadful commandments upon each other . . . as if the task had been left unfinished? As if there had never been any *Lösung der Judenfrage?* Horrors as unspeakable as anything I am going to describe . . . not just certain "unpleasant excesses. . . ."

But since we were the first great modern multitude of Victims of the State, is it surprising that we should have created a modern state of our own in which victimizing others became a way of life?

Murder is always dreadful. Guilt is always shared, although perhaps unequally. But the Supreme One—does He not stand condemned as the Supreme Murderer in our scheme of things? Perhaps that is why people here say they are "Jews without God." To be so secularized is to be unforgiving and to distrust the false alibis of the rabbis, whereas to accept God now one must forgive a Murderer, a Mass Extermination Expert and, if one doesn't believe, it becomes much easier to pin down blame, to sort and in turn be sorted.

Which, of course, brings me back to my uncle's obscene bequest with its stinking legalities and its final disgusting little proviso: Am I still Jewish? I defy you to answer: Are there still Nazis? Are any of us still Jews? Our enemies say we are and that is why we are so haughty when one of us murders or kidnaps or trades in false currency, or asserts himself in any way except the so-called "traditional methods." Strange. Our enemies are mostly Jews like ourselves. But to be defined so is to be defined for our negative qualities. It is just another form of anti-Semitism, another way of perpetuating that tired old affirmative caricature of the noble, long-suffering Jew. What we need to give the world are negatives. Portraits of horror. If you ask I will tell you that the affirmative Jew evades me. "For three transgressions . . . nay for four," cried Amos. Those who served in the "death brigades"—were they Jews? Recently in this country four judges could not decide among themselves without disagreement if a Jew who had converted to Catholicism was still one of us. Some thought the apostate was. Then why must I be judged any differ-

162

ently? What exactly did Uncle Bela have in mind? Am I to be thought any worse than a man who forsook his faith to wear the cassock? But if I tell you no, if I say I still believe in an eye for an eye, among other things, what am I admitting then, when I know that in the "final solution" we *were* the ones whose eyes were gored from their sockets. . . . That we became the blind. For three transgressions, nay, for four. . . . Let me put the question another way.

▊ ▊ ‖ Alex scribbled abruptly in large strokes across a new sheet of paper, feeling as if his whole body had fallen asleep on him, his arms, legs, his eyes and ears —as if they were now pins and needles—even while the sun dipped under a nearby rooftop and flooded his ‖ ▊ ▌ desk with a bright hot flame of light.

Today we know that Plevnitz was a lie, at best an excuse to make what had been planned by the highest authorities reasonable to those charged with carrying out the Fuehrer order. Yes. We know that even such men under such circumstances needed to have reasons. Then, after a while, all reasons were equally good, just so as long as they were available at the right time.

Other things we know too: that, for example, the Slovakian government actually paid Germany a fixed sum for every Jewish soul who was made to leave the mother country on condition that he or she would never be allowed to return. Also, we know that every fourth one of Hungary's leaders vacillated between being Jew-killing zealots and cowardly equivocators, men who could be bribed, cajoled, even frightened into being merciful. We know how the bombings and the Allied broadcasts affected such people; they became even more irrational toward us, found they needed many more reasons to do what they would have liked to

163

do all along. If Plevnitz was staged for the benefit of such Hungarians, we needed to believe in it too. How else could we accept what was happening to us if we could not believe that we had acted and were being punished for what we had done? If we could not say to one another, "For what our foolish neighbors did in Plevnitz we are being punished fourfold," and if we could not argue that the punishment was too severe, then the punishment would, indeed, have seemed unbearable and we might have taken steps to evade it.

Innocent people need to have reasons; yes, even the innocent. I can remember my father explaining to us on the day they took away his automobile that there was a "critical" shortage of fuel. It so happens that there was no such shortage then, so my father learned to modify his thinking. "It would set a bad example," he explained, "if we were to drive an automobile while others were making sacrifices." Then: "I do not wish to cause offense." A fourth time, when it was apparent that people were grabbing whatever they could, that nobody was making sacrifices or taking note of offenses, Father came to this conclusion: "Why would I drive a car? Where is there to go now?" Don't you see: Father always had a wallet full of reasons. Otherwise, how could he have been such a prodigal spendthrift?

Perhaps the major paradox of the Plevnitz *Aktion* was that we —who had not resisted the expropriations, or the ghettoization of Clig, nor even the deportations and the obscene sporadic reprisals of the Arrow Cross—now we needed to believe in a resistance which didn't even exist. For what could we give to it or do within it? Belief is never enough. How can you resist when first an entire town and then an entire countryside turn against you? Facts. I am talking facts. That is the way it actually was. That is why men like my father buried treasures so that they are rotting still and were marched right through the doorways of the crematoria. It was hopeless. There may have been a few nice people among the gentiles but we never saw any of them after 1942. By the time Plevnitz was announced to us in 1944 we were virtually cut off

164

from every contact with our gentile neighbors, although we passed them as before on the streets. If the ghettoization was never so strict that the "races" were separated permanently, it was still possible to look at a man being beaten and pretend you were seeing an oxen.

Even after the war it was the same way. I have told you that I traveled through Europe as a British soldier, but have I told you that these same gentiles who had fallen on us in 1944 were willing scarcely two years later to offer themselves to us as guides, drinking companions, and bedmates? You will not believe the lewd sights I saw: In Feldkirchen, German girls "of good family" fornicating on the streets with black men. In Oberkirchen, flaxen-haired German boys on street corners, painted male prostitutes for the Moroccan troops. Christian or Jew, black or white, foreskin or lack of it, distinctions were no longer made. In Hamburg I saw six young Palestinians waiting behind a parked lorry in front of the British military police headquarters while the widow of a slain Luftwaffe major offered her favors orally for occupation marks.

And all over Europe it was the same, although in Germany this new Jew lust was especially ironic. That Germans who had grown fat off our wasted bodies should now be enticing us to go to bed with them was indeed "quite rich." The blind and the blinded, embracing like lovers; who was to say which was which? If we were still the miserable, the crass, the wretched, and the revengeful, they, peculiarly enough, seemed to us much the same as before. Occasional rapes were welcome. You could get a woman to do anything for you if you had the money. Nobody then worried about race mixing. Our soldiers accepted the favors of Germany's women and, again, even as ovum and semen were mixing in a thousand squalid rooms in a thousand *Gast* houses throughout the battered countryside, it was as if they saw us and looked away, saw right through our naked quivering bodies, saw us and despised us. . . .

And so, Rubin, I am not able to forget a single detail of our walk that day (when Plevnitz was first announced) from the Street of the Oxen to the railroad terminal which, inscribed and seraphed above its entranceway, cast the shadow of vanquished dreams along the narrow streets of Clig, past the brick factory which Grandfather Fass had once owned, where even now four or five workers were lounging about with their lunch pails, eating slowly and not seeing us. They saw us! I saw them! I also saw a number of the unmarried Jewish girls being herded toward the back entrance of those works where kilns liquefied the air overhead; and I could not move until I had ascertained whether Lilo was among them. These workers saw me. They also saw the girls. And they sat against the walls in deep shade, chewing slowly.

Then we continued walking, describing a wide arc around the terminus itself, following the Red Cross signs which led to the baggage sheds on the adjacent streets. Again, as we walked, our neighbors—people whom my father had known many years, the mothers and fathers of children with whom I had recited in school—they stood now outside their tenements and store fronts, shedding crocodile tears for us, but these, we knew, would be the first to see what could be looted once we were, in fact, deported. For three transgressions, Rubin? Nay for four. . . . Or five!

. . . In Transylvania, when the land is suffering from long droughts, the peasants ascribe such a curse to the gypsies who—they say—can make dry weather by occult means to favor their own trade of brickmaking. Now when the necessary rain cannot be obtained by beating the guilty *Tsiganes,* a crafty peasant will often resort to the *Papaluga,* or rain-maiden. He will have a young gypsy girl stripped stark naked, and then cover her up with leaves and flowers, with only her head being visible. Then the *Papaluga* will be conducted around the village four times, followed by musicians playing a weird music, while everybody pours water on her as she passes by. The custom is still very widely spread. In some benighted villages the men are told to

166

urinate. . . . And when a gypsy girl cannot be had they say a Jewess is still the next best thing. . . .

I believe a curious book might be written on the efficacy of nakedness in witch spells, and in other matters as well. My mother used to tell us that if a young girl wanted to know her future husband's name all she had to do was stand naked beside a lake or upon a dung hill with a piece of Christmas cake in her mouth, and when the village clock struck twelve she must listen for the sound of a dog barking. From whichever way that sound came, her lover would appear to her.

I also think the Germans must have believed in such nakedness charms with the same peasant cunning. To stand naked before a man in uniform, they knew, was a mark of humiliation, almost magical in a way. Consider, for example, the methods of your own slave traders with the Ashanti women in West Africa. . . .

So what if the depravities we witnessed were probably not so unique as we believed. Why should that matter? Men are not born relativists. They are just exactly what they think they are at any given moment in time. Waiting in line at the railroad shed and, again, when we entered the examining room, although my father was quite brazen about articulating certain pro-German sentiments which he presumed might do us no harm if overheard, it was *as a naked man* that he confronted the authorities; and even their most perfunctory words of command to him, then, were like scourges against his flesh.

Father was a man of peculiar integrity. He would not, as some had been doing, maintain that he was not of Hungarian origin and demand the rights of a Rumanian national. He was a good Ashkenazi who truly believed that because we spoke the same language as our captors we were of the same culture; and so—*naked as he was*—he gave his birthplace as Clig, but he insisted upon adding that he had a law degree from Vienna. Even naked, Father refused to surrender what he had so obviously acquired. He adopted his most eloquent Viennese when next addressing our friend, that so-called medical major, or the two blowsy nurses who were attending him, or even a certain grimy little warrant officer from the Transport Corps. Father urged me to imitate him, as best I could, but I held back. A truly spirited imitation was more than I could summon up. I just was too conscious of my nakedness. My ribs were showing through my skin and I thought people could see right through my belly.

Father may have thought himself more fortunate in that he still managed to seem prosperous and corpulent and could adorn himself in his nakedness as he had previously worn his finest suit of clothes, but he struck me as embarrassing and somewhat ludicrous. I almost wished not to be identified as the son of such a Falstaff. Here we stood, bare as stones or tree stumps, while the broad flashes of late sunlight glanced off our freckled backs, warmed our buttocks and shoulders, glinting against the sterile medical instruments, and then streamed like a rich dust among the crates and military baggage, the dressing kits split open at the seams with effusions of pussy cotton wool, the swabs, and the great green bottles of corn alcohol. In such a confusion of bodies and objects, I constantly saw the pasty Jewish bodies of my father and myself as if with an inner eye, unused to such displays of nakedness but now naked and grim, as naked as those same harsh streaks of daylight, our chests caved in, our bellies stuck out, stiff in the formal postures of attention, my father jabbering on in German, his genitals tucked beneath his immense corporation, as he attempted to impress our enemies with his knowledge of their ways.

"You are . . . I can tell you are from East Prussia," my father said.

The medical major didn't even bother to look up; he answered, "Quiet!"

Do you know what happened next? You were made to pass naked before him and his two assistants who, in turn, thumped your chest, examined your teeth and noted down the number of fillings. One woman inspected your vaccinations while another squeezed your testicles and then asked you to cough and jump up and down four times, first on one leg and then on another. Next we all had to form a circle with our backs to each other. We were told to bend over while a certain orderly inspected our assholes for hemorrhoids.

Even the delicate Hasidic children were made to stoop over so that their forelocks touched their thighs and the groan that went up from our circle when they protested was precisely like the lowing of certain young heifers when they have been mounted and stuck fast. On that day Jewish modesty perished and Satu Mare covered itself in sackcloth and ashes. The little Yeshiva children were raped by the criminal eyes of medical orderlies.

At the end of this process you formed on line again. Ahead of you were a second pair of nurses, grim-looking creatures with slatternly eyes. They looked like identical sisters, and were separated from each other only by a small foot locker turned on one end to resemble a dressing table on which were all sizes of stoppered brown and green bottles, steel instruments, needles, rubber clamps. You are asked to open your hands with the wrists showing. The first woman sprays you with a freezing-cold solution.

The flesh stings and then turns numb, directly above that place on the wrist where the main artery pulses. "One more," the woman shouts at you. Then a second voice says, "Move on."

You do as you are told. A second woman grabs you and leads you into a small curtained-off area, about the size of a closet. Everything stinks of ether. Little sopping wads of bloody cotton are scattered about. The woman takes your hand. Then you notice a pot-bellied fellow in the shadows. He is wearing just an undershirt and an apron. Before you can cry out somebody has pressed a switch. Motors whir like the sound of a dentist's drill. Your arm is a piece of lead. In just three or four movements of the thing against your flesh the mark is made; and you don't have time to feel the pain.

"One more!"

Again you move on. But not before a wad of wet cotton is pressed against the mark: "Hold this!" You are pushed outside where another nurse seizes your arm, makes a notation on a sheet of ruled paper next to your name, wraps the wrist in gauze; and you are told to dress. For the moment you are to act as if you are dismissed. Only now you have a number on your wrist.

What would you say if I told you my number was 4200424? You are right. I am a liar. The entire process lasted no longer than fifteen minutes, excluding the waiting around before, after, and in-between stages, so that by the time my father and I were ready to be processed these medical people were working with efficiency and dispatch, but they were still not by any means the infallible automatons one reads about in your *Life* magazine. They were bunglers, just like us. They wasted time, made mistakes, were lazy, had to prod themselves to keep alert. And the result was that when we dressed again and waited at the other end of the shed for Maurice (who had been delayed at the rail-head by a troop train) we compared numbers, and I was C107, although my father, only three paces ahead of me on the line, was C104. So now I had to worry about two different sets of numbers! My father gave me one; the Germans another.

Another significant event took place: when my father was slipping his shoulders under his braces the major came among us. From the doorway leading to the main examining room he appeared, rather jovial, a man who knew his way around. Nothing stand-offish about this one. He was ready to make conversation. And we welcomed him like the Sabbath bride. *Just why were we waiting? Did we have any questions?*

"Sturmbannfuehrer," my father asked, probably to be polite, "what can we expect next?"

"What? Are you so anxious?"

Father stood with his braces stretched taut above his shoulders. Some were tittering. One among us found he could no longer control himself.

170

Mendele—Mendele Fittelson was his name, a carpenter by trade, small, homeless, a fellow with a narrow look, deep-sunken eyes, cheeks like a skull, yellow teeth—a sad little thing who had wandered into our town from Lvov with a batch of the usual horror stories during the spring of 1941.

When the major made his little joke at my father's expense, this same Mendele—perhaps through nervousness—looked as if he had dabbed rouge on his sallow cheeks. The fiery points under his skin burned fiercely; his lips turned blue; and it seemed almost that he was about to choke from laughing.

None of the rest of us could tell if Mendele actually thought the major was such a clown, or if he just couldn't help himself once provoked to laughter. Consequently we grew annoyed, stared in a group at him, all of us including—finally—the major.

Mendele saw us, acknowledged us, but still shook like a reed. Now it seemed as if his face was being consumed with fire. Sweat densened above his brow. His bald knees were of extraordinary size beneath the seams of his ragged cotton undershorts. He whispered, even as he continued to laugh: "Forgive me, forgive me. . . ."

"Do I amuse you?" the major asked.

Mendele shook his head, as if dodging a blow. While he stammered silently, he seemed to be struck with a cramp below the pit of his stomach so that his hands went to cover the spot.

Looking down, then, we all noticed that he had grown quite lustful, as if he was carrying a bulky object under his shorts which he was trying hard to cover over, yet again he began to laugh and had to cut himself short.

"What is the matter with me? I cannot imagine. . . . What?" Then he added: "But, of course, what can be the matter with me?"

"*You tell me*," the major said.

Mendele's stomach growled angrily. Just then my father's braces snapped. "What?" asks Mendele, his throat filling with bile. He tries to swallow against the tide and succeeds finally, a pale trembling thing with eyes.

But all that this major saw he took to be a personal affront to his own authority. "What kind of person are you?" he asks. "Answer me. Are you mocking me?"

Continuing to tremble and shake, Mendele was seized with still another paroxysm, as if of gas, and when he claps his hands over his mouth, his throat works as if he had just swallowed a hot potato.

It is also clear that he is still in the aroused state.

The poor goose. "You will stay here," the major tells him, "until we are finished with the others."

It seems Mendele has swallowed a mouthful of ether because he is starting to vomit on the other man's boots. Only later do we learn where he is tattooed a second time—on that same organ which initially betrayed him.

"*Liar!*"

4

"Filth!" Esther continued. He felt her warm body brush against his shoulders. *"Do you see what you have done now? You have another letter from that attorney."* Even as she spoke, Yagodah turned and saw her quickly tearing open the envelope.

His hands gripped the sides of his chair. He felt as if he had been backed into a corner. Alex had not heard the exchange between Esther and the postman. He regarded the long blue envelope which he saw in Esther's hands as a matter of some privacy, but he also found he could not get angry that his wife had intercepted his mail.

Yagodah had been writing: "And that, dear sir, is how I came to be known as IVB C 107 Yagodah," until he heard the door slam and saw the woman coming toward his desk. Then he did the expected, raised his pen so that she could place the sheet of legal stationery across his papers; and he didn't object when she continued to stare over his shoulder.

Dear Mr. Yagodah:

It has been nearly four weeks since this office was able to notify you of the bequest of your late uncle, Bela James (Yagodah).

We are sure that your delay in not replying to our letter is not intentional, and we are looking forward to the receipt of your affidavits so that we can make an immediate and proper disbursement of the funds.

In the course of making inquiries on your behalf it has come to our attention that you have been known variously as Albert Jackson, Alex Jacob and Alex Silk, and that you were—at one time—a member of Her Majesty's Forces in Bavaria. You must realize, of course, that we shall need to have a detailed *vitae* so as to fulfill all of your uncle's stipulations.

The terms of your late uncle's bequest are unequivocal. I had the pleasure of knowing the gentleman personally, and I can assure you that he was most anxious to help his entire family. Since we are also equally anxious to make an adequate and equitable distribution of funds we would appreciate any help you can give us in locating the following persons or their descendants:

Mihaily Erdos
Hilda Weiss
Pepi Weiss
Lilo Gero

We look forward to an immediate reply to this and our previous correspondence.

Very sincerely yours,

Ernest Rubin
Attorney at Law

For lack of anything better to do Alex studied the lawyer's signature. "Ernest?" he went on, in a mocking voice.

"Very sincerely yours, Ernest," Esther put in.

174

Abruptly they found themselves snickering at the same joke. Then Alex asked: "Do you think he will personally read what I have written?" She replied: "There is somebody here to see you."

Alex thought that it must be his friend the manager. Probably Esther had called on him for help. He could detect a shadow in the doorway. Probably the man was standing just outside the entrance. "Tell him to come in," Alex said, without enthusiasm.

A large fellow with fair hair and reddish freckled skin entered the room. Like many men of his size, this one seemed prepared to apologize in advance for his clumsiness. When he entered the shack, he bumped against a doorpost and nodded at Alex, trying out a tiny flicker of a smile on Esther as well. "We are all pleased with your good fortune, Yagodah," the manager said.

"And how did you *all* know?"

Looking as if he had been betrayed, the manager stared at Esther. "However," he continued at last, "as your friend I must advise you that on no account should you overstrain yourself. Our solicitors in Jerusalem are prepared to assist you. There is no point, after all, in dredging up the past. We all know what happened. Why ruin your chances? Do you know what we could do with forty thousand dollars?"

"We?" asked Alex. "*We?*"

"Well naturally," the man stammered, "naturally you are aware that you won't be allowed to keep so many dollars. You will have to turn them over to the State Bank. They will give you our currency in exchange. There will be taxes. And you won't have very much left when all the lawyers and accountants get through with you. Naturally. But if you were to invest it in this cooperative. . . ."

"Is that what you came to tell me?" Alex asked.

"Naturally," the manager said.

"Good. Then you have told me. Now get out of here. Please leave me alone."

His friend's eyes were blinking rapid fire: "You—realize, of course," he said, "what people here think about your malingering. The people at the dispensary, for example. We must all work to survive."

"Get out of here," Alex screamed, "or I will make sure you don't survive!"

He turned toward his desk once more. He was sorry that he had screamed at the manager. The man was part German and quite sensitive about it. He had befriended them, given them a home. Still trembling, Alex took the letter and folded it under a pile of his papers. When he was sure the manager had left, he again picked up his pen and said to Esther, "Do you see what I mean about some people?"

The woman cleared her throat. "Troublemaker!"

Alex added, "All they care about is money. Some people," he added.

"And you?" she asked. "What do you care about? All you know how to do is tell lies."

"Well, I also know how to protect what is mine," he said. As he spoke Alex thought he was having one of his palpitations. He felt a sweat break against his forehead but his hand went up to his heart. "Don't you think certain things should be said?" he asked, after another little while. Esther didn't answer, so he added, "If I have gone this far do you think I ought to hand everything over to our friends on the committee?"

"Do as you please." The floor creaked.

"But if you were so good at protecting your own—" she started. Then: "It stinks like death in here. I'm going to take a bath."

"Go," Alex grumbled.

He listened for her tread on the gravel path. Once she was out of hearing he found the letter again and read through it. "The quartet you ask about are all dead," he scrawled across the piece of stationery before tearing it into little pieces.

Afterward he still felt unsated, unexplained. What would he do

176

with the money? He had never thought about it. Surely there were more serious questions. Fundamental problems. The money was his. What did it matter what he chose to do with it? Alex looked out through the window. In the nearby fields they were having military drill. He saw the manager talking to one of his platoon leaders. They were pointing at his cabin. Surely they had no right to make demands on him. The money was his; not theirs. Alex drew the blinds and switched on the electric light.

At his desk once again, the glow of the lamp was dim and gloomy. He looked through his many pages, and found the one on which he had begun to scrawl. "There are so many liars," he said, but it gave him little satisfaction to be talking to himself. There were still too many hours left before sunset. He lifted a corner of the blind. A group of odd-looking young men in red berets and short pants were doing calisthenics. Alex went to the door and closed it. Presently the air in the shack was very close, but the cramp in his hand had numbed by the time he took up his pen once again. He was staring at his tattoo.

Dear Rubin:

The people you ask about are all numbers. Why didn't Bela leave his money to a set of digits? Names? What do they mean? One can always change a name but when one has a number on his wrist it is a permanent thing. One becomes a perfect solipsist. There are records in the war archives in Berlin, and carbon copies, no doubt, in Budapest, Debrecen, and the Palace of Justice in Clig as well; you are now a living war museum.

Even today I can make out, beneath a matting of cinnamon-colored hair on my arm, the slightly bluish veined numerals on my skin, now faded, almost marbleized, graded and inspected like beef on the hook, a blur of color which has become so familiar to me that I no longer shrink from staring at it. As some might

177

wear an ornament, an expensive watch or a silver bracelet, I continue to boast of that exclusive cluster of numerals which refuse to fade even when I rub or pinch the skin. Yes, we are a rather discriminating club. My stepdaughter calls the thing my "beauty spot." Ofra has not been told why I am so endowed. Nor does she understand the numbers my Esther wears in the fleshy folds between right arm and breast. Perhaps she is even a bit envious, as little children often are of the deformed.

One thing is certain: not too many of us are left in this country who can boast of such things. We are, we joke, easily identifiable after air disasters or on the battlefields, but now, at long last, such a joke takes on a certain hackneyed bitterness which is not unlike acquiescence, acceptance of our miseries. If it had always been that way with us we should have perished for sure; in those days some of us thought we knew better. Even though I did not resist when the mark was made, I was aware, nonetheless, that I was being treated like cattle. I didn't like the feeling. What was my first reaction? Well, you must know that the petty bourgeois instinct in me was still dominant; and so, since my skin was my property, I resented the intrusion. Then, like a good little *chedarist*, I thought I must memorize my new numerals, as if some great teacher had set out an exercise, until it occurred to me: How absurd. When one is in possession of the *ur*-text, memorizing is a foolish waste of time. . . .

If only this had been true with my Latin verbs . . . or the Swiss numbers of dear paterfamilias. . . . In general, though, I was shortly to feel relieved that the process had gone only so far. Suppose they had tattooed the word JUDE across my chest or forehead. It's not likely I would have resisted. Resist when? With what? We were now dismissed, free to go as before. Although our restrictions were too obvious for words, I thought a man could get used to such restrictions, just as he gets used to the size of his body, or the puny limitations of his brain.

Take my word for it. Even the blackest savage also has such a proprietary interest in his own skin that he must, perforce, regard the act of tattooing as a violation and a degradation and yet we know that some African tribes regard these marks as beautifications. Although it is just not possible to be discreet when one has acquired a burning mark on the wrist, it is also true that one is not likely to pour salt on the wound as an act of spiritual regeneration. Fastidious about infection, our German masters had distributed typewritten notes in Hungarian and the local German dialect, warning us—as we departed—not to remove the cheap cotton gauze patches that were on our arms for forty-eight hours, but, as soon as we were outside the dispensary, my father, Maurice, and I—as if by some common signal—tore away these flimsy protective coverings to stare with surprisingly little horror at the elegant calligraphics which had been affixed upon us. Moshe Shad was then the first to complain because his skin had been accidentally scalded by the hot needles, but even he tried to play Zeno. He held his lips clamped together, wincing only slightly with his eyes and forehead at the sight of the puckered skin on my wrist as I took my hand up to the light, turning it this way and that like roasting meat on a spit, hoping perhaps that my scars might still run, or fade, or be washed off like certain tinctures which are used for a heat rash, but, as I recall, feeling also a certain satisfaction at the manner in which the act had been carried off—so quickly and with so little personal inconvenience. One thing is certain: I was displeased with the perfunctory manner of the physical examination, for I can remember asking: "How will they ever know if we are fit or not?"

"It doesn't even matter," my father said. He too was doing nothing but staring at his palm; and the significant thing is that it trembled like the hand of a man twenty years his senior. When Father noticed his own trembling he grew visibly alarmed, tried to stay one hand with the other while he examined the mark more closely. The late afternoon sun was orange, blackening our shadows. There were deep pockets of shadow under Father's eyes. His pallor was of the sort that a clown might apply to his cheeks.

Father had dressed hastily; his clothes were in disarray. I tried to divert him from his thoughts but I simply couldn't find the right words. "Look," I announced, "how ugly it is. Why it cannot even be covered with a glove."

Father examined his hand, matching my comments against his observations, but nodding, finally, stupidly.

Then we heard Moshe Shad: "Do you think they will do this to the baby?"

"What baby?" Father asked.

Then: "We must hurry home."

Father let his hand fall to his side as we quickened our steps.

In the front hall we were greeted by Adam: "Dr. Yagodah, I must of course, I must . . . and cannot wait a moment longer."

Perl's fiancé always used the most respectful forms of address toward the head of our family, as if to shame his rival Maurice, who insisted on the more familiar "Poppa."

As always, too, Adam's voice was so thin and his talk so animated that it was difficult to separate the import of what he seemed to be saying from his rather nervous manner of setting out long strings of words. Really, when he spoke it was like one complete stammering sentence of proper nouns and pronouns which, though it struggled ever forward, clause after protracted clause, never quite seemed to make contact with the verb.

Saint Adam! His usually sallow face was now quite bilious; his narrow bald pate—a slice of cold meat in a platter of garnish—shimmered like poisonous stuff under the light of the one flickering incandescent bulb left in the giant chandelier in our entranceway. Adam's tonsure was like an open wound. He argued with his own shadow on the carpet like some distracted talmudist: "We haven't a moment . . . not a moment to waste, I assure you. There simply isn't any time. Look around you, Doctor. A tragedy is about to happen. Do you think we can stand here talking? I must speak with you in private. May I take the liberty—"

"Speak," said Father. He was losing his patience. "Speak," he repeated, as if to indicate that he now saw no necessity for confidences. "Speak," he insisted, a third, then a fourth time.

180

Clearly Adam wished to be agreeable but his glance couldn't help going toward the front parlor where Perl was looming out of the shadows. Facing us again, Adam tried out a dirty look on Maurice and myself, hoping to convince us to move on, but my father said, "They can stay."

Then he added: "What do you want?"

"Adam will you speak up," Perl added, as she stepped toward our group from out of the shadows. Presently we were joined by my mother and Sarah, and when I glanced up, I observed Lilo at the top of the first flight of stairs.

Adam swallowed air: "My father—he—that is—the apothecary whom you know is my father. . . ."

"What a dummy. Let me explain," Perl said.

Downcast, Adam backed away from our circle as I stuffed my hand into my pocket, hoping to hide the tattoo. "Fix yourself," Father said to my mother, whose hair had come unpinned on one side, like a wig. I saw Sarah go to help her mother. Perl had already started speaking: "I don't see why anybody has the right to sacrifice themselves . . ."

Perl put the matter very simply. Adam's father had been born in the same village with Brunner, a top official in the Hungarian gendarmerie. This Brunner was not a Jew-hater. He had introduced the old man Geiger to Hauptman Zweig, one of the chief officers in the Waffen SS constabulary, a Tyrolean with, apparently, a barbiturate habit. When his usual sources of supply in the SS dispensary evaporated, this Zweig turned to Geiger through Brunner, promising as payment a certain favor should it ever become necessary. Now Zweig was attempting to keep his promise. There were two Salvadoran passports available under the name of Nusweiler. Each cost fifteen thousand pengö. Apothecary Geiger had already purchased one Nusweiler passport for his only son, Adam. He had Brunner's promise that the other could be sold to my father for Perl, since he was not such a wealthy man that he could pay for the pair. If my father was sensible, Adam and Perl could leave that very evening. A note of hand was sufficient. Adam's father had set down a small deposit and would collect the difference from my father after the pair had arrived safely in Debrecen where Brunner would have a covered lorry waiting to take them south across the Yugoslav border. In Slovenia they would quite likely find friendly partisan groups who could ship them across to Italy or east to Turkey, perhaps even to Palestine. The Nazis had little control over Yugoslavia. The partisans were well armed. There was almost daily contact with the Allies. Perl wanted to know if my father would spare her fifteen thousand pengö. Would he agree to such an uncertain arrangement? How could he not?

Perl was no fool. She presented her case rigorously, without stammering and without emotion, ending, finally, paler than usual, her lips wrinkled but set, her forehead quite uncreased.

Then we were all silent, but I could see that my mother had her apron up to her face.

"If it was one of the others," Perl started. "If—"

"Be quiet," Father said.

Then Maurice asked, "What about the child?"

"My baby," Sarah said.

"Be quiet," I echoed my father.

Sarah looked the other way shamefully. She recognized what she had almost done to her sister. Probably she would have made some gesture of atonement but, when she put out her hand, Perl said: "Please!"

Then all we could do was to wait as my father gnawed at a sore on his lower lip. I tell you, Rubin, in my innermost self I suppose I did hope that Father would deny my sister, if only to repay her and Adam in kind for their intolerable arrogance (or perhaps because I felt—as I told myself much later—that the risk was too great), and yet I should have known Father well enough to recognize that he would feel called upon to be generous under such circumstances. What would you have done in his place? Suppose a murderer said to you: "Who do you wish me to kill—

your wife or your daughter?" Would you call that a fair choice? If there is simply no basis for equity in murder, how can I blame the old man? When I saw his lip slip like a piece of rubbery stuff from between the clench of his strong teeth, I knew in his eyes that he would motion Perl and Adam to follow him into his study. Then Sarah and Maurice were moving away; and my mother went back to her chores in the kitchen. Left to myself, I again stared vacantly up the stairs.

Lilo hadn't moved, but was looking down at me soberly. When my sister and brother-in-law came level with her, they separated and were forced to go around her; she wouldn't even move aside; and she didn't nod at them as they passed. Only afterward she spoke: "Alex, why do you let Uncle Newman play King Solomon? Do you really think he has so much wisdom?"

My answer was to start up the stairs, that hand still in my pocket.

"Can't you talk?" Lilo asked. She started to back away, her face the map of surprise. ". . . *What have they done to you?*"

Lilo grasped my sleeve, and began to pull on it. *"Oh, let me see. . . ."*

I clutched at the twill lining of my pocket. I even tried to fend her off with my other hand. Accidentally, once, I swung too hard. My hand was like a slap against Lilo's face. She fell backward with a little cry. But when she tried with her own delicate hand to ward off the next expected blow her wrist was also revealed, and I saw an identical mark, an even larger tattoo with considerable swelling in the general area of the tiny numerals.

"Lilo!"

I tried to seize the hand, to smother it with kisses, to hold my beloved so close to me that we would be fused, as it were, into one wounded, suffering body. She pulled me down against the stairwell with her and we did not speak.

Presently Adam and Perl rushed past. I heard the crashing of a door. Father had emerged from his study. Below us he stood with

183

his head bowed, coughing into his hand to make his presence known. We peered down through the slats of the evenly spaced balustrades. Father was pacing back and forth, like a man in a prison cell.

Lilo spoke: "Uncle Newman, what did you let them do to Shandor?"

"*Let?*" he replied. "*How could I stop them?*"

Father struggled to gain control over his anger and bewilderment by coughing a good deal as he continued to pace back and forth. Abruptly he stopped at the very foot of the stairway, head bowed.

"I am determined not to quarrel with you now," he announced. "You both must dress for dinner. We are bound to make a proper farewell for Perl and Adam."

Dismissing us, he next fished his watch fob out of his hip pocket, selected a key, and went toward the cellar to get wine. We didn't speak. Lilo and I held on to each other still, peering down through the bars of the staircase. After a while I was aware of the awkwardness of my position. Although I continued to extend my arms, she had again slipped out of reach and was padding softly up the stairs to her room.

5

THE spirit of happier times haunted us that evening. Dinner was like a meal one eats upon coming home from a funeral. We simply had no stomach for what we were being served.

But, if memory of the day's events constantly served this apathy, these same emotional memories also managed to admonish us to eat, to stuff ourselves, even though there was no hunger. Each of us seemed to be treating our appetites as if we were the overly anxious parents of anemic children. We coaxed and cajoled ourselves to eat, deceived and frightened ourselves with each new serving.

I was reminded of a certain bedtime story that our housekeeper Magda used to tell us when we were all children. It was about a small boy named Antonin Pfeffernusse who wouldn't eat anything, not even corn-meal mush. Thinking that she hadn't gone to enough pains to please her boy, his mother, Mrs. Pfeffernusse, prepared elaborate courses for him of sweetmeats and carrots, fine stews with fennel, honey, and other spices, but the boy always made a nasty face, saying everything tasted "too sour" or "too sweet," "too spicy" or "too bitter"; and that if he had to eat anything, he would much prefer plain corn-meal mush.

Mrs. Pfeffernusse was a simple woman. Seeing how thin her little boy had grown, she feared he would starve to death. She borrowed a gold coin and went to the miller to have the very finest corn ground. At the dairy she purchased cream so fresh that it was still warm from the cow's body. But when she served this fine delicacy to her prodigy he again refused to eat, even overturned his bowl, and ran from the table.

Finally the poor woman went to see a wise man in the village: "How shall I get my little Antonin to eat?"

The old man thought a moment and then told the housewife to give her son garbage because if he didn't know what good food was that would be one way for him to learn.

Mrs. Pfeffernusse was extremely dubious about the elder's suggestion but she was also desperate. That evening she brought the dust bin to the table and proceeded to scoop out a few portions onto her son's plate. "Here," she said. "You will learn."

Imagine the good woman's surprise when the child greedily devoured every morsel and then demanded even more, eventually sticking his nose into the pail to eat directly from it. "My heavens," the woman said, "what have I done?" But the next day and the next the child grew fatter and demanded more and more garbage until the entire family couldn't produce enough and there was hardly anything for the pigs to eat. In fact, little Antonin became quite greedy. He would crowd among the littlest piglets at their trough and steal their leavings. Then the neighbors began to say that old Ma Pfeffernusse had a pig for a son; and she was so ashamed that she went in desperation again to the village elder.

"You told me to feed him garbage so he would learn the value of good food, so now I have a pig for a son," the good woman berated the wise man, "and it is all your fault—"

"Ah no, housewife," he declared, "blame yourself. I told you to

186

feed him garbage, yes, but *you fed* him garbage, and *he ate* the garbage. . . . Even wise men can't make human beings into pigs," the old man, who was named Nicolas, concluded, *"only humans can. . . ."*

Perhaps, then, it was mother's fault that we continued to stuff ourselves even though we lacked all appetite. Mother had never been content to allow us to get used to our deprivations. As a final gesture, on this deportation eve, she had broken out all her hoardings. There was a special thick soup of dried vegetables, beans and mushrooms, an entree of bread crumbs and drippings, and meat potted with a sauerkraut for the main course. How we suffered over these things which we were urged to consume! I do not doubt that my mother felt she was performing a genuine service when, at eight in the morning, her extremely ardent pleas had convinced butcher Emil Fink to part with some of his last remaining "beef," and without a ration card. Probably my mother had bribed, cajoled, browbeaten and bullied old Fink, even threatening to take what she wanted without his permission, but, over the dinner table, she explained what she had done in somewhat different words: "Fink," she had said, "it is a question of now or never." She also claimed to have explained to her old adversary that she needed to have something special for the men in her family, and she reminded Fink that she was willing to pay in gold. Besides, she had boasted, "I was the first on the queue and I told him: 'Who do you think will be buying your fancy meats after tomorrow—Reichsfuehrer Göring?'"

I doubt if Mother ever said any such thing but her recounting of her adventures brought reluctant smiles to all our faces just the same. We ate with greasy lips, choking down the rich fatty meat and potatoes, slopping margarine on our bread, setting our teeth on edge with the sauerkraut, thankful for what she had gotten us but anxious not to seem overly pleased with ourselves. At least we were no longer trying to hide the strange tattoo marks gracing some of our wrists. There was much less tension of that sort; and perhaps it was my mother's doing. From the way she continued to go on in her deliberately hackneyed manner about Fink it was becoming obvious to me that Father had instructed her not to make too much of our tattoos.

"That Fink," she would say, "a thief. He isn't any good at all. The airs he puts on. You would think he wasn't a butcher but a professional man, an artist. When he as much as slices a liver, veins and all, you would think he was a famous surgeon. Nothing will discourage such fellows. He takes. He takes all he can get. What does he expect to do with it all? I can tell you he doesn't give unless he has to. Such a dishonest person. A Bluebeard! One would have to be a magician with the knife—I assure you children, Newman—to make what the Hungarians have given us of late into liver, but Fink, he goes on and on. Fink has his ways. He knows how to cut corners. He is the entire black market. He would teach a gypsy how to steal, that Fink. Someday I'll give him everything back in kind. Little Mr. Fink with his scrawny pullets, his cat and mouse veal, stringy horsemeat, dog meat, rabbits, even pork he would claim can now be koshered under extreme circumstances. He would say such things. But where is one to find a piece of pork?"

When nobody answered, my mother went on as before: "Such a liar, that Fink! Business as usual for him means you take what he gives you for what he tells you it is, and you can't get a copper off on the price no matter what it happens to be, and *if* you complain it's a personal insult. Bluebeard. You complain too often and he won't sell you.

" 'Fink,' I told him once, 'I need at least three kilos of the side meat (by which I mean beef not horsemeat) and I'm willing to pay any price within reason.' Do you know what the monster said? 'Go easy, Mrs. Yagodah. Tomorrow is another day.'

"Such gall. Do I look like a hoarder? Would I want to serve my family spoiled meat? Tomorrow is another day. As if I didn't

188

know? Bluebeard! To have such things said to you by a fellow who doesn't even know the name of his own father. Didn't you know? Fink was *her* name. The wife. Everybody knows when this fellow came here—from where was it in Dobruja?—he had no proper last name but was like an orphan. A bastard. So now he speaks that way to the granddaughter of Isaac Meyer Fass. War profiteer. The nerve he has. If things continue he'll be cutting all of us up someday and then selling us to our neighbors as first quality kid. Honest little Mr. Fink will bring us home for that Vera of his to make into a stew. . . .

"Such a fellow. Just the other day I sent our Sarah for two and a half kilo lung and giblets, and do you know what he had the effrontery to say to her? All our neighbors were there, even the wife of Frankel, your friend Frankel, Newman, and here comes our Sarah, not asking any special favors, I assure you. She waits her turn, asks nicely for the lung which in ordinary times I wouldn't feed to our cat—and this Fink, this little pimple—whose wife and children ate chicken feet even in the best of times—this blackhead, this monster Fink, he wipes his hands on his bloody apron, he cleans his spectacles, and he says to my daughter so that everybody else can hear: 'That is why I admire your mother. War or peace, nothing is too good for Ilona and her family. . . .' And all I had ordered was one kilo of lung. Can you imagine such bad manners? Gross, I'd say.

"Well, isn't that what he told you, Sarah? You told me he did. Calling me by my first name too. Ilona, no less—"

"Mother Yagodah. Please. Enough . . ."

It was Moshe Shad who interrupted. He directed our glances toward his wife.

Sarah gamely held her fork up to her mouth, but the tears were streaming down across her face, seasoning her still-untouched plate of meat.

"Enough. Can't you see what you are doing to your daughter?" Maurice asked.

189

"And one of your kind is going to correct me, I suppose," Mother replied.

"*Yes. One of my kind.*"

"Enough," my father put in.

Sarah's fork rattled against her plate. "My baby," she said. "My baby."

Total silence. What could one say? How did we still manage to eat? A pall had fallen over our heads, as it had been threatening to do all evening. Our food now tasted like grease; the wine was sour. Outside our doors police dogs howled. Yet we continued to pass the food from plate to plate.

There were eleven of us at table: my father at the head, next to my mother, then myself, feeble Aunt Pepi, and counterclockwise, Maurice, Lilo, Adam, Perl, Sarah, and our two guests, Skirzeny der Schike and Miklos, both sitting at the farthest remove from my father. They pretended to be unembarrassed by our squabbles, acted oblivious to my mother's chatter.

Pigs! Glancing up once after the soup I had caught my rival's eye; beneath his blond lashes he was staring at Lilo, wanted me to see that he was. Miklos flicked a brazen stare my way, making it clear that he knew I had not informed on him, before he returned his gaze upon Lilo.

"Pass the salt, Alex!"

If Miklos felt so sure of himself in our company, what was I to do? Wasn't it enough to make it clear that I detested him? But, if he was not so thin-skinned, all I seemed to be doing was to provide him with even more encouragement to be brazen. Miklos Skirzeny pretended we were old school chums, as if nothing else had transpired in the intervening years. And what, indeed, could I say about that? Along with his stepfather, he was my father's guest. It was believed that they could help us. That was why we were stuffing them with our precious food. Was I so shrewd to offer other alternatives? No! All I could rightfully do was to pout and look hurt, to refrain from conversation as much as possible,

190

and to pass the salt without making too much of a fuss about it.

A fine thing! We sat down to eat with our worst enemies, and nobody seemed to care except me. When we were summoned to the table I had noticed the wine, which was not from one of the drought years, and the two extra places, so I asked, "Who?"

"Skirzeny," my father whispered. "He has a proposition to make."

Shortly thereafter Sarah went to the front door to admit father and son with a house present, a large straw basket filled with field mushrooms.

The Skirzenys gave their basket to my sister. They didn't bother to greet the rest of the family, but took their seats around the long dining table, a trifle ill-at-ease at first when it came to passing things or joining in the small talk, but accepting the good wine which my father served out to them in abundant quantities. In fact, they already seemed quite inebriated upon their entrance. The old man had such a powerful odor about him that Perl was constantly turning up her nose.

But, throughout the early courses, not a word was said about the reason for their visit. Mother had not given anybody else much opportunity to speak, and Lilo was agitated and pale. She fussed with her napkin ring, once letting it clatter onto the greasy gravy in her plate by accident. Shortly thereafter, Perl and Adam began to exchange looks and glanced at their watches. My father ordered Maurice to bring the cordials from his study. Presently Miklos was commenting that our armies had launched a new counteroffensive. He said that by fall the situation in the East would again be "normalized," and asked the Herr Doktor Yagodah for his opinion.

"That would interest me very much," he claimed.

Miklos' slurred efforts with the pretentious jargon of the Goebbels press brought smiles again to all our faces. Why did he struggle so to copy himself after the German pronunciation of the men he heard on the wireless when he was obviously doomed to failure? To see Miklos slobbering, with a mouthful of food, over the niceties of his adopted tongue was both comical and reassuring. Although remaining silent, I lost some of my apprehensiveness, fell to eating my food once again, and was pleased to hear my father remark: "What you tell me is to be hoped for, young man. For all our sakes." *Why?* Because I felt sure Father was being ironical.

But then Miklos smiled back at him, baring his unhealthy gums.

The fruit bowl was brought to the table by Lilo. Skirzeny raised his shaggy eyebrows, questioning. Again, Miklos slowly smiled and nodded, the lines of his face dragged down for a moment so that he looked like a sly, prematurely old man, the father of his unruly bearded companion. He creased his lips. "Elegant. Very elegant," he said.

Lilo must also have noticed the change that came over his face for she was unable to hold onto the bowl of fruit; her hands went up in the air, the poor bruised fruit spilled out and rolled along the floor, under the table, in all directions.

Lilo dove for the floor and I scrambled after her. There was great consternation above us. Beyond the hem of the tablecloth, in a forest of thick ball fringes, legs, cast-off shoes, discarded napkins, crumbs, I reached for an apple and just the touch of its naked skin was enough to bring back the vision of Lilo squirming under Miklos.

Nausea and fainting spells. I clapped a hand to my mouth, but my other hand still grasped the apple. Lilo had disappeared. People were beginning to ask, "Why so long?"

I made a retching noise but brought up nothing solid.

"Come out from under there," Father demanded.

Bracing myself with my knees and hands against the floor, I tried to gain control over my body. By the time I raised my head above table level, Lilo had fled upstairs. Only the men and my mother were still seated. Farnas Skirzeny was speaking.

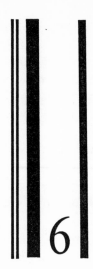

6

"It appears as if they have you up against a wall."

Skirzeny seemed to be uttering a dare. He waited for a comment, poised, a shingle of his coarse, streaky black hair falling across his forehead, his bald spot burning, his tongue darting between his lips, or down across a smidgeon of beard. "Against a wall," he grunted.

Once more the coated tongue flicked forward again and disappeared. He set himself into his chair. "Truly against the wall."

But his sagacity was just a pose. Skirzeny seemed prepared to make an instantaneous disclaimer should one of us argue that *he* and the mysterious *they* were virtually identical. "Who, me?" he seemed to be suggesting by his very posture. But when my father made no such disclaimer but merely nodded his head, more or less agreeably, and ordered more wine, the old drunkard was somewhat taken aback. Skirzeny's mouth fell open. We could see that he was still chewing a cud of beef. Standing over his shoulder, but to one side, my mother tried to pour more wine until he shoved his glass out of reach so violently that it tipped over, spilling its carmine contents against the soft creaminess of her best cloth.

Mother raced to the kitchen to fetch a rag. Skirzeny meanwhile blinked at the mess, staring down apologetically, eyes opening and closing, his expression a shudder, an animal in pain. Words seemed to thicken on his lips:

"Back against the wall, Newman. I don't understand. I shall never understand," he added, glancing up helplessly, "why you pretend with me that all is well when by tomorrow evening who knows where you may be."

Father didn't answer except to shrug his shoulders and grin a little.

"Ech," went Skirzeny. Bearlike, he pawed at the damp table-cloth, giving us the impression once that he could reach across the width of it to touch my father, as if by such a gesture he might jar Father into acknowledging certain brutal facts.

I started from my chair. One thing was certain: this man would not touch my father.

Wonder of wonders, Miklos also seemed to be restraining his father. He had his arms around him too, else the old man might have tipped forward in his chair, overturning everything.

Skirzeny snarled, shrugging off his son's grasp. His features glowered as he pawed again at the spot on the tablecloth, this time with his pocket handkerchief.

"Listen, old friend," he began, "I am sorry for this but you see what I am getting at, don't you? You need not pretend with me. You people are not known to be stoics. Weep and wail if you like. Tear your hair out for all I care but listen to me, please, for I am talking good sense."

Father held up his hand. "You may be talking sense," he said, "but do you also have to rub a hole in the cloth?"

"Of course . . . of course," Skirzeny grunted. "Of course not . . ."

Father made a nasty face. He was unrelenting now in asserting

194

his kind of superiority. It also seemed as if he had lost all restraint. His little quip was followed by a brief, sardonic smile, a promise of things to come should Skirzeny continue to be so oblique. "Silly old fool," Father muttered. Turning his back on Skirzeny, he went to dip his hands in the large fingerbowl on the sideboard, dipping and wiping the fingers and then burnishing in between them, one by one, with a large white napkin. He wasn't even trying now to mask his contempt. When he smiled and was rewarded by Skirzeny's broad grin—a combination of hurt, guile, crass stupidity and cunning—believe it or not—Father asked: "Farnas, just who do you suppose you are grinning at?"

"Why nobody, of course.'"

"Then stop it. I don't appreciate silliness."

I had been staring out of the corner of one eye at Miklos all the while. He, too, seemed hardly able to restrain certain feelings. When his father spoke Miklos seemed as if he were trying to control a giant tic which constantly threatened to contract the right side of his face, and then his shoulders, his rib cage, now throbbing along his neck or pushing his nose and lips to one side; he would brush some longish strands of hair out of those same eyes with a swipe of his hand, a brush of his arm, but the tic would only throb up again, forcing him to hold us all in contempt, frozen by the same aimless, hate-filled expression which he flashed alternately toward his father, toward my father, me, the room, the entire forced atmosphere of congeniality.

Outside our house a train shuddered through the night. Minutes later planes were scratching at the sky overhead. The room was quiet, like a wireless set between transmissions. In the kitchen doorway my mother hesitated, bent over a bit as if with cramp, afraid to enter lest she cause the old fool to overturn another object. A long gray piece of rag dangled from her fist. I stared again at the table. The stain had soaked deep, spreading from a pool in its center where bread crumbs floated on the surface of the still-wrinkled rivulets of the cloth. Glancing at

Miklos again, my thoughts were a blank. His eyes were as aimless and glassy as those in the animal heads mounted on the wall. Then I saw my father folding his hands. Skirzeny quickly imitated him, but Miklos spoke:

"Why are we wasting our time?"

"Do I need your idiocy?" Skirzeny shouted back, causing the table to tremble. My hands went to steady it. "Be quiet," he added.

Skirzeny had been holding his fingers to his mouth, as if to warm them with his breath. When he let them drop a second time all the china rattled. His shoulders sagged forward. "Old friend"—he smiled—"in Serbia, in the Great War, we had a saying: when your back is to the wall you can try to climb over it, or you can tunnel under it, but you just can't stay as you are. Does that make any sense to you? Well?"

"Certainly," my father replied.

Skirzeny nodded. "Very good"—under his breath.

He lurched across the table to poke inside his stepson's shirt front for a cigarette. Evidently he now felt he had made his point, for he smiled and took his time cadging the light.

First Skirzeny brought the bent paper cylinder up to his nose, sniffing the tobacco. Then he wet his lips, slobbered on them with the grainy side of his tongue, rolled the cigarette between both pursed lips until it was sopping at one end. His heavy jaw, with its little beard, like a rabbit's tail, firmed in its strict outlines but then blurred just as quickly once again as his jowls worked nervously on an anxious cud of tongue. When he lowered mother's flaming candlestick toward his jaw to light the end of his cigarette, a streaming rivulet of hot wax dripped down, ran onto his chin, stuck fast, so that his eyes and mouth were forced open wide, an expression of silent, momentarily searing pain. Quickly, he gulped more wine and his fingers tore at his face. Then he tried again with the dripping candlestick. But, as soon as he blew out the smoke, Farnas Skirzeny was talking again.

"Newman, my son thinks me a fool. Don't pretend, Miklos. You

196

think. So that's what you think. What else should you think? Listen, Newman, my friend, this Miklos, he is very different than us. All the young are. They are dangerous. Who do you think are running this war? Young people, of course. My only point is Miklos says the *Aktion* is planned for tomorrow; he wishes to be very logical. When the Yagodahs will no longer be here, he says, you can simply take this place and say it is yours again. He says: 'Who will want to argue with you once the Yagodahs have gone?' And, he says, if the army or the police should try to requisition the place, you have only to point to your loyal service to party and Fatherland to make them let you have your way.

"Miklos," he interrupted himself, "I am afraid you are the fool. You eat goat shit. Don't bother answering me. I know better than you. Haven't I lived longer?"

Momentarily, even Skirzeny came to suspect that his remarks smacked of cant. He hesitated, turned again to my father. Finally he added, "I am an old man."

When nobody seemed impressed, and he was still not able to summon up new arguments, he resolved to be the complete buffoon. Rising, he turned toward Miklos and clicked his heels, the Fascist salute. He next pinched his nostrils, wheeled about, clicked, and slumped down again, a tiny spot of wax still stuck against his chin. The chair creaked under his weight. Skirzeny was like a sack of grain. Rolls of fat bulged from his tunic, spilled out above his waistline. His head lolled against his shoulders, idiot-fashion. His tongue stuck out. He cracked wind at us. Even Miklos was smiling at him. Straightening himself, Skirzeny bellowed:

"Dunce cap! Dung heap! I'll teach you who to respect," he said. "Don't you think our time will come? Are we to pass as so-called Aryans? Do you believe that? And even if we are unharmed, will our German protectors be with us forever? Victory is an illusion. What will happen to us when this war ends like the last and these people come back? What treatment can we expect? Again we will be homeless, only then we shall also be thieves, Miklos. Do you want your wife and your sisters, me, your mother, do you want us all to be war criminals and thieves—common garbage? Zigeuner! Doesn't my honor mean a thing to you? Remember what our lives were like in the best of times. Some of our people still believed in pig worship. The black hen was the offspring of the devil and a Jewish girl. You could cure a headache by rubbing the forehead with special stones or a piece of iron. We mixed potions out of the fat of bears, dogs, snakes, snails, along with the oil of rain worms, spiders, and midges. Remember the slogan: 'After the Jews the Gypsies. . . .'

"No, I tell you you are a fool, Miklos. Haven't you heard any of the broadcasts? Do you know what they will do to us if we are caught?

"I tell you we will be civilized like these Jews and we will still keep this place so that after the war is over not even Mr. Roosevelt can question our rights to it. We will make tit for tat, as they say—"

"Tit for tat for what?" Father interrupted.

"As if you didn't know," Skirzeny smiled. "Listen to me," he began again, for his stepson's benefit presumably. "Let me educate *you* for a change. A little history. At such a moment it is sometimes useful." Skirzeny swallowed air like a frog and spoke again, more softly: "After the Great War, money was a problem. Austrian kronen were still in circulation, although we were no longer a 'Grand Principality.' You remember that much, don't you, Newman? Now, let me refresh you a bit more. When the Rumanians marched in, all that old money had to be withdrawn from circulation and replaced by the new National Bank notes from Bucharest. Remember? For political reasons kronen were being exchanged at the rate of two for one leu when, in the open market, one could easily buy at the time such an exchange was consummated between seven and eight kronen for one little leu. Isn't that so?"

"You have a good memory for figures," Father said. "I had forgotten all that. What is the meaning of this?"

"As if he didn't know," Skirzeny giggled. "But," he went on, "allow me to continue."

Again he faced his stepson.

"Yagodah is right," he said. "I have an extraordinary head when it comes to money matters, but even an idiot can see how fortunes were made on the occasion of the exchange because, for example, a man had only to buy with one hundred thousand lei some eight hundred thousand kronen in the open market, and then present that currency to be exchanged by the new government for four hundred thousand lei. . . .

"Ah, but it was even easier for some. Let me continue. It has been intimated that *some* people had advance knowledge of the two-kronen rate. Who? *Well, if one were on the Board of Trade, for example?*"

Skirzeny gave my father what I presumed to be his most methodical glance.

"Get on with your storytelling, Farnas," he said, brusque as ever.

"I mean," added Skirzeny, only somewhat flustered, "*if* one knew what the official exchange was to be, and *if* one had the capital, he could arrange to bring into the country kronen from Budapest or Vienna, especially if he was on an official government mission. . . . *Now wouldn't that seem likely?* Very likely," he answered his own question. "But one had to be a very special person to make it work. People were using every available means to bring in their currency. The most efficient of all proved to be the airplane. Ah," he sighed again in his buffoonish manner, "I shall never forget one warm night in May, 1921. The air dizzyingly sweet, redolent of pine and rose petals. You would think such a night would lead a young man to thoughts of lovemaking, but Jews love only one thing; it turned out to be very easy for our good old friend Yagodah here to pack an airplane in Budapest full of kronen, have it fly over the border to an arranged point, leave its valuable cargo, and fly back again, without a trace of this most extraordinary exchange transaction. The only trouble was young Yagodah couldn't fly a plane so I had to find him a pilot, and the arranged point happened to be a clearing in our woods. Now isn't that so, Newman?"

Skirzeny picked his chin, nodded, as if to say, your turn, and Father didn't waste a minute. Even as Skirzeny was examining the wax in his fingernails, we heard Father's voice, and our shoulders jerked.

"That was a very long time ago. You must have good reason, Farnas, to bring up such old wives' tales . . . or do you simply want to humiliate me in front of my family? Well? What is it you want? We haven't that much time to worry about what I did in 1923, or was it 1921? What difference does it make? You were well paid, weren't you?"

"Yes," said Skirzeny reluctantly, his finger waving in the air, "but I was a man of honor. You corrupted me." Then, probably realizing how hollow-sounding were his protests, he added: "You are right. What difference does it make? I merely wanted everybody to understand what kind of people we all are, so there won't be any crocodile tears shed . . . so that nobody will be able to pretend that so-and-so is acting badly toward so-and-so. Now, don't you think that's a good idea, Newman? Don't you think we should be honest with each other? After all, as the saying goes, once a thief always a thief . . ."

He was sucking on his cigarette, coming away with tobacco strings on his lips. He studied father and then his stepson, lips curled distastefully. "Goat shit," Skirzeny went again, and Miklos' face sagged. I could see that his shoulders were cast down in an elaborate pretense, a posturing of apology. Now Mother had come to sit beside my father. Skirzeny's guilty glance referred to the tablecloth.

"Go on," she said mildly.

He seemed not to believe what he was hearing.

"*Go on*," she urged, turning shrill.

My father nodded. Skirzeny swallowed air again.

200

"And so, Newman, I shall be simplicity itself," he added, with another hard swallow. The cigarette stuck to his bottom lip as he spread his arms out. "Your back is against the wall. You know it. I know it. We all know. And we know what kind of people we are. And for years, too, as you know, I have coveted this place, once mine, now yours. To say that I merely want to take back what was mine all along is one way to put the thing . . . not completely accurate because, as you must know, there has never been a way for me to get the estate from you legally. Only now does such a way exist. Now your back is against the wall. We know that. You do too. Your back *is* against the wall. You need a shovel, a ladder, dynamite, some way to escape. Along comes Skirzeny. You say: 'Help me, dear friend!' Influential as I am, Newman, I have no way of knowing for sure what your fates may be. A great tragedy seems quite probable. So now you are coming to your dear old friend Skirzeny, whose house you are living in, to ask for help. You offer him money. You have offered him money in the past. Yes, Newman. Don't deny that you did. But what would Skirzeny want with money . . . even a hundred and fifty kilograms of gold? It is not your money he wants. Not Skirzeny. . . .

"I want back my estate!"

"Yes. That would be so," my father mumbled quickly while Skirzeny's words were still echoing about the room. We all looked up.

Even as he spoke, Skirzeny's cigarette had burned to within a sixteenth of an inch of his lower lip. Now, with a gesture of his stained fingertips, he peeled off the smoldering thing and let it fall to the table, where it landed in the residue at the bottom of his wine glass with a tiny sizzle and then went out. The room continued to be silent. Frowning still from the heat of the smoke, Skirzeny said: "I could tell you I want back my honor but who would believe me?" He waited then to see if anyone would contradict him. At last, reaching into the inside pocket of his shabby green huntsman's tunic to remove a sheaf of thickly folded documents which he also threw upon the table, sorting among them with his fingertips, finally selecting one at random and throwing it open with a crackle under the candle flame, Skirzeny squinted down at the writing nearsightedly. "*There*," he groaned.

Skirzeny squared his shoulders, satisfied that he had produced the correct papers. Again the coated tongue flicked at those lips, and his eyes blinked and watered. Skirzeny sniffed, seemed to want another cigarette but didn't choose to ask for one.

"I have gone to great pains," he said. Then he stopped, looked around, a frightened hare: "I have gone to much expense and to no small amount of inconvenience . . . it has even cost me money to have drawn up this set of documents transferring the deed of this property to me and my heirs in perpet—in perpetuity"—he stumbled on—"as it is so here written and set down."

He was smiling, having gotten through the Latin phraseology; Skirzeny the buffoon again. He actually seemed to take a great delight in the legalese of the documents, for he began once more in the same manner without so much as a pause:

"Newman, the particulars are all herein included. You may inspect them now or later, at your leisure. Only do not be too leisurely. I think you know why. Skirzeny need not tell you. Read and sign and you have then only to have Frankel or your future in-law, the apothecary Geiger, notarize the transaction and we can destroy the documents I gave you so long ago and I can have back what is rightfully mine.

"Now then, you see, it is quite legal," Skirzeny continued, offering my father his documents. "Here," he said, "examine. The best legal minds were at work. I have taken very great pains in Debrecen and elsewhere to consult with specialists, experts, and I have been assured by these same gentlemen that what is here set down will stand the tests of any court of law no matter what the future brings for us, for me and mine. As you can see, Newman, the document is in the best traditions. It states . . . states in very plain but correct language that our little transaction is being made without duress or *force majeur* . . . that it is all strictly legal, a business matter, as you would say. Now then, Newman, what do you say?"

Skirzeny was trying to thrust the documents over to where my father was sitting, but, when he wouldn't accept, they fell between the candlesticks onto the tablecloth, covering over a portion of the spilled wine. Fearing that his precious papers would get soiled, Skirzeny lunged across for them once again. "You asked me for help," he said.

But Father's reply was icy: "And just how do you propose to help?"

"*Sign the paper!*" shouted Skirzeny. "*Sign the paper and then you will see.*"

But all his entreaties were met with a silence, all the more stultifying now because my father's quiet shrugging seemed to portend the negative, a definite reply of a sort. Father shrugged and was silent, waited and shrugged again, his hand up to his mouth to hide the curve of his lips, and when Skirzeny saw now that his ancient adversary and partner would not be bullied, his posture gave every indication that he was about to adopt a somewhat different approach to the problem. He belched and then he turned, at the same moment, so that his shoulders were facing me, although his head was still held obliquely on one side. "My stepson has said you have a very pretty fiancée," he declared, in the most neutral voice. "I suppose that was the young lady . . . with the fruit bowl."

He took a napkin to his lips demurely and went again, "Ech."

Miklos was laughing.

"Poppa," I started.

"She is a very pretty girl," Skirzeny explained.

"Poppa, you must listen to me," I said.

"Be quiet, Alex!"

"Ech," Skirzeny went another time.

"Mind your manners," my father admonished him. His face seemed especially haggard, rather ashen by candlelight, too, his lips bloodless, the bald pate sallow, lusterless, as unhealthy as Skirzeny's seemed robust. "Be quiet and behave yourself," he insisted, staring down at his hands while he clenched his teeth and compressed his lips until they were almost as pale as the whites of his eyes, pausing only then to glance up again, assured that his authority was recognized:

"Farnas, will you be good enough to let me see those documents?"

Father's right hand was extended, the palm opened. Halfway between each of the flickering tapers it trembled and throbbed, as if levitating itself. Meanwhile the index finger beckoned, rising and falling from off the mass of tired flesh:

"Farnas, please. This gets very tiresome . . ."

There was a sharp, almost strangulated laugh from Miklos, quickly cut short again with a cough, a harsh rasping swallow, and then :"Well?"

"Be quiet," snapped Skirzeny, menacing his son with his eyes while he again extended the sheaf of papers and let them fall to the table.

What we saw was just as Skirzeny had said it would be: very legal, very proper, a brief description of the property, a map, a search of the title going back as far as the early part of the reign of Empress Marie Theresa, then terms set forth, provisions made explicit, enumerations and liens all indicated and set into a rigid framework of wherefores and whereases.

The little Slovak clerk of Skirzeny's choosing had apparently been a man of conscience, meticulous in setting forth what was Skirzeny's and what was to remain ours. Whatever objects and pieces were not enumerated must have been beyond Skirzeny's recall: our curtains, our rugs, our lamps, our silver, only some of our furnishings. But only some. The enormous armoire in the attic wherein was stored my grandfather's and my father's military uniforms was listed putatively as *one armoire, glass-fronted with side curtains in the style of Louis Quatorze.* It was also noted down that the bath next to my parent's bedroom had a Switzer shower with fixtures of German silver.

Truly a remarkable document. It was made perfectly clear that upon a truce or general amnesty we could lay claim to all such furnishings and personal belongings as we could not now take with us and which were enumerated under a special column headed *Personal Effects Family Yagodah.* There was even a perfunctory disclaimer to the effect that we would have the right to visit our former properties if there were any relatives, servants, or family pets buried thereon, in properly marked tombs, and that under no circumstances would the final liquidation of our holdings imply that we would later have to suffer the accusation that we were trespassers, provided, of course, we applied for our visitation rights approximately seventy-two hours in advance of any intended intrusions.

Truly a noble document, written with a fine hand, tiny in size but also long-suffering, exacting, a hand trained in the old-style script, which in its transitions and circumlocutions seemed as adaptable to new orthodoxies of orthography as it was also to new ways of thinking—i.e., it seemed to accept every one of Skirzeny's rigid demands upon us while still insisting that there be certain slight formulary revisions in the text.

And would you believe it, Rubin—the monstrosity was dated in Latin with an *Anno Domini?* Guileless to be sure, without the slightest reference or hint or even acknowledgment or awareness that such and such a seal might be in questionable taste, considering the nature of the transaction. . . .

God save us all from the law: it can make the inhumane credible, the impossible seem necessary. Laws are like mildly grotesque acknowledgments after the fact that men alone are capable of murder, arson, rape, and genocide. Consider the phrase "legal fiction." In old Roman law *fictio* was a term of pleading, an averment, for example, that so and so was a Roman citizen when, in truth, he was not. The object was to assign jurisdiction, to make the deliberations of the courts possible. But we now use the expression to signify any assumption, *any assumption which conceals*—as, for example, for the purposes of probating Bela's bequest we will assume that a certain Alex Yagodah may still be a Jew. . . .

The fact is, in both cases, not only has the law been wholly changed but the nature of truth has changed equally. *It may simply be a legal fiction if we are still willing to pretend that the word JEW means what it always meant.* . . .

. . . So with all these pronouncements about equity and prudence, these fictions with their graceful scrawls and jargon-ridden texts, they implicate the maker as much as they indict the rest of humanity. And why not? How else should it be? Rubin, I have just realized that for two days now I have been trying to make you believe that we were only mortal, and I am going to fail—I know I am—because, although we may be—that is to say, all murderers—each of us, as they say, each has his own particular methodology and his unique set of victims. Each of us, when he kills, believes in the greatest of all legal fictions—justifiable homicide.

It so happens I have nothing against niggers but somebody else does and somebody else despises fat bald men with halitosis. Each of us, then, glancing up from our own cramped little lives to speculate about the death of six millions (or any other crime of that magnitude) may recognize and abhor the injury, but we are likely to perceive an entirely different set of circumstances or be baffled by such an exotic variety of evidence. To whom should we give the ultimate jurisdiction in these matters? Wouldn't those six million martyrs be equally bewildered if they were to rise from their charnal heaps and view the crimes we are committing daily? They would probably say, "It is just as we had thought. No

206

different. Just as we remember. It is the way we were until our murderers came among us . . ."

Too bad that I have such a fatal tendency toward melodrama. It is the vice of the *auto-didact* and I must learn to watch myself. I don't wish to convince you of a single thing with the abstractions of others. In this particular instance I am the only expert. I am on solid grounds and I must learn to stay there. As I glanced from the document-proud Skirzeny to his son—who was taking no particular solace in his father's fancy set of papers—it was clear to me that we had, at last, pierced through certain rather pedestrian deceits to an eloquence of viciousness; and that there was even honor in the act. That's what I believed that I believed. Some will surely tell you that Farnas Skirzeny and his papers were merely the recrudescence of a vanishing world, of vanishing standards and rapidly disintegrating values (which, although no less vicious than what was soon to replace them, nevertheless proposed a particular way of doing this or that and simply refused to surrender to certain anarchic principles of darkness), but do you see what I am trying to contribute, dear Rubin? I do not bait you merely because you happen to be a practitioner of the law. Every man to his own chicanery, of course. That is not my point. I wish you to see the intention behind the intention, that what those documents marked was the beginning of an entirely novel period of inhumanity for all of us. This was the final relativistic moment when all truly imagined, unlike any other brutal act in the long history of human brutality, that they were copulating with their shadows and fish could sing and pigs bid for *aliyahs* or delivered sermons—when, in short, there is no judgment and no judge, as the Talmud says, and thy Father becomes thy bondslave.

Written, as they were, by a certain fifty-pengö Debrecen clerk, attempting—as they say—to carry out every one of his client's wishes and intentions to the very curlique of a letter, it was such documents which provided for Skirzeny precisely the kind of life style that he had lacked all along. If, to his stepson, they may have seemed like a rather old-maidish and fussy way of doing things, to Skirzeny himself they had the taint and savor of novelty and revelation by which he was empowered with the ultimate truth: the law doing what you told it to do. You were then the master of abstractions. Caught between that way of thinking and the coldbloodedness of people like Miklos (who believed that others had to do what he, the law, told them to do) how could we help but be the innocent, impotent victims?

Were we, therefore, victims of circumstances? We were unique. I would not put the matter so simply, but I will insist upon our uniqueness. I am drifting again and I must finish before nightfall. I simply cannot waste another day of my life with these tedious explanations. All the dead of Europe are standing on my shoulders. The world groans and aches. Its teeth are chattering. If I wish to keep my family, my position, I must be done with you tonight, Rubin, or suffer in a way that even I am not prepared to take on. Allow me, please, to be done with my story once and forever.

Lacking training in the ways of businessmen, or the law, my mother and I (who had crowded behind my father's chair) were able to gloss Skirzeny's documents far in advance of Father who was studying every passage with an exaggerated judiciousness. Poor Mother. She tried to embarrass Skirzeny by outstaring him but when he bruised her glances with the blur of his eyes, she turned to those papers again. Those precise, somewhat familiar, but nevertheless hackneyed phrases, what did they all mean? I was forcing myself to expel breath. Our eyes met. Mother and son shared their puzzlements. She seemed to be saying: *But why, even so, is all this necessary now? Why can't this fellow be like all the others? Why can't he just take?* My first thought was to explain to her that none of the others had hated for as long as the Skirzenys, but I heard my father crinkling papers and then clearing his throat. He was about to speak for me, I thought.

And, for a moment, his voice did seem to float toward us from a different point within the room. Father was like a disembodied spirit: the words he spoke did not seem to be emanating from his rather stolid figure but from a point somewhere to one side, or even above his head. I hastened to my seat, anxious to hear all of what was going on from my proper place and perspective.

" 'And I do entrust to Farnas Skirzeny and his heirs the house, the land, and all its yield, relinquishing him from all further obligations to me and mine . . .' "

Father was merely reading aloud from one of Skirzeny's documents. Seeing me in motion he paused, then looked around and beckoned for my mother also to be seated. He continued reading aloud. " 'Know then that upon signature Farnas Skirzeny is once again master of the estate and all the properties which go by the name of Bellville [or the Frenchman's house], situated on the market place in the City of Clig, Royal province of . . .' " Afterward he said to Skirzeny, "Fair. Very fair," as he handed back the papers. Then he added: "It's very pretty and I'm sure it gave you great pleasure to dictate. But all you needed to say was 'I deed to Farnas Skirzeny, etc., etc.' Too bad. Such a waste. . . ."

Der Schike seemed puzzled. At first, Miklos looked pained, then he seemed exultant. I was silent, waiting for further hints as to what we should do.

But Father now remained silent, rather impassive, or perhaps reflective. Against the tablecloth, his soft folded hands twitched, as if struggling to break free of each other's grasp, but his face was still encased in an expressionless reserve behind which—if a turmoil raged—he wanted it to seem as if that too was under the careful control and scrutiny of his gaze which he had now turned inwardly upon himself.

For a long while nobody spoke. From outside, we heard the sound of marching feet. A patrol. It was past the curfew time for all. The troops stopped, moved on, were ordered to halt again, then moved on once more, banging against our shutters with their fists to signify that they were going past. What courtesies we still observed! It was always rather startling. I saw my father exhale so that the candles were guttered. I expected him to speak. Skirzeny was fussing with his papers to put them in order. Miklos reached across the table, offering me one of his dark cigarettes. I refused. He repeated the offer for my father's benefit.

"Nevertheless," Skirzeny was saying, "I assume you accept my terms, Newman."

Was he really asking a question, or waiting for some confirmation of the obvious? "You realize this is the way I must deal with you," he went on. "Your back *is* to the wall. Now isn't that the case, Newman?"

Father slammed his palm against the table. "What exactly are your terms?" he asked.

If I seemed alarmed, so did my mother. The grudging silences of these two had absorbed us until we had not expected Father to interrupt quite so surreptitiously. Why? When they seemed to understand each other without even bothering to make words. . . .

Or so it seemed to me! I was convinced that merely by the lengths of their pauses, or by the way they snorted, breathed out, and then gnawed, each at his own lower lip, that a strange, almost unholy intimacy was being shared, an accommodation being made. Was it still happening? Clearly Skirzeny seemed aware that the spell had been broken, or that my father had rejected him out of hand; for, even before I could remonstrate with Father to the contrary, the old drunkard was chattering: "Newman, I warn you, not to be such a fool. What is the matter with you? Where is your intelligence that you look at such an offer in the face and sneer?"

I decided to remain silent but my mother said, *"Newman,"* surprised.

"Yes, Newman," continued Skirzeny, "perhaps I have indulged myself but you should think of your wife and family. Take a more responsible attitude. There are others besides yourself. Our little arrangement is just. Why such false pride? From one of my countrymen I might expect this," he said, as if he had already ruled us out in that respect, "but from Newman Yagodah?

"Listen, my friend, we did not just meet yesterday. You and I, we know each other now how long—thirty years or more? And in that time how many businesses have we made together? How many times have I given you my notes and how many times have you lent with interest? Can't I ever get the better of you? Is it even a question of that?

"Old friend, you are hard pressed," Skirzeny declared, rushing his words together now. "I want to help you. I wish to be appropriate. Do you recall how I came to you that time when you first took away the property and begged that you give me just a while longer to make good—another month or two?

"Well, as I recall," Skirzeny added, "you were then living in a house owned by your wife's relatives under very crowded circumstances and you weren't very anxious to be charitable. You were just about to bring the bailiffs after me. What could I do? I have never been an aggressive person. I cooperated. I understood; business was business. You had won, I had lost.

"Did I bark at you? Highly unlikely, Newman. The place was yours on the first of the month. Now isn't that so? Isn't that the way it was? Some other person might have gone to the courts to get a postponement. Not so! Not Skirzeny. His word is as good as gold coins. I decided to deal with you according to your desserts. Now isn't that so, Newman? Isn't it so that—Jew or Aryan—I said we had to be honest with each other . . . and since you were my foremost creditor, I said I was beholden to you and I agreed not to make a fuss? Tell me. Wasn't that the case? So now that the tables are turned and you are beholden to me and the firing squad is all lined up and I make you an offer based on generosity and, as you admit, a sense of Christian fairness . . . what do I get from you in return? Evasion. Evasions. Nothing but evasions, Newman—"

"Oh, Newman," Mother wailed, "Newman! Newman!"

211

Father had been jerking his shoulders in a meaningless way after every one of Skirzeny's little speeches, but now his face was flushed, and he sat up quite straight. "What evasions? What offer? Have you both gone crazy? Farnas, in my opinion, you drink too much."

He spoke so rapidly that when he poked his questions at Skirzeny the old fool could not get in a word of reply. His mouth stayed open; his jaws hung apart.

"Listen to me," my father was saying, "I wish you would stop this play-acting, Farnas. Is this some new delirium? Why then you had better see a doctor. I thought we were being business-like. But where is all this getting us? Ilona," my father said, as she was stifling another wail, "why don't you listen? All of you. I see what I am giving you, Farnas," he added, "but what in return do you offer me?"

Skirzeny clapped his head with his hands.

"Stop that," my father ordered. "Why don't you stop your carrying-on and tell me, please, what you intend to do for me. What will you give us? Money? Passports? Evacuation orders? Immigration permits? Why not plainly state once and for all what you plan to do for us in return . . . if you want your respectabil-ity so badly . . ."

"Why bargain with them?" Miklos said.

"Shut up," his father replied.

"I am glad to see that you have some sense, Farnas," my father said; "I am perfectly willing even now to strike a bargain with you but, as you know, bargaining is a two-way street, and so if I give what you ask I must then have something in return. Now isn't that so?"

He was speaking as if to a small child. Father seemed very calm, still quite assured of himself.

"You claim to know me well," he said. "You even bother to re-peat certain old slanders about me in front of my family. Then how is it you forget so easily? I shall not make speeches. I simply want certain definite assurances. There are eight adults in this family and one infant. By next Sunday we may be scattered in all directions. Do you think I like to sit back and watch the dislocation of my family, the disruption of all I have built here? Well, what have you got to say? Can you promise us passports—enough for all of us, and by tomorrow evening? Can you provide transportation? Can you secure Swiss francs or dollars for my savings, so that we can manage to live where we are sent? These are the things you must consider if you are asking me to sign your papers, little Mister Skirzeny, and bear in mind please I will trust you only under certain circumstances—that is to say, you must attend to all of these things yourself . . .

"Try and stay sober . . . at least for a little while. Farnas! Stop making eyes at me. I am not some streetwalker. And don't go looking to your stepson for help. I will not take his word for anything. No, Farnas, I must have your personal word of honor, more than that—some personal guarantee, an assurance that every member of my family will be helped to safety. Come. Don't frown, Farnas. You can do this if you wish to do it. We are not children. You want something and you know I won't give it to you, even if it means my own misery, unless you act in my behalf. I know just how much influence you have. The war has been good to you. Why must we keep pretending? You must act quickly. Tomorrow may already be too late. Tonight. You must get busy tonight. If you wish to go through with this transaction, you must stop playing the lazy dog. I don't know what you will gain from having us all murdered. But you must make up your own mind, drunkard!"

I think my father insulted Skirzeny so as to sting him back into attentiveness, and then to calmly observe what effect his words were having. Obviously satisfied that he had shaken Skirzeny loose from his son's gloomy, contemptuous frown, Father became more businesslike himself; his manner was dry, quiet, matter-of-

213

fact, his voice hardly ever going above a whisper. In fact, I had to strain forward to hear all that he was saying:

". . . A very foolish mistake," his voice rose and fell. "Bad errors all. . . . Today my son and I and the girls were tattooed . . . no longer possible for us to pretend that we are not Jews.

"People will recognize our marks . . . constant danger of arrest and deportation . . . yes. You must secure papers attesting to the fact that we are a Christian family of Jewish descent . . . Jewish until the last generation . . . a family with much intermarriage . . . you know the kind of family I mean.

". . . Say we have been 'ransomed' by rich relatives in the States, Brazil, South Africa"—Father's voice rose argumentatively until it was now wholly audible again—"and that we are now en route to Zürich from whence we plan to debark by air for Hong Kong or Macao. I can provide you with a good currency to cover any 'gratuities' which may be involved, but you will still have to rely mainly on your own intelligence and connections. You can say, for example, that I have relatives in America. A brother. I can give you the name of the place where he resides. Again you choose, Skirzeny. I don't care whether we are to go to Lisbon or Istanbul. I leave that entirely up to your discretion. Choose the relation and invent the suitable place. Only inform us in advance of our departure. The rest you may carry out independently. . . .

". . . Or perhaps you will wish to smuggle us south across one of those routes you know so well from your little businesses? If that is the only way, then, of course," Father went on, "it will be necessary that we go that way. . . .

". . . Thank God," he added, "our passports need not even be forged. They must simply be validated for emigration. As you well know, Farnas, that is still perfectly in order for certain classes of Jews . . . so you must simply endeavor to provide us with transportation as far as Debrecen and, of course, you must also arrange to get our names and numbers stricken off the deportation lists. *The master list.* I'm sure there must be one. You will see to it. I know you will. . . .

214

"But," Father said, "if it is better to go toward the Russians in Rumania, and if that can be arranged, we will have to take our chances going that way, although I would prefer, of course, to go with my family West.

"Or perhaps we shall have to split into two groups or three. In any event," Father said, "the important thing is to be stricken off the master list."

When he paused again, so that his words might be thought over, Skirzeny was hunching forward, his face in his hands, not saying yes or no. Miklos was also a perfect mask.

I said, "I think I will go upstairs now."

"Stay," Father demanded.

He was speaking rapidly once more to Skirzeny:

"I don't imagine any of this will be so easy for you to carry off, and I am quite willing to go beyond this initial transaction in being generous with you. Farnas"—he leaned forward with a quickening smile—"if you are successful on all accounts, I promise to write from our final destination and to give you, by a certified note of hand, title to all our personal belongings as well, including the furniture, which, you are right of course, we certainly cannot take with us, and which I know you will want to have. Ah, come now, Farnas, you have admired these things a very long time. The heirlooms, the rugs, the pictures, even the gramophone—you will not find such an instrument these days— and it would cost thousands to fill the place with inferior stuff. Under the circumstances, then, as I say, I am willing to make over everything to you and even to add the first year's house money in good currency. If you like we will put it in as an amendment to the deed. So you have everything to gain from working for our well-being. Now then, how does that strike you? What do you say now, my friend? Are you still quite so respectable?"

Father was licking his lips like a cat, evidently satisfied with himself and his performance. He directed my gaze to Skirzeny then, who had turned quite pale, and seemed as if he had been seized by an alcoholic tremor, the whiplash to his previous state of high spirits. Inaudibly, he was grunting at us: "Newman . . . Newman . . . my friend . . ." He didn't even seem to notice our curious glances. *"What am I to do?"* he suddenly protested. *"I am not my own master."*

"Come now, Farnas."

"But what am I to do?" howled Skirzeny.

"Think about it," Father advised him, while he prepared to polish a bruised storage apple across his sleeve. "If you choose the course that is best for you," Father said, "I am confident you will be choosing correctly."

But Skirzeny's head remained bowed. "Why is it," he argued, "why is it you always like to make me eat goat shit?"

He was acting like a chastised schoolboy. Then Miklos made as if to mimic him facetiously; and he wiped his lips with his sleeve, staring at his stepson with undisguised contempt.

"You shut up," he simply said.

Skirzeny drained a final glass of wine and got up from the dining table. He bowed slightly toward my mother, but she was looking away. Again he wiped his lips. "Newman," he said, "you ask too much of Skirzeny. Much too much."

He suddenly wheeled about and went toward the door so that the surprised and agitated Miklos had to hurry after him. "Too much!" he bellowed, turning again so that the son was blocking him from our view.

It seemed perfectly reasonable, then, for my father to reply, glaring at Miklos: "Be sure that little animal keeps his mouth shut."

"Only trust me, *Ur* Yagodah," Skirzeny replied, turning, so formal and subservient that, as he bowed again, he found that he was bowing only to my mother and me because Father had already turned the other way. Embarrassed for Skirzeny, I also tried to look the other way. When I finally turned back it was because the second of our double doors was concatenating against

216

the warm night air like the sound of a gunshot. Outside our window the Skirzenys were scuffling along the pavement—a pair of frightened crabs.

Immediately Father set about to reassure Mother and myself that they would return by early morning. He explained that Skirzeny's greediness would not permit him to be the coward he might otherwise like to be. A fine hypothesis. Satisfied with his little axiom, Father departed abruptly for his study before we could put any further questions to him. "I will be up to bed shortly, Ilona," he simply said. Mother jerked her shoulders as she nodded. Then she got up and began to clear the table. A clock tolled more times than I had the patience to count. The final evening patrol had surely rounded our corner already. Alone now in the big dining room, while Mother padded in and out from the kitchen or the pantry, I tried to focus on one or another of the objects in cut crystal and silver still remaining on the cluttered table, as if by so doing, I could force myself no longer to doubt Father's analysis of the situation, and to consider the possible dreadful alternatives should our mutual friend and "benefactor" decide not to take such a risk, even for such a lavish return.

Mother said: "Go on to bed. You look like you have too much money in the bank." But, of course, my worries were not so benign that they could be soothed by mockery. Once one has tasted doubts about one's father (as I had done even before the Plevnitz affair) the mind is infested with maggots. All life tastes as bitter as alum; the mind is poisoned. This may be a sweetened poison, one which—like certain rich confections—is preserved or suspended in a wholesome jelly of optimism and self-assurance, or a sticky lump of libidinous ego. Still, as one is accustomed to gnawing his way through the crystalline preservatives in order to delight in the questionable fruit, so is one therefore sickened all the more; the mind itself atrophies through infusions of such a

217

questionable substance. No longer can it be sustained by the illusion of its own crystalline simplicities. Thoughts like *Pity,* words like *Truth* and *Father,* once absolutes, indissolubles, identical, guaranteed, meshed together, as it were, and confused like certain rich French confitures, come to the surface of the poisoned mind, only to be skimmed away like a sugary precipitate, so that one is presently forced to crave after even more exotic feelings, differing interpretations of the facts, perverse sympathies; and then, of course, that poison wandering through the bloodstream emits its final rigors, and one expects to be struck dead. Doubting one's father, one soon perceives how it is even possible to worship other gods, or, perhaps, God's mirror-image—oneself.

But why must I put you off the scent again with my unruly metaphors? Let me specify. I shall be as lucid and exact as a butcher's invoice: seated in our dining salon, in the lonely center of the night, I was soon able to see beyond every one of my father's assurances. Presently, I was also framing a series of rather disrespectful questions for him, each more so than its predecessor. I wondered, simply, if paterfamilias hadn't driven too hard a bargain at our expense. Then I ventured to suppose that Skirzeny really wouldn't return but would inform on us, was in fact even now going straight off to the authorities. I leaped across to other conclusions, made new synopses, turned extremely fanciful in my morbidities. Visions now perplexed me of my father lying dead with a neat, black bullet hole through his forehead, in the place between his eyes. Then I saw my sisters dishonored, disgraced, disembowled. The wedding scene of my dreams flooded my reveries so that my ears thrilled to the music and the dances but the bride and groom so happily in each other's arms were again Lilo and Miklos.

Presently I gave in to the horror. I framed my thoughts in neat little pictures, tourist souvenirs of the future, which visions might have prepared me to personally volunteer for the labor forces in order to save the lives of my dear ones. Only see what I was doing now! First I had envisaged an utterly gratuitous but horrible fate for all of my loved ones. Now I was hoping that they, in turn, would volunteer in my place, that we would all be as aggressive in our diffidences as diners in a restaurant sometimes are over the waiter's proffered check.

So that, too, was just another way I had of trying to save my own skin. A poison was sweeping through my veins, and I was corrupt, inert, helpless flesh. I saw myself so clearly that I had to look away, to cover my face with my hands and shut out the light, but even my features were jagged to the touch, as if reflected in those deep grooves and facets of cut crystal. My features also had accumulated a certain grit. Corruption! Cowardice! Ah, but I was only human.

It is a bewildering thing to know yourself finally. Seeing yourself as a potential parricide, you must either shudder or go about your business. I found that I wanted to cry out because of what I was learning but I also found, even more immediate to my needs, was a certain crass hunger. How could I still think of my body and its needs? What kind of low creature was I? Hadn't I eaten my fill? Beast! I was a swine, surely no better than Miklos, despite my pretensions.

When my mother came to take away the fruit bowl she frowned because I had stuffed my pockets with pears and apples, but she brought me a marzipan sweet from the pantry, and sent me up to bed with a cool kiss against my forehead.

That same evening Adam and Perl departed. I could not sleep for fear of more bad dreams; more precisely, for fear that my dreams might reinforce what I thought I now knew about Father and myself. A night of strange bird calls and sudden cries of alarm . . . when the darkness was almost something you could touch, and every glimmer of light was thronged with noises, insects, mysteries of every sort. I shall never forget the experience of being alone in such a sea of darkness. I floated on it, and it bathed my eyes, my every pore. The almond paste had left a sour taste in my mouth. In the next room I could hear Father mumbling to my mother hours after their light was turned out, but I could hardly make sense out of what they were saying, even though I went and put my ear to their wall.

Once it seemed they were copulating, which appalled me. I had not thought of them in that way in such a long time. Moreover, I could not understand their ease with each other at such a moment. Had they bribed me, like a small child, with a piece of marzipan, so that they might carry on as usual? Listening to what I took to be the creaking of their bedsprings, the thought occurred to me that it was Skirzeny, not my father, who was acting like the stud bull with my mother. I wondered what she was like, how it would be to touch her warm body in the act of sex. My depravity knew no limits. I imagined all three elders in bed together, naked, drunk, sweating, snagged among the stained bedclothes like a band of flabby satyrs in the various and unnatural positions of the sexual ballet.

God help me! The only way I could dispel such thoughts was to reach out, as it were, to seize upon the image of Lilo, to cherish it and mull over my desire for her, which only triggered me for the act of masturbation. Overheated, quite helpless and tumescent, if I still didn't attempt to do anything overt it was simply because I had enough decency not to want to flaunt my selfish behavior in front of my family. If my father was the way he was, I would still manage a certain reserve. Somebody had to keep a clear head if tragedy was to be averted . . . by which I meant, no doubt, that I was still a little envious of his illicit stewing in the room next door. How did I know? Perhaps it was not my mother after all. Perhaps my father had Lilo with him. The filthy old goat!

They say an old man is not to be trusted with his son's intended, for love of the son may excite him to lust for the future daughter. Well, I wonder. Although I did not dare to accuse Father aloud, my envy remained, a definitely muted afterthought. But the most prominent feeling I had was still worry, anxiety,

220

concern, and skepticism, if you will. You must believe me that this was the case. Lying awake, I found myself speculating again, as German searchlights crisscrossed in the sky overhead and then went out, leaving my room in total darkness; and I was functioning with an almost deliberately cool detachment. . . .

My father thought we might pass as baptized Christians. Winkleman! Pure Winkleman! Where did he think we were living? Did he think we faced mere social ostracism? I was convinced now that some people were ready to burn us alive. And father thought we might pass as Jews turned Christians.

I don't ever remember having strong religious qualms, as I think I have told you, and I could agree with Father, generally speaking, that we did not look Jewish or act Jewish. Just what did that have to do with our alleged baptisms? Did he think we were seeking to evade the municipal sanitary code? How would such an act save us when even those with four or five generations between them and their Jewishness had been called among us for the deportations.

Father was obviously a very confused man. His confusions could become dangerous and contagious. He had given himself over to lust and self-pity. He was cruel, cold toward me. Now he was abusing my mother. How could I allow myself to be guided any longer by his distorted vision of the real?

At one in the morning a single chime in the clock tower of the Jaroscrag roused me momentarily. A lifetime later the chimes pealed twice. Ponderous and judicial-sounding, they had the resonance of a judgment being handed down to us. So affected was I that my body squirmed, forcing itself further under the covers, as if hoping to be passed over by the certain morning light, left finally to itself.

There was again a muffled tolling, muted, I suppose, by the very thickness of the night. There was a crack of thunder. It dripped rain awhile and my curtains waved in the wet breeze. Then the rain stopped. I lay amnesic for what seemed like still

221

another lifetime, but perhaps it was only half an hour before I heard whisperings in the corridor outside my doorway. Somebody exclaimed, "Push!"

It was my sister Perl. Her voice cut through the silence. She was not alone. Obviously, she and Adam were attempting to make off with some heavy object which they could not quite shove across the landing onto the incline of the stairwell. They were grunting like porters. Going to the door, I pressed my ear against the paneling just in time to hear Adam's voice. "Not you," he was saying. "No. You wouldn't listen to me. You never listen to me."

"Less talk and more push."

"How dare you say that?" Adam replied.

I pulled open the door as Adam staggered toward the darkest corner. "Are you going?" I asked, mildly.

"Going?" mimicked Perl. "What do you think? What do you want?"

By now Adam had joined us. He was teetering next to Perl against the incline as they attempted to brace up an enormous steamer trunk, pasted all over with hotel and railroad advertisements, which had been Father's during his student days. The thing slipped and they struggled with it again until it held firm. Then Perl asked: "Why were you eavesdropping?"

Truly astounding insolence. My sister was obviously attempting to conceal the humiliation she felt at being caught in the act. We stared as if across some deep chasm. Perl was intending to see whether I would accuse her of anything directly. Adam's teeth were chattering. And since it was quite drafty in the corridor (and since I felt quite uncertain of myself, without my reading glasses, standing before these two in just my thin summer pajamas) I held myself back, folded my arms across my chest to keep myself warm, and hoped that it would seem to Perl as if I was trying to make it easier for her, so that she would not feel called upon to attack me again, or to feel bad for sneaking away at such an hour without bidding the proper farewells to the rest of the family. Believe me, I did not care about what she had taken.

But just as I was about to turn away, Adam blurted at me: "We have only taken what is hers. Now that your father intends to give everything to the Skirzenys we feel we have a right to do as we are doing. My father will store these things for us."

"Your father, Adam?" I began to laugh. I couldn't help being a little nasty "Do you expect this to serve in place of a dowry?"

"Why don't you shut up?" Perl said. "It's none of your business."

"No. It is not mine," I said. "Poppa should know what you are doing. You can't just leave without telling him. It can't be done. It can never be done."

"You wait and tell him for us, Alex."

"Yes. I'll tell him everything," I said.

"And make sure that you tell him *everything.*" She stressed the word. "Don't forget anything about Lilo and yourself, and what you have been doing behind the summerhouse."

"Perl," Adam interrupted.

Her eyes drove sharp nails at the man she was going to marry. "But," he trembled, "he's your brother . . . and you may be seeing him now for the very last time."

"And what would you have me do?" she turned on him again. "Rend my clothes? Should I tear my hair out? What?"

Her voice had cracked on her even as she spoke, so that she finally had to turn away from us, while I continued to stand in my doorway, scorching now with embarrassment. At last I said, "Can I help you?"

In a dry, different voice, which was not meant for me, Perl urged next: "Push. Lift. Less talk and more lifting, Adam."

Adam crouched forward from the hips, grunting with the weight of the trunk as he tried once more to incline it against his back. Then his whole body seemed to heave forward; he panted and gasped but the thing did not move. His arms remained taut, unflexed and impotent, like a pair of crippled wings. He dragged himself down the first step. Then the chest wobbled out of his grasp, falling like thunder to one side. Adam whimpered.

"Baby!"

Perl could not control her shrill voice. She clapped a hand to her mouth. Too late! The light had gone on under my parents' doorway. Father was limping along the carpet. I hoped he would not open the doorway, wished he would have sense enough to go back to bed. Indeed. It still seemed questionable what he would do. For, as we stood in our tight circle, as if paralyzed, Father, on the other side of the closed door, was now eavesdropping on our fearful silence. Presently Adam had to clear his throat. The door was thrown open wide. Grinning, Father confronted us: "You didn't want to disturb, did you?"

Perl's tight lips were twitching.

Next he seemed to be assessing my role in the affair. Because I knew that to protest my innocence would be doing my sister a further injury, I said nothing. Glancing from me to Adam, Father smiled. "I don't think you ought to stand here like this, Alex," he said finally, "unless of course you are prepared to help him with your sister's luggage. Put on your robe, son. You'll catch a cold in the night air.

"It is still quite damp," he added. "So if you are going outside I would put something on my feet and I would wear a scarf."

I wanted to explain that it was past curfew time and that we would be seen with such an enormous burden. "Father," I asked, "do you really think it advisable?"

"That," he snapped back, "is Adam's business. It is not my business. Put on your robe," he insisted, "before you catch a fever."

As I withdrew, I heard my father reminding Perl how I had once suffered from a rheumatic heart. A strange business. I went to my closet, selected a dark shabby thing with a sash, and found my carpet slippers. When I returned again, cinching the sash as tightly as I could about my waist, I observed that Perl and Adam had not moved. With my father off to one side of them, they formed a curious tableau beside the battered and overturned trunk. They were each looking in a different direction. Standing to one side, Father shifted from foot to foot on the decrepit landing, managing to glower at them softly. I touched the mezuzah so that they would be aware of my presence. Nearby, a pair of alley cats were brawling.

"I see that Fink is still going out in search of provisions," Father said, making a little joke at which nobody laughed except himself. My sister's lips were twitching out of control.

"Shandor," he declared, "be very gentle as you go down the stairs. The rest of the family is still sleeping. And Shandor," he continued, "go only as far as the alleyway. Be careful. I don't want you to be seen by the order police."

I nodded, groggy and afraid to contradict anything he was saying, even if I felt he was making little sense.

"Shandor," he said then, so that I now perceived that his remarks were intended mostly for my sister's benefit, "be sure to keep alert, son. It makes no sense to rush out into the night when there are so many unfriendly elements about. Be alert now. Don't let your sister hurry you. She will just have to be a little patient with you."

"Yes, Poppa."

In the gloom I felt my way until I came to the farthest reach of the trunk. What if I should fall at the first lift and stumble backward down the stairwell? I wished I could change places with Adam. I turned toward the light, my shoulders jutting into the darkness. At the other end of the trunk, hands in pocket, shoulders slumped forward, already breathing heavily although we had not yet begun to move, Adam slowly began to crouch with me. "I hope there is nothing breakable," observed Father.

Adam was about to rise again to reassure him that there wasn't anything of the kind inside the trunk, but Perl forced him to stay down by saying, "Can't you see my brother is waiting?"

Across her brow the eczema had flared anew. The suddenly

stricken cast of her face when she looked at my father, as if hoping even now to receive a farewell kindness, was more than I could bear. I looked down at the battered trunk with its numerous torn and faded stickers and labels. The only one that was still legible read:

SCHWEIZER HOF
LANDECK

"Well, Alex?" Adam was speaking to me. Embarrassed, I crouched again, to pick up my end of the trunk. It was like a dead shifting weight, as if inside a full-grown body was sliding about between our hands.

Abruptly, then, he shoved. I felt the weight against my chest. We were both heaving forward onto our knees, then a little higher, until—with our legs straightening—he was actually able to move a few steps ahead and I retreated tentatively, slowly, one step at a time, but having now risen to nearly my full height.

Believe me, I was sweating, and my hands ached. "Walk ahead of us," I whispered to Perl, but she did not choose to hear me. Perl remained where she had been, subdued, as if still hoping that my father would say a gentle word to her.

Then Adam screwed up his courage: "You must do as your brother tells you," he whispered. Perl frowned, but began to go forward, stopping herself to look about one last time at Father. Even when she spoke gentle words she remained a curt angry thing: "As soon as we are safe we shall send for the rest of the family."

"Your Uncle Bela said that to me over thirty years ago," Father whispered back at her.

There was no reply, just a brief wavering of shadows on the landing. "You will take care of yourselves?" Adam added then.

"Fool," whispered Perl.

She looked at my father again who had started to retreat inside the doorway. "You do understand . . ." she started.

"Go!"

226

Father waved me forward. He wouldn't let his daughter come close enough to say good-bye.

Which is perhaps why my sister strode over to me as soon as we had come to a rest and were standing together in the alleyway. The air was chilly. Our bodies seemed to be sprouting out of numerous moonlit puddles, and what we could see of the sky was bruised by many small clouds rushing by swiftly.

Perl could not bring herself to be so direct as to attempt to kiss her brother farewell. Perhaps she feared that I might also turn away from her. All she could do was to reach into her purse and to try and force something into my hand, ten pengö. "Buy your sweetheart a present," she said, pressing the money on me. She pushed me to one side, and took up my position beside the trunk. *"Lift,"* she urged Adam. *"Lift!"* When I tried to help her, she was the first to find the handle and she butted me with her hip, forcing me away again. *"Adam, if you don't lift this thing . . ."*

Perl never finished her sentence. Suddenly the trunk was upended. She had to struggle to hold up her side. She and her fiancé moved off together, their heavy burden swaying between their grasps, working more efficiently as they moved along until, as they staggered onto the open street from our alleyway, illumined for a brief instant in that space between our house and our neighbor's house where no shadows fell, they might have passed for any pair of workingmen one saw along the Szemos.

Presently they stopped to rest before preparing to round the corner. They were wiping their hands along their sides, rubbing them together like beggars. A shutter banged against our neighbor's house. A damp night wind churned the air as they fell to it again. Although I had felt sure that their foot scufflings and groanings would be heard as soon as they came out into the open street, I found myself urging the Higher Powers to watch over them once more until they had crossed the street and were again protected by shadows under that aisle of dripping trees that fringed the square.

My final glimpse of Perl and Adam came through the first floor window of our parlor, where I had immediately fled once they had dismissed me so that I could observe their crossing, but only after making sure the front door was secure.

Four bells had already sounded in the Jaroscrag, but about the deserted square the wind was riffling papers, posters, and other rubbish. My eyes roved from one abandoned kiosk where, in happier times, beer and spirits had been purveyed, to the empty streetcar terminal which was also closed, although plastered over with proclamations and other posters.

For a moment I seem to have lost sight of my loved ones. I was staring at an ordinary yellow bench, the kind one saw all over our area before the war, and I did not seem to notice that Adam and Perl had placed their trunk under the bench and were standing like statues to each side of it. Perl was dressed in a man's clothing with a little cap on her head. They seemed like workmen squaring off for a first fight. Or else they hardly even seemed to know each other. Not once did their eyes meet. Nor did they exchange any other visible signs of intimacy. The moonlight invaded their faces. Rain was shaken down on them from the trees. Shivering, they stepped backward into the darkness.

And, as they merged with the night, I remembered how in my childhood, Father and Mother had stood at the very same place, waiting for a taxi to take them to the terminal where they were departing for a holiday in Vienna. I did not want my parents to go away, even for such a brief holiday. Nurse had to restrain me from running outside the house. I was crying. Finally nurse let me watch them leave from the parlor window. She begged me to smile too, for she said I would make my parents very unhappy if they were to see me in such a sad state. "Does baby want to spoil such a holiday?" Of course I relented, forced myself to grin like a jackanapes, just in time to wave good-bye to them when their taxi arrived and their things were loaded aboard and they sped off toward the great terminal. For the entire period they were gone, I pretended that I was sick and, actually, I did begin to feel rather ill and nasty after a while.

Mentioning this incident now, I realize an important similarity to events that evening: although I was most anxious to see my sister get away safely, it is equally true that I felt the same sickly feeling when I had lowered our shades at last, and turned to go up to bed. Perhaps it was because I was so exhausted. I had not had a moment to myself since early morning, and I could not think about anything without yawning. My eyes burned and my teeth ached. The fingers in my hands felt numb, hanging by my sides. I realized then that I might never see Adam and Perl again, but I was too tired to question myself as to whether I was being quite honest about my reactions to their going. Perhaps I did hope that by leaving in advance they would strengthen our chances later, or perhaps I was just envious of their good fortune. In the darkness, I could hear my voice as a child, crying out to my parents when I thought they were deserting me and my sisters. Then I heard another voice which made me cringe: "You will see if Perl doesn't bring it off."

I spun about toward the center of the room. With a glowing pipe in his mouth, Father had folded his great body inside a heavily carved gentleman's chair so that when he spoke, puffing out ash and sparks, I could barely make out the mass of his white nightshirt and cap; a kind of ghostlike presence he seemed, surmounted by the soaring carved wings of his chair. Father kept repeating himself: "They know . . . you will see they know." Then he was silent again.

I wondered what he thought they knew and would he ever finish his sentence. Stubbornly, I was staring at the nest of coals in his crooked pipe. They seemed to breathe when he breathed, to glow a moment before his face glowed, illuminating the cast of his features until it was just a thing of hollows and shadows, a death's head, only momentarily come alive, but, even then, never giving any sign that it would speak to me again.

229

"Just what do they know?" I challenged him at last. *"What?"* My voice was even louder than I wanted it to be.

Father's pipe had gone out. He fussed with his matches, not seeming to hear me. I started to move forward.

"Alex, wait!"

But I was halfway up the first landing of the stairwell, my need for sleep dragging me on. "You are not coming to bed?" I asked.

Again Father didn't seem to hear me, or else he may have thought mine such an impertinent question that he didn't want to waste the breath to answer. "Do as you please," I grumbled. Cut off now from my father by the narrow partition of the entrance-way, I could say anything I cared to say, as I stood high up in the darkness of the stairwell, waiting for his reply to the questions which I dared not repeat any louder for fear of waking others in the house, but fearing, as well, that I might interrupt the silence he had carefully set between us.

Only much later was I to learn that Father had been growing slowly deaf for quite some time, but, just then, turning as I did to peer down the stairwell toward the empty parlor where I presumed he was again smoking his pipe, Father's silence seemed considered, profound, quite sorrowful, and so all-encompassing and yet vague in its borders and outer reaches that it couldn't even be contained by his strangely amorphous shape as he hunched forward again in his flowing white garments, a shrouded corpse, but enveloped also by occasional nebulae of smoke and gray cinders. "Old man, I presume you know what you are doing," I warned him.

To my surprise, Father replied without acrimony: "About Skirzeny—if you mean about Skirzeny—you needn't worry," he was saying. "Skirzeny will not go digging in our garden. He is far too lazy. He merely wishes to act the grand *seigneur*. Believe me, son, I know what I am talking about. Your treasure will be safe here until you return."

My answer was to shrug my shoulders and continue up the

stairs. I felt sure that Father couldn't see me where he was, but I really didn't care any longer. I knew then that I would never be returning to Clig.

Going to my room in the darkness I thought of death, my own and that of others. Strange. I truly believe that until then I had thought myself practically immortal. How much stranger still to be aware suddenly that if your father must perish so must you and that you may never again be feeling the wooden stair railing as something hard and cold against your hand, never again feel the breath catch in your chest, or argue with your own father. What had I possibly done to deserve such cruelty? An entire lifetime passed before my eyes and I was struck by the sameness of all that I saw. Not to have thought about death until then—to have tried one's hardest to live in a half-world of reasonable doubts and optimistic uncertainties—and now to be aware that death and extinction were perhaps the only certitudes—I tell you I found myself shuddering even while my head was nodding like a mechanical object as I considered such a possibility. My dispirited condition was such that, upon closing my door upon the darkness and stowing my robe on the peg in my closet—actions which I continued to carry out by a certain phlegmatic rote—I went immediately to my window, as if otherwise believing that I might suffocate.

The casement had been left ajar so that I felt the night's breath against my face and was momentarily refreshed. But only momentarily so. My room faced the rear of our house. Its one tiny window bulged over that same garden where my father had buried his fortune. As I pushed the casements open even wider, the strong scent of the damask roses was dizzying, almost noxiously sweet, with an air of putrescence. At the outer edge of the darkness the faint blue light of the pre-dawn sky was beginning to glimmer, but our heavy mansard, sloping over the greenery, still managed to shut out all the light so that I found myself looking down into a velvety blackness that was almost palpable, in

231

which the intense petals of the quatrefoils seemed to shimmer and quake, causing a slight rustling noise, after which their perfumes would be sent aloft, ever more heady and condensed.

Thinking again of Adam and Perl with their forged documents, again I heard myself crying out to my parents. The dawn seemed to be coming upon Clig ever so slowly. I wished that it would still be dark a while longer. Hadn't Joshua commanded the sun to remain high in the heavens? Look! The night was already quite diluted at the horizon point. Already I thought I could hear the strains of a distant barnyard. I forced my bleary eyes to search for the sloping outline of my father's various outhouses behind which, I knew, was that place where Lilo and I had been together so often. My slippers creaked. A bird sang at the fading moon. Still concentrating on that outer edge of the darkness, what did I hope to conjure from oblivion? I heard a sound, became aware of the breathing of another person in my room. Perhaps, I thought, my father has followed me up the stairs to continue our conversation. I waited for him to come behind me. Below me, in the garden, a shadow flitted across the turf. I heard the noise of a spade hitting the ground. Then I became aware that that steady rising and falling of breath was emanating from my own narrow bed where, as I turned, I could barely define another form in the turmoil of the eiderdowns.

"Lilo?"

No longer cautious that I would be overheard, I didn't bother to whisper: *"Lilo, is that you?"*

I seemed to be shouting into an abyss. A gray mistiness covered the room through which I could barely perceive another's shape. I feared stepping forward, not knowing who I might then encounter. *"Lilo, answer me,"* I demanded.

The soft slope of her body made me realize she had been dozing. I poked at her gently: *"Lilo?"*

"Alex . . ."

232

The figure stirred: "*Alex*," she said my name again, as if speaking to somebody in a dream.

"Be still," I said then, as I fell against the bed, taking her in my arms so that I inhaled the sleep from off her body, but, when I tried in a perfunctory way to kiss her (and thus to quiet her again), she pulled herself away from me, saying, "Is it morning already? Oh, Alex," she continued, "you cannot imagine what I have dreamt."

I pretended not to be interested. Again I tried to force Lilo to accept my kisses, pressing her face against mine until our lips were touching and I could taste the salt. "Alex," she merely said. "Alex."

And I said: "Don't . . ."

There was very little pleasure for either of us in what we did next. Not having been with each other for so very long, our emotions were those of perfect strangers, grating and gyrating together in a passionless spin. To this day I am not even certain if I came or just simply gave up on myself.

Afterward, we were rather too embarrassed to lie close to one another. Although I considered a renewal of such previous efforts, my halting words, my hesitations, my momentary gestures and caresses, were all quite unwittingly bestowed on Lilo. I would doze and wake abruptly, impotent as ever, then try to kiss her once again, but nothing of what we said to each other can I remember. Lilo had already slipped between the eiderdowns and when I joined her there she didn't bother to move away, although I felt her naked body stiffen momentarily. Then I found myself speaking: "Do you know how pleased I am that you are here?"

"I'm glad," she replied.

It was nearly light outside but we kept our eyes shut fast. Lilo said, "I should be going." After another moment she added, softly: "Do you want me to stay? What difference does it make? Where would I go?" she asked herself then.

233

And though I continued to paw at her arms, touching her hair, rubbing myself up against her backside, dipping my lips down against her shoulders, even as I tried to press myself against her body, Lilo's only response was to bring her forehead for just a moment to the point of my shoulder and then to suddenly expel another mouthful of her breath, her body now so entirely clammy that I felt a twinge of nausea when my hand lighted on the dome of her belly. I pulled away from her but immediately felt guilty so that I was forced to return again, after a decent interval of silence.

By that time Lilo had grown quite passive. She began to talk in a kind of queer monotone, not even seeming to care if I was listening to her. Once she started to tell me a story she had told me many times in the past about a certain girl at her boarding school who had wanted to make love to her. I allowed Lilo to continue until she said, "Can you imagine, Alex?" Then I nodded and her narrative abruptly switched so that we were laughing together about the coldness of the lake near my aunt's house in Lillafüred. It seems that Lilo had almost drowned there once, as a small child, when her paddle boat had tipped over. She claimed to recall that my father had saved her, that he had been very gallant with her: "You wouldn't believe such a thing about your father, would you, Alex?" She prodded me over and over again with such family memories. Now she was claiming that my father had jumped in after her and dragged her helpless to the shore. "You don't know how terrified I was," she announced.

"I know," I said, "I know," touching Lilo again, hoping to interrupt her, or, at least, to renew a contact of sorts. Pretending not to notice my hand, Lilo now spoke about her puppy dog Gustave. Her mother had poisoned him, she said, because he made too many messes in their house. Poor Gustave! He always used to lick her nose in the morning and his breath was like horse manure. Lilo began to giggle.

234

"Will you stay?" I asked.

"Of course," she said, "but isn't it nearly morning?"

She wanted to turn about so as to look out the window but I put my hand over her eyes and drew her to me. Lilo didn't seem surprised. I kissed the back of her neck. "Alex," she started, "what do you think will happen to us today?"

I tried to close her mouth with another kiss. "No," she said, squirming away again. "You must be honest with me. Please."

"We'll know soon enough," I said.

"Soon enough," she echoed. "That really isn't any answer. You are getting to be just like your father."

Then I knew that Lilo still thought she was immortal, and it chilled me to think of her innocence: "Like father like son," I told her as she laughed softly, playful with me again.

Very quickly I added, "We really shouldn't think about these things. It does us little good."

"I know," Lilo observed.

My hand had come to rest on the soft warm mound below her belly. "Don't poke," Lilo said.

"Don't talk that way," I told her. As I spoke, my fingers were parting the fleece, peeling back the lips of her womb, probing and prodding those familiar folds again so as to lubricate them, to ease my way for another penetration. Lilo remained unyielding, however, so that my fingers were locked in the entranceway between her thighs, caught, as it were, in a cold clammy limbo of intimacy. "Let go," I said.

"Not until you tell me what you know," she argued. "Just how will they treat us, Alex?"

I was anxious and tired, not even aroused, but still quite willful. My body was trembling again. I felt ill, quite without any lust for her, as flaccid as a piece of dead flesh. Listening to Lilo pout at me so feebly, expelling her words softly between those clenched teeth, I wanted to insist for her sake that all would be

235

well, that even her present misery could be avoided, but all I could do was to try to make her smile. "If you had your way," I said, "they will kill Father. . . .

". . . And if Father has his way," I added quickly, "Farnas Skirzeny will become cock of the walk and Miklos shall have your dowry for his Bracuta . . ."

". . . And you?" Lilo asked. "What would you do?"

"I should like to make push-push with you all the rest of my life."

This, too, was a lie, of course! Lilo had tried to squirm away and I knew that I must catch her again.

I felt that if I tried to force myself upon her now she would be bound to move away, but, if I could keep her next to me quietly, she would soon be content to let me remain as I was, extended, disappointed, even at the very moment of completion. My hand had fallen asleep. I needed to shift away from Lilo but didn't dare to move. Even though I wanted us to be entirely separate entities again, I feared that any sudden move on my part would only bring on further entreaties and renewed anguish.

Presently Lilo seemed to be dozing. I felt myself turning heavy-handed and going off. Rolling in the bed, my hand slipped away. The fingers were like pins and needles. Again, she woke and grabbed for me. "Why?" she asked, reaching for my privates as well, but I was impotent. "Why?" she asked again.

Once more I forced my fingers to slip deeper. Staring at the brightening sky, Lilo turned to me. Our lips touched and we kissed. "Poor Alex," she said. "Poor little mushy prick."

"Poor Gustave," I sighed. Presently I was asleep.

7

I AWOKE with my pajama trousers down at my ankles. My feet seemed bound together. I was lying on my stomach, my mouth stuffed with a corner of the pillow, one arm warding off the bedclothes. The sound of sirens was still ringing in my ears when I heard Father calling all the family to the cellar. Lilo had already fled. I remained rigid with the consciousness that I might have buggered her in our sleep.

They say you should pinch yourself to make sure if you are awake. Feeling as I did about our future, I refused to bear any further hurts. Let the bombers come. If we were all to be destroyed, why should it matter when or how? Squinting, my hand over my eyes, I tried to recall whether it had been as much as an hour ago or less since I had lain in bed, almost as I now was, watching Lilo dress.

She had shown very little modesty. I remembered the splotches of sunlight against her narrow body, the highlights in her hair when she shook it out before wrapping herself in her dressing robe. The all-clear was heard. As she went to the door, it seemed as if I wasn't even in the room with her; Lilo hadn't bothered to say farewell. Perhaps she thought I was still asleep. Let us hope so. For I did doze off once again until the sunlight became too intense.

Upon my second waking there was much activity about the house. I think my nose was bleeding. As if affronted by the sun's dazzling display against the bright handiwork of my mother's quilted comforter, I lay with my fingers pinching my nostrils, my head thrown back against the pillows. I felt brisk and alert, although a trifle worried about my nosebleed. My few hours of sleep had not affected me adversely, but it took nearly fifteen minutes before the bleeding would stop.

When I was washed and dressed in my best trousers and shirt I went downstairs, hoping to find Lilo at the breakfast table. At the first landing I peered through a patch in our tiny stained-glass window across to our neighbor's garden. The summer sky was cloudless; not a breeze touched the high straight lines of black shrubbery and box hedges. On our neighbor's lawn, a rabbit was eating grass. The walls of our house shook slightly. The rabbit's ears stiffened. Heavy trucks were driving past.

In the dining room Father and Mother were seated, as usual, with their coffee cups between their hands. Nothing about the way they greeted me was unusual. Father's braces were down at his hips. In fact, they both seemed to have dressed rather too hastily, as if they had already been out to pay a call. I observed that Father had brought his inkstand and blotter from the study, and there was a third cup and saucer—along with an untouched plate of biscuits—on the table at a place which I assumed at first was set out for me, since Lilo customarily shared her early morning repast with her aunt in their bedchambers. I greeted my parents soberly, thinking that Lilo would shortly be down among us, and went to sit at the place where this other setting had been laid. Just as I was getting placed, the frosted glass door to the water closet swung open and the overhead light clicked off. Out stepped Skirzeny, blearily nodding at me as he buttoned himself.

Our "benefactor" had certainly wasted no time in coming back to us, I thought. It was hardly half past eight by the clock over the mantelpiece. Skirzeny's manner and his unusually untidy appearance were a sure indication that he had hardly slept that evening. He stood over my shoulder, alongside my place, until I understood that I had usurped his position around the table. Then I moved on to another. "More coffee," he told my mother. She immediately went to fetch the pot from the sideboard.

Then we sat together like conspirators, my father the most restless of all. "Come," he said, after a moment, quite a bit more anxious-seeming then he had allowed himself to appear the previous evening. He leaned across the table, pen in hand: "We are wasting time."

Skirzeny was obviously uneasy about my presence. Not only would he not now speak when my father directed him to, but his fingers continually drummed at the tabletop, and his eyes were marbled with weariness, great agate-colored things which seemed as if they might drop from his sockets at any moment. Once, when I started to go, Skirzeny grinned, a series of quick revolutions of his bristling head on those neckless shoulders. Then my father held me back: "Are we to have more of the buffoon?"

"Suppose we are?" Skirzeny observed.

"Must we?" I said then. "Why is it that you two are always arguing? Have you come to us with good news or not?" I added, turning to Skirzeny.

"Of course I did."

Then he added: "Young man, your tongue is not half as sharp as you think it is."

"Leave the boy alone," my father said.

Our visions crossed once more as Mother was shuffling in with the fresh pot of coffee: "You must let it sit awhile before you pour."

Skirzeny said, "That is true in all things, *Frau* Yagodah," but it was clear that he was speaking to my father and myself. He shrugged his shoulders, and looked quite sly as he placed a cube of crude gray beet sugar between his front teeth. Inhaling the coffee and the warm condensed milk that was in a pitcher nearby, he added: "Nothing is too good for your protector, eh?"

Mother apparently hadn't understood. She pushed both containers toward his place. Then she fetched me a clean cup and saucer, a spoon, and another cube of sugar. "Please," she said to Skirzeny, "let the boy have some first."

He nodded. The pot was placed directly under my nose. He pushed the milk next to it. "There," he said, "you will forgive me if I don't serve you."

"Please," Father said.

As I passed my hands over the warm coffee pot, I could smell the vapors rising from it, but they were not particularly appetizing. Skirzeny was mistaken: this was an *ersatz* mixture, not at all the same as the fine rich stuff from Turkey or Syria which mother had managed to serve us the previous evening, but thin and acrid-smelling, like the smoke of stale Virginia. It made me a little nauseous. I couldn't bring myself to pour such stuff and I could see that Skirzeny, whose lips were slicked flat in anticipation of the fresh stimulant, was getting rather impatient with me for holding back even after the time had elapsed that was necessary for the coffee to have dripped through the pot. Skirzeny was staring at me like a fish.

"If you didn't want any breakfast why make me waste?" Mother was saying.

"Excuse me, *Frau* Yagodah . . ." Skirzeny spoke before I could get in my words of regret. "But why would you save it . . . *now?*"

When he laughed I remained downcast, but Father withdrew his pen. Then Skirzeny removed the two containers and helped himself to some of the brew until it spilled over the brim of his cup. "You pig," my mother said. She went to get another rag. I started to follow her.

"Both of you sit," Father said.

He was stern with us as ever, as if all things were normal again. "This is not such a fine time for any of us," I heard him say in Yiddish. "Still, I advise you to be as you always are. If we panic now we are truly lost. Save your indignation for a proper occasion, Shandor, and if you cannot sleep at night make yourself busy in useful ways. I do not want to find you entertaining your cousin in your room unless, of course, you are prepared to face the consequences for what may happen to her should she now become—"

"Newman, please."

"Ilona, he knows what I am talking about."

Skirzeny was squealing with laughter. He had understood the words, or had pieced together enough of our Yiddish to make sense of the conversation, and it titillated him so that the coffee bubbled out from his lips and began to dribble down his beard.

"You are a very offensive person," Father observed. "You are tactless, Farnas . . ."

Skirzeny seemed troubled by such a remark. He swallowed what was left in his mouth noisily, his eyes narrowing with puzzlement and fright as he assayed the insult for what it might signify, but, before he could take appropriate action, Father was throwing a napkin his way. Skirzeny wiped his lips with his sleeve, and let the napkin fall onto the tabletop. In a muffled voice he inquired: "Why do you continue to treat your old friend this way, Newman? And if you do, why continue to ask me for favors?"

"I want no favors from you," said Father. "Ours is a business arrangement."

"Yes," Skirzeny admitted. "So it is. But in these times even doing business with a Jew is doing him a favor." He pretended a discreet smile, but the insult was blatant enough, and when I looked away from him again to my father, I heard somebody shudder.

241

Father's shirt collar had come unbuttoned. The grey tufts of hair on his chest could clearly be seen. It was probable also that lack of sleep was beginning to make him ill. His eyes were now surrounded by heavy gray folds of skin; his hair, his face, his posture at the table, all gave off a generally frowsy aura. There were yellow pipe stains on his usually well-cared-for hands which, when they were brought together on the cloth, trembled and then fell away from each other; and when he opened his mouth to speak, even from my distance, I could taste the sour odors of his breath, the graveyard emanations of that same sleep-crazed body.

"Skirzeny," he began, motioning with his eyes that Mother should also be seated.

"Skirzeny," he started with a shudder again, but in the voice of one so tired that his words seemed to spill out automatically, without any special emphasis or accent.

A third time he said, "Skirzeny . . ."

But the gypsy held up one hand, not letting Father get any further. "It's not as if I didn't know you were calling me," he said, amused with himself and us.

Then he made us watch while he poured himself more coffee. The heavy tongue dampened his lips, went once across those wild red and black whiskers in his mustache. He said, "Newman, I think we should not go any further with this business until a certain Ujlaki is here."

"Who?" Father asked.

"Counselor Ujlaki," he explained, as if it was the most natural thing in the world. "You know who I mean. He is our friend in the ministry."

"But," said Father, "I thought you were to act in confidence."

Skirzeny had his hand up again: "Surely you can trust Ujlaki. He has himself a little Jewish blood."

"But why must you trust this man?" I asked. "Now look what your great friend has done . . . and yet you are willing to go on trusting such a fellow . . . What is the matter with you?" I asked, raising my voice. "Have you lost your senses? Do you think Mother and I are such idiots? Well?" I demanded. "Is that what you think?"

Father swallowed something with distaste. Then he tried to brush a hair away from his eyes with one hand while, with the other, he continued to grip the tabletop. I was accusing him wrongly again. I knew it, knew that he would not reply. I saw my mother start to say something that was inaudible to me. I got up to go. As if on cue, there was a ringing at the front door. Grinning at me then, Skirzeny bade us all to remain seated. He would admit our new guest.

Helpless idiot! This wasn't Ujlaki. A man with a donkey cart stood at our door. A gentleman from the patriotic society. He was making his rounds. Did we have any surplus fats?

Yes. Fats for the war effort. Render unto Caesar what is Caesar's. . . . There were, apparently, some people still making the effort and poor Skirzeny didn't quite know what to say. First he tried to explain that he was not the master of the house. Then he lied that the Jews had already been deported and that, in any case, as everybody knew, Jews did not use lard, or any other fats, for that matter. "That's not true," my mother said. She was about to go to his assistance with explanations but Father ordered her to remain seated.

"Believe me, fellow patriot," Skirzeny was now saying, "there isn't a bit of fat here. No fat, do you understand! No silver foil. Nothing of that sort. Certainly not! *What is my name?* What difference does that make? I tell you there is simply no fat."

Just then Ujlaki must have appeared. "At last," Skirzeny said. "Will you explain to this idiot that we have no fat? *None—none whatsoever . . .*"

"I will personally certify," the newcomer declared. Presently, our door was slammed again and Skirzeny returned, behind him a small, pale, bespectacled man wearing an antique sporting jacket, a wide-brimmed hat which he didn't remove until he was

243

seated, and long pointed brown and white shoes. The fellow said, "Enchanted," even before he was introduced to Father. He also bowed to Mother and myself.

Ferenc Ujlaki had Asiatic features, eyes like smoked glass, great black pupils, almost no hair. Now that I saw him I knew we had passed many times on the street. If, as Skirzeny insisted, he was really part Jewish, that would explain why he had never been a part of our community. I recalled that he had a son named Archangel with bad skin. The boy had been three years behind me in school. I remembered that he was always chosen to play Barabbas in the Easter pageant. A mean-looking, quite unhappy child, but nobody hated or feared him the way they felt about Miklos.

Probably nobody hated or feared any of the Ujlakis, and yet there was something about such a family which demanded no special courtesies, but, rather, the most cordially demeaning treatment. When Skirzeny's friend took his seat, hat in hand, his large egg-shaped head completely bare and pitted with old pock-marks, none of us thought to fetch such a servile-looking fellow a cup of coffee, and yet he seemed quite pleased with himself to be among us.

Finally Skirzeny spoke: "Ferenc, tell these people what you have learned."

"Not like this," the other man started to protest until he felt the pressure of Skirzeny's hand on his arm, nodded back at him, and then at my father.

"Your son—I believe I know Archangel," I was saying.

Ferenc Ujlaki nodded again, as if deferring to me as well, but he spoke only to Father: "Dr. Yagodah, I do not wish to seem overly inquisitive, but can you perhaps explain why some members of your family chose last evening to go on a little excursion?"

"Excursion?"

Father pretended not to understand. Mother started up from her chair, truly ignorant. "An *excursion*," Ujlaki emphasized the word.

244

"Never mind denying what we know," Skirzeny broke in then. "Your daughter and her friend were found halfway to Debrecen in the back of a lorry—"

"They carried false passports," Ujlaki added. "They were obviously trying to get around the law. When arrested they claimed to be neutrals. Very silly. There are no neutral Jews. The authorities in the village of Carai were not so easily fooled. They immediately telephoned our headquarters. A car was sent out to fetch the pair. They were—"

Skirzeny put his hand again on his friend's arm. "But they were," Ujlaki insisted, "you know they were." He got no further. Skirzeny had silenced him with a nod, and was again calmly assessing our reactions.

What did he expect? My mother was weeping, her face covered over by her hands, a ball of sorrowful flesh. As for my father and myself, we tried to control ourselves better, waiting for the rest of the tale to be told.

Ujlaki was sitting forward in his chair, so anxious to impart what he knew that we all realized he had been rehearsed previously. I went to stand behind Mother's chair. After another moment Skirzeny also got up, and went over to my father. He put his hand on Father's shoulder, would not allow it to be shrugged off. "My son thinks you are a terrible old snob," he said. Then, almost wistfully, we heard him add: "Odd how we grow away from our children."

"*Buffoon!*" Father shouted. Mother was twitching silently against her hands. Luckily Father still pretended to have his wits about him: "Why do you tell me such nonsense?" he asked dryly. "Farnas, what has happened to our daughter?"

Sighing heavily, Skirzeny gave his companion another cue. Ujlaki started to speak, like the prologue to a play:

"Dr. Yagodah, our police think time stands still for them, not being Germans. You can imagine how difficult it is to keep order when one has to depend on such hooligans."

"I'm sure you must have your problems," Father said.

"We do, of course," Ujlaki went on.

"But they are not my problems," Father added.

"Yes. Of course . . ." Ujlaki seemed about to apologize to us. "Of course they are not. Who ever said they were?"

"Go on with your story," Father broke in.

"Why, yes, of course."

"Of course I will," Ujlaki continued. In the silence, he fumbled with his hands, starting up again in what seemed like the middle of a sentence:

". . . The escape was managed in such a way that by the time our people arrived at Carai, your daughter and her friend had outwitted or overpowered their guards, two foolish peasant boys, and were nowhere to be found. A general alarm was then sounded. Presumably the couple had fled into the mountains. There is a wilderness nearby. Do you know the place? I didn't think you did," Ujlaki went on, with the faintest of smiles. ". . . And I only say presumably because early this morning—not more than an hour before I came here—we received word at the Ministry that a border patrolman had shot and critically wounded the man, as he was attempting to crawl across a mine field. I believe that would have been . . . your future son-in-law. . . . In any event," Ujlaki was becoming more brazen, "the poor fellow told his interrogators that he had been separated from his lady friend who was, I might add, also manfully attired. That is all we know. Only that. No more. He died before we could learn the direction in which she might have wandered off so . . . so . . ."

"So? Is that all you can tell these people? So?" Skirzeny broke in. "After such a terrible loss!" But he turned himself on my parents then, just as quickly: "Ah now, no weeping," he went on. "I'm afraid this fellow is not a very good storyteller, but it is quite likely, Newman, that your daughter found her way across the border, and in Greater Hungary it is not too difficult for a young lady to lose herself among the populace. So I think it is foolish for you to mourn or give up hope now. You should have thought of such risks earlier.

246

"However," he added, clearing his throat, after another moment, while looking out at us over the top of his fist, "there is some occasion now for concern. One doesn't like to predict such things but it does seem quite likely, doesn't it, that such a little adventure won't sit very well with Zingesser and his aides. Well now, doesn't that seem likely to you?

"Very likely. In fact I have no doubts," Skirzeny went on, without even pausing, "before noon I haven't the slightest doubts that you can expect official visitors. And then what will happen?"

"What will you say to such visitors?" echoed Ujlaki.

"They will not be coming to collect fats," Skirzeny added. He was going on so rapidly that it almost seemed as if he was making jokes to himself. I heard: ". . . This little worm knows . . . your back is really up against a wall now . . . adventures . . . top of the lists . . . twice as difficult for us to strike our bargain . . . this bit of goat shit knows . . . And so," he said, slowing himself again, "I bring Ujlaki with me. We shall need outside help which, of course, means that additional arrangements will have to be made. Am I making myself quite clear to you, Newman?"

When a man dies all the future corpses breathe a sigh of relief. What could any of us do, then, but continue to stare back at Skirzeny as if his news had struck us dumb? But that we were not, in fact, senseless to what he was telling us is proved by the fact that I became extremely irritable at the way he continued to tap at the table and smile. In fact, I cannot remember when I had felt so disoriented, and I seem to remember a sharpening of thought momentarily—as if some great plan had been laid out before me and I could see from end to end. The probable murder of their daughter Perl had not, apparently, destroyed my parents utterly. As I glanced at Father and Mother, it was clear that if they were struggling with any great astonishment, it was still only on the surface of their minds, as if—once again—somebody had sprayed that freezing solution over them. To be sure, all of us had suffered a loss. Unfortunately, the human tendency at such moments is to seek to identify gains. Were we truly bereaved or had we merely been divested of one of our dear ones? And wasn't that also to be expected if one was forced to deal with people like the Skirzenys? Thank God, I can recall myself saying, Adam and Perl were not a party to our negotiations, although, of course, I continued to pretend—along with my parents—that my lips had been sealed with an unutterable remorse.

Know, therefore, that I believe our silence was eventually quite unnerving to Skirzeny, for he grumbled: "*Well, you do understand, don't you?*" Then, as he was about to roll a fresh cigarette against his lower lip, the villain added: "So?"

"You are referring to my daughter?" Father asked.

"He is referring to Ujlaki," said the other fellow.

"You have made yourselves quite plain," Father smiled.

Skirzeny struck a stick match against his fingernail. "Under the circumstances," he began, "I took the trouble before coming here this morning to rouse the poor young man's father. Geiger was convinced to notarize our little transaction in advance. I didn't even allow him to look at the papers. You will admit that was a clever thing for a fool like myself to do, Newman. . . .

"But now," he added, "we must think about our friend Ujlaki here. He, too, must be recompensed, and he says he doesn't want to share in the property. Furthermore, I do not want to give him any of it. But his wife, she, he tells me, has never worn a proper wedding ring and he says everybody here knows about your lady's diamonds. Apparently the little monkey would like some diamonds for his wife. Come now. Don't be shy, Ujlaki. Have I said the wrong thing?

"Of course I haven't," Skirzeny continued. "If that's all the wife of this little worm wants you ought to help her. It shouldn't be too difficult for you, Newman, since Ujlaki, in return, is prepared to cross you off the deportation lists. Now then, what do you say? Will you and Ujlaki be man and wife? And shall we have a single- or a double-ring ceremony?

"Oh," said Skirzeny, as he considered his afterthought, "what sacrifices we make. How noble we are."

"Must you?" Father asked.

"*Yes,*" he said. "*I must, and I will.*"

For a moment his nose seemed to grow to a preposterous size and distortion, like the beak of some great evil bird, and when he spoke to us he pecked at his words: "I will. I will until I no longer wish to do so. And you are in no position to stop me, Newman."

Skirzeny's talk made my neck stiffen. I found myself staring at Mother's hand. Where it trembled open against the cloth of the table, the flesh was deeply creased and wrinkled so that I noticed the white scar of her finger where the ring had been only after I heard the clatter of metal against a plate and saw my mother push the sparkling object toward that Ujlaki.

"There," she said. "Take it."

Ferenc Ujlaki did as he was told. He held the thing up to the light, closed one eye, brought the thing back and forth between the light and his other eye, and, like a true expert, still pretended to be a little dubious, unsatisfied. To our surprise now, we saw him staring at the pair of solid gold earrings with antique pearl circlets which my mother always hung from her pierced ears. The wretch! They had been among my father's booty from the Lespedii campaign. I would teach him to covet what was not his.

"Ujlaki," I began.

"Shandor, please," Mother spoke. She placed a hand on mine for just a moment; then she attempted with the other to remove the things from her swollen lobes.

Presently Father volunteered to help. There was much silence, even a certain embarrassment, while he struggled to twist the loops from her flesh without causing any further pain. Once even Skirzeny was forced to look away but Ujlaki evinced no shame. He accepted each of the earrings after they had fallen to the table, held them up to the light, weighed them in his hands like a grain merchant sifting flour, and finally grunted that he was satisfied.

"So now," Skirzeny said presently, "all you have to do, my friend, is sign my papers . . . that is, once we can all agree on the newly revised terms . . ."

"What new terms?"

"What . . . terms?"

"Terms? What new terms?"

First Mother, then Father, then I was asking the same question, mere echoes of one another, except that Mother had her hands up to her ears like a child who has just been boxed for some unpleasantness. I noticed that my mother's eyes were crowded at the corners with a fluid which threatened to spill over if she but blinked at us. "For heaven's sake, what new terms?" she repeated, straining to keep her eyes wide open as she uttered her question.

Father would say no more. He was hunching forward, breathing hard, waiting to learn of this further blackmail. It seemed as if he could no longer look at my mother, as if he felt he had dishonored her. His glance was restricted to an arc that ran from myself, past Skirzeny, to where Ujlaki—still fondling his baubles —sat, baring unhealthy gums. I said, "Such impudence . . . such impudence . . ." Until I heard Father's voice like the whispering of a thousand ghosts: "Still he is not satisfied. What does he want from us?"

"Only what I am entitled to," the gypsy replied. "After all," he added, "who takes all the risks?"

"Go on," said Father.

Skirzeny was running his eyes along the many deep ridges in his hands: "I find your stipulations of last evening perfectly in order but my friend and I, we simply cannot do now as we may have once wished to do. It is simply impossible at such short notice to arrange the transportation of eight adults and an infant, to secure travel permits, ration cards, rail coupons, not to mention all the various currencies you will need. And at such short notice? Impossible, Newman. These are difficult times. It is not as one might hope it would be. We are all hard-pressed. Not only you Jews. All of us, the Germans no less so than ourselves. People are simply in no mood to be cooperative. Correct me if you think I am mistaken. Newman? Ujlaki?"

He looked up again as Ujlaki spoke: "True enough, I'm afraid."

"Newman, whether you know it or not, you are looking at two very influential men," Skirzeny continued. "If I have certain connections with the high officialdom, so does our friend over here. Men like ourselves . . . you cannot find them just anywhere. I am telling you all this because—"

"—Obviously you wish to bully me," Father said.

"Certainly not," protested Skirzeny. "Bully you? Why should I want to waste my breath on that? I am quite fond of you and your family. Bully him," he pouted. "Skirzeny a bully. Never. I merely wish to impress upon you the difficulty of our task."

He took one of our fine table napkins and blew his nose into it. Seeing mother's grimace, Ujlaki copied his friend. But Father only said that he wished to proceed. "Precisely," went Ujlaki, baring his gums again so that a kind of dog's smile appeared; and I was forced to hold myself back once more from attempting another unseemly act of violence. To do so I had to actually get up from the table and pace about, and my solipsism was such that by the time my ears were attuned to this new situation, Skirzeny had already begun another part of his strange recitation:

". . . Seven is not to be sneered at . . . count yourselves fortunate . . . a lucky number. Seven of you and no more than seven . . . one less than eight, and you can't imagine how much influence went into such a bargain. . . . A variety of friends, acquaintances, connections . . . I have put a lot of sentiment into what I did for you. You can't imagine how much. Think, Newman . . . seven of you free to go where you choose. . . . By two in the afternoon all seven and the infant saying farewell to this place . . . don't sneer. . . . Don't argue. . . . The best I can do. . . . All one can hope for. Seven. . . . Take it or leave it."

Ujlaki started to protest: "And don't argue with me," Skirzeny cut him short. "We cannot change any arrangements now; it is all settled. And if it must cost this family an extra fifty thousand to do the job even on such a limited basis of success, why then I am sure they will pay us and not complain. Besides, you are already well treated, Ferenc . . ."

"I know," the little man said. "You did not think I was complaining?"

Skirzeny waved at him to be quiet. "I do not wish to have you embarrass us with our friends at this late date," he said to Father. Then he added quickly: "So? You do understand?"

"I understand," Father said, but I assumed that his words and his nod were more or less involuntary gestures, mere tics, not necessarily signs of any acquiescence. Skirzeny, apparently, felt differently, for he signaled to his accomplice to go on with the arrangements.

Ujlaki spoke in a soft measured voice: "You will, of course, not be permitted to take anything other than a few personal belongings, some clothing, perhaps your books and articles for prayer—if you are so observant—and you must be ready to leave the house one at a time in any order of preference you desire. You must say your farewells before, however, for we shall all have to move quickly. Here is what you can expect: between the hours of twelve and one a common brewer's lorry will come to your side door. First, you must have signed Skirzeny's papers so that you can hand them immediately, along with whatever monies you have agreed upon, to the wagon master. Only after he has received such from you will he then allow you to dispose yourselves one at a time, inside the wagon, as he so instructs you. It will not be comfortable. . . . The best we could find at such short notice. Bombings, you know. There are very few private vehicles anywhere, and we had to find a man with the necessary travel papers. I think I should also caution you against talking with the driver, and there is the matter of your own travel permits. . . ."

"Ferenc, thank you," Skirzeny said. After interrupting Ujlaki, he waited a moment, as if hoping that he would now go away. "Thank you for everything, Ferenc," he said again, but Ujlaki's attention was fixed on a further point of contentiousness. Although his face was cast down, mock-serious perhaps, his long nose quivered at the point with excitement as he sucked at the spaces between his teeth with his tongue, again revealing those unsightly gums.

At last Skirzeny had to make his meaning quite explicit: "That will be all for now, Ferenc."

Ujlaki's surprise was such that he rose to his feet and began to back out toward the doorway, bowing so that he was nearly up-ended for a moment in backing over our threshold and had to grasp for a nearby chair to avoid a complete spill. "And you think I am foolish," Skirzeny started to laugh. But, when nobody answered the question, he was at us again even as his accomplice was fleeing from sight.

"Now Newman," I heard him speaking softly, as one might to a child who has been naughty, every word a condescension, "as to the person who must remain behind with us. The poor unfortunate one. Ah, but why should I put it that way? Am I not also remaining behind? Won't he or she take comfort in remaining with us? There will be no danger if we are all intelligent about these matters."

He stared at me as if suggesting that I solve everybody's problem by volunteering. "You see," he added quickly then, "Skirzeny has given some consideration to the problem and" (here I thought he was pausing to wink deliberately at me) "I have consulted with my wife and my eldest, my stepson. Now as to who that person must be this much should be obvious. It cannot be one of the men. Why? I shall tell you why. You are well-known and numbered. You are also needed. There are the labor drafts to be considered. It would not go easily for one of you if you were caught evading your responsibilities. If you think I am speaking foolishly you have only to say so."

Here, again, he held himself back for just a second, as if hoping to catch one of us in a contradiction, but there was nobody prepared to interrupt him.

"Well, then, by the same reasoning," Skirzeny went on, "it should be quite clear that the older women must also be eliminated. They would be of no help to us or to themselves in the months to come. And the infant doesn't matter. It would perish without a mother's care. Certainly. I do not want to have that kind of thing on my conscience.

"Therefore, Newman, under the circumstances," (again the pause followed by the wink and the pouting of those lips as if he, Skirzeny, would also test my father's so-called selflessness) "as I was saying. But where was I? Oh, yes, of course. At *under the circumstances*. How original of me. No matter. Under the circumstances, as I was telling you, Miklos and I both feel—and I am sure that a man of your wisdom must also agree—that the boy's cousin is, of course, the logical choice."

"*Infamous!*"

"Why, yes, of course it is, young man," smiled Skirzeny then. "You are so right. It is infamous. I am merely trying to do you a dirty piece of change. But," he added, "it is also your only choice.

"Your cousin is young," he went on. "She is passably pretty too. She gets along with people, and she could easily pretend to be one of us. If need be we would say she was our servant girl, or hide her at our cabin in the woods, or say she was only an eighth Jewish. Those kinds of papers are not hard to come by. A baptism can be arranged, and afterward your father will be good enough to reimburse me and mine for whatever expenses we may have, although . . . don't I understand that she has a fortune in her own right? No matter," he said hurriedly, "I am not after the girl's

254

riches; I am here to help. And my choice is logical, although, I admit, it involves a certain risk. But, again, no matter. I am more than willing to take such a risk and I promise you faithfully, Newman, that I shall endeavor to make certain that no harm shall come to the young lady even if she must be hidden some place . . . or . . . heaven help us . . . marry among us.

"What have I said now, boy? Why are you staring at me that way? Newman, haven't you told the lad how cousins breed idiocy? Oh, Newman, my friend, don't you turn idiot on me. This, I tell you, is the best possible arrangement. A proposition I am offering you and you must take it or leave it. As you well know, of course, the *Aktion* is scheduled in all events. I haven't much time to waste with you if I am to make the final arrangements. I have other business. So? Give me your answers? Will you now sign these papers? *Damn me. What do you say, man?* Hasn't Skirzeny dealt with you honorably? All in all, when you consider the thing as a whole, I have given you fair value. Yes or no? I expect you still have a tongue. Use it, man. Use your tongue, Newman. There. What do you say? Speak!"

Although Farnas Skirzeny was slapping the table with his palm like some petty apoplectic official in the Ministry of Taxation, nobody would give him his answer.

Have you any idea why?

Surely, if you don't understand that much, I am banging my head against this wall of language foolishly. I cannot go on, Rubin. I bang my head again and again and with head bleeding I withdraw. Then I must proceed again which I just can't do. It is not my purpose in life to instruct the ignorant. The morally smug will have to learn from bitter experience.

If you construe the silence of my dear father as a conspiracy (or even as acceptance of such impossible terms) then I am afraid you are condemned to your *amerikanishe* stupidities; and I pity you—washing machines and all. Yes. Pity! In this prison house of language it may sometimes seem that we were all bewitched by Skirzeny's rhetoric (and that I am even now bruising my reason against certain hidden implications) which is simply not so. None of us were so foolish or so callous to believe all that he told us, word for word, stipulation by stipulation, or to dare to entrust such a fellow with one of our own. I tell you we were civilized people, especially Father. He was Lilo's guardian. In law he was responsible. His inability to contradict merely proved his powerlessness and impotence and not some truth about his character *per se*.

In truth *per se* my father knew only too well that no man can trade lives for lives, or this one over that one, one above the next. We were enlightened people. All life was precious to us. We thought such choices are never permissible. As it is written: "Love thy neighbor as thyself . . ."

I swear to you, moreover, that my father was a wise, a just, a liberal and a decent man, with a keen sense of the social realities, ruthless only by necessity but certainly not one who would let mere expediency determine his behavior. Why should I have to defend such a man? He has proved his innocence. He is dead. Times have changed a good deal since there were men like my father controlling people's destinies and perhaps, being a bit of a parvenu, you are not even shocked by such an alternative. Then you are the one who is bewitched, or else you have never lived by the pretenses that were ours.

Good for you! If you have never had to pretend or to worry about your pretenses being violated, it may be easier to deal with certain superficial types of reality, not to be consumed by life's hell fires but to warm one's hands, as it were, over the dying coals. That was never possible for us. Try to understand. Never before had any of us been confronted with such a choice. We had always put pretense between us and such choices. We were sentimentalists. We believed. This perverted alternative cut us into little pieces.

You must believe that on all previous occasions, when—for

example—the deportations first began, my father had argued in a principled way that it was better for our own people to make the choices than to allow the Arrow Cross to do so because, he said, "We can at least be more gentle and helpful than they are and consequently make our friends' ordeals a little easier." Does that sound to you like barbarism? Do you think it was pleasant for such a man to have to say such things? As it is written in Proverbs (11:26): "Him who monopolizes grain the people curse—but blessings upon the head of him who distributes it." And in Isaiah (10:1-2) it is set down: "Woe to those who enact unjust statutes and write oppressive decrees." But how my head aches with these language games! If only I could describe, no more explanations. If only it were possible to draw the curtains on the past with its rules and principles and to perform for you now like certain acrobats of light, or to tell you merely how we felt. You must understand, however, that it was never possible to do so when one felt it as an obligation to cast aside personal feelings and emotions and to act in a principled way, out of a sense of "superior duty."

Even now, as I sit here rereading all of Skirzeny's cajolements and wheedlings, his bluffs, his hesitations, all his stilted attempts at warmth, courtesy, grandiloquence, I feel bruised in every part, as offended as if I had been slapped hard in the face, and by what he was to suggest, as well as by what we finally were to do. I tell you, Rubin, our fate *was* "the interaction of the perpetrators and the victims." That is why I have strained so hard to reproduce every twitch of language, all that Skirzeny and Ujlaki had to say, the unimportant as well as the important things, their gestures, ours, the way we slurred at each other, slowing ourselves down and speeding up again as determinations flagged. I want you to try to find your way in this language jungle not because I wish to inflict our punishment on you but because I need to make you understand the kind of adversaries that faced us, to bring some light into the darkness of that time. Only so will you finally be less glib. At last you will understand that what was destroyed

257

was not a house of cards, and that it did not happen through some momentary quirk of fate but was the culmination of our history.

That is the solid barrier on which I bruise my skull. Skirzeny's mercy toward us was the mercy of one who felt we were "determined by fate to perish." And were we any less convinced believers in such a dream? We shared the same deliriums, woke and then went to bed again, bound together by the same tremors. The myth was that we were "doomed" to "race extinction." Perhaps it was but another "legal fiction" or perhaps there was some truth to such an ancient religion, but if either is the case, your late client's question can now be answered: There are simply no more Jews anywhere.

Hard to believe it when it is put that way, I know. Harder still to disprove, however. You would like me to say I am such-and-such and let the matter rest there, with all due respect for its pettiness, but is that possible for me, Rubin, caged as I am by language, by history, by myself? No. You will have to let me play my own little tunes on the fiddle. Then you may criticize the fingering. But try to bear in mind: these pages can only reflect the naked brash ultimatums of those minutes together when it still seemed to all of us that a soft word, a smile, a shrug, a twitching of the eyes, could help to soften the harsh profile of reality and make it seem more credible in terms of what we were and could reasonably hope to be. My father had known Farnas Skirzeny nearly forty years. Was he now to suddenly stop trusting in him? To disbelieve in Skirzeny meant that Father could no longer believe in a part of himself, in his own life. Likewise one must mention the Germans. As we felt toward Skirzeny, so we wanted to feel toward every German. When one lives in a cesspool, those who walk along the gutter seem like kings. Do you see what I mean? What would you say if I told you that we just had to look at our experience through the other fellow's eyes? And if you ask me what did we actually think, how did we actually respond, that, I'm afraid, is another matter, not so easily set down in the imperfect first person.

To begin with, let me say that from that moment my father was to adopt a new identity, a new personality. The honest man of affairs became a murderer. You could see it in the way he walked. Father's crime was implicit in every one of his gestures from that day on, as if he had felt a sudden blow across the legs. My poor father. Forty years he had slept with a devil, and thus was conceived the incubus or dybbuk or what-have-you who was later to be his murderer. And you wonder how one can be bewitched by language? Poor Father. Our murderer. . . .

I suppose Mother was more fortunate because she had always been allowed to seem the weaker of the two, and had her supposed weakness to disguise herself; when Father began to play his little tune Mother did not dance with the rest of us. She surrendered to a yielding, a softness, to frequent outflowings of tears, fits, brief moments of naked unguarded hysteria, the final diminution of her person. Whereas Father slowly crumbled from within himself, corroded and consumed by his own complicity, Mother merely wept when she was spoken to, keeping her feelings that way at an arm's distance from herself. In the days to come she was hardly ever lucid. If the loss of Perl was simply too great to be endured, she thrust it away from herself, pretending it had never happened, shrugged her shoulders, wept, and began to speak to us in parables that never quite came the full circle to touch on some meaning.

My father was trying to live with his loss (as he might accommodate himself to anybody) by acting as if his life was a ruthless business of sorts which did not allow its dealings to be disguised by sentiments, but Mother was all suffering and sentiment, withdrawn inside a circle of grief no bigger than the span of her arms; here she was herself intact, and here she suffered. Here, too, she was able to preserve herself from my father's kind of anguish. Strange, to see the two of them together in those days. Sometimes

Mother would cry without provocation, when nothing at all was being done to her. I am sure Father wanted to rush to her at such times and shake her by the shoulders, or slap her face, but he did not; he held himself back. Mother was never disciplined and Father was never contradicted.

The worst thing of all was that Sarah and myself both chose to ape him at this point; we were weak yet we too tried to face up to the real and merely bruised ourselves against it, failing to see what was finally there. Sarah grew melancholic; I became agonizingly placid, hating myself as much for not wanting to shed crocodile tears as for the ways I truly acted. I had a continual siege of tightness and soreness of the throat but no purgation of sorrow. The misery of it all.

Perhaps I am being too vague, too general, in what I say. Bear in mind, please, how painful it still is for me to do otherwise. I feel as if all my senses have been drained away. My eyes are imbedded in concrete. They are full of sand. My neck is also stiff and grimy; I cannot turn from side to side to put what I am seeing into its proper perspective but must look straight ahead, toward a blank wall. How can I be specific? To be so at this moment is to tell you who said what to whom and then how the other party replied, and so on and so forth. You say it would be an act of very great courage, stamina, not a torture for me, I suppose, but possibly requiring more resources than I can conceivably summon, but you are such a naïve young man. Nonsense! How can I talk to myself as if I were you? Forgive me, Rubin. You would not believe it but I have been living on little besides black coffee, scraps of bread, raw fruit. Physically I am exhausted. I do not truthfully know how much longer I can keep myself going. I want to splash cold water on my face, to walk out into the cool night and sit under the stars, to have my Esther rub my neck and shoulders, to lie back and smell the scent of the desert with its soft feathery breezes, to plunge into the icy waters of the Szemos. Here all is tepid water and sweat, and if I do as my instincts direct me I shall only be disappointed. Moreover, I shall never want to come back to this desk again, to look at these crabbed pages, to think, to remember.

Surely you must have noticed how, when I try to recall the exact course of events on that day so long ago, memory boggles. Yes. Though my recall seems otherwise quite as it should be, I find in this matter alone that I must continually resort to self-justifying slogans, generalizations, obfuscations. It is as if I no longer knew how to be specific. A man of my class. What am I trying to avoid? A man with my intelligence.

I should tell you that whereas my frontal lobes are not highly developed I know from my training as a technician that mine is an extraordinarily well-developed mind, a brain capable of great subtleties. As if you hadn't guessed that much on your own initiative.

I should also tell you that I don't believe in guilt. Did I tell you I did? Yes. I am a liar. We are all guilty! What am I trying to avoid? Were we truly like oxen being led to the block? Did we truly object when this one rather than that one was picked out? How? What did we say?

You know I am really not an honest man but a whore. I don't know the difference between true and false or whether I'm thinking or not. And when I try to discard all these lugubrious sentiments and attitudes, hoping in that way to locate in myself what may be real, I find the shadow of only another catch phrase and I cannot seem to jump over that gossamer thing and know with any certainty what lies beyond it.

Don't you see what this may mean? It is as if we too had been distorted by the so-called "language rules" of SS and SA, as if we—not they—are now bearers of certain secrets—about events in our own lives. An Eichmann could be more frank than people like myself because, as he said, he was never touched in an intimate way by what he chose to do. Eichmann was a Nazi! What am I? What was Father? Thus we have the spectacle of a man standing aside to survey the spectacle of his own ugliness.

Adolf Eichmann put on a show for the court. He enjoyed doing so. I know whereof I speak. I too would enjoy doing these things if I could but suspend a *frisson* of memory. But, you see, I don't dare. I have never dared. That was my trouble. Yes. I have never dared. My mind is a granary, filled with human-interest stories so colorful and vile that they could fill a hundred novels, if only I could set them down as I think of them. But I am unable. Not me. I can't. I am as humble as dog shit. It is as if all those specific instances ran along a different groove in my memory, and such a recorded memory was proof against reason, argument, self-knowledge, all that we think of when we speak about the paraphernalia of the civilized man. I just don't seem to want to remember what I can never forget. My compulsions are no less real because they wear the disguises of reticence. I know, for example, a man in this settlement who pretends he is deaf. It so happens he is only hard of hearing. They punctured his eardrums at one of the camps, a medical experiment. Yet because people think he is deaf they have stopped talking to him and do you know—he has stopped listening for their words. Thus the man is as good as deaf even though he still hears. The poor man. I understand him well. He is one of us. Why should he try to hear if somebody has taken the trouble to puncture his ears? Why should we try to recall what was turned into cinders and fertilizer?

Why are you forcing me to remember these things?

That Lilo's mother's father was called Spitzer. . . .

That Skirzeny's other children were named Zoltan, Imre, Mary, Eva, John . . . and Paul. . . .

That the road from Clig to Debrecen was the color of blood after a rainstorm. . . .

Or that Grandfather Fass had carved on his tombstone: "I acknowledge all!"

You could make a tape recording of all my memories! What would you learn of relevance? That when my father felt put upon (or when there was too much tension) he sometimes had the nasty habit of sniffling mucus through his nostrils.

Yes. It's true. It doesn't mean he felt guilty, or wasn't civilized.

262

Some people probably thought my father was asthmatic, or took snuff. Nonsense. He was an extremely temperate man in all important respects who, unfortunately, would only let this habit get the better of him in moments of real stress. Then, and only then, an expression of evident distaste would mask his calm face as he would taste what was leaking into his mouth and throat. If nobody was looking, he might also spit into a handkerchief. What we children hated the most was when he would occasionally try to swallow the stuff. It is contemptible to watch your parent doing such a thing, but the gesture was so characteristic of Father that he would do it even when he was well, had no catarrh, no running nose, or problems breathing. Father was the type of man who would rather eat his own fluids than make a big show of things by expelling them in public.

I wish to stipulate this because it is a fact that when Skirzeny had presented his ultimatum to us, Father exaggerated his usual nose-sniffling performance, and my mother, as was customary with her, reached over to hand him the handkerchief. Father's frown then made her swallow loudly; his haggard features were directing a constant warning to all of us that we should not be too familiar with him.

Meanwhile I was trying to find a way to be courageous. I would have liked to formulate some way of telling Skirzeny unequivocally that we were going to refuse his offer. If necessary, I would have liked to say that I would stay behind in place of Lilo. Thinking of my beloved I found myself shamefully aroused again, although my mind was wandering beyond our initial sex together to moments in our childhood at Lillafüred and elsewhere. I thought I heard Skirzeny coaxing Father to come to a quick decision. To this day I cannot tell how long it was that we sat together silently, but I recall my mind like single frames in an old motion picture, flashing quickly past the naked figures of Lilo and Miklos, past the crowded square and the mobs churning together as if in a whirlpool while "the song of the good comrade" made a mockery of our community, and, in the course of all these

263

ruminations, I finally chanced to glance up toward the doorway to the kitchen. "Poppa . . ." I stammered, aphasiac with grief "Poppa, look please, Poppa look!"

Lilo was rocking against the doorjamb.

Prisoner of my own blushes, I thought I heard Skirzeny bid her good morning. What did I hear? What did I truthfully see? It was as if a curtain on a stage had abruptly parted and an ugly thing was disclosed which everybody knew had been hiding there from the beginning.

Lilo held me in her gaze, forcing me to repeat my chant of "Poppa . . . Poppa." What was the use? She was indiscreet. She had come at precisely the wrong time. If Father was aware that Lilo stood behind him, he still did not turn around. "Come in. Be seated," he merely said, as if to anybody.

Then Mother uttered a shrill, stifled animal squeal and I went to her, but Father was still acting as if he had heard nothing. Skirzeny was also silent, as if fascinated by the knottiness of the situation he had helped to shape. He seemed to want to appear inconspicuous, did not look once at Lilo. Nor she at him. But her eyes were burning holes in my father's back.

"You should be seated," I whispered then, unaware that my words might be construed in the wrong way. Lilo remained stubborn. She would not come forward. I left my mother to go for her, to force her to come with me around to the other side of the table.

Lilo waited until I came close. Then she slapped me hard across the face and rushed the other way, behind Skirzeny's chair until she came to a place alongside my father, in my former seat. Pretending a cynical indifference to all, she next folded her hands on the table, a mocking imitation of my father's posture. She also sniffled and her voice was quite shrill, as if in exaggerated imitation of her real anger.

"We deserve everything," Lilo said. "Look what we would do to each other."

264

"But," I tried to explain, "Skirzeny was only making a proposal and we were merely listening to the fullness of what he had to say."

"Quite right. Excuse me," Lilo said, after another deadening moment of silence. She gave me a look, the innocence of a doll's face: "I hope I didn't interrupt you men of affairs.

"And Uncle Newman," she went on in her strange unblinking coldness of tone, "I know surely you have been kind enough to suggest certain alternative possibilities to this filth. . . .

"I'm sure you have already done that," Lilo said.

Only Skirzeny responded to her words with a shudder. Growing red in the face, he seemed to want to reach out for her folded hands, as if to paw at them like an animal. The truth is he very near touched her before I intervened.

"Don't you dare!"

"Shandor. Mind yourself."

Father was routed from his reverie. He seemed alarmed but when Skirzeny said, "I was merely being humane, like you," Father bowed his head and was silent again.

I was kneading my hands together. Lilo pretended to be amused. Skirzeny lit a fresh blond cigarette, and blew the smoke at my face. "You are a monster," I started to say.

But my father was also speaking: "Lilo, even if we do what this fellow asks of us it can only be for a little while . . ."

"Even?" she asked.

"Even?" went her voice a second time, her eyes widening now and also turning bloodshot.

I said, "Father, do you mean by that . . . that you . . . you will possibly . . ."

Father was nodding quickly, hoping to interrupt.

"But," I said, "possibly to consider such a matter. . . ."

"So you have considered the matter and decided," Lilo remarked flatly.

"Please," I went. "Please."

"You would consider leaving me with these people?" Lilo demanded.

"Please. Please. Please, Father. Please."

"You would do this to me . . . now . . ." Lilo said.

I was gripping the edges of the table with both my hands. My anger pricked inside me until it blossomed into a shout: *"I will not leave Lilo. I will stay. I will not leave. Oh please, Father, please. We cannot leave her behind. Let me stay. Don't treat me like this. Let me stay. I must. Please. Oh please. Let me be a man for once in my life!"*

When I could think of no further variations on such a plea, I let my head fall into my hands, crying out: *"Why? Why can't I?"*

Skirzeny spoke first: "He is already quite gallant."

"You," I said. "What do you know?" But my father was also whispering at me:

"Shandor, what would you be accomplishing now by risking your life? Stay if you like. You are certainly old enough to make that decision by yourself. But don't let this girl fool you. You cannot do her any good by staying. Indeed. You will only be making it more difficult for Lilo . . . as well as your whole family . . . but stay if you like . . ."

"How can you tell him to stay?" my mother demanded. She turned on my father to repeat her accusation: "How can you tell us such things?"

"There now," Lilo said. "There now, Aunt." She took my mother's hand in hers and would not let her twist it away.

"Don't hate me, Aunt," she went on, fondling the splayed fingers. "You must not hate me. Why should you?"

Lilo took note of the streak of blanched flesh where my mother's wedding ring had been; she jostled the hand in hers, as if weighing it. Presently Mother seemed calm again. Lilo spoke next in a matter-of-fact way. The room seemed to shudder. She was addressing Skirzeny:

266

"Your son is a demented animal. Do you understand me? If we were not in the presence of loved ones, I would tell you some things about him. Your son is a criminal. He should be destroyed, just like a criminal. Would you have me stay as your guest, believing such things? Wait. You will listen to me. If I stay behind I shall have nothing to do with your son. If he comes near me again I shall kill him, no matter what the consequences may be. Will you tell him that?

"*Will you be sure to tell him that?*"

My father said, "Skirzeny has sworn he will protect you."

"*Shut up, old man!*"

She was trembling as if with a seizure: "*Will you tell him that he must leave me alone?*"

The great shaggy head dropped once with a nod. Lilo didn't wait for further assurances. "I want to speak with Alex," she said next.

"Alex," she began, but her staring at me made me quite uneasy. I felt a queasiness in my stomach. Mother was whimpering. I dared not acknowledge Lilo. "Alex," she said, "your father is perfectly correct, as usual. He is correct. I am the least likely person to suffer here. Ask King Solomon over there. He knows what is right and wrong, now doesn't he?

"Why yes," she volunteered. "Isn't that so? Isn't that just as it should be? Am I not right, Alex? I know you think I ought to stay only you don't want to say so. Now isn't that so? Well? Don't you? I know your reasons, Alex. You have said to yourself somebody has to be the one. You have said, how long can such a war last before we are all together again? You don't really believe what they did to us yesterday, now do you? Well, isn't that so, Alex? And, you say, what harm can come to a girl like Lilo if Skirzeny volunteers to protect her—as, indeed, he has given his word that he will. Now isn't that also so, Alex? Isn't that the way you have been thinking? Come. Be honest with yourself. If you

267

felt differently you would have acted differently. Isn't that so? Don't be afraid to tell me. Lovers should not keep secrets from each other . . ."

After such a harangue, what could I do but affirm that which even Lilo knew to be a lie. All of the older people were staring at me as if their faces had been pressed against a glass window. I could hear the plumbing yawning, the humming of the electric bulbs, Lilo's soft breathing: "I will stay. I will take your place," I said.

A bold smile had frozen on my beloved's face. Her voice was very childlike. "So," Lilo said. "Skirzeny was correct. You are a liar. I have always fancied you for that. Thank you, dear cousin. But you are a liar." She turned next to my father: "Yes," she said. "You are correct, as usual. I will stay. But don't think it will be any easier for you because you have gotten rid of me."

8

PROBABLY you know the rest of our story, following—as it does—along certain quite common blood lines from here on. Suffice to say that a bargain was struck: goods for blood and blood for goods—as Eichmann was supposed to have offered little Dr. Kastner. And all my dear ones, all the dear little ones, they were poured down a sewer. . . .

What did they ever do to earn such a terrible fate? It is too late to question, too late for somebody like yourself to "put yourself in my shoes." I have left a bloody trail behind me. I have walked through puddles of blood. Have pity on the victims, the living and the dead.

That same morning, in the alleyway alongside our house, from the canvas-covered van of a brewer's lorry, my family and I say our fare-thee-wells to Lilo, and climb aboard. Before departing Father hands Lilo an envelope stuffed with currency and a box of her mother's jewels. We are then the very last to leave. First goes Sarah and her family. Half an hour later the wagon is back and it is my mother's turn to go, along with Aunt Pepi. Only we remain behind like prisoners in a dock, speaking to each other or looking at each other just to accuse. Presently, Father goes to his house to gather a few personal belongings. Lilo and I are alone for a very few moments. The ceremony of betrayal is then completed. We are unable even to indulge our sentiments indiscriminately. Neither one prates at the other person. There are no more outbursts, no anger. Yet it is painful to be so alone with Lilo, as if we were now sharing nothing but the silence which she constantly interrupts with her chattering.

"And, of course, you think you will be writing me every day?" Lilo says once more, "even though there are no more letters!"

Another time I hear her inquiring about my clothing: "You have taken warm things. This time of year it is likely to be cold in the mountains . . ."

Still another time she says: "I can't say I envy you. It isn't going to be a very comfortable trip. And your father looks so tired. The poor man . . ."

I don't even answer Lilo. What can I say? These are not questions which can be answered. Clearly Lilo is trying to bait me into making some admissions which I see no point to making; she is referring obliquely to feelings which we both once may have shared, but cannot now. How can I help myself from being resentful of her? I simply can't wait for the lorry to return once again. In my father's back garden I pace about in circles near the stinking carp pond and, when the lorry does come at last, I help Father aboard, pretending to be very efficient, businesslike.

The sun is now at its zenith. I also smell the stench of our compost piles. Father is huddling in a dark corner of the vehicle, partially hidden by bunches of oily rags, pieces of canvas. He shivers and groans, with eyes closed, as if it were already midwinter, but I am sweating fiercely. "Get out of the way," I say, but after swinging my own body aboard the wagon, I must reach down toward the ground again for my own small valise. Lilo touches my hand. I can see her staring up at me. One of her combs has

270

slipped loose. Behind her straight hair the hollows of that stricken face are hidden.

"You must not worry about Miklos," she says. "He will never again be touching me."

I try to tell Lilo that I have never worried. "Never about that," I say. "About other things . . ."

It's as if I haven't really been speaking words which form sentences. Just making sounds with my lips. Little gurgles and noises of varying frequencies. Lilo listens patiently. Then she asks: "And do you think you have ever touched me?

"Do you think," she adds, "it will go easy for you now?

"Do you think," she said, "do you think I am such a fool?

"You are unfit, Alex. Impotent little thing. Do you think what we did mattered to me? That was as nothing also. And if it were not for my poverty, dear cousin, do you think I would have allowed you to touch me. You and your father both!

"Do you think I could have ever loved you, Alex?"

Our wagon starts to move. Even as she speaks we are lurching farther away from her, and I feel as if I want to jump out of the thing again, to seize this girl in my arms, to remonstrate with her until the vehicle has moved out of sight and I have been left behind with her, but Father is holding on to my waist, gripping me tightly so that I am forced to stare helplessly at Lilo from out of the darkened hollow of that wagon as she backs away from me—or we move on—I cannot now remember which.

All I can remember for sure is when presently the carter tells us to lower the tarpaulin because we are coming out onto the street. I have to do as I am told. My last glimpse of Lilo is of her rushing forward again, toward us, hands clawing at her face, as she stumbles against the deep ruts in the alleyway.

Then we are in the midst of traffic. For a moment I see another figure and I tell myself it is Miklos, racing out of my father's house to find Lilo. Can it be so? I don't take the risk to find out.

271

We are stalled in the middle of the gutter in front of our house by some drovers and their flocks. Air-raid sirens are heard. People are running past our wagon. The horses panic. They gallop forward. The sheep begin to bleat. My father's body lurches against a post. He groans. When I go to him he is unconscious.

Again I crawl to the rear of the wagon. We have climbed the hill above the brick factory where only a week or so later nearly all our Jewish friends were herded together and machine-gunned to death. Below us the town lies as if deserted. There is nobody in the streets. The cook fires of the great houses waft up toward the perfect blue of the sky where already I can see the first shadows of the aircraft moving across the ground below. There is the hollow noise of doors being slammed, a series of great explosions. The terminus is in flames. More planes are moving overhead. They veer off in formation and move across the open countryside toward Bucharest or perhaps Ploesti. The all-clear sounds against the mountain sides. People are emerging onto the streets. We begin to rock forward, slip once against a deep grade, and proceed along our way.

All the rest of that day, when I was able to stare out through the back flap of the wagon, I saw Lilo's figure, jolted into sudden focus by the moving countryside, transposed, as it were, in front of buildings, wandering across meadows, in silhouette on the adjacent hilltops. Always her hands seem to be clawing at her doll-like face. It is a vision I have never discarded. Some may remember the belching smoke of the crematoria or the ornate gateway leading to Auschwitz, but I carry with me always that tiny cameo of betrayal, the excess baggage of lust and memory, carry it with me as some people carry photographs in their wallets. I never saw my fiancée again, and did not learn that she had perished in that raid until years later. Perhaps she still lives but I prefer to believe it is not so.

Rubin, you realize of course that I came back to Clig when the war was over, in borrowed civilian clothes, furtive and circumspect as I wandered about in what was then a fief of the Soviet Union. What could I expect? What compelled me to return to such a cinder heap? Nobody seemed to know what had happened to Lilo. The Skirzenys? Yes, some said, they had moved away, some even said to the Western zone of Germany. Ujlaki was in a forced labor camp somewhere within the Soviet Union. His children had disappeared. I could not bring myself to revisit the square where our house had stood for fear of finding some traces of my former life there; and I left as I had come, ignorant and troubled, only hours after my arrival. Later, here in Israel, I made further inquiries, as many of your immigrants do, and I was processed in the files of a certain bureau, awaiting pending research. Truly. Our disaster must be remote if we can set historians to work on it.

But, you may still care to know, what happened to me and my parents? How did we, in fact, manage to survive? The truth is we did not—not all of us together. If I thought any still survived—Lilo or even my father—I would refuse your money, never to write a single word. But I am convinced that I am the "survivor surviving," as you would say. Therefore, briefly:

When my father and I arrived at the farmer's cottage in the hills above Clig where we were supposed to meet up with the lorry driver who would convey us to Debrecen, we were met by Skirzeny who informed us, in his usually harried manner, that he had sent the rest of the family on without us. We thought he was merely being ingenious. When my father complained at being kept in such ignorance Skirzeny took great pains to explain to us how it was necessary to travel in small groups. He then suggested that we remain overnight in the farmer's cottage. A fast auto, he insisted, would be picking us up early the next morning and taking us to the house in Debrecen where our papers were being made ready for us.

Skirzeny was a convincing fellow, especially when he made it clear that you had no other choices. The farmer's wife gave us cheese and milk, and we were put to sleep in the barn that night in exchange for some gold coins which my father still had on his person. After dark it rained. We huddled together, cold and wet. I did not sleep well. I remember the eyes of the mice in the place. Much later I heard the procession of autos coming to a halt in the upper pasture. I went to the door. Through a crack in the wood I could see flashes of light, as if electric torches were being waved about; moments later I distinctly heard the crunch of boots on the gravel walks. My first thought was: Skirzeny has betrayed us. Perhaps I should have woken Father but our journey had so exhausted him that I was afraid he would slow me down. Halfway out the barn door, I heard him whimper: "Shandor, you must rest. You should not wander about all night."

"Go to hell, you old bastard," I whispered. Then I crept behind the farmhouse on all fours until I came across the tiniest of meadows to a small wooded area which led first to a stream and then across a large private estate into the fastness of a forest. I started to run immediately.

For the next weeks or months I was to wander about like an animal, never knowing where I was going, eating leaves and tree bark, and the worms which appeared from the earth's fissures after a good rainstorm. Eventually a peasant family found me and gave me a beating for rooting about in their vegetable garden, but, when they saw I was feeble, they took me in.

Indeed, they were not bad people but simple-minded. Their cruelty—it was a part of the air they breathed and the way they lived. Probably they were still much as they had been at the time of the Voivodes. Distrusting me, suspicious, they saw I had a gold watch and they wanted what I had. But they were guileless about their cravings.

Chiefly I remember the father of the family, whom everybody called Bad News and who looked not unlike a cruder version of my own father, but there was also a girl named Hunchback. The father told me once that his daughter had been frightened by a

274

spirit. He also believed she would someday be well again. And since it was thought that she was bewitched, she was feared and respected by the rest of the family.

The girl was not so ugly as her name might indicate. She was dark and close-eyed but her voice was soft and she had a good smell. I was made to do chores for her and she was insufferable in all ways. But if Hunchback bullied me at first, it was because she had picked me out to be her lover. For my food I was made to do many odious things with her. I could not always resist, for she knew I was a Jew and threatened to turn me over to the authorities.

Hunchback believed that by coupling with me she would be cured. I tell you she wouldn't let me out of her sight, and I would not have had the courage to venture very far away alone. The woods were thick with horrors. She spoke of spirits and enchanters, called me her "little Isaac" when we were alone, and was especially cruel to me in front of her family.

When it was clear that her condition was not to improve despite our efforts together, Hunchback wanted me to come with her to the priests at Dej. Bad News grew angry. He did not like us to go off together. I think her father was afraid he might lose a servant, so she went off to Dej one night alone, shortly before the harvest moon. Presently Bad News sent for me to fetch tinder wood. A band of partisans surprised us. They thought I was a Russian deserter, but, when I showed them my tattoo, they agreed to accompany me to the Soviet lines. There, too, I was treated with suspicion. Some thought I was a spy. It was almost the firing squad. At last I was made to serve as orderly for a political commissar.

When my strength failed me I was sent to a recuperative home near the Black Sea. Then I was allowed to go on to Turkey where the Joint Defense Appeal arranged for me, as a stateless person, to come to Palestine in secret. Old enough by then to volunteer for military service, I was trained with the so-called Palestine Brigade, was sent briefly to Europe, was demobilized shortly before our War of Independence, served in one of our underground organizations, and was granted an amnesty after the creation of the State, although, even now, there are people in Tel Aviv who would kill me if they met me alone on the street. . . .

Which is one very good reason why I am still reluctant to make the trip to your representatives.

When you write again, tell me if there isn't some other way for me to get my hands on Uncle Bela's money. Perhaps it can be sent to some good Swiss bank where I can go to retrieve it. I do not fancy paying taxes on such a large sum. Haven't I earned the right to this little bit of dishonesty?

Or perhaps you can arrange for us to come to America where the money will be waiting for me and my family. Surely we must make other arrangements. I do not want to give up a cent more than we have to. I have a wife and a daughter. It would amuse me to pamper them. I think I would like to live in America for just a little while, and I will not accept any of your Zionist lectures, Rubin: if you are not prepared to send the money to Switzerland, then at least arrange my emigration to the States.

But there is still my uncle's question which cannot be avoided: *Am I quite Jewish?*

My answer is (and I will swear to it) that there are no more Jews. I cannot answer you any more faithfully or explicitly than to say that. *There are no more Jews!* But, if there are, I am one of them for sure. What other meaning would my life have? I am a Jew. What else should I call myself save *victim?*

Through the same agency which brought me here I have learned this much about the rest of my family:

My mother was arrested at Debrecen, shipped to a detention camp at Mauthausen, from thence to Auschwitz.

Father died in forced labor during a typhus epidemic, at a later date in another section of the domains of Dr. Mengele.

Aunt Pepi perished of "heart failure" shortly after her apprehension by Slovak border guards.

No doubt Sarah will tell you her own story. As can Perl.

Strange, that my uncle of all people should have liberated me from this obligation. It is still very much like a bad dream, yet when I reach out in my sleep to grasp these solid everyday realities, I am reassured by the void. How does the horse transcend the glue factory? *How?*

Still I want that money, Rubin, and I am now ready to swear to anything. Understand, I am not threatening you in any way, but if I am not given my just share I will have to take positive steps to assert my rights. My rights, you understand. It is not simply a matter of money any longer. I want the money, yes, but I want my rights; and I will swear to anything you say. You have no cause to make exceptions. If my sisters are to be bribed, so must I. I refuse to accept my sentence here. Nothing but victims here. It's like a prison. Yes, I want the money, Rubin, and I am now ready to swear to anything: that blood is thicker than water. . . . That Miklos and I were brothers. . . . That we inhabited a house of the blind in a country called death. . . . Or that I—the survivor surviving—self-consciously wish to affirm my kinship with dung heaps and ashes.

Why must this be denied? At Clig in 1944 the doors to the Ark were kicked open and gentiles wiped their arses with the scrolls of the Law. Who invited them into the synagogue? Nobody seems to know. Nobody seems to care. It has happened before. It may happen again. Heaven help some Jews if it doesn't. Those who have nothing to affirm save their blindness. Those who still believe in the God of Abraham, Isaac, and Max Winkleman. From the Land of Milk and Honey I send greetings to my sisters, wishing you also a good health and a long life. *Ego te absolve . . .* or, as we say here, *shalom!*

He signed his name with a series of broad sweeping strokes, first in English, then quickly from right to left, a second time, in Hebrew. Glancing up then toward the window screen, where hundreds of dying insects were now clustering, he saw once again that it was dusk.

His body ached with cramps. He knew that the sun had been on his face far too long, for he could hardly move his cracked lips to smile. The thought that he might part the curtain and be among his family once more was then quite sweet to him, but, upon doing so, he saw that Esther had her back to him. Seated in front of the stove, Ofra was the first to look up.

"*Shalom,*" Alex said. The child seemed to be staring at him as if he were an intruder. "*Shalom,*" he repeated. Her spoon fell out of her hands and dropped against the plate. Esther scolded: "Eat your supper!"

She rushed to set a place for her husband around the table, but he waved her away. "I have made arrangements for us to go to America," he said. "New York City perhaps. It's my choice. There will be no arguments. The money will help."

"Yes. It will help," she said.

"What have you got against money?"

Then Ofra spoke: "People say we are going to be rich, that Yagodah is writing such memoirs and they will be published in New York and all the Jews there will read them and we will have a fortune. Is that true, Alex?"

"Quite true," he said. As he sat down at last at the table to pick at his dish of cold food, he heard the woman again: "Liar!"

"Why yes, of course," he smirked, reaching for the little girl. "Isn't that so, Esther? Why certainly. Of course. Somehow I just forgot to mention that. Stupid of me. How considerate of you to remember. . . .

"But you needn't worry," he added, hoisting Ofra onto his lap, "because I am sure to be found out. Sooner or later. It just isn't possible to remain such a liar all your life. . . .

"No. They will find me out. You will see if they don't. . . .

"It's only to be expected. I am prepared for it. . . ."

"You are lying even now," Esther said. "You have never learned to tell the truth."

"How true. How true." Alex was stuffing Ofra's mouth with tiny bits of bread. Every other bite he would pop into his own mouth, chewing ferociously, so hard, in fact, that his jaws started to ache and there were tears forcing their way down his cheeks: "How true. How absolutely correct you are, *Estherleh*. . . . How marvelous of you. . . ."

Upon hearing her pet name, the woman was startled. Ofra had hidden her face against Yagodah's chest, a soft warm bundle. It was night again. Esther went to light the lamp: "It isn't as if I blame you, Yagodah—"

But he cut her quite short: "I do . . . yes I do indeed," only it was very much as one might shrug one's shoulders to a wind. Outside it seemed very still, as if their entire settlement was already asleep. Alex was speaking to the girl again: "The money comes because I'm Jewish. A consolation prize. Your great-uncle Bela has died in America and for that I am to get forty thousand dollars. . . ."

"I'm sorry." The girl had turned her face up to his to speak in the tone of one who truly wasn't quite sure whether to seem happy or sad.

"Don't bother," Alex said finally. The light from the lamp pained his eyes. He pushed the girl's head against his chest. He would have fallen asleep with her in his arms except that he was just too tired. "Numbers were the religion of our fathers," Alex was saying: "Swiss Bank Corporation . . . Basel . . . 4200424 . . . Can you remember, child?"

But either Ofra was already asleep, or else she was pretending. In any event, she didn't say anything. Close against his chest, the child lay with her eyes shut, her hair warmed by his breath. The room grew draughty and she pressed herself even closer. To a stranger, then, it might have seemed as if Alex and his stepdaughter were lovers exchanging confidences, but Alex was thankful that the child had not heard him, had not even wanted to hear. At that moment he felt himself quieting as the night quieted.